USA TODAY bestselling ⬚⬚⬚⬚⬚⬚⬚⬚ north
Texas with her ve⬚⬚⬚⬚⬚⬚⬚⬚⬚⬚⬚⬚ three
beautiful chi⬚⬚⬚⬚⬚⬚⬚⬚⬚⬚⬚⬚⬚⬚⬚ ⬚ard
poodle mix⬚⬚⬚⬚⬚⬚⬚⬚⬚⬚⬚⬚⬚⬚⬚ In
her downtim⬚⬚⬚⬚⬚⬚⬚⬚⬚⬚⬚⬚⬚⬚ ⬚uch
of her time o⬚⬚⬚⬚⬚⬚⬚⬚⬚⬚⬚⬚ She loves
interacting with⬚⬚⬚⬚⬚⬚⬚⬚⬚ r their support.
You can reach he⬚⬚⬚⬚⬚⬚⬚

Nicole Helm grew up with her nose in a book and the
dream of one day becoming a writer. Luckily, after a few
failed career choices, she gets to follow that dream –
writing down-to-earth contemporary romance and
romantic suspense. From farmers to cowboys, Midwest
to the West, Nicole writes stories about people finding
themselves and finding love in the process. She lives in
Missouri with her husband and two sons and dreams of
someday owning a barn.

Also by Barb Han

Texas Kidnapping
Texas Target
Texas Law
Texas Baby Conspiracy
Texas Stalker
Cornered at Christmas
Ransom at Christmas
Ambushed at Christmas
What She Did
What She Knew

Also by Nicole Helm

Summer Stalker
Shot Through the Heart
South Dakota Showdown
Covert Complication
Backcountry Escape
Isolated Threat
Badlands Beware
Close Range Christmas
Wyoming Cowboy Marine
Wyoming Cowboy Bodyguard

Discover more at millsandboon.co.uk

TEXAS ABDUCTION

BARB HAN

MOUNTAINSIDE MURDER

NICOLE HELM

MILLS & BOON

First Published in Great Britain 2021
by Mills & Boon, an imprint of HarperCollins*Publishers* Ltd
1 London Bridge Street, London, SE1 9GF

www.harpercollins.co.uk

HarperCollins*Publishers*
1st Floor, Watermarque Building,
Ringsend Road, Dublin 4, Ireland

Texas Abduction © 2021 Barb Han
Mountainside Murder © 2021 Nicole Helm

ISBN: 978-0-263-28361-7

1121

TEXAS ABDUCTION

BARB HAN

All my love to Brandon, Jacob and Tori,
the three great loves of my life.

To Babe, my hero, for being my best friend,
greatest love and my place to call home.

I love you all with everything that I am.

Chapter One

When you reach the end of your rope, tie a knot in it and hang on.

Cheyenne O'Connor couldn't count the number of times her mother had repeated the line from a past president, but the one that had stuck in her memory happened moments before her mother closed her eyes for the last time. This morning, as Cheyenne pulled the covers over her head, not yet ready to face another day, guilt racked her for letting her mother down. She needed to figure out a way to get out of bed despite the feeling of heavy weights on her ankles that made moving her legs seem impossible. Not even the promise of caffeine or the shining beams of sunlight streaming through the mini blind slats could break those shackles. Or the fact that her friend was probably home from working the nightshift at the hospital with a ready smile and the promise of a fresh brew. Ally Clark had been a lifeline.

Cheyenne glanced down at her stomach and the bump that was no longer there. Big mistake as emotions brimmed and a devastating sense of loss filled her. Crying wouldn't change a thing and yet she prayed for the sweet release it could give.

It was strange someone she'd never actually met could cause this much pain when she was gone. Except that

Cheyenne had known her baby. She'd felt movement right up until the day of her delivery—a delivery that she'd been told had gone horribly wrong.

All she had left now was a drug-induced blur where there should be memories, and empty arms where there should be a bundle of joy.

Shouldn't she feel something if the life force that had been growing inside her was suddenly snuffed out? Shouldn't she *know* her little girl was gone? Shouldn't she somehow sense it? She'd never put too much stock in a mother's intuition until now, when she'd become one. *Almost*, a little voice in the back of her mind reminded.

"Take care of my little girl," she said under her breath as she fingered the ladybug bracelet on her left wrist, a final gift from her mother.

Cheyenne reached for a pillow and hugged it to her chest, trying to find a way to fill the void. Her body ached to hold the little girl she'd imagined meeting so many times over the past eight months. What would she look like? What color would her eyes be? Would she inherit Cheyenne's blue eyes or Riggs's mocha brown? Bar none, Riggs O'Connor had the best eyes. She could stare into them all day. She'd wanted her daughter to get those from him. Mocha brown eyes with Cheyenne's blond locks. Now, that would be a combination.

Keep lying here thinking about it and you'll run out of rope.

Cheyenne forced herself to sit up. She glanced over at the two-carat princess-cut diamond ring next to her cell phone. Habit had her reaching for it first thing. She stopped herself midgrab, diverting to her cell instead. She'd shut down her phone before bed last night, too lazy to get the charger from the next room.

Staring at the screen while her eyes tried to focus, she

hit the power button. A few seconds later, the screen came to life. The first thing she noticed was a text from Ally.

On my way. b ready. I have news. There was a firework icon beside the last word. Ally always did that when she thought something would blow Cheyenne's mind. Using it in this context left Cheyenne with an unsettled feeling in the pit of her stomach.

When did Ally send the message?

An hour ago.

Strange. Cheyenne hadn't heard her best friend come in and Ozzy would have barked until the cows came home. The little yapper went off at just about anything that moved, and she herself woke at every noise. Two weeks had already passed. She still wasn't used to living here.

Cheyenne figured it best to get up, splash some water on her face and track her friend down to find out what Ally was talking about.

After freshening up—and avoiding the mirror as best she could—Cheyenne walked into the hallway. She stood in front of a closed bedroom door. Ally had a habit of closing her door when she left for work but normally left it open when she was home, even when she was sleeping.

Cheyenne knocked and leaned in so she could hear as Ozzy came gunning down the hall full force, his tiny legs working double time. He barked his greeting and maybe disapproval that Cheyenne was standing at the door of his fur mom's room.

There was no response on the other side of the door. Since the message indicated urgency, she cracked the door open and called out. Again, there was no response.

Ozzy was at her ankles, losing his mind from barking. "Okay, little guy. Calm down." She was a dog lover, but he didn't exactly fit the bill. He was more purse accessory than anything else. And yes, he was adorable with the little blue bow on his head, but he was also the most annoying creature she'd ever come across.

Her head raged at the spot right between her eyes—eyes that were so dry they were the equivalent of west Texas dirt.

"Shhhh." She bent down to pick him up. The hospital was less than half an hour's drive from here. Twenty minutes at this time of day. Shouldn't Ally be home by now?

A quick tour of the two-bedroom bungalow revealed Ally was nowhere to be found in the house. Her car wasn't outside on the parking pad, either. Had she taken a detour on the way home? Gotten distracted? How important could her message be if she didn't race home?

Cheyenne's mind snapped to a darker possibility. She gasped.

What if Ally *was* speeding home and got in a wreck? Terrible things kept happening to the people she loved. Why should this time be any different?

She retrieved her cell phone and responded to the text. Ally always had her phone tucked inside her pocket. She would either answer in a few seconds or a few minutes, depending on whether or not she was delayed by a patient. But she always answered and a glance at the clock said her nursing shift was already over.

When five minutes ticked by with nada, Cheyenne's heart raced and her concern level shot through the roof.

COULD THIS YEAR get any worse?

Riggs O'Connor gripped the steering wheel of his pickup a little tighter as he navigated through traffic, thinking of everything that had befallen. He'd lost his wife a couple of weeks ago after losing their daughter during childbirth. Since the events happened within hours of each other and were 100 percent related, he lumped them in the same category—utter devastation.

Before that, his father had been murdered on the very cattle ranch he'd built as a family legacy. His father received a medical diagnosis that meant his days were numbered. Because of this eventual death sentence, he'd decided to reopen an investigation into his daughter's kidnapping, and was killed in the process. Digging into the case, Riggs and his brothers realized their father had opened a deadly can of worms by renewing a thirty-year-old search to find out what happened to his daughter. Caroline had been the only O'Connor girl born into a family of seven kids.

Although four of Riggs's brothers worked in law enforcement, leads on finding their father's killer had been drying up until his brother Garrett uncovered a link to an alpaca farm that was a front for an illegal adoption ring that had since been raided. Progress on the investigation was still slow.

Life didn't discriminate when it delivered a bad hand. Even good folks were thrown unfortunate circumstances and sometimes the biggest jerks got off scot-free. Riggs wasn't much for self-pity. Anger— now, there was an emotion he could relate to. But this general lack of enthusiasm for doing something as routine as getting out of bed in the morning was foreign.

"Long on questions, short on answers" pretty much described his entire existence. A few nagging questions wouldn't quit, though. Why had an otherwise healthy baby been born "sleeping" as they'd called it? Why had Cheyenne pushed him away after suffering the devastating loss? He couldn't think of a time when they'd needed each other more. Cheyenne's best friend, Ally Clark, had been working in the hospital that night in the ER. He'd assumed

Cheyenne moved in with Ally after telling him *he* would be better off without her in the long run. Did Cheyenne really believe that? He'd been informed of her plans to divorce him via a text message. *A text message.*

She'd returned none of his calls. And then, out of the blue, Ally had reached out to him an hour ago. She'd asked him to stop by, saying something about important news that she needed him to hear directly from her. She also asked him not to tell anyone she'd contacted him. He was still scratching his head over that part. Then again, much of his life was one big question mark lately.

He parked on the pad in front of the two-bedroom bungalow, debating whether or not this was still a good idea. The sedan that belonged to his wife—soon to be ex-wife, once she filed the papers in court—was parked around the side of the home, confirming his suspicion that Cheyenne was with Ally. It was only a matter of time before he heard from her lawyer. If she wasn't grieving so hard, and he didn't doubt for one second that she was, he probably would have already. It frustrated him to no end that he couldn't speak to her one-on-one. Not that there was anything he could do to help her, especially while he was burning up with anger for being shut out in the first place.

The soft spot he had—the one that had him wishing there was something he could do to ease her pain—was another question mark. He shouldn't care what happened to her now that she'd turned her back on their marriage. He didn't even know if he could help her other than to accept the fact she didn't want to be married to him anymore.

And yet, part of him believed there was a solid reason she never returned his texts. To his thinking, she knew that if she faced him, she couldn't hold the line, which gave him hope she didn't want to dissolve the marriage in her heart of hearts. Was it ego talking? An ego that couldn't accept a hardline rejection from someone he loved? Maybe.

There wasn't much he could do if she wouldn't speak to him. It took two people to make a marriage. His parents had been successful at it, and he'd hoped for the same in his union to Cheyenne, despite the rushed circumstances. Rushed to marriage and now he'd be rushed to divorce, he thought wryly.

Ally's car wasn't outside, so he sat in his truck with the engine running. Curiosity was getting the best of him and he wanted to know why she'd asked him to come. Cheyenne wouldn't be happy to see him. He issued a sharp sigh as he glanced over at the door. His gaze skimmed the car seat in his truck he didn't have the heart to remove and the baby blanket draped over that his mother had knitted.

He owed it to his little girl to find out what happened at the hospital two weeks ago. Administration was still conducting an internal investigation into the ordeal and why there was no body to bury. Mistakes happened, they'd said, promising to get to the bottom of it.

Biting back a string of curses, he cut off the engine and then exited the pickup. A moment of hesitation made him pause as he stood on the porch. And then the anger that had been burning him up inside raged. He flexed and released his fingers a couple of times to work off some of the tension.

He took a step forward and fired off three rapid knocks. Ozzy went nuts, barking up a storm on the other side of the door. For a little dog, he had big lungs. He also disappeared a little too fast, which meant someone was home. His guess was Cheyenne.

Did Ally set them up to try to get them in the same room together so they could talk? Nah. She wouldn't surprise her best friend like that. The two were close enough for Ally to know Cheyenne wouldn't want to be ambushed.

No matter how much he wanted to speak to her, there was no amount of talking that could change a mind that was already made up. Frustration caused his hands to fist. Frustration from being so angry at her that he wanted to shout from the top of his lungs. Frustration from feeling sorry for her because he knew, without a shadow of a doubt, she'd been looking forward to the baby as much as he was, if not more. Frustration from the overwhelming feeling that he was letting her down in some way by not figuring out how to get her to talk to him.

No one came to the door.

Wasn't she a little bit curious as to who was outside? At least one of his questions was answered quickly when the curtain moved. His chest squeezed. His heart turned out to be a traitor because it beat a little faster at the thought of her being so close.

The door, however, didn't budge.

Riggs knocked again to no avail. He didn't drive all the way out here only to turn around without knowing what was so important Ally had him cut out of work in the middle of the workday and make the drive over. It was eight o'clock in the morning and he'd already been up and at it since four.

He reached up to knock again, figuring he'd give it one more shot before giving her a call, when the door cracked opened.

"Riggs," she said. Her eyebrows drew together and stress lines formed on her forehead. She was clearly caught off guard by his presence. "What are you doing here?"

All the anger that had been building inside him for the past two weeks took a back seat the minute he saw the depth of pain in her pale blue eyes. All the arguments died on his tongue as to why she should tell him exactly what happened that night. All his frustration over the way she'd told him about her plans to divorce him fizzled out feebly.

Standing in the doorway was a beautiful woman who was doing her level best to keep it together and be strong.

"I got a text from Ally," he said by way of defense. His tone was stiffer than he'd intended.

She stood there, mouth open, shock stamped on her features.

Chapter Two

"Ally hasn't come home from work yet. And now I'm seri-ously worried about her." Cheyenne frowned despite how fast her pulse raced at seeing Riggs standing not five feet in front of her. It wasn't like her best friend to pull a stunt like this. Ally would never ask Riggs to come over with-out running the idea past Cheyenne first.

Seeing him standing there, all six feet three inches of male glory, sent Cheyenne's pulse racing. Sweaty palms. Butterflies in stomach. The feeling like she'd just dived off the face of a mountain with nothing more than a bun-gee cord around her ankles engulfed her. He was excite-ment and sexual chemistry times a hundred. All of which explained how fast she'd fallen for him and how far down the rabbit hole she'd gone once she did.

As much as she wanted to blame stress for her body's reaction to him, she couldn't. Riggs had always had that effect on her.

Ozzy was going crazy at her heels, barking rapid-fire, and that wasn't helping her headache one bit.

"Cheyenne," he said in the low timbre that had a way of reverberating through her and disarming her defenses. "What is all this about?"

Since that was a loaded question, Cheyenne decided to

take a step back without answering. She cracked the door open a little bit more. "You can come in and wait for her."

Without waiting for a response, she opened the door a little more before turning around and walking away. Seeing him again was doing a number on her senses.

Besides, her coffee was getting cold in the kitchen and she figured half the reason for her headache was a complete lack of caffeine. She brought her hands up to her temples and tried to massage some of the tension out.

No sound came from behind her except for Ozzy. No way would Riggs be afraid of that little yapper.

Cheyenne turned around, despite wondering why she hadn't heard the screen door open yet. In the sliver, Riggs stood there like he was debating whether or not he should come inside. His cell phone was out and he was staring at the screen like his life depended on him memorizing the contents.

Her heart surged. It would be so easy to get caught up in the man standing on the other side of the screen. It had been so easy to forget how cursed her life was before she met him. Too easy? The whole fling had felt like the fairy-tale version of life. Girl meets down-to-earth and ridiculously gorgeous and almost obscenely wealthy rancher. Falls in love instantly—something she never once believed was possible for anyone before. But this guy is different. He's tall and muscled with rough hands from working outside. He's grounded. So much so that it became too easy to forget he was one of the wealthiest bachelors in Texas, and that was saying something in this state.

Not only that, but he had the kind of billboard-model good looks that made her pinch herself when he'd asked her out. And that was just the outward appearance. The physical attributes that got noticed when she first met someone. An initial appraisal that ticked all the boxes.

Talking to him had rocketed the attraction into a whole new stratosphere. He was quick-witted. He was funny. He was compassionate despite a tough exterior. He lived by a cowboy code that set him apart from other guys she'd dated. Combine all those qualities, wrap them up with his devilish charm, and he was irresistible.

Reality was settling in now, and it was a hard, cold one. He deserved so much more than she would be able to give. She could see that clearly now. Looking at him as he stood there, she knew without a doubt that shortchanging him wasn't an option. Not once in the past year had she stopped long enough to think about what being in a relationship with her might do to him. How the dark cloud following her would rain on him, too. She'd been caught up in a whirlwind fantasy and wanted to blindly trust that everything would magically work out.

Life had handed her a different reality. One she must've known she had coming, because fairy tales weren't real and men like Riggs didn't exist. And the rare few who did? They deserved something better than the bad luck that stalked her.

She'd also neglected to assess how devastating the consequences might be for her when she left after giving away her heart.

He glanced up before reaching for the handle. Her heart skipped a couple of beats when he stepped inside the living room. And all she could think to say was, "There's coffee if you want some."

An awkward silence filled the room before he finally said, "Yes, please."

His manners had always been spot-on, but she knew him well enough to realize anger brimmed under the polite surface.

"You can come on in and find a seat," she said, motioning toward the bar stools and then the kitchen table. "Sit wherever you like."

"I can't stay long," he said, and her chest deflated. She had no right to be disappointed. In fact, she should celebrate because her resolve to keep him at arm's length wouldn't last long if he tried to get close to her.

Rather than dwell on it, she fixed him a cup of coffee and walked it over to the counter in between the living room and kitchen.

"I got a text from her, too. She said she had news and to be ready, but she didn't explain. She said we'd talk about it when she got home and the news would blow my mind." Cheyenne palmed her own cup.

Riggs thanked her and then stared at the cup in her hand for a long moment before finally asking, "Since when did you start drinking coffee?"

"Recently." She shrugged, not ready to admit the real reason.

Riggs eyed her suspiciously before picking up the cup, and took a sip. He set his phone down presumably where he could keep an eye on it in case Ally called or sent another text.

"When did she contact you?" Cheyenne asked.

"About an hour ago." He confirmed what she already suspected.

"Same here," she said.

"You don't think she would be trying to get us to…" His voice trailed off when he seemed to think better of finishing the sentence.

"No. I don't." Cheyenne was clear on that point. Her best friend would never pull a stunt like this to shock her out of her funk. "Something is wrong. I can feel it."

The last time she said those words, she'd ended up in the ER and then in labor and delivery. An icy chill raced down her spine at the memory. She shrugged in an attempt to shake it off.

"We can take a ride up to the hospital to see if she's still there and got sucked into working another shift," he offered without meeting her gaze. Riggs O'Connor wasn't afraid a day in his life, so she doubted he was scared to make eye contact. Was he trying to shield himself from the disappointment their relationship must represent to him now? She wouldn't blame him one bit. She also took note that he hadn't so much as looked at her stomach. Was it too painful a reminder?

"I don't know," she hedged, not wanting to be in close quarters with the one man who caused a dozen butterflies to release in her chest without doing much more than glancing at her.

"I'm fresh out of ideas, then." His frustration came through in his tone. "We can sit here as long as you like but she might be on the side of the road somewhere."

"Okay," she said without thinking it through. If Ally was stranded, she would call. If she had access to a phone, she would return a text. If she was going to be stranded at work, she would let them know. Plus, the two of them were struggling to talk as it was, despite a growing piece of her that was comforted by his presence. Riggs was like that. He was the sun, and everything else orbited around him, drawn to his warmth.

"Ready?" He cocked an eyebrow.

"Yes." These one-word conversations ranked right up there as the worst. They were a stark contrast to all the nights they'd missed sleep while lying in each other's arms and talking about the future they were going to build together. A future that died alongside their daughter.

"I'll wait in the truck."

She nodded. At least they were up to five words now. It

was her fault. She'd been the one to tell him she was going ahead with a divorce, breaking the promises they'd made to each other. This might be best for Riggs, but it sure left a hole in her heart the size of Texas.

She would learn to get by. Hadn't she always picked herself up by her bootstraps and forged ahead? Hadn't she always found a way to keep going even when it felt like the world was crashing down around her, grabbing hold of the rope, tying the knot and then holding on for dear life?

She instinctively reached for the ladybug bracelet that was her mother's favorite piece of jewelry. Fingering the delicate lines and jewels brought her heart rate down to a decent level after panic caused her pulse to jump.

Reminding herself to breathe always helped in these situations. She watched, unable to move, as Riggs walked right out the front door.

Breathe.

Ozzy ran to the door and back. He ran circles around her feet. It took a second, but she finally caught on to what he was trying to tell her. He wanted to go outside.

"You're a smart doggo." She reached down and picked up all six pounds of him and brought him nose to face. "Okay. You're in. Only because Ally will be so happy to see you and not because you're starting to break down my resolve to not get too attached to you."

She realized she'd just had a longer conversation with a dog than with the man she'd promised to spend the rest of her life with. That pretty much summed up how her life was going these days.

Setting him down, she fed him before letting him out in the small backyard. She took another sip of coffee before moving down the hallway. She threw on her favorite yoga pants and cotton shirt, and then pulled her hair up in a ponytail. Socks and tennis shoes were next. So, basically, the most nondescript clothes she could find. The dark colors matched her mood.

She grabbed the leash on the way out the door before shouldering her purse and locking up.

Riggs sat in the driver's seat, engine running, as another dark-cloud-hanging-over-her-head feeling nailed her. She held Ozzy a little closer to her chest, and then hopped off the porch, figuring this was going to be the longest drive of her life despite the hospital being less than half an hour away.

RIGGS WAS USED to being with folks who didn't feel the need to fill empty air with meaningless words. But the chilly twenty-plus-minute ride to the hospital with no conversation ranked right up there with one of the most awkward moments of his life.

What was he supposed to say to someone who was hurting so much she couldn't speak? It was impossible not to feel like he'd let her down in some way. Then there was his own anger to consider. Anger that had him chomping at the bit to release all the fury he held inside. At least they hadn't found Ally in a ditch somewhere unconscious and therefore unable to call.

"She usually parks on the east side of the lot," Cheyenne finally chimed in as the hospital building came into view.

"It's the closest to the road leading home." His voice came out a little gruffer than he'd intended. His finger itched to reach over and touch Cheyenne again. But what would he say to her? There were no words that could cover their loss, and the divorce he knew was coming was nothing more than insult to injury.

Even so, he couldn't rightly walk away without knowing there was no chance of a reconciliation. Anger or not, he'd made a commitment he didn't take lightly. Based on the look on her face and her closed-up body language, she'd rather move on.

As much as he wished things had turned out differently, he wouldn't try to convince her to stay with him when she so clearly couldn't wait to be as far away from him as possible. As it was, she sat so far on the opposite side of the bench seat that her right shoulder pressed against the door.

"Do you see her car?" The parking lot was less than half-full, about thirty cars and trucks mostly huddled up toward the entrance. He drove up and down each aisle, searching for the cherry red Mustang Ally drove. He'd met her a few times and had been threatened to within an inch of his life if he ever hurt Cheyenne.

He'd promised not to and that was the second promise he broke. The first was to love and protect her. Not being able to protect her from the kind of pain that would cause most to curl up in a fetal position and give up had his hands tightening around the steering wheel.

Guilt racked him for not being in the room with his wife when she'd had their child. He'd been called out onto the property after someone spotted poachers. She'd gone into early labor. He was in an area without cell coverage, none the wiser. So yeah, he felt like a jerk for not being there for his...for her.

"It's not here," she finally said after studying each vehicle like she was going to be tested on it later.

"Does she ever park anywhere else?" he asked. Being back at the hospital where she'd lost their child two weeks ago caused stress lines to crease her forehead.

"I suppose it's possible." She frowned.

"We can take a lap around the hospital. Check the other lots." He navigated around the white-and-glass building, not ready to leave empty-handed. There were four lots and he drove each aisle as concern mounted for Ally with every minute that ticked by.

Cheyenne had been right earlier. Her friend wouldn't call them together and then ditch.

"I can call my brother and ask if there have been any accidents in the area," he offered. They would have seen something on their way over, though. There was only one main road from Ally's house to the hospital and a couple of side streets, so it wasn't like there were a lot of options.

"Okay." There was a lost quality to Cheyenne's voice that nearly ripped his heart out. She was holding Ozzy close to her chest with one arm while chewing her thumbnail to bits on her right hand.

He pulled out to the edge of the lot and parked, leaving the engine running. Colton's number was programmed into the truck, so all Riggs had to do was press the screen on his dashboard to call.

"Hey, what's up?" Colton answered on the first ring, barely covering the concern in his voice. It came as no shock that everyone was worried about Riggs and he appreciated his brothers for their concern. The O'Connor family was a tight-knit bunch. Always had been and always would be. Even their rogue brother Garrett had come around recently after their father and family patriarch's death.

"You're on speaker. I'm with Cheyenne and we were supposed to meet her best friend after work. You remember Ally?"

The line was dead quiet for more than a few uncomfortable beats.

"Yes," Colton finally said, not masking the confusion in his tone as well as he probably thought he was.

"She requested a meetup. Gave us the impression it was

important and that she had news to deliver that had to be kept hush-hush," he said to his brother, the sheriff.

"And you believe this information is related to your daughter." Colton was sharp. There was no doubt in Riggs's mind his brother would catch on to the implication without spelling it out for him.

"I do." He didn't want to speak for Cheyenne. Although she was nodding, hunkered over in the corner. "She didn't show up at her residence. We're at her place of employment and her vehicle is nowhere to be found. We didn't observe any accidents between her home and usual route to work."

"Which is?" Colton was all business now. This was his territory, and he was good at his job.

Riggs rattled off street names after giving both her address and the name of the hospital.

"I can be there personally in—"

"No need." Riggs appreciated his brother for wanting to show up for him. But he really did just want to know if any accidents had been reported.

The click-clack of a keyboard sounded.

"Hold on a second," Colton said in a distracted voice. He was no doubt staring at the screen, waiting for results.

"Nothing in your area has come up on the radio and I'm not getting anything in the system, either," Colton reported. "Have you spoken to anyone inside the hospital yet?"

"No."

"Someone might have needed to borrow her car last-minute." Colton's suggestion was a reach. Ally would have her cell phone on her and would have contacted either Riggs or Cheyenne.

"I can ask around, but it doesn't seem like she'd leave us hanging like this," Riggs said.

"Hold on for a second." Colton must've muted the call because he went radio silent.

After a few tense moments, his brother returned to the line.

"No accidents reported. I'm sending a deputy over to make the drive and I've contacted a group that volunteers to use drones in searches." He exhaled. "With the information we have right now, I'd say she probably stopped off somewhere along the way for a drink to force the two of you in a room together. Or it's possible she ran into the grocery store and happened into an old chatty friend."

Riggs compressed his lips to stop from refuting his brother's ideas. Colton was coming at this from a seasoned law enforcement officer's point of view. In many cases, he was probably right. He also probably wouldn't even send a deputy or dredge up drones if he wasn't talking to a trusted source. Riggs needed to keep perspective and hold his frustration in check. He was already ticking through possible stop-offs along the route home. If they had to visit every business to find her or convince his brother she was missing, so be it.

"I appreciate your help," he finally said.

"This is just a starting point. There are other things I can do if she doesn't turn up from these efforts," Colton assured him. His wheels were turning, apparently.

Riggs thanked his brother and ended the call.

"She wouldn't do this on purpose." Cheyenne tapped her fingers on the armrest. "She's in some kind of trouble and it's somehow related to us. Ally would never just disappear like this without contacting us first."

The thought was sobering.

"Where do you want to start?" he asked, figuring they could backtrack but also needed to check out any of her favorite haunts.

"Anywhere but the same hospital…" She didn't have to finish the sentence. He didn't want to go inside the place they'd lost their daughter, either.

Chapter Three

There was one grocery store, three restaurants and two gas station/convenience stores in between Ally's house and the hospital. Cheyenne remembered one of the gas stations as Ally's favorite, and the convenience store where she herself had stopped for coffee the other day. And yes, she'd started drinking coffee two weeks ago instead of her usual chai tea.

Ally's red Mustang was nowhere to be found. Hers was distinguishable by the color and the personalized license plate, IAM NRSE.

An hour and a half later, they were right back where they'd started, in the hospital parking lot. Pulling up to the hospital building, knowing she was about to walk through those cold, white-tiled corridors again, filled her with dread. She wasn't sure what to do with herself, let alone Ozzy.

"Think I can get away with putting him in my purse and sneaking him inside?" she asked, motioning toward her best friend's dog.

"Might as well try." Riggs had been quiet along the way, which was never a good sign. In the short time she'd gotten to know him, she realized how often he closed up when he was frustrated.

Then again, he wasn't her business anymore. After they located Ally, he would go back to the ranch and she would figure out her next step. The timeline and the circumstances of the pregnancy hadn't been ideal, but Cheyenne was surprised at how quickly she'd adapted to the news and pivoted to welcoming full-time motherhood. Now she needed a job. The nearby community college where she'd worked as an admissions counselor had already replaced her. Her emergency funds would only get her through the next three or four months, and there was no way she was asking for any of Riggs's money. Seeing him again had already stirred up feelings she needed to keep at a safe distance. Safe? There was nothing safe about Riggs O'Connor when it came to protecting her heart.

The time had come to tie a knot in the rope.

Shouldering her purse, she tucked Ozzy inside so that only his head peeked out. Staring down the building was the hardest thing for her to do. But she hadn't survived this long by hiding from things that might hurt her. She would have to face this pain at some point. Was she ready? No. But Ally was worth it.

With a deep breath meant to fortify her, she exited the truck. While wrestling with her own thoughts, it hadn't occurred to her how much this might be affecting Riggs. A quick glance at him was the equivalent of a punch in the solar plexus.

His chin was jutted out, and his gaze was focused on the entrance as he stood there waiting for her to come around the truck. He was strength and courage personified, so to see him struggle, even for a brief moment, was a direct hit to the heart.

She stood there, just out of sight, giving him a minute of privacy.

"Ready?" he asked after glancing over at her.

"Yes." She couldn't muster enthusiasm and she couldn't stop the flood of emotions engulfing her. She didn't cry no matter how much she wanted to. Instead, she tucked her chin to her chest and took it one step at a time. She could take a step. And then another. She could cross the circular road and then step up on the curb. She could walk inside the double doors that opened with a swish.

Her heart pounded with every forward step until it felt like it would bust through her rib cage, but she could take a step onto the sterile white tile.

"May I help you?" An older voice, a gentle voice, caused Cheyenne to look up.

A four-foot-high counter separated her from a lovely older lady. The woman, whose name tag read Grey, had the warmest smile. Her long white hair was pulled up in a bun on top of her head like she was an aging ballerina. She had the kindest pale blue eyes, which stood out against age-worn skin.

"We're visiting a friend who works here," Cheyenne piped up. She could only hope Ozzy would behave in her handbag and not start barking. He had a habit of getting in trouble, and yet strangely, he seemed to have settled in there.

"Do you know the floor?" Grey asked. Cheyenne had become fascinated with names while trying to find the perfect one for her daughter.

"Yes," she said.

"Have a good day," Grey said.

Cheyenne started to walk away and then stopped. "You have an unusual name. Do you mind me asking what it stands for?"

Grey smiled and it warmed her face. "Greyson. My daddy wanted a boy. He got four girls. He'd planned on giving a boy my name." She laughed and it filled the space with more of that warmth. "Everyone calls me Grey for short."

"It's a beautiful name." Cheyenne loved rare or unusual names with a story behind them.

"Thank you." The older woman beamed.

Cheyenne smiled before casting her eyes to the floor, and then headed toward the elevator bank. She'd go anywhere but labor and delivery on the seventh floor. Lucky for her, Ally worked on three.

The bell dinged. A set of elevator doors opened, and Riggs put his hand in to keep them from closing. He nodded toward Cheyenne to go first. He'd always been a gentleman. She thought of him more as a Renaissance man. His Southern manners, which gave a lady the option to go first, were always appreciated in her book. Did she need someone to open doors for her? No. She was capable of doing that for herself. And yet there was something nice about having the option, about being spoiled just a little bit. It was one of the perks of living in Texas among cowboys and ranchers, and she hoped it stayed in style.

She pushed the number three, thankful they had the elevator to themselves. She wasn't one for crowds on a good day, preferring curling up in bed with a good book over drinks at a crowded bar or dinner at a busy restaurant.

Ozzy tried to climb out of her bag.

"No. No. You're okay," she soothed.

The little guy jumped out before she could stop him. Riggs caught Ozzy before he crashed to the ground.

"Hey, there, little guy. You need to stay put and keep your head down so you don't get us kicked out of this place. We're trying to find your mama." His voice caught on the last word and he seemed to notice how it sounded. He cleared his throat and whispered an apology. He'd always had the kind of deep timbre that threaded right through her, traveling over her and through her.

Even now, when she couldn't afford to let it.

THE ELEVATOR BELL DINGED, indicating they'd reached their floor as Riggs tucked the little dog in Cheyenne's bag. He pulled back his hand the minute it grazed Cheyenne's creamy skin—skin he couldn't afford to think about for how off-limits she was.

The doors opened and he waited for her to go first. He didn't have the first idea how to talk to her about what had happened on a different floor inside these same walls. She might have been the one to close that door, but he didn't know what to say anyway.

In the first couple of days, he'd naively believed she needed time. She'd refused to take his calls, so he gave her the space she needed. Was that a mistake? Would it have made a difference if he'd shouted from the rooftops that he wanted to be there for her? That she didn't have to go through any of this alone? An impenetrable wall had come up around her, a fortress he'd had no idea how to break down or break through.

Riggs held out his hand to keep the elevator doors from closing. Then he followed her.

Ozzy's ears peeked out. Cheyenne was doing a good job of keeping the squeaky little barker under wraps. As long as the little guy cooled it, they should be fine.

Cheyenne walked up to the nurse station where three nurses were working on separate tasks. One studied a computer screen. She was facing them but so engrossed in what she was doing she didn't look up. Another stood with her side to them, writing in a file. And the third stood at the back of the station with her arms folded, looking down at the tile.

Cheyenne waited for someone to acknowledge them, rather than draw attention. The old saying it was easier to catch bees with honey than vinegar came to mind. Interrupt the nurses while they were deep in thought or busy doing their jobs, and they might be uncooperative.

Rude people rarely ever got more than base-level information or service. Besides, these were Ally's coworkers. He didn't want to appear a jerk and he was certain he could speak for Cheyenne on that front.

The one mesmerized by the computer screen broke her trance and then looked up. "Oh. Sorry. I...uh...can I help you?"

Her eyebrows drew together and an emotion passed behind her eyes that he couldn't quite pinpoint. Shock? Fear?

Couldn't be.

He was probably seeing things. He didn't know this woman from Adam. She had no reason to be afraid of him.

"We're looking for Ally," Cheyenne said. "We were supposed to meet for breakfast and figured she got caught up here."

The nurse shrugged. "I didn't see Ally today when I started my shift. I can ask around, but I doubt she's still here."

"That would be great, if you wouldn't mind," Cheyenne said. Ozzy started moving around inside the purse and he might get them booted out if they weren't careful.

The nurse didn't seem enthused about the request.

"Sorry to bug you about our friend." Riggs stepped forward and placed a hand on Cheyenne's lower back. The nurse locked onto Riggs and her face flushed, a reaction he'd never get used to.

She smiled and brought a hand up to tuck her hair behind her ear, a sign of flirting that would have upset

Cheyenne a while back. Now she didn't seem to care who looked at him or when. Crazy how the tide could turn on a dime.

Much like a rogue spring thunderstorm, Cheyenne's feelings had changed course in a flash. Again, there wasn't much he could do if she was unwilling to sit down and talk about their future. To be fair, she'd said she didn't see one for them anymore. And yet, part of him couldn't believe she meant those words. Couldn't believe or couldn't accept? an annoying voice in the back of his mind asked. Because there was a big difference. None of which mattered at the moment. His priority had shifted. He wasn't much for worrying, but Ally's disappearance was troublesome. He also made a mental note to ask Cheyenne about Ally's personal life. He wanted to know if she had other friends, a boyfriend, or had started a new relationship. While he was at it, he wanted to know if she'd had any disagreements with anyone recently, a falling out or a breakup. Riggs's brothers who worked in law enforcement were beginning to rub off on him.

"It's not like her to leave us hanging." He leaned an elbow on the bar-height counter and smiled.

The cheesy move worked, because the nurse winked at him before rolling her chair back a couple of feet.

"Hey, Sherry. Have you seen Ally today?" she asked.

"Not me." The nurse didn't look up from her file. Her name tag read: Renee.

"How about you, Becca?" she asked the nurse at the back of the station without making much of an effort to make eye contact.

Becca continued to study the tile but shook her head.

Renee rolled her chair back to its original position. "Doesn't look like anyone here knows where she is."

Funny. Cheyenne hadn't asked if anyone knew where her friend was. She'd asked if anyone had seen her today. A coincidence? Or was the nurse holding something back?

Chapter Four

"Thank you for your time." Cheyenne knew when she was being stonewalled and saw no point in sticking around the hospital. She turned to leave when a nurse rounded the corner. The young woman froze in her tracks, a horrified expression on her face.

Riggs seemed to catch on. He started to say something when the nurse glanced up at the camera in the corner of the hallway before scurrying off.

He took Cheyenne's hand in his and then gave a quick squeeze. On instinct, she jerked her hand back. She didn't dare look up at him. She couldn't look into those eyes one more time—eyes that showed pain no matter how well he tried to cover.

"Let's get out of here," he said low and under his breath. His voice had the same gravelly quality she loved. Correction, *used* to love. She couldn't afford to love anymore.

"Okay." There was no point in waiting there when the nurses seemed determined not to give them any information.

She followed him down the hallway, into the elevator, and out the same door they'd come in twenty minutes ago. As they walked to the parking lot, she caught sight of the nurse from the hallway a few minutes ago.

Of course, the nurse would know a quicker way down

to the parking lot. She would also know where Ally parked and might have guessed they would do the same. These were a lot of assumptions and yet they were logical.

The mystery nurse pulled something from her pocket. Metal glinted in the bright sun. For a split second, Cheyenne's pulse leaped into her throat. On instinct, she grabbed Riggs's arm. He stepped beside her, using his considerable size to block Cheyenne from the nurse. And then he almost immediately sidestepped so Cheyenne could see the woman had pulled out one of those electronic cigarettes. She gave a weary look, glanced from side to side, and then waved them over.

Cheyenne wasn't 100 percent certain the woman could be trusted, especially with the way she kept checking the parking lot every time the wind blew. They were short on options, though. Mystery nurse was their best shot at progress.

It was then she realized the woman stood in the blind spot of a pair of cameras attached to the building. Riggs must have noticed the same thing because he nudged Cheyenne with his elbow and then made eyes toward the cameras.

"You can stay here or head to the truck. You don't have to go with me," he said quietly.

"I'm good now that I know she's not carrying," she said, careful not to squeeze her bag since Ozzy was still inside. The half-demon dog turned into an angel inside a handbag. Maybe that was where he felt the most secure. Everyone should be so lucky to have a place that made them feel safe. Cheyenne would have said she had Riggs's arms before...

She didn't want to go there while they approached the nurse. Being with Riggs already caused the world to tip on its axis and Cheyenne needed to check her balance, not throw it off even more. *Tie the knot, Cheyenne.*

The woman stood a little shorter than Cheyenne and had mousy brown hair in a ponytail that swished from side to side as she moved her head. She was of petite build and had an oval-shaped face. She kept twisting her hands together and searching around, looking like she'd jump out of her skin if someone said, "Boo."

As Cheyenne and Riggs neared, the doors swished open. A woman came out. Face down, she barely acknowledged the two of them. The nurse, however, tucked the e-cig back inside her pocket, mumbled an apology, and then scurried past them and back into the hospital.

They stood there for a moment, frozen, not wanting to draw attention. When the woman walking toward her vehicle in the parking lot turned toward them, Riggs pulled Cheyenne into an embrace and then kissed her. His lips still tasted like dark roast coffee, just like she remembered. Her favorite flavor.

Her breath caught and her pulse skyrocketed. His lightest touch caused her stomach to free-fall.

Kissing her had been a maneuver. Something to deflect attention from the woman walking by. It was a smart move on Riggs's part. And yet, so dangerous for Cheyenne's resolve. Because she could get lost in his arms. She loved the way his lips felt when they moved against hers. And she loved breathing in his spicy scent.

Her hands fisted at her sides. She knew exactly what *she* wanted. It would be so easy to be selfish right now. It would be so easy to be with Riggs again. It would be so easy to tell herself the only thing that mattered was the here and now. Would that be the best thing for Riggs? The long answer was no. The short answer was no. No. No. No.

Pulling on all her willpower, she took a step back. Glancing to her right, she saw the back of the woman's head as she climbed into her sport utility.

Riggs didn't immediately move, and she could only guess what must be running through his mind right now. Hers raced.

"Think we should head back to the truck?" she asked, thinking there wasn't much more they could do.

"My first thought was to follow the nurse back inside." He shook his head. "Wouldn't do any good, though."

"As much as I want to march inside the hospital and demand answers, I agree with you." Based on her experience with Renee, Sherry and Becca, doing that would be as productive as planting summer crops in December. With a sharp sigh, she walked back to the truck with Riggs.

Inside, he didn't seem in a hurry to start the engine or pull out of the parking lot.

"Cameras are probably watching us as we speak," Cheyenne pointed out. Her nerves were shot. She checked the sky for the drones Colton had promised and didn't see any. She reminded herself it would take time to get resources in the air.

"Let them. We aren't doing anything wrong in sitting here. A deputy will be here in a little while, and he'll be on our side." His voice was a study in calm. In fact, he was too calm. It was the calm before the storm.

She shifted to one side and then back to the other. Ozzy peeked his head out of her purse and she reached over to scratch him behind the ears. He ducked in time to miss contact, back to his old tricks. Little squirt. Or maybe he *should* recoil at her touch. Did he know on instinct to keep a distance from her? Did he have a sixth sense for cursed people? Because she had to be cursed. No one had this much bad luck in one lifetime.

"Who does Ally socialize with from work?" He pulled out his cell phone and she assumed the reason was to take down names.

"To be honest, I have no idea." The admission stung. Cheyenne should know who her best friend had been hanging out with. "I've been so wrapped up in my own life for the past year and getting ready for the baby that I haven't been staying in touch as much as I should have."

He nodded.

"Do you know if she was seeing someone?" There was no judgment in his voice.

"She used to date someone in Dallas, but I don't remember his name and I think it was a long time ago." Cheyenne blew out a frustrated breath. There were fuzzy memories of Ally coming home in the mornings after work, coming into Cheyenne's room to check on her. Her friend talked about her shift as Cheyenne drifted in and out. "Look. I haven't been the best friend to her lately. I got so caught up in my relationship with you and then the pregnancy that she and I didn't talk as much as we used to." She threw her hands up in the air. "There was a time when she was going back and forth to Dallas for a guy, but I couldn't tell you if that was still the case and for the past two weeks all I've wanted to do is stay in bed twenty-four seven, so it's not like we've been having sleepovers to catch up."

She blew out a breath and apologized.

"I'm frustrated with me, not you. Please don't take what I'm saying the wrong way," she said. "I remember something about work… I can't remember what, though."

"It happens to friendships," he said and his attempt to comfort her shouldn't make her even more frustrated. "And it was probably just her needing to talk about her shift."

"It shouldn't, though. I care about Ally. I just never really worried about our friendship before. It's not like we talk every day. We've gone weeks, sometimes months, without talking. Then we just pick up where we left off. Except this year has been the longest break we've ever taken." And she wanted to add it was her fault. She also wanted to remember who Ally complained about from work. A doctor? It would be another angle they could follow up on. And yet nurses grumbling about how a doctor treated them wasn't exactly new.

"I'm sure you two would have picked up again once the baby was born." Again, his attempt to let her off the hook shouldn't infuriate her more. Except that was exactly what it did.

"How? From everything I read, babies are more than a full-time job," she said with a little more heat than she'd intended. She pinched the bridge of her nose to stem the headache threatening. "I would have just let our longstanding friendship slip away. And now, something might have happened to her and it's because of…"

She stopped herself right there before she went all in blaming herself. This wasn't a pity party by any means. She had a very real sense of annoyance that she'd let her friend down—a friend who had been there for Cheyenne during her darkest days.

"I won't pretend to know your friendship with Ally, or how it works. All I can say is that I'm guilty of the same thing with my brothers." He didn't have to tell her how close his family was. She'd seen it firsthand while living at KBR, Katy Bull Ranch. "It can be easy to take the ones we care about most for granted." He put his hand up before she mounted an argument. "I'm not saying we have to do it that way, but it's more common than it should be."

He wouldn't get an argument from her there.

"Why is that, Riggs?" She leaned her head against the headrest. The headache from earlier threatened to return.

"You tell me and we'll both know," he said. It was one of his favorite sayings while they were together. A smile ghosted her lips at the memory. There were others that tried to follow but she shut them down.

"All I know is that she's out here somewhere and if I was a better friend, I'd know where. I'd be able to find her and help her," she admitted before she had time to reel those words back in.

Riggs didn't immediately respond. In fact, he took so long she slowly opened her eyes and turned to look at him. When she did, she saw something else…

Movement in the background caught her attention. The mousy-haired nurse was back, and she was standing in the same spot as before.

"Well, look at that." Cheyenne nodded toward the woman.

"She must have something she wants to say to us," he said.

"What if she was just trying to bum a lighter?" Cheyenne couldn't afford to get her hopes up.

"I don't think e-cigs work that way but I don't exactly have personal experience to draw from," he said. Then he turned to lock gazes with Cheyenne. "Only one way to find out."

"True." She opened the door, exited the vehicle, and met him around back.

They approached the nurse together. She had the same e-cig out. Cheyenne figured a smoke break must be her excuse to leave the building while on duty.

"Come closer." She took a drag off the e-cig before glancing around again. "I need this job and I'll get fired if I'm seen talking to either of you."

"Why us?" Riggs took the lead.

"Don't you know?" The nurse's name tag wasn't on her left pocket like everyone else's. Had she removed it?

"I'm drawing a blank here." He threw his hands in the air for emphasis.

"Your friend is in trouble," she said like it was plain as the noses on their faces.

"Why?" Cheyenne asked.

"Because of you. She went poking around where she shouldn't, and now she disappeared just before her shift was over. Have you seen her?" the nurse asked with a cocked eyebrow.

"No. I haven't," Cheyenne said. "I was hoping you could tell me where she was."

The woman shook her head. "That's not a good sign."

"Her car is gone," Cheyenne pointed out. "Did she leave on her own free will?"

"All I know is that she was poking around in the files on your birth, asking around about Dr. Fortner," the nurse said. "Then she was gone, and Sherry, the head nurse, starts asking if anyone can fill her shift tomorrow."

Sherry knew?

Riggs reached over and squeezed Cheyenne's hand.

"Is there anything else you can tell us?" Cheyenne asked. "Please. My friend might be in danger. Anything you can tell us might save her life."

The nurse's eyes widened to saucers. She pushed past them and tucked the e-cig inside her pocket. "I gotta go."

"That's it?" Cheyenne asked. "What about Ally?"

"I've already said too much. I'm sorry. I have to worry about me and my kid." She twisted her hands together.

"Can I ask why you're here talking to us, then?" Riggs asked.

"Yeah. Because any one of us could be next." She stormed off and disappeared around the corner into the building.

"She knows more than she's telling us," Riggs said.

"I know." Cheyenne reached in her bag and pulled Ozzy out. He immediately started barking. She placed him back inside, figuring she was right about him feeling the most secure there. She might not be able to help Ally right now, but she could take care of Ozzy.

They headed to the truck with the confession spinning in Cheyenne's thoughts. Riggs walked her to the passenger side and opened the door for her. She could open it for herself but her hands were busy with Ozzy, and she appreciated the gesture.

She thanked him and then climbed inside the cab. After situating the dog and securing her seat belt, she exhaled. "Something sinister is going on here."

"It sure is." He started the engine and then put the gearshift in Reverse.

"Something about the birth." She couldn't bring herself to say the words *our daughter*, despite them sitting right there on her tongue. After feeling like her heart had been ripped from her chest, she couldn't dare to hope there'd been some kind of mistake. Although rare, mistakes did happen. Could their daughter have been sent home with someone else by accident? Babies switched at birth? Those kinds of things made the news. As tragic as it was for all parties, mistakes happened.

"Yes," he agreed, clearly not wanting to get his hopes up, either. They would be crazy to, and both seemed to realize it.

"Which doesn't mean there's a different outcome," she quickly said. "It could be something as simple as Ally figuring out someone messed up the birth. That it wasn't all my fau—"

"Hold on there a second." Riggs hit the brake. "These things happen in life. And as awful as they are, no one person is to blame."

Did he really believe that? Because she didn't. She was the one in the hospital in early labor. She was the one who was supposed to be able to give birth like so many other women did every day of the week. And *she* was the one who'd lost their daughter.

The black cloud hung over *her* head, not his.

Judging from his reaction, telling him so wouldn't change his mind and there was nothing he could say to change hers. So she left it at that, figuring it was time to redirect the conversation back on track.

"Where do we go next, Riggs?" she asked, hoping he would let it go.

He sat there silent, with the engine idling for a long moment before shifting into Drive, looking like he had a whole lot to say. He seemed to decide on, "Let's go back to the house. She might be there waiting already."

"Do you really believe that after what the nurse just said?" Cheyenne asked.

"Not really, but I'm grasping at straws as much as you are," he admitted.

"I'm not saying I don't believe the nurse. But it wouldn't be the first time Ally's cell died after a long shift." Evidence pointed to the contrary, but she wasn't ready to embrace the thought something permanently bad had happened to Ally. "On second thought, do you think we should circle back and try to get more information out of E-cig Nurse?"

The woman had disappeared a little too fast. She knew something she wasn't sharing.

"If it's true that she has a kid, she won't tell us anything else. She barely told us anything as of now. And we don't even know her real name." He navigated out of the parking lot and onto the roadway back toward Ally's bungalow. "We'll give Colton an update. The nurse will talk to law enforcement and so will Sherry. I'd like to hear her explanation as to why she seems to know Ally won't be coming back to work in the next few days."

The obvious answer was that Ally was going somewhere and asked for time off. But Ally wouldn't. She didn't. And yet Cheyenne couldn't prove it.

"I'd like to be a fly on the wall when the nurses talk to law enforcement." The thought of going back to the bungalow to wait for Ally with Riggs made breathing a challenge. *Slow down. Breathe.*

Tie the knot. Hold on. Her new mantra had to work because Riggs was most definitely going home with her. She couldn't turn him away when the investigation involved finding out what had happened to his daughter.

Cheyenne picked up her handbag and held Ozzy to her chest. Instead of trying to snap at her, he leaned his head against her neck and nuzzled her.

"You like car rides?" She kept her voice quiet. Talking to the dog was one thing. Figuring out what to say to her soon-to-be ex was a whole different ball game, especially since her pulse pounded so loudly he had to be able to hear it.

Being around Riggs did things to her heart she couldn't afford right now. She needed all of her determination and resolve to find out what had really happened to her daughter. To *their* daughter. The unfairness of shutting him out slammed into her. She'd been so caught up in trying to protect him that she'd hurt him even more.

Cheyenne took in a deep breath. She had to figure out a way to find the words to talk about what had happened.

Riggs deserved to know.

Chapter Five

"No sign of your friend." Riggs pulled onto the parking pad in front of Ally's place for the second time that day. A few thoughts circulated through his mind and a picture was emerging as he hopped out of the driver's seat after cutting off the engine. Cheyenne blamed herself for losing the baby. He suspected it was at least part of the reason she'd told him that he would be better off without her. There could be more to it, but something told him this statement carried most of the weight.

"No." The sadness in her voice nearly cut a hole in his chest.

The passenger door swung wide open before he made it halfway around the front of the pickup. She'd been quiet on the ride back. Too quiet for his liking. It meant she'd gone inside herself again and he had no idea how to reach her. It had happened twice during the early months of their relationship. The first time wasn't too long after she'd told him she was pregnant. He'd given her space and she'd come around after two long weeks. The second came midway through the pregnancy, when she'd shut down on him. Again, he'd given her space, and she'd come around with a little bit of time. This time seemed different.

Riggs headed toward the bungalow as Cheyenne shut the door to the truck. She stopped on the porch and turned to face him. The way she bit the inside of her cheek before she launched into whatever she was about to say caused a knot to form in his gut.

She shifted her weight from one foot to the other and her fingers traced the house key in her hand. A sense of dread for what might come next tightened the knot.

"Is there any chance you can stay for a while?" she asked, not making eye contact.

Cheyenne's question caught him off guard.

"I can and planned to," he said. Nothing inside him wanted to get back inside his truck and drive away while there were so many unanswered questions anyway.

"Good." She turned around before unlocking the front door. "We need to talk."

The second surprise struck with her last comment.

Riggs closed, then locked the door behind him and nodded toward the kitchen. "Mind if I get a fresh cup of coffee?"

"Be my guest." She shrugged. Tension radiated off her in waves. "I can get it for you. It wouldn't be any trouble."

"I sort of remember where everything is," he said, figuring he needed something to do with his hands as much as the caffeine boost.

Cheyenne followed him into the next room. Ozzy was still tucked inside her purse and he seemed to like it there. He'd stopped yipping, so that was a step in the right direction.

"You want a cup?" he asked.

"Sure." Cheyenne kept her distance, looking like she was working up her nerve to tell him something. If he moved toward the fridge, she took two big steps backward. Five feet seemed to be her "safe" distance from him.

Hell, it wasn't like he was going to bump into her despite the small space. He had no plans for intentional contact. Granted, the kiss from the parking lot still sizzled on his lips. But he didn't foresee the need for a repeat. It had gotten them out of a tricky situation.

Telling her to relax would most likely increase her stress levels, so he let it be, forcing himself not to think about the fact they normally couldn't be in the same room without near-constant contact even if it was just outer thighs touching while seated on the couch.

Riggs fixed two cups and handed one over. Their fingers grazed, causing a familiar jolt of electricity to shoot straight to his heart. He stared at the cup for a second longer than he'd intended, and she seemed to do the same.

After taking a sip and then a breath that was apparently meant to fortify her, Cheyenne apologized.

"It's not easy for me to talk about that night," she continued, referring to the birth. "But that's no excuse. It has dawned on me that you deserve to hear what happened."

He nodded as she glanced at him. Suddenly, the rim of her coffee cup became very interesting to her.

"I panicked when I couldn't reach you," she said.

"Why didn't you grab someone else at the ranch?" he asked.

"Because I wasn't there." She started working the ladybug bracelet her mother had given her, another sign her stress levels were climbing.

"The doctor didn't think it was a good idea to be away from the r—"

"I'm aware," she cut in, her voice laced with more of that sadness. "I should have been home and probably in bed. At the very least somewhere with my feet up."

She flashed her eyes at him.

"I was going stir-crazy at home by myself and I don't know the rest of your family well enough to—" she took in a slow breath before continuing "—to ask someone to go to my mother's favorite place with me."

"You hiked Harken Falls alone?"

"There were technically park rangers there, but yes." Another emotion was present in her voice. Shame?

"What made you decide to go there?" This wasn't the time to pour on more guilt, so he checked his frustration.

"I knew the baby was coming soon and I—" her voice dipped low "—missed my own mom, so I went to the place we spread her ashes."

"It's understandable." He knew her mother had died many years ago. Other than that, Cheyenne didn't say much about her family. Any time the subject came up, she got quiet.

"Is it?" she quipped. "My water broke and I went into labor. There was no one around to help and I had to hike down the falls area. I ran in between contractions. Once I got in cell range, I called 911, but it was irresponsible of me to go there by myself."

She'd tried to call him almost a dozen times. He'd missed every single attempt. Reminding her of that now didn't seem like it would help much. So he held his tongue.

"You couldn't have known that would have happened, Cheyenne. We both know you would never do anything on purpose to hurt the baby." His words didn't seem to sink in. She appeared determined to punish herself for the mistake.

"The EMT gave me oxygen and I was in pretty bad shape by the time I got to the hospital. I guess I dehydrated out there faster than I realized I would." She turned her face away from him and it took every ounce of strength inside him not to walk over to her and offer comfort. "That's about as much as I remember. I was too far along for the epidural and then there were complications with the birth. The rest is all like a nightmare. I have fuzzy bits of being told the baby was breech. Another of a masked doctor leaning over me right before everything went dark."

Riggs sat there, listening to what had to have been one of the worst moments of his wife's life. Knowing full well that he should have been right beside her. Guilt was a knife stab in the center of his chest.

"People make mistakes, Cheyenne," he said after a few thoughtful minutes. "You never would have done anything to hurt her," he repeated, hoping this time he could convince her what happened wasn't her fault.

She glanced up at him with red-rimmed eyes. Her chin quivered but not a teardrop fell.

"You did everything right. You couldn't have known how events would unfold. What happened isn't your fault," he said in a low voice. He couldn't deny that he was being a hypocrite. He absolutely believed everything that had gone wrong with the birth and his marriage had to be his fault.

She wiped away a rogue tear and stood up straighter. A sip of coffee seemed to be what she needed to regain control of her emotions. "I owed you that conversation, Riggs. But now I'd like to move on to talk about Ally before it's too late."

Everything Riggs wanted to say died on his tongue as her walls came up again.

"You don't really believe what you said about Ally earlier, do you?" he asked, wishing they didn't have to move on from the first real conversation they'd had about that night.

Her eyebrow shot up as she took a sip of coffee.

"That her phone is turned off or ran out of battery." He figured the subject of the baby was off-limits from here on out and this didn't seem the right time to ask why she'd pushed him away after losing their little girl. Cheyenne was right about one thing. All of their attention needed to go toward finding Ally.

"Wishful thinking," she admitted. "I'm at a loss as to where she could be, though."

"Without her cell phone records, we don't know who she spoke to or texted with other than what she sent us," he said. "The nurses aren't talking but they are covering for someone. E-cig Nurse brought that point home."

"My guess is the doctor who delivered..." she flashed eyes at him before continuing "...made some kind of mistake and they don't want word to get out."

"Tight-knit communities have a habit of sticking together," he pointed out. He should know. He'd grown up in one. Katy Gulch was a cattle ranching community that had each other's backs. Not to say there weren't disagreements or that people always got along. It was a lot like having siblings. They might mess with each other from time to time but no one else could. Period. Riggs had five brothers who would prove his comment true and he felt the same about them. Even his most troubled brother, Garrett, had come back into the fold recently. Now that their father was gone, they needed all hands on deck in order to run KBR, as well as be there for their grieving mother.

Granted, Margaret O'Connor was one of the strongest people he'd ever known. She would balk at the idea of needing help and would never ask Riggs or his brothers to give up their lives to work the ranch out of obligation. And that was one of the most beautiful things to come out of everything that had happened. Each brother had come home because he wanted to and was wrapping up other work obligations to transition into working the ranch full-time.

Riggs had always stayed at KBR. There'd never been another job for him. He loved the family land and had a great deal of pride working in the family business. His side job as a volunteer firefighter was something he did to give back to the community.

But there'd never been a question in his mind of where his heart truly was. And clearly, that was all he knew in life because it was the only thing that made sense to him now.

"I know nurses stick together. Ally has mentioned they have to, with some of the doctors who can be jerks," she said, breaking into his thoughts. "Now that I think about it, there was a traveling doctor who could be a real horse's backside."

"He probably didn't think he had to worry about making nice if he only worked there to cover for other doctors," he said.

An idea he couldn't afford was forming in his head. One that gave him a sliver of hope there was a mistake somewhere that meant his daughter was still alive. Riggs shut it down before it had time to take hold. The ache in his chest and the hole in his heart told him he couldn't bear to lose her twice. He'd already lost her mother. Based on the dead look in Cheyenne's eyes, there was no hope of resurrecting their marriage.

Shame, he thought. He might have been doing what he considered to be "the right thing" by asking her to marry him six and a half months ago, but he took the vow he'd made seriously. Sickness and in health. Richer or poorer. 'Til death do us part.

That was the deal.

Cheyenne had to make that decision for herself. She'd been clear that she'd only married him because of the pregnancy, despite convincing him otherwise when she'd taken the ring—a ring that was no longer on her finger, he noticed. He couldn't make her want to stay married to him. And to be honest, his ego didn't want to have to.

Riggs's cell buzzed. He fished it out of his pocket and checked the screen. "It's Colton."

Cheyenne moved a few steps closer, still keeping him at arm's length as she white-knuckled her coffee mug.

"Hey, what's up?" he asked Colton.

"I have news." The sound of Colton's voice caused Riggs's stomach to drop.

"Let me put you on speaker," Riggs said with a quick glance toward Cheyenne. She was chewing the inside of her jaw, a nervous tic he'd noticed during their marriage. He held the phone in between them and hit the screen. "We're both here."

"You might want to sit down first," Colton warned.

Cheyenne didn't argue. She immediately walked over to the small dining table next to the kitchen, and then sat down. She removed her handbag from her shoulder, placing it on the back of the chair. Ozzy seemed content to stay inside, not bothering to peek out.

Riggs took the opposite seat, breaking the five-foot rule Cheyenne seemed to have imposed on their proximity. He couldn't help it. The café table wasn't but two feet around.

"We're sitting," Riggs said to his brother.

"Community Friends Hospital came up in connection with the alpaca ranch we've been investigating." Colton paused, letting those words sink in.

A baby ring connected to the hospital where Riggs's daughter was born.

Cheyenne looked more confused than ever, so he gave her the quick rundown that his brother Garrett had been investigating their father's murder and was led to an alpaca farm that was a front for an illegal adoption ring.

"Does that mean there's a possibility she's alive?" Cheyenne immediately asked.

"I don't know what it means yet. I won't stop investigating until we find out, though," Colton said.

"Ally's text message was hopeful," Cheyenne said, her voice laced with some of that hope. "She said my mind would be blown. I assumed it meant I would be happy."

Hope was dangerous. Losing their child had knocked her completely on her backside once. Riggs didn't want to give false hope and yet he couldn't bring himself to quash the only life he'd heard in her voice since the birth.

"And I remember hearing her cry in the labor and delivery room," she added. "The nurse said I probably wasn't remembering right because of the medication I was under, but I swear I heard my baby cry."

Hearing those words for the first time was a gut punch. The air in the room thinned. The hole in his chest widened. Without realizing, he'd fisted his hands. Cheyenne had heard their daughter cry?

The little girl could very well be alive.

Chapter Six

"Do you remember the name of the nurse who assisted with the birth?" Colton asked.

Riggs wondered if the information would be on her discharge papers.

"There was a shift change. I think. My mind isn't so clear on the order or some of the details. Okay, most of the details," Cheyenne admitted. She stared at the phone on the table like it was a bomb about to detonate. "But that doesn't mean what I do know isn't true."

"If it's any consolation, I believe you," Colton said.

"So do I," Riggs agreed.

"It means more than you could know." Chin up, she brought a hand up to cover her heart.

Riggs didn't want to point out there wasn't a judge in the state who would take the word of someone who'd been given enough drugs to make her thoughts blurry and lose the chain of events. She'd be deemed an unreliable witness and any decent attorney would have a field day with her in court if she pursued a civil case against the hospital. Most prosecutors would refuse to take on the case to start with.

Riggs had access to the best lawyers in Texas and he'd have no qualms about draining his bank account if it meant bringing his child home alive or making certain this didn't happen to another family. It was clear something was up with the hospital and the nursing staff. He didn't have to be in law enforcement to suspect Ally must have uncovered something others didn't want to get out. E-cig Nurse had confirmed their fears there.

The question lingered in the back of his mind. Could his child be alive?

Was that the reason for the medication? Had Cheyenne really needed it? Or was she given it to numb her mind and dull her senses? It sure was a convenient excuse. It gave the hospital an out, too, because all anyone had to say was that she was under the influence and her memories couldn't be trusted. Now that he really thought about it, he should bring in the family attorney to put some heat on the hospital's internal investigation.

"Didn't you say your regular doctor wasn't on call the night of the delivery?" Riggs asked.

"That's right. I asked them if we could wait but everything was already happening so fast the nurse said we had to get going or risk losing the baby." Cheyenne exhaled and her shoulders slumped forward.

Riggs had to fight every instinct inside him not to reach out and be her comfort. He quickly reminded himself his touch was the last thing she would want. She'd been clear where the two of them stood. Divorce.

The kiss didn't change anything.

He tried to convince himself the only reason he wanted to protect her came down to the same basics of why he would try to help anyone or anything in need. It was ingrained in him to help someone who was suffering. His family always went out of their way to offer aid. It was part of Riggs's DNA—a part he had no qualms with.

"Do you remember what the nurse on duty looked like?" Colton asked.

"Not really. I think I remember hoop earrings. Like

from the 1970s." She squeezed her eyes shut like she had to block everything else out to concentrate. When she opened her eyes, she frowned. "Sounds like someone from a hallucination, doesn't it?"

"Don't be hard on yourself. Every memory is important. All it takes is one detail to blow a case wide open," Colton said reassuringly.

Cheyenne nodded and compressed her lips. She was clearly frustrated with herself.

"Can you make a guess as to her age?" Colton asked.

"Not young," she said quickly. "Not too old, either. I'd say somewhere in her late thirties to early forties."

"Good." Colton was quiet for a few seconds. "What do you remember about the doctor on duty?"

"Sandy-blond hair. He had blue eyes, cobalt," she explained. "He was definitely older. Maybe early to mid-forties. His name was Dr. Fortner and he only works at the hospital on a rotating basis. He'll be easy enough to look up on my discharge papers."

"Does that mean he works at other hospitals, as well?" Colton asked.

"I believe so. Honestly, once I was told my baby died, I blanked out on everything else going on. I went into a state of shock that I seriously doubt I've recovered from yet." She chewed on the inside of her cheek while staring at the phone.

A hammer slammed into Riggs's chest at hearing the details. He did his level best not to let his anger show. Right now, he needed a clear head. Flying off the handle had been Garrett's gig. Riggs used to have a temper, too. He'd watched how it could destroy relationships between friends and brothers, and had forced himself to get his temper under control. This situation tested his resolve.

In fact, he wanted nothing more than to plant his fist

through a wall to release some of the tension that pulled his shoulder blades taut. A blinding pain hit square in between his eyes as white-hot anger engulfed him at the thought there could be foul play when it came to his child.

The pain Cheyenne must have been in during that moment wasn't lost on him and he suddenly understood the dark circles cradling her eyes. He still didn't like the fact she'd pushed him away in the process but at least he was developing an understanding of the depths of her pain.

He'd lost a child, too. And a wife in the process. So he knew about pain.

"Is there anything else you remember about the hospital, the staff or the birth?" Colton continued.

Part of Riggs wanted to stop this conversation right here and now. Watching Cheyenne relive what had to be one of the worst moments of her life twisted the knot in his gut. Not being able to take away her pain or make a difference messed with the knot even more. He'd asked for a meeting with hospital administration and that was still pending their internal investigation. His lawyer should be able to get things moving.

No one should have to watch someone they cared about recount the loss of something so wanted, so loved.

Strangely enough, it was Riggs who'd had to talk Cheyenne into keeping the baby. Early on, she'd brought up adoption as an alternative. He still remembered the moment she'd told him she was pregnant, like it was yesterday. The look of shock on her face was still etched in his thoughts. She'd sat on his couch, her feet tucked underneath her sweet round bottom.

"I have to tell you something and I have no idea how you're going to react."

He'd set a cold beer down in front of her, her favorite longneck. Instead of picking it up, she'd stared at it with a look that said she wished she could partake but wouldn't be for quite some time.

The move had puzzled him.

That was when he'd really looked at her. There'd been something different about her from the moment she'd walked into his house, weeks before that, too. Something he couldn't quite pinpoint. Glow wasn't the right word. Although, looking back, it wasn't a bad place to start, either. There was a flush to her cheeks that made her even more beautiful. Her eyes looked a little tired but that only made her more attractive to his thinking.

Then it had dawned on him. *Pregnant.*

He'd let her tell him the news in her own time. It had taken her twenty more minutes to work up the courage. He'd reassured her that everything happened for a reason and a baby was always a good thing. No, it wasn't planned or expected. In fact, they'd been careful to avoid this very thing. Birth control had failed and he figured he shouldn't be having sex with someone he couldn't handle the risks with.

So yes, it came out of the blue. Yes, it was a huge surprise. But no, it wasn't a bad thing.

In fact, he'd been planning to tell her for days by then that he'd fallen in love with her. After hearing the news, he'd figured he might as well go all in and ask her to marry him. They were stupidly in love. At least he was.

The second she'd thrown her arms around his neck and told him she loved him he'd been hooked. Hooked on her. Hooked on getting married. Hooked on starting a family. And the same candle that had burned so brightly burned out just as fast.

CHEYENNE COULDN'T RISK HOPE.

There was no way she was going to nurse the possibility of her baby being alive before getting absolute, undeni-able proof. And yet, her heart argued against such caution. It wanted to believe the baby had somehow survived. But that also meant she'd been taken from Cheyenne. In a hospital. With multiple people either directly involved or looking the other way. White-hot anger boiled her blood as she suspected a conspiracy.

Strange as it sounded, she'd heard stories on the news that made this seem not just plausible but likely. Or was that her heart running after what it wanted to be true? She settled on likely.

Riggs filled his brother in on their encounter at the nurse station and then the nurse who met up with them outside the building. Colton promised to follow up.

"A deputy is almost at the hospital. He got sidetracked on a call earlier. I'll update him before he arrives." Colton didn't hesitate and she appreciated her brother-in-law's fast action.

She blew on the surface of the hot coffee, watching the steam form a sail before returning right back to where it started. She welcomed the burn on her throat as she took a sip of the fresh brew. Coffee was a funny thing in times of stress. She hadn't started drinking it until two weeks ago. Strangely, it had given her something to do and made her miss Riggs a little less. *Put on a pot of coffee* had been her mantra recently. Maybe it was time to adopt a new routine. Take up tea drinking again. Something needed to change, because her mind was wandering into dangerous territory, speculating her daughter could have lived, and she needed to shake things up.

She glanced over at Riggs. She'd been unable to look at him much of the time when she was speaking to his brother. The way he clenched his back teeth and his hands fisted, she realized how much he must be hurting, too.

The realization hit hard. She had somehow been able to convince herself he would be relieved that she was letting him out of the marriage. She had told herself that he wouldn't be as devastated about losing their child. Well, now she really did feel like a jerk.

Of course, he would be hurting. Based on the look on his face now, she had hugely underestimated how much he would be affected. Didn't change the fact she knew in her heart of hearts he'd be better off without her in his life. Despite her heart trying to play devil's advocate, she wouldn't go back on her decision to let him out of the marriage commitment.

Riggs ended the call with a promise to let Colton know if by some chance Ally showed up.

"I feel like I should be doing something more," she said to Riggs.

"You are," he said. "You're here, taking care of Ozzy while we figure out our next move."

Her stomach growled despite feeling like she wouldn't be able to get a bite of food down.

"The other thing you can do is make sure you're keeping up your strength," he said without missing a beat. "Is there anything in the fridge to work with?"

"To be honest, I haven't really checked," she admitted. "I've been kind of checked out ever since leaving the hospital. In fact, I could probably use a shower."

"Why don't you go clean up while I poke around in the kitchen to see if there's anything in here to throw together for a meal." He stood up and walked over to the fridge, moving with athletic grace. She forced her gaze away from his strong back—a back that she'd memorized. Every curve and scar was forever etched in her mind.

Rather than let herself continue down that road, she pushed to standing and headed for the shower. She stopped in the hallway. "You'll come get me if anything happens, right?"

"Of course. Take your time. I'm here. I've got nowhere else to be," he reassured.

Somehow, she doubted that. His family ranch boomed with activity and he'd been checking into his father's murder along with the others. Finn O'Connor was a great man. She wished she'd spent more time getting to know him. Now she wished she'd had more time with her father-in-law.

"Thank you," she said. "For sticking around. I don't have a right to ask anything of you, so it means a lot that you're willing to stay."

The look of disappointment on his face as he nodded got her feet moving in the opposite direction. She needed to put some distance between them before she let her guard down even more. Being around Riggs was dangerous. Just being in the same room with him started chipping away at her carefully constructed walls.

No good could come of making herself vulnerable. Nothing about their situation had changed. She was done with trying to have a family and Riggs was just getting started.

Twenty minutes later, she was showered, toweled off, and dressed in something besides joggers. The sundress hugged her curves and fell midcalf. She threw on a little lip gloss and concealer. With just those two moves, she started feeling better. There was something about getting out of bed and putting on a little makeup that lifted her spirits even just a tiny bit. She reminded herself that when this was over and she and Riggs went back to their separate lives, she needed to force herself to get out of bed and get moving. Tie the knot. Hang on.

That, of course, could only happen if Ally turned out

to be all right. Where could she be? It was well past four o'clock and her friend was still missing.

They'd driven past all the possible stop-offs. It was already coming up on dinnertime and there was still no word. Part of Cheyenne wanted to sit down at the table with her phone and call every business up and down the roads leading to the hospital.

Colton was a good sheriff. She had to give him time to do his job. She trusted him. All the O'Connor men were trustworthy, even Garrett, whom she knew the least. From everything she'd seen and heard, he was a good person underneath his tough exterior. Of course, he'd met the love of his life according to Riggs, and that had caused him to turn a new leaf. Good for him.

Cheyenne ran a brush through her still-damp hair before straightening her dress. This was as good as it got, she thought, before joining Riggs in the kitchen.

"I noticed you barely touched your coffee. I can heat it up or grab a glass of water for you instead." He motioned toward the full mug.

"It's okay." She took in a deep breath. The smell of food was actually making her hungry despite the nausea she'd felt in the shower a few minutes ago. "Something smells amazing in here."

"It's a breakfast skillet. My mother used to make these when we were little. You basically throw any chopped vegetables you can find along with some spinach and green onion into a pan of eggs and sausage."

"We have sausage?" she asked.

"You had ham, so I made that work."

This reminded her of all those late Sunday morning breakfasts shared out on the back patio. Or in bed. The latter was her favorite. Then there was the homemade pizza in bed after a long session of making love.

She sighed. She'd really tucked those memories down deep in the last couple of weeks. Seeing Riggs in the kitchen, watching him as he moved so effortlessly, caused her chest to squeeze. She thought about the phone call she needed to return from her divorce attorney to keep the ball rolling. She couldn't make her hands move to pick up the phone if her life depended on it. There was too much going on, and it didn't make sense to push things forward until they knew what happened to their daughter and brought Ally home safely.

So she made a decision. There was no harm in asking if Riggs was on the same page. She would respect his position. Either way, she needed to know.

"I was thinking that while we're investigating this… *situation*…maybe it's for the best if we put the divorce on hold," she said and then held her breath.

He didn't turn around, so she couldn't see his reaction. He stopped what he was doing for a few moments and she had second thoughts about what she'd just said. The last thing she wanted to do was cause him additional pain. They were already knee-deep in it.

"Look, I didn't mean that we should stop altogether, it's just…" She couldn't find the right words.

"The investigation seems more important right now." His tone was unreadable. "Is that how you really see it?"

She searched for any signs of judgment in his voice and decided she couldn't find any. He had his poker face on.

"Yes. But we don't have to wait. I was just thinking out loud," she said. More like she was speaking on impulse.

"I didn't have any interest in divorcing in the first place. This has all been your idea." He shrugged a shoulder like it was no big deal. Was that true? She couldn't imagine it being so. And yet it felt like someone sucked all the air out of the room.

"Okay," she said.

"Okay," he confirmed.

The divorce dropped in priority. Nothing was more important than joining forces to find out if their daughter was still alive. Could she risk hope?

Chapter Seven

"There you go." Riggs plated his culinary masterpiece and set it down on the counter-height bar along with a bottle of sriracha. Cooking had distracted him for a few minutes from all the thoughts circling in his mind. Concentrating too hard on one subject was the fastest way to stay stumped. He always did his best thinking out on the land, away from distractions. Out there, his mind cleared all the clutter and answers came to him.

"Would you mind handing me a fork?" Cheyenne asked. He couldn't count the number of times she'd said the same thing when he'd cooked breakfast on the ranch.

"Where are they?" Walking down memory lane was probably a bad idea.

"Second drawer. Or you could just grab one from the dishwasher." She fidgeted in her seat like when she was out of her comfort zone. Any time he'd tried to do something for her in the past year she'd done the same. He understood on some level, considering she was one of the most independent people he'd ever met. She'd been an only child with working parents and had learned to do things for herself early on. But they were a couple and couples did little things for one another.

He located the drawer, grabbed two forks and then handed one over. Once again, when their fingers grazed, electricity shot through him. He chalked it up to residual attraction and did his level best to put it out of his mind, which was difficult with her in the room.

During their marriage, he'd made a vow to himself that he would get her used to letting someone else do for her every once in a while. Although she was one of the most giving people he'd ever met, he'd been caught off guard at how bad she was at receiving. He'd attributed it to her fierce need for independence and left it at that.

Now he wondered if there wasn't something more to the story. Because she seemed downright uncomfortable accepting help, which would make sense if he was a stranger. Not so much considering they'd signed up to be partners in life.

Then again, if they saw life through the same lens, she wouldn't be asking for a divorce in the first place. When times were tough, the O'Connors came together. Garrett was living proof that no matter how far someone strayed from the fold, he or she would travel as far as necessary to come home and help out during a crisis. It was as much in their DNA as chivalry and working the land.

He fixed his own plate, opting to stand in the kitchen and eat.

"I didn't think I could eat a bite and here I've cleaned my plate," Cheyenne said after a few minutes of silence. "At least let me do the dishes."

True enough, her plate was empty.

"It's no trouble," he said. There were only two plates, a couple of forks and a skillet. "Won't take but a second to rinse these off and put them in the dishwasher."

"It's clean," she said.

He cracked a smile and shook his head.

"Don't tell me you emptied it…"

"I was looking for a pan." A tiny burst of pride filled

his chest that she sounded pleased. He'd been brought up to be self-sufficient just as his brothers had. He shouldn't want to make her happy and told himself it was nothing more than reflex.

"Well, thank you. You didn't have to do that." Cheyenne moved from her bar stool and then brought her plate around.

In the tiny kitchen he could breathe in her clean and citrusy scent. To clear his head, he moved past her and managed to bump into her in the process. Not his best move. More of that electricity rocketed through him, awakening parts that needed to stay dormant.

What could he say?

He was affected by Cheyenne. It was half the reason he'd gone ahead and proposed to her the minute after finding out she was pregnant. Had he been freaked out? Yes. Did he know what to say or do? No. He'd gone with his heart and the fact that he'd never met a woman who could knock him off balance with one look before. The instant he'd laid eyes on her, he knew she was going to be important in his life.

People talked about love at first sight and he used to believe they were crazy. Then he'd met Cheyenne. He'd been hit with something so different there wasn't anything to compare the feeling to. He'd tried and failed numerous times. There was no rhyme or reason to the heart.

Looking at her was the equivalent of a lightning strike on a sunny day. Actually, more than that, but he struggled to put the feeling into words. Riggs was a man of action. So he'd gone out on a limb and asked her to marry him.

Being married to Cheyenne had been heaven on earth. At least on his side. Clearly, she felt differently. It might be pride talking, but he didn't want someone to stay married to him out of obligation. Their relationship had been the real deal to him.

"I better let Ozzy outside," she said, exiting the kitchen as fast as humanly possible after loading her plate into the dishwasher. She scurried over to the table and pulled him from her handbag. She must have as much rolling through her thoughts as he had, especially after the news about the alpaca farm.

The little dog started yelping.

"You need to do your business," she said to him, holding him tightly to her chest. She walked out the side door and immediately heard the sound of tires burning rubber.

Riggs jumped into action, bolting toward the door. Adrenaline kicked in and his pulse thumped.

Cheyenne dove inside and he caught her before she landed, softening her fall with his body. For a split second, their eyes met and locked. Hers were a mix of fear and something else…regret? Or maybe Riggs saw what he wanted instead of what was really there. It could explain their marriage and recently paused divorce. Ozzy had been spared from being accidentally tossed across the room by Riggs's fast thinking.

Not wanting the vehicle to get away, Riggs rolled onto his side. Cheyenne scrambled off him and comforted the little dog, who stood there shaking. No need to take him outside again. Ozzy had done his business right then and there.

Riggs hopped to his feet in one swift motion. He bolted to the window. Swiped the curtain to one side with his right hand. Too late. There wasn't a car or truck in sight.

One good thing to come out of this situation was that no one was hurt.

He fished for his cell phone and updated Colton via text.

"Someone is watching the house," Cheyenne said. Her voice was stilted. Shock?

"I should have seen this coming," Riggs said along with a few choice words he didn't care to repeat in mixed company.

Colton's response was instant. Get out of the house.

"No one tried to shoot." He'd expected to hear a shotgun blast.

"That was my first thought, too." Cheyenne picked up the little dog and took him to the sink. She gently cleaned him before returning him to her handbag.

By the time she returned to the living room, Riggs was already on his hands and knees cleaning up after the little guy.

"Here. I can—"

"It's not a big deal, Cheyenne. Seriously. Cooking up a little breakfast and cleaning a pan and a pair of plates are nothing to make a fuss about, either." The words came out a little more bitter than he'd intended. What could he say? He was taking the breakup of his marriage hard and his mind was reeling after all the new information they had.

"Oh." She stopped in her tracks.

"Stay below the window line in case someone comes back on foot." He motioned toward the front windows.

"Right." She dropped down almost immediately. "I wasn't trying to offend you, by the way. It's just..."

"What? Weird for the man you married to make a meal for you?" He sat back on his heels. He shouldn't have said that. It was out of bounds. Their situation was complicated, and he didn't want to make it worse. For the time being, they were working together. "Forget I said that, okay?"

"I can't." She folded her arms across her chest like she was defending herself from the world. "Like I can't forget a lot of things said between us in the past few weeks."

"What has been said between us? You haven't given me the time of day in case you hadn't noticed. I've been told I'm getting a divorce and I'm still scratching my head as to why you went down that road." He issued a sharp sigh, needing to get a handle on his outburst. It sure as hell wouldn't make anything better between them and he didn't want to ruin all the ground they'd been making today.

But what could he say? He couldn't exactly take any of it back and wouldn't want to anyway. Part of him needed her to know exactly how he felt. It wasn't like he'd been given the chance to clear the air before the call from his attorney came to let him know what was going down.

"Mind if we have this conversation at a later date? Right now, all I can think about is finding my friend and possibly getting answers to what happened to our daughter." There was no anger in her words, just resolve.

"Why not." It wasn't like he had any easy answers, either. Even if they could get back together and that was a laughable *if*, how would he ever believe her again?

CHEYENNE GOT ON her hands and knees beside Riggs and finished wiping up Ozzy's mess. Being this close to Riggs was a problem, but she needed to learn to deal with it. If she wasn't attracted to him or didn't feel a pull so strong her body ached to touch him, she would be worried. There'd been enough attraction and chemistry between them for her to throw all logic aside, decide to have a baby together, and get married.

Thinking all that would dissipate overnight would be downright crazy. Even now, her stomach clenched and her chest squeezed in his masculine presence.

Taking in a deep breath, Cheyenne tried to rebalance but only ushered in his scent. He was all outdoors, campfires, and dark roast coffee. Speaking of the latter, it had always tasted better on his tongue. He was the reason she'd taken up coffee drinking because she missed tasting it on his lips so much her heart ached.

"Where do we go now?" she asked sitting back on her heels.

"We could go back to our house."

She started shaking her head before he could finish. It was one thing to be around him for the foreseeable future. It was quite another to go back to the home they'd shared on the ranch that belonged to his family, a ranch she'd loved.

"Hotel. There's a decent one over by the highway that has suites. We could rent one of those just until we get answers or Ally contacts us," he offered.

"I'll leave her a note…in case." She stood. "I've already sent a few texts, so no need to go down that road again. Once she turns on her cell, she'll know I've been trying to reach her. I know the odds of that happening aren't great, but I have to find some reason to hope she'll turn up."

It was wishful thinking on Cheyenne's part to believe it could be that simple. That Ally would somehow magically realize her cell was off, turn it on, and return home with one of her you-won't-believe-how-stupid-I-can-be stories. Ally had managed to lock her keys in the car while it was still running. She was probably half the reason most new cars made it impossible to do that now.

Riggs nodded.

"There was this time Ally decided to cook Thanksgiving dinner," Cheyenne started. "She invited me and this guy she had a crush on to eat with her. She wanted to do everything and wouldn't even let me bring dinner rolls. So I walk in with a bottle of wine that I could barely afford because we were being grown-ups, and I couldn't figure out why her house didn't smell like the holiday. You know?"

He cocked an eyebrow, clearly confused as to where this conversation was going. It was one of the many things she appreciated about him before. She could come out of the blue with a topic and he would go along with it until she made sense.

"I couldn't figure out what was missing. There were a few familiar smells, but it wasn't as if I walked in and was hit with the amazing food aromas like when my mom was alive and we did Thanksgiving. I chalked it up to my memory being faulty." She paused long enough to finger the charm on her bracelet. "At Ally's there was corn heating on the stove, and she'd bought a pumpkin pie for dessert. She'd made the green bean casserole the night before. The stuffing was in the bird, so I just went with it. Then she goes to take the turkey out of the oven and realizes she never turned it on."

She chuckled as a stray tear streaked her cheek at the bittersweet memory.

"And that's Ally, you know?" she continued. "When she was on duty at her job, she was on point. Nothing got past her, and she was there for her patients. Sure, a couple of doctors gave her a hard time now and then but that was the nature of her work. Once she walked out of that hospital, totally different story. So much so, that early on I refused to allow her to bring candles in our dorm room in college for fear she would burn the entire building down because she forgot to blow one out."

Riggs studied her thoughtfully. There was no judgment in his eyes now. Just a hint of compassion.

"You're hoping this is one of those times despite what we already know," he finally said, catching her drift.

"Maybe she got sidetracked or forgot to tell us that she was still with the guy in Dallas. Maybe he called and she's on her way there. Maybe the battery ran out on her phone."

Chin to chest, she tried to hide the tears that rolled down her face. The thought anything bad might have happened to her best friend ripped her insides out. The fact Ally was trying to help Cheyenne wasn't lost on her. The weight of it was crushing.

In the next second, Riggs was there. He looped his arms around her and hauled her to his chest, where she felt the most at home she'd ever felt. "I've never been one to believe in miracles, but I sure wouldn't be against being proven wrong this once."

Cheyenne nodded. She wiped away a few more rogue tears as they sprung from her eyes.

The sound of a car pulling into the gravel drive broke them apart too soon. Riggs's movements were smooth and predator-like as he bolted to the window. Crouching low, he peered through the window, barely moving the curtain.

"Someone's using the drive to turn around," he said. "It's a sedan loaded up with a family."

Cheyenne let out the breath she'd been holding. A miracle was probably too much to hope for.

Wherever they were going, they needed to get to it. The thought someone had been watching the house and could still be sent an icy chill down her spine.

She wondered if they had been followed home from the hospital?

"I find it interesting that someone started watching the house after our visit to the hospital," she said to Riggs.

"I'd like to know what Renee, Sherry, and Becca have to say to law enforcement." Riggs walked over to the kitchen and drained his coffee cup. "Pack up whatever you need and let's head out of here. Colton requested the place be looked after by local police. Manpower is limited and there's only so much cooperation he can get while also requesting his deputy be permitted to interview nurses."

"As sheriff, can't he investigate anyone he wants to?" she asked.

"He's certainly able to follow a lead wherever it takes him, but gaining local support gives him more resources to work with." He set the coffee cup down and gave her the look she recognized as needing to get a move on.

"I'll be five minutes." She circled back to her bedroom and, true to her word, had an overnight bag filled in the time she'd promised. She closed the door to her bedroom and paused in front of Ally's room. It dawned on her there might be a clue inside.

The door was ajar from the time she'd opened it this morning. It seemed wrong to go snooping around in her best friend's bedroom, but if she could find one clue, it would be worth a few minutes of discomfort.

Inside was dark, with the blackout curtains still closed. Ally flipped on the light thinking her roommate would be all kinds of angry if she walked through the front door about now. Since the probability of that happening was about as high as Colonel Sanders pulling up out front to personally deliver a bucket of chicken, she shut down the guilt and pushed ahead.

The bed wasn't made. No surprise there. Ally normally jumped out of bed and ran straight to the shower. Her habits hadn't changed all that much. Her laptop sat on top of her bed.

Cheyenne walked over and tucked it inside her bag. She might be able to figure out the password. Guilt got the best of her, so she pulled out her cell and tried to text Ally one more time.

I'm going through your room.
Sorry.
Taking your laptop.
Pls respond.

No response came. Cheyenne issued a sharp sigh. At least some of her guilt for going through Ally's personal belongings eased after reaching out.

A dark thought someone might have Ally's cell phone and be reading the texts struck. It wouldn't be a good idea to lay out their plans. Cheyenne decided not to mention anything about leaving.

A handwritten note would do the trick.

She moved to Ally's dresser and found a scrap of paper along with a pen. She clicked the pen and scribbled a message. *Leaving for a few days. Call me. Text me. I'm worried.*

The note was cryptic enough not to broadcast Cheyenne's next steps and yet got the point across. The creepy feeling someone could break into the house and read the note raised goose bumps on her arms. The whole situation was surreal. This kind of thing only happened in the movies. It didn't happen to normal, law-abiding citizens.

And yet, she knew on some level crime didn't discriminate. Criminals were everywhere and would take advantage of anyone. But an O'Connor? Surely the name would be a deterrent.

It dawned on her that she was still using her maiden name. Would that make a difference? No one would mess with an O'Connor baby. Or would they? She thought about what had happened to Riggs's sister.

Wouldn't the person be in touch to demand some type of ransom by now if that was the case?

Chapter Eight

Riggs caught himself tapping the toe of his boot on the beige tile in the kitchen. Impatience edged in when Cheyenne didn't return after the promised five minutes. Ten passed before the toe tapping had started. He realized he was gripping the bullnose-edge granite like a vise at the fifteen mark.

Fighting the urge to traipse down the hallway and see what was taking so long, he started whistling. The next thing he knew, Ozzy scampered over and sat at his feet. Looked like the little yippy dog had some training after all.

Riggs bent over to pick up the small animal. Ozzy growled before backing away.

Maybe not.

Riggs's thoughts shifted to the events of the day. He had no idea what Ally's personal life was like. Cheyenne had mentioned her best friend a few times before arranging a meetup. His impression of Ally had been good. She promised to be an amazing godmother after Cheyenne had asked.

Ally had the kind of personality most would describe as bubbly. Cheyenne joked that only happened after a decent amount of caffeine, which Riggs could relate to. The three of them had chatted easily about plans for the baby. Cheyenne had apologized to her friend for what felt like a dozen times for not having a traditional wedding or having Ally as maid of honor.

To make up for it, Cheyenne had asked Ally to be godmother to their child. Ally accepted and did nothing but support Cheyenne as far as Riggs could tell. He'd had a good feeling about his wife's best friend, and he was usually spot-on with his assessments when he met people. Ally was what most would call a pure soul. The thought of something bad happening to her was a gut punch. Not just because she was Cheyenne's best friend, although that was part of it. Because Ally was a good person who deserved the life she wanted.

He stopped himself right there before he got too far ahead of himself. They didn't know anything for certain despite his gut telling him this situation had gone south. The chilly reaction he and Cheyenne had received at the nurse station and then with E-cig Nurse outside drove home the point. Not to mention the fact Ally had gone off the grid. No cell phone contact after sending the texts to him and Cheyenne. No witnesses so far. No sightings.

And now the vehicle that had been watching the house.

So yeah, he expected the worst when it came to news about her and prayed like the dickens he was wrong. Despite her strength, Cheyenne could only handle so much. There was a something in her past that he hadn't been able to break through while they were together. He'd figured they had a lifetime to get to know the nuances of each other's personalities.

When they'd first met, she'd reacted more like a wounded animal who needed protection and was the last to know it. Every time he got close to her, she backed away. It was okay. He understood being broken after her mom's death. He understood needing time. And he certainly understood needing space. The last thing he'd wanted to do was spook her away by trying to get too close too fast. Because he also knew in his heart that when she truly opened up to him, she would absolutely be worth the wait.

"I found her laptop." Cheyenne bounded into the room and patted her weekend bag. She no longer looked like she'd jump out of her skin at the slightest noise. It was progress and he'd take it. Getting her to relax and trust him might just get her talking about why she thought she was protecting him by pushing him away.

"Any chance you know the passwords, too?" He walked over and took the bag so she wouldn't have to carry that and her purse once she put the devil dog in it.

"I wish. I know her personal information like her birthday and first pet name. Maybe I can make an educated guess," she offered as Ozzy started running around her ankles, threatening to nip. "What's wrong with him?"

"No clue. I whistled and he came. When I tried to pick him up, he went psycho." Riggs was normally good with four-legged critters. Dogs were his favorite and there were several on the ranch who preferred living in the barn and bunkhouse. He didn't have time for one of his own. Maybe someday he would. He'd been thinking of surprising Cheyenne with a puppy once the baby came.

"Ready when you are," she said, picking up the devil dog and then tucking him inside her handbag where he settled.

Riggs took note of the behavior. Dogs were den animals, and this guy must feel out of his element now, with Ally gone and a strange male in the house. Not to mention the fact he didn't seem too keen on Cheyenne being there. Based on what she'd said so far, it didn't appear like she'd left her room much except to heat a leftover or grab a cup of coffee or take the occasional shower.

Under the circumstances, Riggs would cut the little guy some slack.

"Keep the dog in your purse. He settles down inside there. I'll go start the pickup truck and then text you when it's safe to come out."

She cocked her head to one side but then nodded with a confused look on her face.

Good. That meant she hadn't caught the underlying meaning in what he was saying. Yes, it was dangerous to leave the house. It was also risky to start his vehicle and he planned to perform a couple of safety checks before hopping in and starting the engine.

"I won't be but a minute." He waited for the okay, which she gave, before heading outside.

First, he stepped outside and beside his truck to block anyone's shot from the road. There were a few cars on the street zipping by. For his taste, this was a busy street, but he lived on a ranch where he didn't have to see another vehicle or person for days on end if it suited him.

By town standards, the street would probably be considered normal. Nothing looked out of the ordinary, but he'd learned a long time ago not to trust appearances. If someone wanted to climb on top of a roof and hide behind a chimney, he could be picked off without ever knowing what hit him.

He ran his hand along the bottom of the truck, feeling for anything out of the ordinary. If someone wanted the two of them dead, a bomb would do the trick. It would be messy, but it would blow up the evidence along with them. He rounded the front and then popped the hood.

A quick check gave him the confidence to take the driver's seat and risk starting the engine.

It hummed to life as he listened for any unusual sounds that might come right before a big boom. When he was certain it was safe, he palmed his cell and fired off a text for Cheyenne to join him.

She came out of the house so fast she forgot to lock the door behind her. Once she settled into the passenger seat, he asked for the house key.

She blinked at him and then embarrassment heated her cheeks. She was even more beautiful with her face flushed, but this wasn't the time to get sentimental or take another trip down memory lane. Their relationship was in the rearview. For now. They had come together as interested parties in an investigation. He needed to remember that when he was staring into those blue eyes or noticing how beautiful she was.

"Right. I didn't even think…" She placed the key on top of his opened hand. "Are you sure you want to get out of the vehicle?"

He didn't say better him than her. Instead, he went for "I got this."

CHEYENNE HELD HER breath waiting for Riggs to return. Her nerves were shot, and she couldn't even go there about something bad happening to Ally. The thought alone gutted her. But this was also the first time she'd felt alive in days. Weeks?

Riggs did that to her. Being around him again reminded her how much she enjoyed his company and how safe she felt around him. This situation was far from ideal, yet it felt right to do this together.

Of course it did. He was the father of her baby. An annoying voice in the back of her mind reminded her that he deserved to know what happened as much as she did. It was, after all, the reason he was here.

Being near him again also reminded her of all the things she could never have. Not because she didn't want them but because her life just wasn't designed that way. Call it destiny or fate but having a happy homelife—with kids running around and a husband who adored her even when she woke up first thing in the morning and was a hot mess—wasn't in the cards.

And, man, did Riggs deserve all those things. Even now, he stood beside her, opened doors for her and took the heavy bag so she could walk a little lighter. He was kind, considerate and wicked smart. He wasn't hurting in the looks department, either. The man was pure billboard-worthy hotness. And the only reason she thought about any of those things right now was to remind herself he deserved much more than she would ever be able to give him.

How many times had he teased her, saying he wanted enough kids to field a football team? More than she could count. He even had names for half a dozen of them already picked out despite swearing he'd never thought a day about having his own children until her pregnancy.

How could she rip his dreams, his future, out from underneath him? Because she didn't ever want to have kids again. What kind of a selfish person did that to another human being, especially one she loved?

Loved?

Did she love Riggs? It had been so easy to convince herself she did while pregnant with his child. Living together had been the definition of perfection. She'd found herself opening up to him little by little only to have it all ripped out from underneath them by losing the baby. Without a doubt, Cheyenne knew she would never try to have another child after what happened.

What if her daughter was alive, though?

Cheyenne couldn't go there yet. Not now. It was too soon. She would pull herself up by her bootstraps and soldier on. She would get back into her career as a college admissions counselor, the career she'd put on hold to have a baby. She would force herself to get out of bed every morning and get back into life.

Strange that she'd only known Riggs for a less than a year and yet the thought of a life without him nearly broke her. He was that special. More proof that he needed to be with someone who could give him a football team of kids. He needed someone who could fill the ranch property with little ones running around, and maybe even a dog or two. As much as she might care for him, that person would never be her. She was fine with it, except for the part about having to walk away from Riggs forever. That was the tricky part.

"Now we're ready." Riggs reclaimed his seat.

"I forgot Ozzy's food." Cheyenne was most definitely not used to taking care of an animal.

"Keep your cell in your hand and have 911 on speed dial," he instructed. "Make the call if you see anything suspicious."

"Got it." She fished her cell out of her handbag and made sure she was ready.

"Lock the door behind me. I'll leave the truck running in case," he said.

She locked the door the second he exited. The street was quiet. There were no pedestrians and only a few cars that occasionally zipped past.

She searched for any signs of movement near houses or in the landscaping. A cat stepped out of shrubbery and she nearly jumped out of her skin.

She gripped the cell so tight she had to remind herself to relax her fingers for fear she might crack the screen. The area was almost too quiet. A few minutes ago, there'd been almost too much activity.

A second wave of relief washed over her the minute the

door opened and Riggs slipped out. He locked it before returning to the truck with a small grocery bag in hand.

"This should keep him fed for a couple of days," he said as he checked the neighborhood one more time before slipping the gearshift into Drive.

A couple of days? The reality of the situation pressed down on Cheyenne. She would, at a minimum, be with her soon-to-be ex for the rest of the day. At a maximum, she might be looking at several days. The pull toward him was difficult enough to resist in the short term.

All she had to do was remind herself that her actions were for his own good. What she wanted wasn't important. All she could think about was how selfish she would be to trap him in the marriage now. The pain he might be experiencing from the loss would be temporary. In a few months, he'd be recovered and a whole lot better off.

Short-term pain for long-term gain. That would be her new mantra.

Chapter Nine

The suite hotel off the highway was basically two rooms and a bathroom. It came standard with a full-size sofa bed, a kitchenette and a square-shaped dining table. The bedroom housed a king-size bed with a decent-sized bathroom attached that included four rolled-up towels, face soap and shower supplies.

The place had a decently modern vibe and smelled clean, which was a bonus she hadn't been sure she could expect when they'd pulled into the lot. The recent renovation was advertised in the lobby with a large sign. Although it fit the bill of what they needed for now, there was nothing homey about the place. The suite would meet their needs, but it also made her realize how much she missed the ranch.

A growing part of her prayed her phone would ring and Ally's name and picture would fill the screen. The ache in the pit of her stomach said she wouldn't.

"Is there anything else we can do?" Today felt like a week instead of a day. A lot had happened, and it was already getting dark outside. Her hopes of this all somehow being a big mistake were dashed.

"Afraid not," he said. "We have to give Colton a chance to work the investigation. Right now, no one at the hospital is talking to us and I'm pretty certain the one nurse who did would run the other way if she saw us again, especially since a deputy is probably finishing up interviews as we speak. I've already updated Colton on what happened at Ally's house before we left."

"Sitting here and doing nothing is awful." Cheyenne twisted her hands together. Then she remembered the laptop. "Hold on." She grabbed it out of her bag and moved to the kitchen table. She opened it and powered up, realizing she'd forgotten the power cord.

The battery was almost fully charged. Thank heaven for small miracles. It would give her time before she had to figure out a plan B. Going back to the house without Ally seemed wrong and dangerous. It was clear the place was being watched and they could probably buy another one. Had Riggs's truck being parked out front deterred a would-be assailant? A shiver raced down her spine at the thought, and an idea sparked.

"Here's hoping I can find something on her laptop to make sense of all this." She glanced at Riggs before exhaling and testing the waters. "How many tries do you think I'll get before I'm blocked?"

"I'm probably not the right person to ask about technology. My best days are spent out of cell range." He seemed to catch himself when he shot her a look of apology. He'd been out of cell range when she'd gone into labor. "I think it's three tries before you'll get locked out."

Three tries. Great. That sounded right.

The first attempt netted a zero. Same with the second. She chewed on the inside of her jaw and tapped her fingers on the edges of the keyboard. If he was right, and she figured he was, this would be her last try.

"What have you done so far?" he asked, seeming to pick up on her hesitation to go for what might end up a third strike.

"I played around with her birthday and her name," she said.

"Try Ozzy," he offered.

"Would it be that simple?" she asked, typing in the name and then hesitating before hitting Enter.

"It's possible."

Inspiration struck before she dropped her right pinky finger on the button. "Her lucky number is six. I remember her saying something once about her passwords always being plus 06."

"It's worth a try." Riggs sat down next to her and she could breathe in his spicy scent, which reminded her of campfires and home. It reminded her of late Saturday nights lying in his arms. And it reminded her of having felt for a while that she might not be cursed after all.

Cheyenne typed in 06 after the dog's name and squeezed her eyes shut.

"You're in," Riggs said, his voice traveling over her and through her.

"Seriously?" She risked opening her eyes. He was right. "Yes." The first win in what felt like a very long time was sweet.

"Let's see if she left any clues," he said.

"First off, I think we should check her email." She figured it was an easy place to start.

Riggs nodded.

There were more ads than anything else in Ally's inbox. If she was dating anyone in particular, they didn't exchange messages over email. But then, everything was on the phone these days. Text. Social networks.

"Oh. I should check her social media page," she said. "See if I can find anything there."

"And her browser history," he added.

"Good idea."

The browser didn't reveal much. Ally mostly shopped online with her laptop. She must live off her phone. Come to think of it, the laptop was old, whereas Ally got a new phone every couple of years. Okay, so there might not be anything here to work with.

She moved on to social media. Ally's page hadn't been posted on in months. Her relationship status was single.

"What about those apps that text certain people," Riggs said.

"I'm not on those, so I wouldn't know." Cheyenne had ditched those years ago. She couldn't blame Ally for lacking a social media presence. Cheyenne was in a similar boat. She didn't live her life online like some. But then, she'd always been the quiet type, preferring one close friend to several surface-level acquaintances. She had no judgment about people who liked a big circle. She just didn't have time to keep up with one. She'd never been the join-a-sorority type, either. Then again, she'd never been much of a joiner of anything. A simple life was all she craved. So much so that her only real wish was to own a horse someday. She'd much rather be on horseback than in a car, despite not having ridden much in far too many years.

"She didn't use this a lot," Cheyenne said as she closed the laptop, figuring she needed to save battery for the time being. "Give me her phone and we'd be talking about another story. That thing was practically glued to her hand."

"I don't think most folks even own a laptop anymore unless they use one for work," Riggs admitted. "I wouldn't have one if not for keeping records. Plus, it just seems easier than staring at my phone or setting up a desktop in my house."

"You never did like bringing work home anyway," she

said, smiling at the memory. He'd explained much of a cattle rancher's life was spent doing paperwork.

"Home is sanctuary in my book. Once you step inside the front door, you have to learn to leave the rest of the world behind," he said. Then added, "Easier said than done during calving season."

She laughed out loud. It wasn't even that funny, but the stress of the day was catching up to her and she needed a release.

His eyebrows drew together in confusion.

"Sorry. Calving season isn't funny except that all it made me think about was how many places I found you asleep while fully dressed. And once buck naked." Again, she laughed. "I think the last count was eleven."

"Very funny. And it was twelve if I remember correctly." His face broke into a wide smile in a show of perfectly straight teeth. He had the kind of mouth that had never known braces, and confounded dentists. Perfect white teeth. But it was his lips that had always drawn her in. Lips she didn't need to be thinking about right now.

"You're right. Then there was that one time I found you sitting on the porch, passed out. Who were you waiting for?" she asked.

"Cash, I think. Who can remember? Calving season is a blur."

"And there was the time I found you snoring standing up. You were leaning against the wall in the bathroom with the shower running. I walked past and there you were. Door open. Buck naked. Dead asleep." She laughed so hard she snorted.

And the embarrassment didn't end there. She laughed so hard about snorting that she double-snorted.

Riggs was already holding his side, trying to gain his composure. He lost it after the double-double.

This was the first time she'd laughed in what felt like a really long time. Everything at the ranch had become tense after his father was murdered and then found on the property. She barely knew Finn O'Connor but he'd accepted her and the pregnancy without hesitation. Losing him was a blow the family found difficult to deal with and accept. She tabled that thought, too. It didn't seem right to think about his father when the two of them couldn't stop being silly.

After they'd laughed so hard literal tears fell down her cheeks, Cheyenne took in a few slow, deep breaths. "I don't know what it is about stress that can make you laugh."

"Better than the alternatives. Holding it in makes you sick. Crying…well, that's never been my thing," he said.

"Is it weird that I'm exhausted right now? Mentally. Physically. And every which way." She'd been that way since losing the baby.

"Not at all." His voice was full of reassurance. "In fact, it might do some good not to think about the current situation for a little while."

"How do you propose we do that?" she asked.

"We could watch TV. See if we can find a movie," he offered.

"Turning it on might be a useful distraction." Her mind was spinning out and she needed to think about something else for a little while.

It didn't take more cajoling to get her up from the table and onto the sofa. She settled on the couch as Riggs grabbed the remote and figured out how to find a movie. Easy-peasy, considering there was a room charge.

"Before we get started, Ozzy probably should be taken out." She started to push to standing but Riggs waved her off.

"I got this." He grabbed the bag and produced a pad. "I'm guessing that's what this is for."

"Your guess is as good as mine." She had no idea. Wow, had she really been in that much of a funk that she didn't know what food Ozzy ate or if he used one of those pads on a regular basis?

The short answer? Yes.

Cheyenne slipped off her shoes as Riggs set up the pee pad by the door on the small patch of tile. She curled up with a pillow on her side and settled in to watch the movie.

"Mind if I join you?" he asked.

"Be my guest," she said.

They settled on something light and she barely remembered the beginning before she conked out. By the time she opened her eyes again, the sun was up.

How many hours had passed? Her vision was blurry, and she felt like she was in a fog. Nothing seemed familiar. Where was she?

Cheyenne sat bolt upright as fear gripped her.

"You're all right." Riggs reached over to touch Cheyenne's leg out of instinct. He wanted to ground her to reality after what must have been a shock, waking up disoriented with memories flooding back.

"What time is it?" She gasped for air and clutched her chest, clearly in distress.

"It's early. The sun is barely rising and I'm right here with you. You haven't missed anything," he reassured.

She searched his gaze with wild eyes. Then she eased back to sitting.

"Where's Ozzy?" she asked.

"He's inside your handbag again. I set it on the floor so he could come and go. He seems to be more comfortable in there and I'm guessing it has to do with being a den animal," he said. Watching her wake up in a complete panic sent his blood boiling. She shouldn't have to wake up scared. They should be at home instead of in this suite, together with their newborn.

Wishful thinking. Dangerous territory, too.

The past twenty-plus hours had planted a seed of hope inside him. One that he knew better than to water. After all, there wasn't a piece of solid evidence yet that pointed to their child being alive. Foul play was a whole different story.

"Is that coffee I smell?" she asked, still sounding a little hazy.

"Fresh brewed fifteen minutes ago." He regretted making the noise now. It was probably the reason she had woken up. "Is everything okay? Did you have a dream?"

She nodded. "I need caffeine first."

"Stay put. I don't mind. Besides, I never did get up to pour mine." He stood, ignoring the electricity lighting his fingertips on fire on the hand where he'd made contact with Cheyenne.

Electricity had never been a problem for them. Sex had never been a problem for them. He was beginning to realize he didn't know her as much as he'd convinced himself that he had. And he was paying a price for it.

Not that he would go back and do anything differently if he could. He couldn't regret the past year with Cheyenne. Or the baby. Both had brought happiness to him like he'd never known, and pain to depths he never wanted to hit again.

The question still burned in the back of his mind. Was their daughter alive?

His cell buzzed, causing Cheyenne to nearly jump out of her skin.

"It's okay," he tried to soothe as he scooted off the couch

to retrieve the phone that sat on the table. He checked the screen. "It's Colton."

Cheyenne sat ramrod straight. Her right hand came up to cover her lips as she seemed to stop breathing. The look on her face told him she was desperate for good news and yet too afraid to want it too badly.

"Good morning," he said to his brother. "What's up?"

"I'm afraid I have news." Those words combined with the compassionate tone in Colton's voice sent Riggs's blood pressure racing. His back was to Cheyenne and he didn't turn around on purpose, not until he knew exactly what he was dealing with, for fear she would be able to read him.

"Go on," Riggs urged, realizing his brother's hesitation meant one of his worst fears was about to be realized. He sucked in a sharp breath.

"It's Ally Clark. She's been found." The finality in Colton's voice sent fire through Riggs's veins.

Chapter Ten

"And?" Riggs's tone caused Cheyenne's stomach to clench. His silence was not good.

No. No. No. Cheyenne had a sinking feeling the news was going to be crushing. The fact Riggs hadn't turned to face her had been her first clue.

Riggs was quiet. He nodded his head a couple of times and said a few uh-huhs into the phone while Cheyenne prepared for the worst.

It only took a few seconds for him to end the call. A couple more for him to deliver the news that shattered her heart into a thousand pieces. Ally's vehicle had been found in the field near the hospital with Ally inside.

Cheyenne's hands fisted at her sides as she stood up and crossed over to the window. She flexed and released her fingers several times before pulling back the curtain to look out over the highway.

So many people zipping up and down the road, busy with their lives. Many without a care in the world, driving to or from work. It struck her as strange how life just went on. The first time she'd had the thought was after losing her mother. The second occurred when she'd been told her daughter was gone. Her world had stopped and yet others kept on, going about their day like nothing had happened.

It had been a strange and surreal realization both times and one she wasn't ready to embrace again.

So many emotions threatened to consume Cheyenne. She could easily let them burn her from the inside out. Anger surfaced first. Disbelief was a close second. She wanted to question what she knew deep in her gut had to be true.

So many feelings were bearing down on her all at one time. It would be easy to give in, curl up on the sofa and block out as much of the world as possible.

There was one very big reason why she could never allow herself to do that. Ally. Her best friend deserved justice. Letting emotions rule, despite the tears rolling down Cheyenne's face at the moment, wouldn't be fair to her friend. Cheyenne needed a clear head and she needed to stay as logical as possible. She'd gone emotional after losing her daughter and had made bad decision after bad decision. Yes, blocking Riggs's pain out of her mind had been a huge one. There'd been others, too. Most involved her treatment of her hus—soon to be ex-husband.

Pulling on all the strength she had left, Cheyenne wiped away the tears and took in a deep breath to calm her racing pulse.

"Hey," Riggs said from close behind her. He was so close, in fact, she could feel his presence before he spoke.

"I'm fine," she said.

He brought his hand up to her shoulder. "It's okay if you aren't."

"I have to be." She sniffed back a tear. It would be so easy to lean into him right now and let him be her strength.

And then what?

How would she be able to go back to the way it was a few minutes ago? To the place where she managed to keep enough of a distance to hold her emotions in check? To the place where she would be able to walk away from him permanently once this was all said and done?

"I want to go to the scene," she said, tensing up for the argument that was sure to come.

"I know." There was a whole lot of resolve in his voice.

The fact he didn't argue showed how well he knew her. There was nothing, short of being called away to find their daughter, that would keep her from that crime scene.

"I'll let Colton know we're on our way, then," he said.

"Thank you." She was half-surprised he hadn't already told his brother they'd be there as fast as possible. She turned to find Ozzy standing next to the door like he wanted to go out. Did he know they were talking about his owner? Ally said he was the only responsibility she ever planned on having other than being a godmother.

Ally.

A few deep breaths and Cheyenne walked over to pick up Ozzy. She nuzzled him to her chest despite his low warning growl. "I won't abandon you, little guy. I'll take care of you."

Ozzy continued to growl but he was all bark and no bite. She wondered how much dogs picked up on human emotions. Probably more than anyone would ever know.

And then Ozzy settled down, nuzzling his head against her. She walked over to her handbag, picked it up and placed him inside. Shouldering the bag, she grabbed her cell phone and then headed to the door without another word.

Riggs picked up his wallet, keys, and phone before following her out the door. After a quick coffee stop, he drove off the main road onto a side road near the hospital. The road dead-ended and then there was nothing but a field that seemed to go on forever. Had Ally been this close to the hospital the whole time?

There were half a dozen emergency vehicles around. There was an area at the back of the field, a heavily treed part that was cordoned off with yellow police tape. The scene made her head spin. And yes, Ally's cherry red Mustang was parked in the field.

A law enforcement officer had all the doors open, including the trunk. He was making his way around the vehicle, snapping pictures from just about every angle. One minute he was on his feet, the next he was on his back, snapping pics from underneath.

She spotted Colton, who was making a beeline toward them as they exited the truck. His serious expression confirmed what she already knew even though she didn't want to accept it as truth. This whole scene was going to take time to process. Answers would have to wait.

Riggs met her at the front of his truck, reached for her hand and then linked their fingers. She ignored the electricity shooting up her arm from contact as it was quickly replaced by warmth.

Colton immediately brought his brother into a bear hug. She'd always admired how close the O'Connor men were. They were tight knit before their father's murder and had only become more so since his death.

Colton surprised her by bringing her into a hug next. "I'm sorry about your friend."

She nodded, taken aback by the show of kindness. She wasn't sure what she'd expected from Colton. Anger? Defensiveness? Definitely not this.

"Thank you," was all she could say as she reached for the comfort of Riggs's hand after hugging his brother. The second their fingers linked she could exhale again.

If Colton was shocked by the move, he hid it well.

"A teenager called it in. Raven was riding her bike across the field to go to the convenience store for breakfast tacos when she came upon the scene. She'd stayed up all night playing video games online with a friend who was supposed to meet up," Colton said. His gaze moved from Cheyenne to Riggs and back like he was checking to make sure it was okay to keep going.

Riggs nodded as Cheyenne skimmed the small crowd of people for the teenager. She must have been so shocked to come up on a crime scene like this...being the one to find a...

Cheyenne couldn't bring herself to finish the sentence. It was too horrific.

Her gaze stopped on a woman who looked to be in her early forties and was wearing jogging pants and a sweater. She was leaning against a deputy's sport utility, smoking. Inside the SUV, a young person sat hunched over with a blanket around her shoulders. Her shoulders shook like she was crying, and it took everything inside Cheyenne not to march right over there and bring that poor kid into a hug.

"She was out without her mother's permission, wasn't she?" Cheyenne asked. "Raven."

"Her mother claims so, but the teen said she does this all the time," Colton said.

"The mother is embarrassed?" she asked.

"That's my guess," Colton said. "She doesn't seem to want to admit to allowing her daughter free access to come and go as she pleases."

Shame.

"Did she see the...?" Again, Cheyenne couldn't bring herself to finish the sentence. Her stomach clenched so tightly she was nauseous.

"Yes," Colton confirmed. "She dropped her bike and ran to the hospital. She came screaming into the ER and one of the orderlies immediately called 911."

Cheyenne thought about the kind of mark that would leave on this teenager.

"They tried to give her something to calm her nerves, but she refused to take it. Said it would interfere with her Adderall," he continued.

The medication sounded familiar. Then it came to her. She had a friend in middle school who used to take it for attention deficiency disorder. It also explained why the teen might have been up all night. What day was it anyway?

Cheyenne realized it was Saturday. Wow. She'd lost track of the day of the week. Hell, she'd lost track of the month, too. All time had stopped in the past two weeks.

"Is she going to be okay?" Cheyenne hated the fact this would scar this teenager for the rest of her life. At the very least, for many years to come. The mother didn't seem like she was being a whole lot of help, either.

Normally, Cheyenne would mind her own business when it came to a parent-child issue. This was sticking in her craw for reasons she couldn't explain.

Riggs squeezed her hand for reassurance and more of that warmth shot through her. She took a slow, measured breath. The move meant to calm her did its job. Her pulse kicked down a couple of notches. Her heart went out to the teen. Same for her gratitude.

"She was in hysterics at the hospital but she's doing better now. Her father is on his way. The minute she got him on the phone, she started calming down. Apparently, the parents divorced and it was hard on her. She lives with her father by choice and spends every other weekend with her mother. I get the impression the relationship is contentious on a good day," Colton admitted.

Cheyenne couldn't help but think about her relationship with her father. How they had drifted apart after her mother's death. How she barely knew what to say to him anymore now that he'd remarried a woman named Virginia and gone off to tour the country in an RV. And how it had taken him almost a week to respond to her text letting him know his granddaughter was gone. A surprising tear sprang to her eye. She coughed to cover.

A girl never stopped needing her father, even if he wasn't perfect.

RIGGS KEPT A careful eye on Cheyenne. She was stronger than just about anyone else he'd ever had the pleasure to meet. Too strong at times and it made her stubborn. She had the kind of strength that also made her try to fix all her own problems, like she didn't want to trouble anyone else even if they volunteered. And yet everyone had a breaking point. Was losing their baby hers? Or would it be losing Ally?

Her eyes were sharper today, not like the distant stare she'd had when he first saw her at Ally's house. This also meant she was tucking her feelings somewhere down deep. He could be accused of doing the same thing far too often. Talking out his feelings wasn't something that normally ranked high on his list.

Except with Cheyenne. He missed talking to her every day in the two weeks since she'd been gone. He missed waking up beside her, that long blond hair of hers spilling all over her pillow and his. He missed the warmth of her body against his first thing in the morning and when he went to sleep at night, and the sense of the world being right when she was in the room.

"How long before her father gets here?" Cheyenne asked. Her motherly instincts seemed to have kicked into high gear. She looked poised and ready to fight off a bear if it got in the way. She was going to make an amazing mother someday despite her many arguments to the contrary.

Colton checked his watch. "Soon. He should be here in the next fifteen minutes or so. He's working the graveyard shift over at the meatpacking plant as security to keep up two houses so Raven's mother doesn't have to move out of the place they shared."

The teen's father sounded like a real stand-up guy. Someone who could use a hand but probably would never take one. Riggs made a mental note to circle back to get information about the man's character. If he turned out to be the person Riggs believe him to be then Riggs planned to set up an anonymous donation to pay off the man's mortgages. He would set up a college fund for the teen, as well. There was no use in having all the zeroes in his bank account that came with the last name O'Connor if he couldn't use the money to help out decent people—people who would never ask for a dime and yet deserved to hold the world in their hand.

He squeezed Cheyenne's fingers and she rewarded him with a small smile. It was in the eyes more than anything else. Those serious blue eyes that reminded him of the sky on a clear spring morning. Eyes that he'd loved staring into.

"You should know the scene looks as though it's been staged." Colton made eye contact with each of them.

"What does that mean exactly?" Cheyenne asked.

"There are empty beer cans loose in Ally's vehicle. All over the floorboard in fact," Colton supplied.

"Ally doesn't drink beer," Cheyenne said without missing a beat.

"Ever?" Colton asked.

"Nope. She likes those fruity wines and she's recently been into Prosecco. She raves about it." Cheyenne seemed to catch her almost smile at the memory before it could take seed.

"Interesting." Colton pulled out his favorite notebook

from the pocket of his shirt and took down the note. "This whole scene has been made to look like she had a rendezvous with someone, a male."

"She texted to meet up with us," Cheyenne said. Riggs confirmed with a nod. "There's no way she would change plans."

"Is it possible she was trying to get the two of you in the same room together?" Colton asked.

"We already considered it," Cheyenne said, "but dismissed the idea. There's no way she would do that to us. And there's no way she would text us and then secretly meet up with some random guy."

"Did she ever do any online dating?" Colton asked.

"Not that I know of." Cheyenne shrugged. "But to be one hundred percent honest, I can't say that for sure. She could have. It doesn't sound like her, though."

"She never mentioned it?" Colton asked.

"Not to me. I've been wrapped up in my own situation for the past year, though. Still, I feel like Ally would have told me at some point," she said. "She wouldn't have felt there was anything wrong with online dating, but she was afraid of her own shadow. She wouldn't meet up with a stranger who wasn't carefully vetted first. We had friends in college who used to try to set her up on blind dates with acquaintances and she wouldn't consider it. Not unless the person had a long history."

"What about dating at work?" he asked.

"I don't think she was against the idea." Cheyenne snapped her fingers like she was trying to recall something that was just out of reach. "I think I remember her complaining about a visiting doctor and I can't remember if he was hitting on her or just being a jerk."

"I'll follow up with her coworkers to see if she mentioned it to any of them." Colton stood there for a moment like he was debating his next question, which caused Cheyenne's pulse to pound in her throat.

"I apologize in advance for the question as we shift gears." Colton locked gazes. He must've decided to go for it. "Did you actually see your daughter when she was born?"

Cheyenne searched her memory. She shook her head and gasped.

"I was shown something wrapped in a blanket. It's all fuzzy." The possibility she'd been lied to, tricked, pressed heavy on her chest. She hated not having clear recall with someone so important. She remembered the blanket. It had been pink. And the nurse who dipped down to give Cheyenne a glimpse of the bundle but…

"No. I didn't see her clearly. All I remember being shown was the pink blanket," she finally realized.

Riggs squeezed her hand. She looked up at him and saw all the questions forming behind those mocha eyes.

Chapter Eleven

Riggs wished he'd been the one to ask Cheyenne the question about whether or not she'd actually seen what was inside the pink blanket. The chance, however remote it might be, that their daughter was still alive slammed into him with the force of a runaway train.

Questions raced through his mind. Thoughts he had to shelve for now while Colton finished the interview with Cheyenne. Riggs would have to circle back later when he was alone with Cheyenne and could really talk.

Colton jotted down a couple more notes before locking eyes with Riggs and nodding. "My deputy spoke with the nurses. It's clear to me there's foul play here. I don't for a minute believe Cheyenne's friend was murdered while on a random date. The evidence says otherwise." He paused. "In fact, it almost shouts it from the rooftop."

"Too obvious?" Riggs asked, but it was more statement than question.

"Yes. The beer cans, for one. Someone Ally's size and weight wouldn't have been able to knock down all these. There are flowers, too. Roses. The kind anyone can pick up at the supermarket without much trouble. She was found inside the vehicle in a way that was very unnatural. She was stabbed by a kitchen knife, which indicates pre-meditation. Forensics will piece together more of what happened yesterday morning when Ally left from work, her time of death..." Colton apologized for his bluntness when Cheyenne sucked in a breath. "Based on the texts she sent the two of you, the possibility exists that she was killed because she discovered information someone didn't want leaked out of the hospital."

She exhaled slowly, and then urged him to continue.

"What about the flowers?" Riggs picked up on something in his brother's voice when he mentioned the roses.

Colton's gaze flashed to Cheyenne, who had brought Ozzy up against her chest. She was speaking quietly in his ear, no doubt whispering reassurances to the dog. The little dog was growing on Riggs. Or maybe it was just his situation. He no longer had a caregiver. The one person who'd promised to care for him was gone through no fault of her own. It wasn't the animal's fault or Ally's. Bad luck.

Ozzy wasn't the best fit for ranch life, but Riggs figured he could find a home for the guy if Cheyenne couldn't take him. Damn, it was strange to think of Cheyenne and his separation as permanent. He would respect her wishes, though, no matter how much it gutted him. There wasn't much of an alternative. He shouldn't have to convince his wife to stay with him.

Watching her while she took in the news their child might be alive, no matter how small the possibility, he could see how guarded she was being. No one wanted to be crushed twice, not with this kind of pain.

"They were 'arranged' in a heart shape around her face and torso to look like someone was obsessed with her." Colton's gaze dropped to the ground. He shook his head.

"I didn't find anything on her laptop to indicate she was seeing someone," Cheyenne chimed in. "Did you find her phone?"

"Not yet. The whole scene feels off," Colton admitted.

"We'll follow the evidence and see where it leads. Word of warning, though. Investigations take time. It's not like on TV where answers pop up almost instantly. Of course, I do get the occasional gift of speed. I just don't want either of you to count on it."

Riggs knew this firsthand, having several of his brothers work in law enforcement. The statement was aimed at Cheyenne. Of course, Colton wouldn't want to get her hopes up. Not once he took a look at how hard she was taking the losses. Losses that were stacking up.

"She knew something," Riggs said. "She requested my presence at her home ASAP. By the time I arrived, someone had made certain she would never make the meetup."

"Interviews with security haven't revealed that she left work with anyone," Colton admitted.

"The cameras," Cheyenne stated. "The ones aimed at the parking lot. E-cig Nurse seemed afraid to be seen on them. She stood in a blind spot when she waved us over."

"That's right," Riggs confirmed.

"The images are blurry, and even if they weren't, security doesn't keep the videos overnight. The system resets at midnight. Otherwise, there'd be way too much recording to keep track of plus space on the system. The hospital doesn't have the most storage, so the head of security said it gets deleted every night," Colton said.

"Why have cameras at all, then?" Riggs couldn't for the life of him figure out how any of it made sense.

"According to security, it's meant for backup if there's an immediate situation. The team can pull the data and hold onto it. They just don't do it routinely," Colton admitted.

"What about the nurses? What did they have to say?" Riggs needed to hear from his brother what he already feared. The interviews came up with nothing.

"Not as much as I would have liked. I think I know

which nurse you're talking about when you say E-cig Nurse. Her hair is mousy brown, and she has a small, pointed nose. Right?" Colton asked.

Cheyenne confirmed with a nod.

"She wouldn't talk, and she seemed scared," Colton said. "We've told the nurses that we'll be arranging for a lie detector test just to give them something to chew on."

"Is it possible someone got to her? Maybe even threatened her?" Riggs asked.

"It is likely," Colton confirmed. "I got the impression she wanted to talk but someone or something was causing her to hold back."

"She's a single mom," Cheyenne pointed out. "Said she needed this job."

"Is it possible someone threatened her child?" Riggs added.

Colton nodded before taking down notes.

Cheyenne shifted her weight from one foot to the other as she waited. He reached out to link their fingers to stop her from twisting her hands together. She rewarded him with a smile so brief he almost questioned whether or not he'd seen it at all.

"I'll check into it personally," Colton finally said.

"Any chance you'll let me walk over to Ally's car?" Cheyenne asked. Her voice shook and her hands trembled.

"I would if I could." Colton issued an apology. "I can't allow witnesses on a crime scene. It might seem like my deputy is being careless by moving around so much but he's methodical and the best forensic investigator I have. Plus, there's a lot of blood and you'll never be able to unsee the scene."

Cheyenne nodded despite her frown.

"It probably wouldn't be good for Ozzy anyway." She exhaled and her chest deflated.

Riggs needed to get her out of there as soon as possible.

"Is there any chance the person in the vehicle wasn't Ally?" Cheyenne didn't look up at Colton when she asked. This was her tell she wasn't 100 percent certain she wanted to know the answer to the question. She would never make it in a card game, which was another reason Riggs couldn't accept the fact she didn't love him anymore.

Pride could be to blame for his reasoning and yet deep down he felt like he would have known if their relationship had been fake. And no, he wouldn't be better off without her despite what she seemed to believe. No matter how rushed their marriage might have been, he'd never been more certain of anything in his life.

Was it pride keeping him from telling her how he really felt?

"I'm afraid Ms. Clark has been positively identified by a co-worker. There's no possibility of mistaken identity." Colton lowered his head in reverence. "I'm sorry for your loss, Cheyenne."

"What about her parents? Do they know?" She ducked her head, chin to chest, and turned her face away. Riggs took note of the move she'd done a couple of times already. Was she hiding tears?

"Yes," Colton confirmed.

Cheyenne coughed before lifting her face to Riggs.

"Can we go now?" she asked.

Riggs shot a look toward his brother, who nodded.

"I'll check in with you later," Riggs said to Colton. He needed to find out from Cheyenne what was causing her to need to leave right away.

EMOTIONS WERE GETTING the best of Cheyenne and she needed to leave the place before she lost it. The morning had started to wear thin and all she could think about was going somewhere safe so she could lie down. Some of her best thinking came when she slowed down. The morning slammed into her like a train going a hundred miles an hour.

Riggs walked beside her, hand in hand, back to his truck. He took her over to the passenger side and then waited while she took Ozzy out of her purse to let him do his business. The little dog glanced back at her before bolting toward the crime scene.

"Ozzy, no," she shouted after him.

"I'll get him," Riggs said, chasing after the little guy as Cheyenne stood there feeling useless.

Since that was about as comfortable as wearing wet clothes in church, she did the same. Ozzy zigzagged across the field, diverting left at the last minute.

He ran another five yards outside of the crime scene area that had been cordoned off and then stopped.

"What is it?" Cheyenne asked through labored breaths. She'd been way too inactive lately to run as fast as she had without her sides hurting and her lungs screaming for air.

"A piece of cloth." Riggs stopped, bent over and studied the ground. "A bandanna." He put a hand up to stop her from coming all the way over. "There's blood on it."

Cheyenne moved close enough to scoop Ozzy up and hold him to her chest. He was breathing heavy and his eyes were wild, which made her believe Ally's scent might be on the bandanna. The blood most likely belonged to her, as well. Cheyenne thought she might be sick. It was one thing to know her friend had been murdered and quite another to see the evidence, the blood.

Riggs motioned for his brother to come over. Colton set off jogging toward them almost immediately.

This seemed like a good time to take a couple of steps toward the truck. Cheyenne backpedaled as Colton reached the spot. He pulled a paper bag out of his pocket and a pair of tongs. He picked up the bandanna and examined it.

Nausea nearly doubled Cheyenne over as anger filled her. So much senseless loss. A spark of determination lit a fire inside her. Ally's death would not be in vain. There was no way Cheyenne planned to let the jerk who did this get away.

The person responsible had set this up to look like a date gone wrong. Why? What issue could a person possibly have with Ally other than the one that came to mind… Cheyenne's baby and a secret someone was willing to kill to protect.

Thoughts raced through her mind about what kind of person would do this. Dr. Fortner came to mind. He'd been there in the delivery room. Were there other possibilities?

This person would be someone who had something to lose. Was a career or family on the line? The latter begged the question as to whether or not Ally would engage in an affair with a married man. Cheyenne would bet against it. Internet dating was out. One of those swiping apps wouldn't surprise Cheyenne but the circumstances weren't right. All roads led back to Cheyenne and the baby.

"Excuse me, Colton." The answer to this question was one that couldn't wait. "You said Ally's phone is nowhere to be found, right?"

"That's correct," he confirmed.

Whoever killed her would probably be smart enough to take it and dispose of it. She glanced around the ground, figuring the perp might have dropped it, too. Or thrown it.

Cheyenne remembered what Colton had said about not stomping all over the crime scene. She figured the perimeter had just expanded with the find.

"Let's get you out of here," Riggs said, and she wondered what else the lawmen might have spotted.

Fighting the urge to argue, she walked next to him on the way to the truck. Both were careful to stick to the same path that had brought them to the bandanna.

"Ozzy might have just discovered an important piece of evidence," Riggs said as she climbed into the passenger seat. He reached over and patted Ozzy's head. His fingers grazed her neck and she ignored the electric impulses rocketing through her at his lightest touch. All her senses were on high alert. She chalked her body's overreaction to that and did her best to move on.

Her cell buzzed in her purse. She gasped before digging her hand in to locate the noisemaker. For a split second, she thought it might be Ally. She reminded herself to breathe as reality struck. It was a cold, hard reminder her friend would never call again.

Cheyenne could so easily get lost in the sea of emotion that came with losing her best friend. She couldn't allow herself to go down that path. For Ally's sake. Cheyenne needed to keep a clear head because the person who killed her best friend needed to be brought to justice. She realized she was gripping her cell so tightly that her knuckles had turned white. She checked the screen as Riggs reclaimed the driver's seat.

Unknown caller.

Didn't those two words send a chill racing up her spine? She fumbled to touch the green button on her screen. A click sounded, and then a recording came on the line telling her she needed to extend her vehicle warranty.

White-hot anger filled her. "It's bad enough these jerks call our personal cells. First of all, that information should be ours and ours alone. No one, and I mean *no one* should be able to telemarket us on our personal phones. It's wrong and someone should put a stop to it."

As anger raged through her, Riggs sat in the driver's seat as calm as anyone pleased.

Suddenly, she was mad about that, too.

Rather than let her words rip unchecked, she clamped her mouth shut and felt her face warm. He probably thought she was crazy at this point and she probably shouldn't care as much as she did.

"You don't have to stop on my account," he said quietly.

"Stop what?" The words came out a little too harshly.

"Ranting," he said and there was no judgment in his voice.

"Is that what you think I was doing, because I can tell you one thing… You're dead wrong. And I mean no one has ever been more wrong in their life than you are right now if you think I'm rantin—"

Cheyenne stopped herself right there. He was right on target. And she had so much more frustration built up she didn't know what to do with. One thing was certain. She couldn't hold her tongue any longer.

"Okay, fine. You sure you want to hear this?" She asked the question infusing as much indignation in her voice as she could. He needed to know what he was getting himself into.

"One hundred percent," came the confident response.

It was all the urging she needed.

"I am mad as hell Ally is dead because of me." Those words stung. The truth hurt.

"She isn't—"

"Come on, Riggs. You don't actually believe that, do you?" she bit out.

He didn't respond. He just sat there patiently.

"If I hadn't called Ally or brought her into this, she would be alive right now. If I hadn't run to her instead of going home like I should have after the baby was born, she would be home sleeping off a long shift. If I hadn't been so selfish, Ozzy would have her instead of being stuck with me for the rest of his life." Those last words broke her. She released a sob before sucking in a breath and holding her head high. *Chin up* had been her motto when her mother died. It would get her through this rough patch, as well. It had to, despite how much the losses were stacking up.

Tie a knot in the rope, Chey.

Riggs continued to stare out the front window even though his hand found hers. His fingers covered hers, causing a sense of warmth to spread through her. That was just Riggs. He was always a steady calm no matter how rough the waters became. He had a rare ability to make her feel like the world might not fall apart despite evidence to the contrary. Cutting herself off from him had been about survival on her part because she would never be able to walk away while he was her life raft in a raging storm.

"I'm sorry for—"

"Don't be," he said, cutting her off. He shook his head as though for emphasis. "I'm the one who should apologize."

Now she really was confused.

Chapter Twelve

"Hear me out." Riggs had had no idea, until now, how much Cheyenne blamed herself for the loss of their child, until he heard how pent up her emotions were. "I should have done better by you."

The look she shot him said she thought he was crazy. He'd seen that look before, so he put a hand up to stop her from objecting.

"You are carrying around the weight of the world on your shoulders, Cheyenne."

"Which isn't your fault," she defended.

"I needed to be a better husband to you. I wasn't," he admitted. "I got caught up in the surprise of becoming a father and husband, and volunteered for extra work on the ranch rather than come home and figure out how to talk to you about what you were going through. I told myself that if I just kept my head down and worked, everything would magically work out between us. That we'd figure out how to talk to each other and everything would be hunky-dory. Believe me when I say that I'm usually not that naive."

"The pregnancy news came out of the blue. We were just getting to know each other, Riggs. You're being too hard on yourself." The words rolled off her tongue like she didn't even have to think about them.

"Am I?" He didn't think so. In fact, he wasn't being nearly hard enough on himself.

"Yes. The whole marriage and family idea takes some getting used to," she said.

"Did you get used to it?" For some reason, it mattered.

"Not really," she admitted. "We rushed into it. I guess I expected a transition but then with a baby it seemed like being an instant family was going to be a tough hill to climb."

"Yeah." He couldn't have said it better himself. "I'll be one hundred percent honest right now. I wasn't ready to be a father. Not when I first heard the news and not a few weeks ago before the…"

He stopped himself before saying *the birth*.

"And now all I can think about is her…*us*. I'd give my right arm to go back to the way things were before," he admitted.

"What would you do different?" she asked.

"I'd be there for you in the way you needed me to. I'd be a helluva lot more excited about the birth. You would not have been in an ER alone," he said.

"I wasn't alone. I had Ally," she pointed out.

"You should have had me." He started the truck and put the gearshift in Reverse, backing out of the field.

No one spoke for half the ride back to the motel room. And then Cheyenne said, "I'd like to go back to the ranch if the offer still stands."

Few words could have shocked him as much as those.

"It's your home, Cheyenne. You'll always be welcome," was all he said in response. Despite her arguments to the contrary, he should have been a better husband. There was no excuse in the book good enough as far as he was concerned. But at least the two of them were talking now and he'd let go of some of the pride that kept him from telling her how he really felt. "Anytime you need to get something off your chest, talk to me."

He shouldn't have let it build up to the point she was ready to explode.

"I appreciate it, but—"

"No 'buts' about it. If we'd talked more about what we were really feeling while we were married, then we probably wouldn't be talking about divorce now," he said. The words came out a little more aggressive than he'd planned, and he regretted it, but they needed to be said. It might be too late for them to reconcile, even though his heart argued the opposite, but he'd needed to say his piece.

"Okay, then. Honesty it is." She surprised him with the response.

"And full disclosure," he insisted.

She nodded.

"We might not have made the marriage thing work, but I'd like to stay friends." He had no idea how she would react to his request. He had no idea how two people went from the kind of sexual chemistry that would light a house on fire in the rain to casual acquaintance, but he couldn't stand the thought of losing her, either.

"Friends it is." There was no conviction in her words. He appreciated them just the same. Trying counted for something and she was making an attempt to build a bridge over the river between them.

The rest of the ride to the motel was silent. They picked up her things and tossed them in the back seat of the truck. The drive to the ranch went by surprisingly fast. Riggs's thoughts were all over the map. He kept circling back to one question. Was Ally killed because she'd discovered his daughter was alive? And if so, where was his little girl? The text she'd sent to Cheyenne indicated mind-blowing news.

Cheyenne had to be wrestling with the same thought. She seemed unable to fully discuss the possibility. At least she'd raised her voice earlier and let out some of her frustrations. She'd been like a teakettle about to blow, before the outburst.

Riggs parked in the garage of their two-story log-style cabin. He hadn't truly taken possession of this place until Cheyenne came along. Before, he'd been content to sleep in the bunkhouse with the other men during the week. He only came here on Sundays. The place was far too big for one person.

There was an open-concept living room and kitchen. An office and the master suite rounded out the ground floor. The upstairs had a game room with a flat-screen TV that practically covered one wall. There was a nursery and two other bedrooms. Cheyenne had decorated one of the rooms as a guest room for her father and his wife. They'd promised to come for a visit soon and that was the last he'd heard of it. They made an excuse to miss the wedding and he had yet to meet his father-in-law.

The place had been decorated to Cheyenne's liking and Riggs wouldn't have it any other way. He wanted her to be comfortable in her new home. It was already asking a lot to have her live at his family's ranch. He'd wanted this place to be her retreat. Thankfully, she liked soft colors and couches big enough to sink into. Her taste had been a perfect fit for him. To be fair, though, he'd lived there with not much more than a leather sofa downstairs, a couple of bar stools at the granite island, and a king-size bed in the bedroom. He hadn't taken the time to pick out dressers or coffee tables, let alone linens and knickknacks. All he really needed was a shower, bed and a stocked fridge. And a flat-screen.

To be honest, the place had never felt like home before

Cheyenne moved in. Before he got too sentimental, he cut the engine. After hopping out of the driver's seat, he grabbed her belongings.

When he'd first listened to the message from her on his phone saying she was in labor and headed to the hospital, an image had flashed in his thoughts. It was an image he couldn't erase no matter how hard he tried, the snapshot of his family. The first thought he'd had was the next time they walked through these doors, they would be parents.

In that moment, he'd realized how ready he was to become a father. Much to his shame, he hadn't been so sure before. He knew that he'd fallen hard for Cheyenne. There was something deep inside that told him she was going to be important to him when they'd first met, something he couldn't explain if he tried. It was more of a feeling than an instinct. Instinct told him the best place a poacher would make camp on the property. This was more like his world had clicked into place—a place he'd never known before.

The sensation had intrigued him from the get-go. The news she'd become pregnant had caught him off guard, but the next step seemed as natural as breathing. She was special. He'd known that from day one. He didn't want to be with anyone else and he assumed the feeling would last forever. Most of the experience was a mystery.

If one of his brothers had asked him if he believed in love at first sight before Cheyenne, he might have laughed. Now he'd changed his mind. The instant he set eyes on her something new and different had stirred in his chest. It would be too easy to chalk it up to attraction or lust. And it would also be wrong. It was so much more.

"Mind if I take the couch?" She interrupted his deep thoughts as he followed her into the kitchen.

"You can have the master." He had no problems sleeping upstairs in the guest room when the time came.

She hesitated, looking like she wanted to say something but decided against it.

"If you don't tell me what you're thinking, I'll never know." Those words covered so much more than this conversation.

One look into her eyes said she caught on to the deeper meaning.

CHEYENNE STOOD THERE for a long moment without speaking, in the kitchen of the home she'd created for their family. For a split second, she thought about closing up and going inside herself again. But what good would that do?

Her marriage had already been destroyed and the child she loved more than life itself was gone. Now she'd lost her best friend. Staying quiet held little appeal.

"I don't like to admit to being afraid…" She took in a fortifying breath before continuing. "So, if you plan to sleep upstairs tonight, I'd like you to teach me how to load the shotgun before you go."

"I'm not going anywhere this minute. It's just now noon, but I thought you'd be more comfortable in our…your bed. And I didn't think you wanted me anywhere near while you slept," he said with brutal honesty.

The truth hurt but she was also learning that staying quiet destroyed.

She walked over to the granite island and sat on one of the bar stools. She'd already forgotten how uncomfortable this chair was right up until sinking into it. She put her elbow on the island for leverage because exhaustion threatened to land her on her backside.

"Tell me what you want, Cheyenne." He set the bags down and walked over to the vacant chair beside her.

She slid the band of her handbag onto the chair. Ozzy was curled up inside. He blinked his eyes open when the purse was no longer against her body. She reached down and ran her hand along his back to soothe him.

"I'd rather you be close to me, if that's okay," she said to Riggs. "The reason is stupid because there's no safer place on earth than the ranch. I know that logically. And yet, when I think about being down here alone and you upstairs—" she flashed eyes at him "—I can hardly breathe."

Riggs brought his hand to cover hers and the instant he made contact, more of that warmth spread through her.

"I know," he started and then stopped like he was searching for the right words. "Relationships change. They take different forms. But I hope you know that I will always be here for you. If you ever need anything, just ask."

She nodded. His kindness washed over her. And maybe it was the losses that were racking up or the fact that her only living relative still hadn't made her a priority that had her thinking she wanted to be back in Riggs's arms if only for a few moments.

"I have a question." She couldn't meet his gaze because suddenly she felt vulnerable. With him, and for the first time since losing her mother and her family breaking up, she didn't feel alone.

"I told you. Ask anything," came the quick response. His gravelly voice traveled over her and through her.

There were plenty of reasons she shouldn't continue...

"Kiss me."

Riggs leaned toward her and brought his hand around to cradle the back of her neck. His thumb drew circles around the sensitized skin there. He issued a sharp sigh before bringing his forehead to rest against hers.

"You have no earthly idea how much I want to." He paused and she braced herself for the rejection. "Is this a good idea?"

She let a few moments of silence sit between them.

"Probably not," she finally said. "But it is what I want."

That seemed to be all the encouragement he needed. Before she could talk herself out of it, his lips gently pressed to hers. He sucked in a breath before his tongue teased her mouth. A dozen butterflies released in her chest and her stomach dropped in a free fall.

The world tilted on its axis in that moment and everything seemed like it was going to be okay. She'd had that sensation very few times in her life and didn't take it lightly. Right now, though, she wanted to focus on how tender his kisses were and how much each one caused the tide of emotions welling in her chest to gain momentum until a tsunami was building. She wanted to shut out all her sorrows and frustrations and get lost in Riggs. It was so very easy when all she had to do was take in a breath to fill her senses with his spicy male scent.

She spun her legs around to face him, planting her feet on the stool's footrest. In the next second, she brought her hands up to rest on his muscled shoulders—shoulders she'd mapped and memorized a hundred times when they made love.

Sex with Riggs was the best she'd ever experienced. There was something out of this world about the moment they joined together and the perfect way their bodies fit before her belly grew big and uncomfortable.

Without a doubt, she would never find another person who fit her to a T. Logic said there was no way the chemistry would last and yet her heart argued the opposite. Some stars burned bright, not out.

Why couldn't they be the first kind?

Not that any of that mattered now. And she didn't want to focus on anything but the way his tongue excited her as it dipped inside her mouth. Or the way she felt when his teeth scraped across her bottom lip.

Before she could debate her next actions, she moved to standing in between his powerful thighs. Her body was flush with his. Her breasts against a muscled chest. She ran her fingers across the edges and grooves of his shoulders and chest.

He released a low growl when she let one of her hands drift down to the snap on his jeans. She rested her finger on the warm metal.

Cheyenne shut down logic because it wanted to argue that nothing had changed. That this moment happening between them would make it next to impossible to walk away when the investigation was over and they both needed to go back to their lives.

Heat rushed through her body, making it impossible to think. The fog that was Riggs O'Connor encircled her in the best possible way, so she let go. In his arms, everything else faded. All the stress. All the loss. All the pain. Nothing broke through except the two of them and the sensations rocketing through her body. Sensations that created a firework show that would rival any Fourth of July.

With his mouth moving against hers and his tongue delving inside, she could taste the hint of coffee from earlier still on his lips.

And then his cell buzzed, breaking into the moment. Panic this could be more bad news gripped her.

Chapter Thirteen

For a split second, Riggs considered not answering his phone. Pulling on all the strength he could muster, he scooted his chair back and stood up. His breathing made it seem like he'd run a marathon.

"Hey, Colton. What's going on?" Riggs asked in between breaths, hoping his brother would let it slide and not question why it sounded like Riggs had just sprinted to the phone.

"You might want to come to my office and bring Cheyenne with you." The sound of his voice sent a chill racing down Riggs's back.

"What's this about?" Riggs asked.

"No time to explain. Meet me there?" Colton asked.

"Okay. We're on our way," he promised.

Cheyenne's eyebrow arched as she reclaimed her seat. Her chest heaved at the same pace as his. She reached down to check on Ozzy and Riggs figured she was going to be better with that dog than she realized.

"Colton wants us to meet up at his office. He didn't say why," he told her.

She frowned before jumping into action, securing her handbag on her shoulder with Ozzy inside. "Do I have time to feed this guy and give him some water?"

"We'll make time," he said.

Cheyenne took care of the little dog while Riggs grabbed a couple of sandwiches for the road. His stomach was growling, and she needed to keep up her strength. He threw in a couple of pieces of fruit to give her options along with a pair of power bars he kept with him while out on the land.

Ten minutes later, they were out the door and inside his truck. He set the lunchbox he'd packed in between them and told her to help herself.

"I'm not sure I could eat anything if I tried," she admitted.

"Will you at least try? I'd be happy if you could get down a banana," he urged. It might not be his place to take care of her anymore, but he couldn't erase from his thoughts the months they'd belonged to each other.

Cheyenne nodded as he pulled out of the garage and onto the gravel road leading past the main house. She pulled out a banana and polished it off with surprising speed. Not a minute later, she reached in and grabbed a sandwich. In the half hour it took to exit KBR, they'd cleaned out the lunchbox.

After Cheyenne suppressed her third yawn, he said, "Feel free to lean your head back and rest on the drive over."

"That's a good idea. I think better when I power down anyway." She tilted the seat back and then closed her eyes.

He had to fight the urge to take his hand off the wheel and reach out to her. They were talking again. This time, they were sharing their frustrations and what was on their minds. They'd talked about something real instead of walking on eggshells or tiptoeing around a hard conversation. Or working longer than he had to in order to avoid dealing with conflict. He'd take the progress. They were taking small steps.

Besides, he liked talking to Cheyenne. Before her, Riggs wouldn't categorize himself as one for long-drawn-out conversation. He said what needed to be said and then got out of there. With her, he wanted to know the details. He wanted to know what she was thinking. He wanted to hear how something made her feel. The more drawn out, the better.

Go figure.

Pride swelled in his chest that she had food in her stomach and looked to be resting peacefully in his truck. After hearing the account of what had happened at the hospital and witnessing firsthand how shifty the nurses were being, he could only imagine what Cheyenne must be experiencing. It was obvious she blamed herself for losing the baby—a baby who might be alive.

The thought burned him from the inside out. The implication that a doctor, or nurses, or both could have drugged Cheyenne and taken their baby sent another hot poker through his chest.

He was reminded of one of his father's favorite sayings—*What happened in darkness always came to light.* It was the line Finn O'Connor had fed his children from a young age as to why honesty was always the best policy. Even when people thought they were getting away with something, they rarely were. They might for a time, but there'd be a reckoning. The saying proved gospel time and time again.

Finn O'Connor had never been able to expose the darkness that led to his baby daughter, firstborn and only girl, disappearing from her crib more than three decades ago. Right up until his death, he was trying to shine a light on what had happened.

Now that Riggs had become a father, he better understood the devastation of losing a first child. He could relate to the intense pain of losing a daughter. And he could not allow history to repeat itself.

A deer leaped from behind a tree and then darted across the road. Riggs slammed on the brake. His seat belt caught, stopping him from smacking his head into the steering wheel.

"What happened?" Cheyenne gasped. She grabbed the strap on her seat belt, clearly shocked.

"Deer. It's okay." His pulse skyrocketed and his heart jackhammered against his ribs despite the verbal reassurance meant as much for him as for her.

Cheyenne took one look at him and said, "Pull over."

There were no vehicles on this stretch of roadway, so he complied with her request. He put his blinkers on to give others fair warning from a distance.

She wrestled with the seat belt for a few seconds after it had locked on her. She managed to finagle out of it and then scooted over to him.

"What are you doing?" he asked as she wrapped her arms around his neck.

"Tell me what's going on with you right now," she said. Those pale blue eyes of hers were filled with so much compassion. "And I don't mean what just happened on the road. I mean in here." She pointed to the center of his chest.

Revealing the parallels between his family's greatest tragedy and their situation didn't seem like the best move right then. Him making the link was bad enough. He felt ten times worse at the thought his daughter might have been kidnapped right out from underneath them. Much like in the case of his sister, no ransom note had shown up. Much like his sister, the baby seemed to have disappeared into thin air. Much like with his sister, there were far more questions than answers.

Opening up to Cheyenne might cause her even more

pain. The last thing she needed was to hear the thoughts rolling around in his head. They would only upset her. However, a voice in the back of his mind warned against holding back the truth.

On balance, he'd hurt her enough. He couldn't continue, not when he wanted to protect her more than he wanted to breathe.

"I'm running through all the times my brother had the same tone in his voice and trying to figure out just how bad this news might be." It had been his first thought, so he wasn't being dishonest. He was simply neglecting to tell her where his thoughts had gone next.

She stared at him and for a few seconds he felt like she could see right through him. Hope followed by something that looked like disappointment colored her eyes. A wall came up and it was too late to go back and recapture the moment.

"What did you decide?" She moved back to her side of the cab and clicked on her seat belt.

"I can't figure it out." Again, he was being honest despite not sharing the whole of his thoughts. The small voice in the back of his mind told him he'd just messed up royally. There'd been a window of opportunity to really talk to her and he'd lost it. There was no backtracking now as he turned off the emergency flashers and put the gearshift in Drive.

He navigated back onto the roadway.

"We'll know soon enough." The disappointment in her voice struck him square in the chest. *Too late* were his least favorite pair of words.

CHEYENNE DRUMMED HER fingers on the armrest. She'd miscalculated the moment with Riggs. There'd been a time when she had a better handle on what he might be thinking. She'd lost her touch. Or maybe losing the baby had changed their connection.

Her mind snapped to Colton and the fact they were barreling toward his office after what could only be described as one helluva morning. Powering down had only caused her to go over her last conversation with Ally repeatedly, trying to remember any and every detail about what had transpired. There was a whole lot of day left and she was already exhausted.

"I keep thinking about Ally's parents and how they had to learn their daughter was murdered today. And how much I want to contact them to offer my sympathies and support, but I don't think I can pull it together long enough when I hear their voices." She pinched the bridge of her nose to stem the headache threatening.

"I can't imagine the pain they must be experiencing," he agreed. "No parent should have to lose a child." He seemed to realize what he'd said and how much it applied to their current situation when he shot a look of apology.

"You don't have to be sorry, Riggs," she said. "When I lost her, I blamed myself and shut everyone out, including you. I convinced myself that I was protecting you by not letting you see me in the state I was in, which was pretty awful."

"What changed?" he asked.

"Thanks to Ally, you showed up at the door. Then, talking to you. Realizing that you were in just as much pain as me, and that not talking about her with you wasn't going to make me feel any better. I can't protect you from the hurt that comes with losing a child." She paused for a long moment before continuing. "And I realized I was punishing myself even more by shutting you out. I didn't think I deserved your compassion or kindness."

"You suffered a loss, too. I'd argue yours was bigger

than mine, considering I had yet to meet her and she'd been growing inside you all along. You were already connected to her in ways that I hadn't experienced yet," he said.

Those words were balm to a wounded soul.

"Thank you, Riggs." That was all she said. All she needed to say. She meant those words and he seemed to know it.

"I've said it before, but I couldn't be sorrier for not being there for you, Cheyenne." This time, she didn't try to stop him. Saying the words out loud probably helped him in some way.

He pulled into the lot of his brother's office where a dozen or so vehicles were parked. He found a spot and started to exit when she reached over to him, placing her hand on his forearm.

"I know you are, Riggs." She knew he would never make the same mistake if given the chance, which was the kicker. The dark cloud over her head wasn't going anywhere and there was no way she could try to have another child. "We'd both do things a lot different if we could go back."

He nodded.

"But we can't." Those words hurt more than she wanted to admit. She picked up her handbag and held it against her chest, securing Ozzy.

Riggs exited the truck and came around to her side as she climbed down. He held onto her arm to steady her before closing the door. For a minute, they stood there, staring into each other's eyes. He searched her eyes as if to see if she was truly ready for whatever waited for both of them inside.

She did the same, nodding when she found what she was looking for—confirmation.

After a deep breath, she hooked her free arm around Riggs's and headed into the building.

The lobby had a desk on the left, where she knew Gert Francis, Colton's secretary, sat, and a long counter on the right. There were glass doors that required a special ID badge for entry. Once behind those doors, they were in a building shaped like a U. Colton's office was to the right and down the hall. The route to the interview room was behind another locked door to their left, as best as Cheyenne remembered. She'd been here once before with Riggs.

Gert rounded her desk to greet them. She was in her late sixties and had been described as lively by Riggs and the others. She definitely had a twinkle to her brown eyes and a grandmotherly smile that could be disarming. Behind her back, folks had nicknamed her Oprah for her ability to get people to spill their secrets, like the popular TV host Oprah Winfrey.

After a round of hugs, Gert led Cheyenne and Riggs through the locked doors and down the hallway to the witness room, which was roughly the size of a walk-in closet.

The lights were dim and there was a small speaker with a box and a button. She presumed the button was used to communicate orders to the people inside the interview room, which was on the other side of the two-way mirror.

"I'll let your brother know you're here," Gert said with a wink before ducking out of the room.

"Why are we here?" Cheyenne asked quietly. All she saw was a young girl, who barely looked old enough to be in puberty, sitting opposite Colton. She recognized Garrett standing next to her, but not the woman on the other side of the girl.

"Missy?" Riggs asked under his breath. "What's she doing here?"

"Isn't that the girl from the alpaca farm?" Cheyenne

tried to piece together why she and Riggs needed to be present at what looked like the questioning of the young lady. The girl sat there, twisting her hands together. She looked to Garrett and then to the woman.

"Yes. Garrett and Brianna are foster parents to Missy. She'd been locked up and made to go without food for the slightest infractions," he said. Those words nearly gutted Cheyenne. Her hands fisted at the thought of anyone abusing this timid child.

"How old is she?" she asked.

"Sixteen," he said.

Sixteen? Cheyenne could scarcely believe the number was true. Her stomach twisted in a knot as she thought about the cruelty of some people.

"Rest assured the people who held her captive will live out what's left of their very long lives in jail, where they belong. Justice will be served." Riggs's reassurance didn't stop her heart from hurting for this kid. "A private search is being conducted to find her parents."

"She was kidnapped?" she asked.

"Seems so. Several children have already been reunited with their families from that farm," he said.

"Didn't you say that your father was investigating a kidnapping ring when he was murdered?" The connection started to sink in. Colton would never have called them there if the news coming out of Missy's mouth didn't apply to both of them. He hadn't asked for Riggs to come alone. He'd asked for her, too.

And that must mean he'd found out something about their baby.

Chapter Fourteen

Gert knocked on the door of the adjacent room before poking her head in. She nodded and Colton immediately turned to glance at the window before turning back to Missy.

"Can you repeat what you told me over the phone?" Colton asked. His body language indicated he was calm and relaxed.

"Yes." Missy's voice shook. She looked like she was suddenly back in grade school and had been called on to read when she wasn't ready.

"Take your time," Colton said in a tranquil voice Riggs rarely ever heard. His brother was a damn fine sheriff and had a pair of twin boys who lit up any room with their smiles. He was also a solid investigator whom Riggs trusted with his life.

Missy looked down at her feet. She twisted her hands together a few times before taking in a breath. Brianna took one of the girl's hands in hers and she exhaled like she was taking a breath for the first time. It was impossible not to feel sorry for the kid even though Riggs didn't normally do pity. Most folks made their circumstances and needed to learn to live with the consequences. Kids were the exception. They didn't have control over their lives, not until they were old enough to go off to college or work. Some ran away, which he didn't condone but certainly understood in extreme cases. There'd been a few ranch hands over the years who said they were of age but clearly weren't.

This kid looked like she had a heart of gold and that frustrated him even more. No child deserved to be abused or taken advantage of. White-hot anger roared through him, so he decided to force his thoughts in a different direction. When it came to families, this kid had just hit the jackpot. Garrett and Brianna were devoted to her. She was receiving counseling. She had a good home now and would be getting plenty of food and nurturing. Brianna was going to make an amazing mother someday, just like Cheyenne would have.

Might still get the chance to, a voice in the back of his mind pointed out. All hope was not lost when it came to their daughter.

"There was a newborn who came through the farm about a week ago," she admitted, turning her face toward the floor again like she'd done something wrong. Kids had a habit of blaming themselves for everything that happened, he'd noticed. Thinking back, he'd probably done the same. His brothers, too. Like they might have done something differently and their sister would come back to them.

It was a strange thought to have and yet he knew how common it was. The truth didn't have nearly enough influence when it came to kids and their emotions. After experiencing his own loss, he also realized how strong his parents were. His mother had been a rock over the years despite never giving up on Caroline coming home one day. Did that keep his mother going? Would Riggs fall into the same thinking if his daughter proved to be alive? Or would despair dig a hole too deep to crawl out of?

Pain. He hated it.

Both he and Cheyenne sat up a little straighter at the news.

"She wasn't more than a week old at the time," Missy continued with Brianna's encouragement.

"Can you describe her?" Colton asked.

"She was tiny, like usual. This little girl didn't cry. They said she was born early, and we needed to take special care of her." She squirmed in her seat.

"How premature did they say she was?" Colton's voice was a study in calm whereas Riggs's pulse was climbing.

"A few weeks. Maybe four," she said. "They don't really tell us very much. I listened behind the door to find out any information I could to help the baby."

"That was very brave of you to do. You could have gotten into a lot of trouble," Colton pointed out.

The compliment rolled off her as though she didn't think she deserved any praise. It broke Riggs's heart a little bit more to imagine her situation and what she'd endured.

"It was the only way to be sure I could keep the baby alive. I mean," she glanced up at Brianna and then Garrett, like she was looking for permission to continue. She started working the hem of her shirt in between her fingers of her free hand. "They didn't care. Not really. They called them 'goods' and talked about 'transactions.' They didn't look at them...*us*...as real people with families."

Missy stopped talking and stared at the wall. Her gaze became unfocused, like she'd gone inside an invisible shell where she was lost. Riggs's hands fisted at his sides. He flexed and released his fingers a couple of times to work out some of the tension.

Cheyenne must've picked up on his mood because she reached for his hand and slipped hers inside. He clasped his fingers around hers, needing the connection more than he cared to admit to her or anyone else.

How ironic would it be if the investigation into Caroline's kidnapping led him straight to the place his daughter had been taken? He thought back to Ms. Hubert's death a couple of months ago and how that opened the door, just a crack, for investigators to use. Ms. Hubert was the local who was murdered in her front yard. The investigation into her death prompted questions about Caroline's kidnapping.

Had his father been right all along? The investigator Garrett had hired to look into his sister's disappearance had tracked down a connection to the alpaca farm. Now, three decades after Caroline's abduction, could the same farm be in business? The short answer was yes. It might not have been an alpaca farm all these years, but Riggs would put money on someone making certain that the farm was transferred to a person or couple in on the scheme.

He didn't want to think about how frustrating it must be for law enforcement to know this operation had been running thirty-plus years at a minimum.

More hope his daughter was out there somewhere both safe and alive took seed. Cheyenne had been clear about her position. She couldn't afford hope. Riggs understood that on some level. But he'd watched from the sideline with his family's ordeal and had realized hope was all they had to go on for most of it. Life also had to go on, he realized. He had even more respect for his parents after realizing how damn hard that must've been.

But then what were the options?

Fold up the tent and stop living? His mother had soon found out she was pregnant with Cash. She was far too strong a person to let her child suffer. No, his mother was the type to pluck up the courage to keep moving. When he really thought about it, Cheyenne would have done the same. She wouldn't have stayed stuck and miserable. It was a knife stab that she'd intended to go on without him...

A thought struck. He'd been protecting his pride by not

sharing his feelings with her earlier. He'd tried to convince himself that he was doing it for her benefit. Was that true?

Hard questions deserved real answers.

"When was the last time you saw the little girl?" Colton asked.

Missy shook her head. "She was in and out. I overheard them say she got a high price because she came from a good family. They said something about good breeding and revenge…"

The young woman stopped and took in a breath. A pin drop could be heard for how quiet both rooms became.

"They said she wouldn't be missed because the parents got married to save face anyway." Missy dropped her face into her hands, breaking the connection she had with Brianna.

"You didn't do anything wrong, Missy," Colton soothed.

The young girl's shoulders shook, and she refused to look up.

Brianna wrapped an arm around the young girl's shoulder before locking gazes with Colton.

"She's done for now. Okay?" Brianna's expression could best be described as tense and tortured. On the one hand, she wouldn't want to let Riggs and Cheyenne down. On the other, she had taken on the responsibility for the young girl who was anguished by what she'd been through. Asking her to talk about anything connected to her past must be a trigger.

"It's okay," Missy said with a little more umph than he'd heard from her so far. She straightened her back and took in another breath. "I can't let them win."

Those words sent a fireball raging through Riggs's veins. He tightened his grip on Cheyenne's hand, realizing for the first time that she was trying to be his support. Guilt slammed into him for not telling her what was on his mind earlier. He made a promise to himself to do better if given another opportunity.

Would there be a next time?

THE LINK WITH Riggs was one of the only things keeping Cheyenne calm as she listened to the account from the young girl. Sixteen wasn't so young, and yet it was difficult to believe the girl sitting at the table in the next room was a teenager, let alone a sophomore in high school. She barely looked old enough to babysit and yet it was clear she'd been forced to care for newborns. Had the young girl held Cheyenne and Riggs's baby?

More of those dangerous seeds of hope blossomed inside her chest. Could her child...*their* baby...be alive? Deep in her bones, she believed the answer to be yes. Now her attention turned to finding her daughter.

"I heard them talk a lot about someone named Miss H," Missy continued. "This new baby was supposed to be revenge."

"After my dad's diagnosis, he reopened the investigation," Riggs said quietly. "I think he wanted to give my mom peace of mind before he died. At that point, he had time left."

Cheyenne squeezed Riggs's fingers before nodding.

"Miss H might refer to Ms. Hubert. She was part of the kidnapping ring linked to Caroline's disappearance," Riggs said. He issued a sharp sigh. "Looks like this crime has come full circle."

"Someone took our child to get back at your father?" Cheyenne couldn't hide the disbelief in her voice.

"It's possible." He turned to her and locked gazes. "I'm so sorry you got caught in the middle of all this."

Before she could answer, Colton asked, "To your knowledge, is the baby still alive?"

"I'm not sure," Missy admitted. "She was when I last saw her."

"Do you know what happened to her?" Colton continued.

"She was most likely sent to her new home. Austin, I think. But I'm not sure. They didn't all make it to their homes. One…" Missy started crying. "We lost one and I never found out who it was before the raid."

Cheyenne's pulse was through the roof. Her heart pounded the inside of her rib cage as disbelief tried to take hold. She shoved it aside for Ally, for the baby, and for Riggs. She needed to keep a clear head. She'd been blaming herself all this time for what had happened. Hearing the shame and guilt in Riggs's voice just now made her second-guess being so hard on herself.

One of the kidnapped children didn't make it. Her heart literally cracked in half at the thought. Didn't mean it was hers and didn't have to be for her to be broken about the loss of life or the fact someone's child had died.

"Do you know what happened to the baby who lost its life?" Colton was calmer than Cheyenne could be. As it was, her hands trembled.

"They always took them away separately. Bert and Ernie came to get them." She looked at Brianna and then Garrett. "Those weren't their real names. They liked to talk in code and said never to reveal the truth."

"Did you ever see Bert or Ernie?" Colton continued.

"Yes." Her body shivered at the admission.

"Can you give a physical description of them?" Colton asked.

Missy nodded. She went on to describe a pair of men who were similar height and weight. One had brown hair and the other golden brown. The two looked like they could be brothers with their sharp noses and beady brown eyes.

Colton scribbled notes feverishly. "Did someone different drop off the babies?"

"Most of the time, they came in at night when I was asleep. I'd be told to get up and then I'd be handed a child to care for," she revealed. "There was one guy, though. He came a few times but his visits were always spaced out. I was sure he brought babies but I never saw him carry one inside the building."

"I'd like to bring in a sketch artist," he said to Missy when she was done. He glanced at Garrett before turning his head toward Brianna. "Would that be okay with the two of you?"

Brianna seemed to be thinking seriously. Cheyenne understood the need to protect someone so young, who clearly had been traumatized. Under normal circumstances, she wouldn't want to push for more information. But her child's life might be hanging in the balance. "Okay."

"I know she cried," she said quietly. The echo of her baby's cry rang in her ears.

"You were right all along. Not that I doubted you." Riggs's words offered more comfort. She wasn't ready to cool down just yet, because a fire raged inside her. She was angry at the lies from the nurses and hospital staff. And she was exhausted. Her emotions were wrung out. Bed sounded amazing even though she doubted she could get a wink of sleep.

At this point, her body ached. This was the most physical exertion she'd had since delivering her daughter. *Alive*, a little voice in the back of her head stated loud and clear.

"Are you finished with questioning for now, Colton?" Brianna asked, a torn look on her face.

"Yes, I am." He turned to Missy. "The information you've given me here right now is very important. You've made a big difference in my investigation and I know none of this is easy for you. Thank you for coming down here in person to talk to me."

Missy's bottom lip quivered, and Cheyenne had to fight the urge to barge into the next room and bring the girl into a hug. It wasn't her place to, and Brianna beat her to the punch anyway.

Cheyenne teared up to see Missy enfolded in Brianna's loving arms. Brianna was clearly going to be a very protective and nurturing mother someday. It warmed Cheyenne's heart to see the tenderness among the trio in the next room. Garrett looked like he'd strangle anyone who tried to hurt Missy or Brianna. Who would have thought the wildest O'Connor brother would turn out to be a family man?

He came from good genes, she thought. Granted, he couldn't come close to Riggs in comparison, but she was happy to see Garrett looking so natural as part of a family, and so protective over his fiancée and Missy.

"Are you ready to get out of here?" Riggs asked and she realized he'd been studying her as she stared at his family.

"Yes."

Chapter Fifteen

Riggs had a lot to think about on the drive home. Cheyenne was quiet. Ozzy was still content in the handbag. The little yapper wasn't as bad as Riggs had chalked him up to be when he'd first met Ally.

He couldn't go there about her murder. He'd overthink it until the cows came home. Chew on it over and over again, which wouldn't do any good. In fact, he needed to take a step back in order to clear his thoughts.

More times than not, the answers to any problem came to him while he was distracted. Normally, that meant working extra hours on the ranch. He was also a volunteer firefighter but had put that job on hold during the pregnancy.

Before he realized, he was pulling into the garage.

"How's the tiny tot in your purse? Does he need to go out?" he asked as he cut the engine off. "I can take him."

"I can go with you," Cheyenne offered, and he realized how much the dog meant to her. Ozzy was the last she had of her best friend. The way she held on to her handbag meant someone couldn't pry that dog out of her hands with a crowbar.

"Someone should stay with him at all times because of the coyotes and I'd enjoy your company." There were other dangers for an animal of that size, none of which needed spelling out tonight. It had been a long day by any measure. The dark circles underneath Cheyenne's eyes said she needed to sleep.

Riggs kept the garage door open and walked beside her to the grassy patch of lawn in front of the house. She lifted Ozzy out of her handbag and then set him on the ground. He did his business almost immediately. Two seconds later, he pranced over to Cheyenne and looked up at her expectantly.

Cheyenne picked him up before nuzzling him against her cheek. She mumbled something about making sure he would be well taken care of. The whole scene struck a nerve in Riggs for reasons he couldn't explain. A question arose. Was it seeing Cheyenne dote on the dog that reminded him what an amazing mother she would have been...*correction*...was going to be when they located their daughter? Because he was now more convinced than ever that she was still alive.

On a sharp sigh, he turned and walked toward the garage. Her footsteps sounded on his heels and a wave of comfort washed over him that she didn't hesitate to follow.

"You take the master if you want to try to rest. I'm fine sleeping on the sofa tonight," he said before reassuring her, "I won't leave you alone downstairs."

"Thank you, Riggs. It means a lot that you're willing to be there for me even after everything that's happened between us," she said.

He wanted to tell her that in his mind she was still his wife. Would that bring up more walls between them? No one should have to *ask* their wife to stick around. The vow they'd taken should have implied it.

Rather than let his pride run wild, he nodded.

"I'll always be here for you, Cheyenne. All you have to do is ask." He meant it, too. She could leave when this was all over. He didn't like the idea, but it was true. She could walk away from him and he would still be here for her if she came back and asked for a favor. It was the vow he had taken and had no intention of breaking. Call it cowboy code, or whatever. Riggs O'Connor wasn't brought up to renege once he gave his word.

Cheyenne stopped. She bit her lip like she was trying to stop herself from saying what was on her mind. And then she headed toward the master.

Riggs needed a shower and there was only one on the first level. He would give her a few minutes to get settled before knocking. He didn't want to startle her or catch her getting ready for bed.

The interview with Missy rolled around in his thoughts as he took a bottle of water out of the fridge and downed it. The terrified look on her face would haunt him. The kid had been through a tough ordeal, to be sure. She'd been taken from her family some time before the age of four, according to Colton. For some reason, she was kept at the alpaca farm. An adoption gone bad? Had she been returned by adopted parents who'd decided they didn't want her after all? She had no memories of the events, according to what Colton had said. Just fuzzy details here and there, confused by a child's developing mind.

Was it possible his child would suffer the same fate?

Missy had been neglected and treated poorly physically. There'd been no signs of sexual abuse, which was the lone bright spot in her situation other than the help she was getting now. Brianna and Garrett had pledged to get her the help she needed and find her family. Garrett of all people would know how important that was. It was unimaginable to think a young child had been separated from her parents this long. Riggs clenched his back teeth. He couldn't fathom going sixteen years without knowing what had happened to his child.

Fanning the flames of anger would only serve to distract him from what needed to be done to find his own child. So, with heroic effort, he managed to shove his feelings down deep and focus. There was no way he could rest under the circumstances despite not sleeping a wink last night, so he might as well use the time to be productive.

He retrieved his laptop and made a cup of instant coffee. He had one of those rarely used fancy machines in the kitchen that Cheyenne had fallen in love with. She'd taken to waking up at three thirty in the morning to make him a cup of coffee before he headed out to work for the day. It was something she'd insisted on doing despite the fact he was fully capable of figuring out the machine and making his own brew.

She'd told him not to worry. Her favorite part of the day was kissing him goodbye with the taste of coffee still on his lips. And then it dawned on him. Was that the reason she'd taken up drinking coffee in the last two weeks?

Did it mean she missed him more than she was letting on?

Deciding that was another trail he didn't need to go down, he set up his laptop at the granite island and took a seat. The kiss they'd shared at this spot had him getting up to retrieve another drink of water.

Riggs wasn't really sure what he was looking for online. Sitting around doing nothing would have him pulling his hair out. He sent a text to Garrett thanking Missy for bravely coming forward. The response from his brother was almost instant.

We'll find her.

Riggs set his phone down and stared at it, unable to believe history was repeating itself in his family. Colton needed to be left alone so he could continue to conduct his investigation. He'd call the minute there was another development. Plus, two investigations had kicked into high gear. There were three actually. The murder of Ally Clark was one. The disappearance of their sister, Caroline, was another. And now the abduction of Riggs's daughter.

Three intertwined cases.

It wasn't lost on Riggs that Ally had been killed within a stone's toss of the hospital where she worked. No doubt Colton had already received the reports from his deputy. E-cig Nurse from the other day was afraid of someone. She had information that could be damaging to one of the people she worked with, or for, but clearly, she also had a conscience, or she never would have called Riggs and Cheyenne over in the first place.

Not that it had done any good. E-cig Nurse had panicked when a woman walked out of the hospital and clamped her mouth shut after. So there was a whole lot of haze around what had really happened when Cheyenne was in the hospital.

E-cig Nurse had a kid. She was trying to protect her child. With investigators swarming the building after the discovery in the field, was the nurse in real danger?

Riggs made a mental note to follow up to make sure she and her kid were safe. There wasn't much he could do at this point. He picked up his coffee cup and took a sip. Cold. He nearly spewed the contents. Lots of folks loved iced coffee. He didn't see the appeal. Give him a hot brew any day.

Opening the laptop, he sent an e-mail to the family attorney to research Raven's dad and if he checked out to set up an anonymous fund to pay off the nightshift security guard's pair of mortgages and a college fund for the teenager who'd chanced upon Ally's body.

Cheyenne must've fallen into a deep sleep, because he didn't hear so much as a peep from the master bedroom as he paced in the kitchen. Dinner came and went. He heated up leftovers. He fed Ozzy and saw to it the dog did his business outside. Then he returned to the bar stool.

How long had he been sitting there churning over his thoughts? After forcing himself to get up and make another cup of coffee, he glanced at the clock on the wall. Two thirty in the morning. In an hour, several of his brothers would be waking for the day. An hour after that, the ranch would be kicking into gear. Assignments would be given out and everyone would disperse.

Riggs loved the ranch. He loved being an O'Connor. What he didn't appreciate was the burden that sometimes came with his last name. The thought his daughter was abducted in order to get back at his father for investigating Ms. Hubert was a knife stab straight to the heart. Whoever killed Ms. Hubert was responsible for kidnapping his child. He'd long considered his last name a blessing. The thought of it being a curse nailed his gut.

He couldn't let himself go down that road. There were pros and cons to everything. He'd always been proud of his family name. He prayed Cheyenne could forgive him for it. He couldn't read the look on her face when they'd learned the crime was linked to his family. Had she convinced herself this was all somehow her fault?

He'd seen her touch the ladybug bracelet several times during the interview and since. It was a go-to move in times of stress. Did she even realize she did it?

Colton was most likely asleep at this point, but Riggs needed to send his brother a text asking him to get in touch when he could. He wanted to know what Colton had learned from the interviews with the nurses and he needed to get E-cig Nurse's name out of his brother if he could. The person who murdered Ally might go after the nurse next. She deserved protection. Riggs couldn't allow any more bloodshed of innocent people tied to this case.

He picked up his phone and sent the text to Colton. Riggs's cell immediately vibrated, indicating a call. With the device still in his hand, he checked the screen. Colton.

"Hey. What's going on?" There had to be news, or his brother wouldn't have called in response to a text.

"I've been wanting to call all night but didn't want to wake you." Colton's voice had the spark that said he was making progress on the investigation.

"I'm wide-awake. Couldn't sleep. What did you find out?" he asked.

"The coroner reported the time of death. Seven thirty yesterday morning," Colton supplied.

"The text from Ally came in twenty minutes prior," he said quietly. This confirmed she was murdered after she reached out to him and Cheyenne. It was as close as they'd been so far to being able to link her murder with whatever she'd found out.

"There's more. The flowers have been traced to a nearby grocery store. They were sold at quarter to nine," Colton reported.

"The killer bought them *after* he killed Ally," Riggs said out loud. The perp must have figured out Ally's plans and decided to get rid of her on the fly. "He had time to wash the blood off and change his clothes. He had to have resources close by, like a shower and change of clothes."

"Gert is on the phone to area motels, asking for single male registrants. A man is the only one who would be strong enough to move her body. He would have rented a place that didn't require him to walk through a lobby with blood on him."

"Makes sense," Riggs said. "Is it possible the perp

worked at the hospital? He might have access to a back-door that isn't widely used."

"I've been doing a lot of digging into the visiting physician who delivered your daughter. Two nurses at hospitals where Dr. Fortner has worked came forward last night to say they believe there have been suspicious circumstances around births he's attended," Colton supplied.

Riggs needed a minute to absorb what he was hearing. His heart hammered his ribs.

"Is that so?" he finally asked.

"Yes. They're willing to come in and speak to me or one of my deputies. Dr. Fortner doesn't fit the description Missy gave of the farm visitor or the one given by the clerk at the grocery store who remembered selling flowers to a tall guy in a hoodie," Colton said. Then he added, "I don't want you to be discouraged, though. This case is blowing open, Riggs. We'll get to the bottom of what really happened sooner rather than later. I promise."

"Do you believe my daughter is alive?" Riggs had to ask the question outright.

"I hope she is. I can't confirm either way, except to say I have questions about what really happened that night." Colton never pulled any punches and Riggs was grateful for the honesty.

"What about the flowers? Do you have a name?" Riggs asked, figuring the perp might have used a credit card.

"No, the perp paid with cash."

Of course, he would. The murderer wouldn't want to leave a trail.

"Do you have any idea what Dr. Fortner looks like?" Riggs asked. "Cheyenne didn't remember much about his face. She said the details were fuzzy."

"I do. I'll send over the photo from his badge the hospital provided," Colton promised. "Or, if you want it faster than that, his photo is on the web."

"Right. Good point." He should have thought of that sooner. "What about the nurse who tried to talk to us outside? The one I told you about. She panicked and stopped talking real fast. With what you're telling me now, I believe she's in danger."

"Let me see." There was a paper-shuffling noise in the background for a few seconds before Colton's voice came back on the line. "Loriann Fischer is her name."

"Are you sending someone over to protect her?" Riggs asked, figuring he already knew the answer to his question.

"I don't have the resources." Colton's voice was low. It was obvious he didn't like it any more than Riggs did.

"What about her number? Can you give it to me? I'd like to check up on her and make sure she's okay. Maybe get her to a safe place until you catch this guy," Riggs said.

"I can't—"

"She mentioned a kid, Colton. What if the perp goes after one or both of them?" Riggs couldn't live with himself if he didn't do everything in his power to ensure their safety.

"I doubt she'd appreciate a call in the middle of the night," Colton argued.

"What if she isn't sleeping? The way she looked yesterday morning when Cheyenne and I were talking to her… you should have seen it. She was afraid, Colton. And now Ally's body has been found. That has to be all over the hospital grapevine by now."

"How about this. I'll give her a call and ask if you can check up on her. I can volunteer your phone number, but I can't promise she'll use it," Colton reasoned.

It wasn't exactly what Riggs had asked for, but it was better than nothing.

"Can you call her as soon as we get off the phone?" Riggs asked.

"That I can do."

"Then I guess I'll talk to you later," Riggs said.

Colton hesitated. "This is really important to you, isn't it?"

"It is," Riggs admitted.

"Then you didn't get this number from me. And please don't let it come back to bite me." Colton supplied the number.

"I'm not sure how I'll ever repay you, but—"

"Just try not to get me fired," Colton shot back. His joke lightened the mood.

"Yes, sir," Riggs teased, appreciating the break in tension. It wouldn't last long.

"Let me know if she needs protection," Colton said. "I might be shorthanded, but I'll figure something out."

"Will do." Riggs could do one better than that. He had every intention of seeing to it personally.

The brothers ended the call. Riggs glanced at the clock again. Twenty minutes had passed since the last time he looked. For most folks, this was a ridiculous hour. Not so for ranchers, bakers and people in a handful of other jobs that required early mornings or twenty-four-hour days.

Besides, if E-cig Nurse, aka Loriann Fischer, was as stressed as she had been earlier, there was no way the woman was asleep. She might not answer a call from an unknown number in the middle of the night, though. So he sent a text first, telling her exactly who he was and why he planned to call. Despite the late hour, he had a hunch she might not be able to sleep. Acting on it, he tapped her number into the keypad. Loriann picked up on the first ring.

"How did you get this number?" she asked with a shaky voice.

"I needed to make sure you and your kid were all right." Riggs intentionally didn't answer her question.

"Oh." She sounded suspicious. "How did you find out my name?"

"Through the investigation of the murder of my wife's best friend." It wasn't a lie.

"Sad about what happened to the other nurse. I shouldn't be talking to you right now," she said. The panic in her voice was palpable. "It's not safe."

"Have you already spoken to investigators?" He knew the answer. He was trying to get her to see reason. Folks in a highly charged emotional state weren't known for making the best decisions. Based on the sound of her voice and the fact she was up in the middle of the night, he figured she'd been chewing on yesterday's events.

"Yes," she conceded.

"Then you need additional protection for you and your child," he stated like it was as plain as the nose on his face.

"Where am I supposed to get that?" Her voice trembled with fear.

"I'm here to help. I apologize for not introducing myself yesterday morning. My name is Riggs O'Connor," he said.

"I know that n…" She drew out the last consonant. It was like bells were going off inside her head and she couldn't figure out why.

"Go ahead and look me up. I'll wait," he urged.

"Hold on." The line got quiet for a couple of minutes and he was pretty sure she'd used the mute function. When she came back to the line, he could hear her breathing for a moment before she spoke. "Why would someone like you help me?"

"Because you helped us. Your statement will help nail

the person who killed my wife's best friend and, more important, it's the right thing to do." He meant every word.

Loriann was quiet. Stunned? A question hung in the air. Would she accept his offer?

Chapter Sixteen

"That's mighty nice of you, Mr. O'Connor, but I don't think—"

"Accept my help for your child," he interrupted before she could get too much momentum on the rejection.

"I don't know," she hedged but he could tell his statement had made the impact he'd hoped for.

"Do you have a boy or a girl?" he asked.

"Boy," came the response.

"How old, if I may ask?" He'd learned a long time ago that he got more done with honey than vinegar, as the old saying went.

"Six years old." She blew out a sharp breath.

"I'm guessing he's asleep right now," he continued.

"Yes, that's right. He is," she acknowledged.

"Let me help you keep him safe, Loriann. My wife and I would like to come pick the two of you up and bring you to my family's ranch, where you'll both be protected until the person who murdered our friend is locked behind bars. No one at the hospital who is willing to speak up against him is safe until that happens and you know it." He'd made his plea. He couldn't and wouldn't try to force her to take the help. At this point, he could only hope she would see reason.

"I wish I could. But I have to work tomorrow." The anguish in her voice caused his heart to bleed for every single parent who had to balance being able to put food on the table versus ensuring the safety of their child.

"What if you could come to work on the ranch? Get paid what you normally make at the hospital to help out around here?" he asked.

"Well, I guess that could work. But I'd lose my benefits if they fire me," she said. Based on the change in her tone, he was making progress.

"What if I told you my family could ensure that didn't happen? If going back there would cause you any discomfort, we could set you up in a new position at another hospital," he said, doing his best to radiate confidence. For his plan to work, she needed to believe him. Most wouldn't trust a random stranger but the O'Connors had built a strong legacy of honesty. One that he was hoping to capitalize on now.

"You can do that?" She nearly choked on her words. Then she said, "Of course, you can. I'm not used to keeping company with people who can make a difference like that."

Riggs was never more reminded how fortunate he was in being an O'Connor, and how rare it actually was to grow up in a household with two loving parents who had the financial means to move mountains if need be. His folks had had an admirable marriage. One he'd believed he could repeat with Cheyenne despite the rushed nature of their wedding.

"We don't take our privilege lightly," he reassured her. It was true. Being an O'Connor meant honor and holding up the family name—a job he'd been born to do and welcomed with open arms. "And it would be a waste if we couldn't use our resources to help others who deserved it."

The line was quiet. He could tell that Loriann was proud and not the kind to take what she would view as handouts from others lightly. This situation was different, but he respected her for her convictions.

"You say you'll keep my boy safe until this situation is sorted out," she finally said.

"Yes, ma'am," he said quickly. She needed to know how serious and committed he was. No hesitation.

"Do you know where I live?" she asked.

"No. I do not," he responded.

She rattled off her address before saying, "It might be my imagination running wild but I'm pretty sure a two-door gray sedan has circled the building three times since we started talking. Get here as quick as you can."

"On my way, but it'll be about an hour. Call the law and report a suspicious vehicle." He didn't want to wake Cheyenne, but he would look in on her and leave a note beside the bed for when she woke. "You have my number now. Call me if anything changes."

"Okay."

The line went dead. The gray sedan might be nothing, but he wasn't taking any chances. He grabbed his shotgun from his gun cabinet in the closet underneath the stairs. And then decided his holster and 9mm wouldn't be a bad choice, either.

A couple of seconds later, he scribbled out a note to Cheyenne and then headed to the master. He tiptoed inside the room, praying he wouldn't disturb her, and then he realized that wouldn't do. He'd promised not to leave her alone while she rested and she'd been asleep a long time. Plus, he'd told Loriann that he and his wife would be picking her up.

The light flipped on as his resolve to wake her grew. Cheyenne sat up, hugging her knees to her chest.

"Where are you going?" She blinked a couple of times like her eyes needed a minute to adjust to the light.

"To pick up the nurse we spoke to yesterday morning. Both she and her child might be in danger. I convinced her to come to the ranch for protection until Ally's killer is behind bars." There was no reason to hold back. "I wrote a note explaining but I planned to wake you up and tell you. Make sure you were okay with me leaving."

"I'm coming with you." Cheyenne threw the covers off. He forced his gaze away from those long silky legs of hers revealed by the sleeping shirt she wore, which was one of his old T-shirts.

He picked up a pair of her favorite joggers that she'd left behind during the move, no doubt by accident, and then tossed them over to her.

"Thanks." She caught them and shimmied into the pair.

He opened her dresser and threw a pair of socks next, realizing the movers had left quite a bit behind in their haste. But then, she might have instructed them to grab what they could see and get out.

No one had checked the laundry room when he'd stood by and watched drawers be emptied one by one in their bedroom. He wasn't about to point out places that had been missed. The memory caused his gut to clench. He chalked it up to one of the worst days of his life.

In the span of two weeks, he'd lost a child and a wife. And in the last twenty-four hours the world had shifted again. To say life was unpredictable would be the understatement of the century. It had more twists and turns than a multimillion-dollar roller coaster and all the ups and downs to go with it.

Cheyenne finished dressing, turning her back to him when she changed her shirt and put on a bra. He respected her privacy.

"Ready." She hopped on one foot as she slipped on her second tennis shoe.

She gathered up Ozzy and tucked him inside her handbag. He figured he'd buy her one of those carriers to make them both more comfortable once this was all over.

In a surprise move, she reached for his hand at the door. He didn't pull away even though he probably should have. There was no reason to confuse the issue of why she was staying there and why they were together... Ally. In fact, if Cheyenne's friend hadn't reached out, the two of them wouldn't be in the same room right now. Add random to the list of life's attributes. Without that arbitrary idea of Ally's to have the two of them listen to her at the same time, Cheyenne would still be at her friend's house and Riggs would be working at the ranch.

The thought struck hard. He wanted his wife to be home because she couldn't stay away. This was a good reminder to keep his feelings in check. At present, they were all over the map. As levelheaded as Riggs normally was, this situation couldn't be more extreme. The stakes couldn't be higher with his wife and child hanging in the balance.

This time, he'd give himself a break for the slip that had him wanting to bury himself deep inside the woman he'd married and not let go of her again.

He released her hand as they entered the garage. She shot a questioning look, but he didn't acknowledge it. Keeping himself in check was his new marching order.

CHEYENNE PUSHED DOWN the hurt from Riggs's action with the realization the two of them were wading through shark-infested waters. It was good to keep guards up and some distance. She respected his boundary, figuring it wouldn't hurt for her to strengthen her walls, as well.

If they were going to be parents, and she hoped they would with everything inside her, she realized the baby showing up wasn't a magical fix. Their relationship had been strained over the past few weeks. She'd asked for a divorce and no matter how confusing life had become, neither could go back and pretend none of it had happened.

He was right to pull back, even though it stung.

On the drive to Loriann's apartment building, he filled her in on his conversation with his brother and how he'd convinced Colton to let him have Loriann's cell number.

"The gray sedan is worrisome," she said when he was finished.

"Let's hope it's a coincidence. I doubt Loriann is usually up at this time of night looking out the window, so it might not be as strange as she thinks," he said.

He was right.

"We both know I can't watch a scary movie before bed," she agreed. "Plants too many ideas in my imagination and it just runs with it."

"Like the time you thought there might be a ghost in the laundry room," he said. "Which turned out to be a squirrel that had gotten in through an opened window earlier in the day."

"How was I supposed to know the little guy was in there? We didn't exactly have any pets," she defended.

"You'd just watched one of those horror movies…which one?" He tapped the steering wheel with his index finger. It was a habit she'd missed in the two weeks they'd been apart. It was crazy how much she missed the little things about her husband. The first kiss in the morning before either got out of bed. It wasn't romantic so much as sweet. Or the way he always picked a single flower for her while they were in season before he walked in the door. She'd set it inside a jar on the table, keeping a constantly growing and changing bouquet.

Relationships were a lot like that. Leave a spoiled flower in the jar too long and suddenly the water was moldy. They took constant pruning, especially in the early years, according to her mother. Cheyenne thought about how much her mother would have loved Riggs. And she would have been blown away by the ranch. The place was glorious by anyone's standards, and her mother had been one of the least picky people on the planet.

Her mother had loved the little things in life. A ladybug crawling on a blade of grass. Ladybugs had been her favorite, thus the bracelet.

"What are you thinking about?" Riggs's deep, masculine voice washed over her and through her.

"My mom." She fingered the ladybug, rolling it around in between her thumb and forefinger.

The next thing she knew, the delicate clasp broke and the bracelet fell apart. Pieces of it flew in opposite directions, on her lap and on the floorboard. Cheyenne's chest hurt as she tried to breathe, realizing she'd just ruined her mother's legacy.

She gasped and probably cursed but she couldn't be 100 percent certain. All she could think about was the loss.

"No," she said loudly. She fisted her right hand and then slammed it on the armrest, drawing it back the minute she connected. Pain shot through her pinky.

Riggs put on his turning signal and hit the brake.

"No. No. Keep going. I'll find the pieces later. We can't stop now," she said.

"Cheyenne, are you sure?"

"Yes. It's too late." Those words were knife jabs to the center of her chest. She repeated them over and over again in her thoughts as she bent forward to find what she could.

"Use your phone. The dome light won't do much good," Riggs urged.

She reached for her cell, disturbing Ozzy, who made no secret of how unimpressed he was with the move.

"Okay, okay. Settle down, little guy." Breaking her promise to her best friend wasn't on the table no matter how much the dog overreacted. "You're good." She lightened her tone and Ozzy responded by curling up and lowering his head to rest on the side of her handbag. He'd warmed up to her and yet she couldn't help but think he was in survival mode.

His eyes—those sad eyes that made her want to cry—stared up at her brokenly.

If ever there was a time for wisdom, this would be it. Except that none came. She patted Ozzy on the head and then scratched behind his ears until he went back to sleep.

There was no way she was leaving this truck without finding the ladybug. The rest of the bracelet could be replaced.

She ran her fingers along the floorboard. The piece she was looking for was so tiny and the cab of the truck was so big. It didn't help that this was a work truck, so it wasn't exactly empty. There were rags and a couple of empty water bottles on the floorboard in the back. And there were clumps of dirt. One fooled her into thinking she'd found what she was looking for as she reached underneath the seat.

"I hate to stop what you're doing, but we're here and I need you to take something." Riggs pulled into a parking spot and then handed over a 9mm handgun. "Can you handle this?"

"I can," she assured him, figuring she better qualify the statement. "My parents took me to a shooting range when I was a teenager, so I'd know what to do if I encountered a gun at a friend's house. Shotguns are a different story. I've never used one. And I didn't load any of the weapons I shot that day."

It felt strange that she hadn't told him that story before

or that her husband didn't know all the little things about her. After discovering the pregnancy and then jumping into marriage, they'd gone straight to getting ready for the baby mode. They'd only been dating a short time before the pregnancy news came.

Riggs nodded.

"I have to find the charm first," Cheyenne said.

He seemed to catch on immediately. This was important to her. He gave a quick scan of the parking lot before taking hold of the cell while she resumed her search.

Cheyenne reached for the chair release lever. Her fingers landed on a button. She played with it until she figured out how to move the seat back. Then she moved onto all fours to be eye level with the floor.

"I can't find it, Riggs." She didn't bother to hide the desperation in her voice.

He moved the flashlight around, and then she saw it.

"There." She reached underneath the seat. Warmth spread through her as she picked it up and held it on the flat of her palm.

Tap. Tap. Tap.

The metal barrel of a gun beat out a staccato rhythm against the driver's-side window.

Chapter Seventeen

Riggs froze. His back was to the driver's-side window where the taps came from.

"Gun," was all Cheyenne said as her eyes widened in shock and fear. She quickly dropped the ladybug inside her handbag.

The 9mm was still in his right hand. He'd used his left to hold the light for Cheyenne. Could he turn fast enough to surprise the person on the other side of the glass?

It was a risky move. Too risky. One wrong flex of a finger and disaster could strike. The sound behind him was at too close a range to miss and it would take Riggs a couple of seconds to swivel enough to get off a shot.

"What does he look like?" he asked Cheyenne.

She put her hands in the air as she rose to her knees. "I can't tell. His face is covered, and he has on a dark hoodie."

The same description of the rose buyer from the grocery store. For a fraction of a moment Riggs thought about drawing down on the guy. But Hoodie was already in position to fire and the second or two it would take Riggs to position his weapon could cost Cheyenne her life.

After issuing a sharp sigh, he released his grip on the 9mm, letting it tumble onto the seat and then put his hands in the air before slowly turning around. A gun wasn't the same MO as Ally's murder, which meant multiple people could be involved or the original perp could be getting nervous. Ally had been stabbed, a bloody and personal way to die. It fit with the date-gone-wrong ruse.

Riggs's thoughts immediately jumped to Loriann and her kid. This person couldn't be random. He had to be connected to the case. Nothing else made sense.

Was this the guy from the gray sedan?

Hoodie took a step back into the shadows and motioned for them to exit the truck. It looked as though he was working alone and that would give Riggs and Cheyenne a possible advantage. Two against one were numbers he'd like better if he was the one in possession of the firearm.

If he could get close enough to the bastard to safely take him down, he wouldn't hesitate.

"Can I count on you to stay behind me?" Riggs asked Cheyenne.

"Yes." There was no conviction in her response, but this wasn't the time to dig around for clarification.

Keeping his hands in the air, he motioned toward the door handle. He would have to lower his right hand out of the perp's view to open the door. Again, he tried to figure out a way to capitalize on the opportunity but came up blank.

The perp also had on dark pants...slacks? He had on surgical gloves. Dr. Fortner? Or someone else from the hospital?

"Does this guy seem familiar at all?" he asked Cheyenne quietly.

"I can't see anything," she said.

The perp stepped forward and opened the driver's-side door before moving approximately fifteen back. The guy had on surgical gloves. He was too far away to make a move but even at this distance Riggs could see the perp's hand shaking.

"Come out," came the demand. Riggs didn't recognize the voice.

Did he plan to shoot them outside the truck? Make it look like a robbery gone wrong? Or set up some other scene like the one he'd tried to use to cover Ally's murder?

Murder-suicide?

The silencer on the end of his gun would minimize noise. Folks wouldn't be any the wiser as they slept through the night. Except Loriann, who was waiting for Riggs and Cheyenne. He couldn't let his mind go to a place where this jerk had already gotten to her and her son. Anger ripped through him. She'd been watching out the window. Was she now?

He'd parked across the lot from her building so he wouldn't run into the driver of the gray sedan.

As he was about to climb out of the truck, Cheyenne reached for his door. She held it where he couldn't move. It only took an instant for him to realize she meant to use it to shield them as she brought the 9mm around and aimed at the perp.

A second later, Riggs felt the shotgun being shoved at him. He gripped it and took aim as the perp darted between vehicles, firing a wild shot. A warning?

Riggs was momentarily torn between chasing after the guy and checking on Loriann. Her safety won out. That, and the fact he didn't want Cheyenne chasing a guy with a gun, and she would insist on coming with him. Not to mention the fact he couldn't very well leave her in the truck.

The sounds of screeching tires came a second before a gray streak shot out of the lot and in the opposite direction. At this point, Riggs was at a full run to get to Loriann and her child. He vaguely remembered slamming his truck door closed and locking the vehicle.

Cheyenne was right behind him, gripping her handbag with Ozzy inside, as they raced to Loriann's unit. Her apartment was on the second floor. Riggs made as little noise as possible as he took the steps two at a time. As he and Cheyenne made it to the door, it swung wide open and a scared-looking Loriann stood on the other side.

Relief he couldn't begin to describe washed over him.

"Come in quick." She ushered them both inside, then closed and locked the door behind them. "The gray sedan couldn't get out of here fast enough. Now I know why. He was coming for me, wasn't he?"

"Yes. We got here as fast as we could," Riggs said as he tried to catch his breath.

"I'm just thankful we got here in time," Cheyenne added.

"Me, too." Loriann stepped forward and brought Cheyenne into a brief hug. "I called the police to report a suspicious vehicle like you said, but the dispatcher didn't seem too thrilled. She said they'd been getting calls about teenagers joyriding, and I couldn't prove any different, so I just let it go."

"You did the right thing," Riggs reassured. "The guy in the gray sedan had a gun with a silencer on it and he wore surgical gloves. I doubt he was planning to let you leave here alive."

Loriann shook visibly.

"What was he waiting on?" she asked. Something passed behind her eyes that Riggs made a note to ask about later. Right now, all he could think about was getting her and her son to safety.

"My guess?" Riggs asked. "An opportunity."

"Makes sense." She shook her head like she was trying to shake off the creepiness of the close call. "I packed a bag for me and Zachary." She looked from Cheyenne to Riggs. "I wasn't real sure how long we'd be gone."

"We can get whatever else you need at the ranch," Riggs said. "Let's get out of here before he decides to come back."

As it was, they got lucky. The perp must have realized he was outnumbered. Cheyenne's move had been brilliant. There was no way Riggs could have pulled it off while the guy was focused on watching him, viewing him as the bigger threat. The man never saw Cheyenne's move coming and, to be honest, neither had Riggs. His wife had always been strong and quick-witted, so he wasn't shocked. His admiration for her grew leaps and bounds, though.

Cheyenne O'Connor was a force of nature. One he admired and respected for her strength and courage, which wasn't going to make it any easier when they went their separate ways. Of course, if their child was alive out there and they found her, they'd be bound together for the rest of their lives.

"Give me your suitcase. I'll run them down." Riggs handed the 9mm over to Cheyenne. "If anyone besides me walks through that door, shoot first and ask questions later."

"I should go with you for cover," Cheyenne said with a pensive look.

"I'd rather you stayed here with Loriann and Zachary." Riggs had no doubt Cheyenne's protective instincts would kick into high gear since a child was involved.

Loriann rolled a large suitcase into the room. "He has a favorite blanket and teddy, but I wouldn't be able to pry those out of his fingers if I tried."

"It's fine. We'll bring those with him," Riggs said. "Will seeing guns scare him if he wakes up?"

"I'll tell him we're playing pretend cops and robbers," Loriann offered.

"Lock the door behind me," Riggs said before heading out the door.

The look of concern from Cheyenne had him wanting to figure out another way. This was their best bet, though.

CHEYENNE'S ADRENALINE WAS jacked through the roof as she locked the door behind Riggs.

"He's a good person," Loriann said.

"Yes," Cheyenne responded.

"A good husband, too?" Loriann asked.

"Yes." Her admission wasn't helping Cheyenne keep an emotional distance. Did she want to stay married to him? The short answer was yes. If only it was that easy. Life was complicated now that she'd pushed him away because she could never give him children, only to find out their daughter was alive.

The thought of Anya—that was to be their daughter's name—being out there somewhere with another family sent a tsunami of emotions roaring through her. She had to shove them aside to focus on getting Loriann and her son out of the apartment in one piece.

"You should probably go and get your son now," Cheyenne said to Loriann, figuring they would be on the move the second Riggs returned. She moved to the window with the view of the parking lot. She cracked it open and readied the gun. If the gray sedan came back, she wouldn't hesitate to shoot.

From this vantage point, she was able to keep watch over Riggs. When he returned, he brought the vehicle with him, blocking three parking spots so he could be as close to the stairs as possible.

Relief like she'd never known washed over her as she watched him take the stairs. She closed and locked the window. The floor creaked behind her, indicating Loriann had returned. Cheyenne dropped the barrel of the gun, hiding it behind her leg in case the little boy woke. She didn't want to frighten him and had no idea if he'd been around any type of weapon like this before.

"I can't thank you and your husband enough," Loriann said quietly. The boy in her arms was more than half her size. His head rested on her shoulder and she bounced like she had an infant in her arms. The sweetness of the mother-child scene slammed into Cheyenne's solar plexus. It hurt to breathe.

The fact Loriann kept referring to Riggs as Cheyenne's husband wasn't lost on her. There was no reason to explain how complicated their relationship was. And if she thought she could give him what he wanted...*deserved*... there'd be no talk of divorce. Make no mistake about it, Riggs O'Connor had been the best thing that ever happened to Cheyenne.

Riggs tapped on the door three times. Cheyenne raced to open it and usher him inside. After closing it behind him, she reached up on her tiptoes and gave him a kiss partly for luck and partly because recent events showed her how little was guaranteed in life.

He brought his hand up to cup her face before feathering a kiss on her lips. There was something so tender about Riggs's kiss that it robbed Cheyenne's ability to breathe.

A second later, the moment had passed, and they were wrangling Loriann and her son out of their home.

"You lead the way," Riggs said to her. "I'll take the back to ensure no one is lingering."

Cheyenne nodded and did as requested. Thankfully, it was a short trip to the truck. She opened the passenger door and helped Loriann step inside. The boy in her arms stirred, opening his eyes for the briefest moment. He had the sweetest brown eyes. His cheeks were flush and his lashes long. He had the face of a cherub.

Loriann positioned in the back and her son sprawled

out on the bench seat, holding tight to his teddy. Cheyenne helped with his blanket as he rolled over. Then she hopped into the passenger side and secured her seat belt. Shotgun at the ready, Riggs reclaimed the driver's side.

The sun came up on the drive back to the ranch, giving Loriann the ability to see the full glory of KBR as they drove through security. A bunkhouse in one direction and barns in the other created a kind of grandeur that still wowed Riggs today when he slowed down.

"This is where you live?" Loriann asked, wide-eyed. The place would be considered grand by anyone's standards. A guard at a security stand controlled entrance to the paved road leading to their massive white house.

"Technically, my mom lives in the main house. Our place is another half hour's drive from here. I'd like to get the two of you situated before heading home," Riggs said to Loriann.

"Are you sure it'll be all right for us to stay here?" The wonder and disbelief in her voice was a little too familiar to Cheyenne. It was difficult to believe people who were this well off could be as kind and generous as the O'Connor family.

"Believe me when I say I had the same reaction the first time Riggs brought me home to meet the family. They'll welcome you and Zachary with open arms. No questions asked," Cheyenne said. It was true. She'd never met people like the O'Connors before. Part of her had been losing faith in the goodness in the world until Riggs.

He parked in front of the main house.

"I hope you'll be comfortable here. Like my wife said, my mother will be pleased to have the company. She's always complaining about rattling around in this big house by herself now that her children are grown," he said. That seemed to put Loriann at ease.

As they started the process of exiting the vehicle, Cheyenne's cell buzzed.

Riggs froze.

"Go on inside without me," she said. "I'll be right there."

He nodded even though he looked reluctant to leave her there. She shooed him away, fishing for her cell phone inside her handbag. Besides, she had to give Ozzy a chance to stretch his legs.

Being at the main house brought back a whole slew of memories. His family had been nothing but welcoming. It was impossible not to feel like she let them down in some way. She hoped they realized she was hanging onto the end of her rope as best she could.

A quick check of the screen told her that her father was on the line. She caught the call right before it headed into voice mail.

"Hey, Dad," she said. "Is everything okay?"

"I came as soon as I could," her father said. His voice had lost the spark it once had. Hearing it again shocked her into the reality of what her future might look like without Riggs.

"Hold on a sec. What did you just say?" she asked.

Chapter Eighteen

"I'm here, knocking on your door. I see your car right there." Cheyenne's father spoke like she was standing on the porch with him and he was pointing it out.

"I texted you two weeks ago," she said as panic gripped her. He'd come to Ally's place?

"I'm sorry I couldn't drive any faster," he explained.

"You should have texted me back or called." What if the driver of the gray sedan was watching Ally's house? He might be expecting Cheyenne to come home where he could ambush her.

"Listen to me very carefully, Dad," she began. "Leave right now. Okay?"

"What? Why?" Her dad's confusion wasn't helping with her fried nerves.

"You have to get out of there. It's not safe," she warned, praying he would listen to her and not question it. She might be overreacting, but she wasn't willing to take a chance.

"What's not safe, honey?" There was real concern in her father's voice and she appreciated him for it.

"I don't have time to explain right now. Get in your RV and start driving. You can come out to the ranch or—"

"What are you doing at the ranch? I thought you were

staying here. Is everything all right between you and Riggs?" Her father sounded confused.

"Yes," she said for lack of something better. It would be easier to explain once she got her father on the road and away from Ally's place. "Drive right now. I need to see you."

"Oh. Well, then. I'll just get off the porch here, and walk back to the RV. I'm parked on the street." As he'd gotten older, he'd developed a habit of giving her a play-by-play in situations like these.

"Yes. Hurry. It's been too long since we've seen each other, and I need my father right now." She let the emotions coursing through her play out in her tone. It was a ploy for his sympathy, but she didn't have time to explain. She would do or say just about anything to get him out of harm's way. The two of them might not be as close as they once were but she couldn't risk anything bad happening to another person she loved.

"What's the address?" he asked.

"Get in the RV and then give the phone to Virginia. I'll direct you once you get on the road," she urged.

"Well, all right. If it's that important to you we'll head on over," he conceded.

"It is, Dad. It's the most important thing you could ever do for me." She wasn't afraid to pour it on thick.

She heard him tell Virginia to stay in the RV. Virginia grumbled but she went along with what he said.

It was impossible in times like these not to compare Virginia to her mother. The two might resemble each other in looks but they couldn't be more different when it came to their personalities.

Cheyenne let Ozzy run onto the lawn while she waited for her stepmother to pick up the phone. Rustling came over the line before the sound of the engine kicking over.

She sighed with relief when she heard the two of them arguing about where they were going. She shouldn't be surprised and yet it made her sad. Her parents had had one of those magical relationships. They rarely ever disagreed. Their house was filled with laughter and her mother's happy squeals as she was being taken for a spin around the kitchen after supper.

She didn't recognize her father's life anymore. Now that she'd experienced loss, she didn't blame him for wanting to fill the void. It struck her as strange how the two of them reacted in completely opposite ways to their grief. When Cheyenne was told her daughter was gone, she'd decided never to try to have children again, whereas her father had married the first woman he came across who looked like the wife he'd lost. While she couldn't fathom trying to replace her child, she suddenly wondered if they were both equally wrong. Had they gone to opposite extremes?

"Hello, Cheyenne?" Virginia sounded like she half expected someone else to be on the line.

"Hi. Yes. It's me," Cheyenne responded, never quite sure how to speak to her stepmother.

"I'm sorry about your…*situation*." Virginia sounded sorrowful.

"Thank you." Cheyenne realized it was the first time she'd spoken to Virginia since losing the baby.

"I lost a pregnancy once and couldn't get out of bed for a month," her stepmother continued. "It's awful."

"I'm sorry to hear." Cheyenne appreciated the sentiment. Virginia spoke more sincerely than she usually did. "You're right about one thing. It's the worst feeling."

"It sure is." The cold edge that had always been in Virginia's voice softened.

The thought occurred to Cheyenne that it couldn't possibly be easy to step into another woman's shoes. And her dad was far less sad now that he was remarried. He'd been gutted after his wife's death.

"Sounds like you guys are on the road now." Cheyenne needed to change the subject and steer the conversation back on track. "This is going to sound like a strange question. I promise to explain later."

"Go on," Virginia urged.

"Is there a gray sedan anywhere near you?" Cheyenne held her breath while waiting for the answer.

"Let's see." There was a moment of silence before Virginia said, "No. Not one in sight."

Cheyenne released the air in her lungs with a slow exhale. She rattled off the address of the ranch and told her dad to call when GPS said he was getting close. He mumbled something about finding an RV park first. She ended the conversation, picked up Ozzy and then turned to face the main house. Her chest squeezed.

Riggs's mother must be inside. Margaret O'Connor was about the nicest woman Cheyenne had ever had the pleasure of meeting. The thought of hurting someone who had already experienced the worst possible pain didn't sit well.

If Margaret gave Cheyenne a chilly reception, she wouldn't be surprised or place any blame. It would be nothing more than just desert for hurting Riggs and letting the family down.

With a heavy heart, she marched to the front door. As she arrived, it burst open and Margaret stood on the other side, arms wide open.

"It's so good to see you," Margaret said as she brought Cheyenne into an embrace.

Shock robbed her voice. This warmth was so unexpected and, to be honest, felt undeserved. All Cheyenne could say in response was, "I'm sorry."

Margaret pulled back and shooed the comment away.

"There's no reason for apologies. You're here now and I don't want to waste a minute."

Cheyenne couldn't stop the smile from curling the corners of her lips.

"Who do you have here?" Margaret motioned toward the handbag.

"This is Ozzy." He popped his head out as though he knew he was being talked about.

"Oh my goodness. What a sweetheart." Margaret cooed at the little dog and Cheyenne could have sworn he made the same noises back.

"Do you still like to drink that chai tea?" Margaret asked, returning her gaze to meet Cheyenne's.

"Coffee is my drink of choice now," Cheyenne admitted.

"How about a cup?" Margaret asked. "I can figure out how to work the machine while Riggs gets our new houseguests set up in one of the guest rooms."

"Sounds good to me." Everything about being back at the ranch felt right. A couple of weeks away suddenly felt like an eternity.

Arm in arm, she walked with Margaret into the expansive kitchen. She'd rarely come to the main house during her pregnancy and yet the place felt like home. Her house with Riggs was the same. She'd moved around a lot as a kid, so it surprised her how much she fit at the ranch the minute she arrived.

Ozzy whimpered inside the handbag.

"What's wrong, little guy?" Cheyenne freed him.

He wiggled like a baby who didn't want to be held.

"Okay if he runs free for a few minutes?" Cheyenne asked Margaret.

"Fine by me," came the response as the older woman went to fix the brew.

Cheyenne set Ozzy down on the tile floor. She squatted next to him. "Is that better? Do you need to stretch your legs?"

Ozzy half ran, half hopped over to Margaret, and then lay down by her feet.

RIGGS CLOSED THE door to the guest suite where Loriann and Zachary were settling in. The little boy was still asleep and Loriann was unpacking their suitcase when he left. Riggs would be lying if he didn't admit to taking a hit at seeing the mother and son together. Loriann's love for her son made him wonder what it would be like to hold his own child in his arms.

As it was, he could only imagine how powerful a moment that might be. He had yet to meet his daughter and he already knew he'd move heaven and earth to make her comfortable.

They had to find her. Period. There was no other outcome in his mind.

Riggs had learned a long time ago to shut out all other possibilities when he went after something. Whether it applied to work or a personal goal, the same tactic came into play. Singular vision gave him clarity.

Whoa. He thought about that for a moment and applied it to his relationship with Cheyenne. When she'd told him about the pregnancy, he'd set his sights on becoming a family. Technically, that wasn't the same as becoming a good husband. A strong relationship required communication. And what had he done when she'd seemed stressed? Given her space. He figured everything would magically work out once the baby came. That was as realistic as cooking an egg on a December sidewalk in Texas.

He could say the same for when she tried to talk to him in the cab of his truck. He'd decided telling her the whole truth would cause more harm than good. Part of his thinking was meant to protect her. But she needed to know what was on his mind. Otherwise, they'd never get to know each other on a real level. He'd lost some of her trust when he didn't communicate. He'd seen the change in her eyes the minute he lost her. The eyes never lied. He had some work to do to gain her trust again. His mistakes were racking up.

Riggs veered into the kitchen. The smell of fresh coffee quickened his pace.

When he stepped onto the tile, his heart squeezed. There his mother stood nuzzling Ozzy, chatting easily with his wife. His two favorite people in the world looked like they were old friends. A growing part of him wanted to fight for his marriage no matter what else happened with the investigation.

The annoying voice in the back of his mind picked that time to point out she'd pushed him away when they needed each other most. What would stop her from doing it again?

Again, the concept of communication came to mind. Looking back, he could have done a better job.

"Are either of you hungry?" his mother asked. She had a special radar for when one of her boys walked into a room. There was no hiding from Margaret O'Connor. Maybe that was the by-product of bringing up six rowdy boys. He smirked, figuring he owed her a couple of apologies for some of their antics as kids.

Cheyenne turned toward him, and it was like the sun breaking through the clouds after weeks of rain.

"We should do what we can to up our strength," he said, figuring he needed to catch his mother up to date with all the new information.

"Take a seat at the table and I'll whip up something," she said like it was nothing.

"Why don't the two of you grab chairs and let me stumble around in the pantry for a change," he offered.

"I'll take you up on that after fixing a cup of tea." His mother beamed. She'd brought up all of her boys to be able to fend for themselves in the kitchen when necessary. Her guidance had come in handy all those times he had nothing but a skillet and a campfire as tools and a small bag of groceries to sustain himself when tracking poachers.

"Let me get the tea. You have your hands full already." He motioned toward Ozzy and one word came to mind… traitor. The little dog was as happy as a lark. He'd come alive. Cheyenne didn't seem to mind the slight despite becoming closer with the little yapper after Ally's death.

Speaking of which, Riggs went over the basics in his mind as he heated the stove and grabbed enough ingredients to make breakfast tacos. Eggs were basically his staple and he hoped Cheyenne wasn't tired of them yet.

Cheyenne had finally rested. Before coming home, he doubted she'd slept more than a few hours. Based on what she'd said so far, he didn't get the impression she was getting a whole lot of quality rest for the past couple of weeks. He could attest to the fact she hadn't been sleeping well in the last month of her pregnancy. The middle-of-the-night trips to the bathroom had multiplied. So had the back pain and cramps. Pregnancy didn't seem to be for the faint of heart.

And yet, every time she talked about the baby, she brought her hand down to gently rub the bump. Was that her subconscious at work? He figured so. Long before the child would come into the world her mother had bonded with her.

Riggs didn't have that same instant connection, but he would be ready to love the child once he met her. She was still an idea in his mind. Not real until he held her in his arms, a move he'd been anticipating more and more the closer the due date got.

Breakfast was served and eaten in a matter of minutes. Cheyenne bit back three yawns while praising his cooking, despite having conked out for almost twelve hours at the house before he woke her at three o'clock this morning. Almost four hours later, he wondered if he could get her to rest while Colton did his job.

"What do you think about grabbing one of the guest rooms here at the main house and taking a quick nap?" he asked, clearing the table.

She stood up and joined him before glancing down at Ozzy.

"My father and stepmother are coming, and I doubt I'd be able to sleep while waiting for them," she said. "They did say something about finding an RV park first, so I'm not sure when they'll be here."

Riggs wouldn't mind meeting his in-laws for the first time.

"I'd be happy to take care of this guy to give you a break," his mother said before cooing at Ozzy again. The dog practically purred. "You could relax at the very least."

"I'll take you up on the offer for Ozzy," Cheyenne said with a half smile.

"Good," his mother said.

"I'll get you settled and then come back for the dishes." Riggs prided himself on his self-sufficiency. Had he gotten too used to living alone? Taking care of himself and letting no one else in?

"You'll do no such thing," his mother said. "You fed me. And quite well if I do say so. Dishes are the least I can do."

He opened his mouth to argue but Margaret O'Connor was having none of it. She shooed him out of her space like he was a fly buzzing in her ear.

"Okay, I'm going," he said, appreciating a little levity in what had been some of the heaviest days of his life. He'd given his mother the two-cent version of what had happened, and she'd told him Colton had been sending updates. Thankfully, Riggs didn't have to go into it in detail.

Mentally, he was whipped, and he could use some down time to process. He also wanted to think about his next move. He knew full well investigations took time. His brother was working this case on steroids, throwing as many resources as he could toward it. There would be a breakthrough. There *had* to be one. Progress was being made.

The thought of Riggs's daughter, if she'd lived, sleeping one more night away from her parents, from her home, caused anger to rip through him. Did the family who had her know the adoption was illegal? He shook those questions out of his thoughts as he walked Cheyenne to his old bedroom on the second floor.

"This is it. I think you'll be comfortable." He stopped at the door. "Use anything you want. The bathroom is attached. I'll be in the room across the hall if you need anything else."

She grabbed a fistful of his shirt and tugged him toward her. Those pale blue eyes of hers locked onto his, sending heat swirling through him in places he knew better than to think about with her standing so close.

"Will you stay?" Her voice was steady. And yet he realized she wasn't trying to hit on him. There was a lost quality to her, too, and he figured she didn't want to be alone with her thoughts.

He wrapped his hand around the doorknob and twisted. "I'm right behind you."

Chapter Nineteen

"Thank you for sticking around." Cheyenne meant it. "Everything you're doing for me is above and beyond and I wanted you to know that it's not going unnoticed or unappreciated."

"You deserve it." He waved her off like it was nothing.

Her cell buzzed in her purse. The call was from her dad. She fished her phone from her purse and answered. "Everything all right?"

"Yes, honey. It's fine. You told me to call you when we get close. We found a nice little park where we can hook up the RV. We've been driving a long time and I thought it might be best if we rest and come to you refreshed," her father said. Was he avoiding facing her?

The thought sent a dagger into the pit of her stomach. From all accounts, he hadn't been identified as her relative, so a park should be safe. And honestly, she could use a couple of hours to gather herself.

"If you think you'll be more comfortable," she said, figuring arguing wouldn't do any good.

"We will." The emphasis her father placed on the word *we* made her think this might be his wife's idea.

Either way, Cheyenne could use some rest of her own, so she wouldn't argue.

"Call me when you feel up to it," she said before ending the call and then staring at Riggs.

"What was that all about?" he asked.

"He's not coming," she said.

Riggs took a step toward her, closing the gap between them. He cupped her face in his hands before pressing a tender kiss to her lips. "I'm sorry."

Those two words spoken with conviction eased so much of the hurt inside her.

"He was an amazing dad at one time," she said by way of defense.

"What do you think happened?" Riggs asked, taking her by the hand and leading her to the bottom of the bed where he sat down and tugged her onto his lap. He encircled his arms around her waist and then waited.

"My mom died, and it shattered him." She'd never said those words aloud. Some of the pressure that had been weighing on her shoulders lifted. "She was the glue that kept our family together."

"He still had you," Riggs said.

She sat there for a long moment without speaking. How could she make him understand? *Show him.*

"Have I ever shown you a picture of my mother?" she asked.

"No, I don't believe you have." His dark brow arched.

Phone still in hand, she pulled up a photo of the three of them.

"You're the spitting image of her," he said. "She was a beautiful woman."

"Inside and out," she said.

And then it seemed to dawn on him.

"Every time your father looks at you, he sees her," Riggs said, catching on.

"It's the only reason I can think of for him to take off

with his new wife and leave me behind," she admitted. A rogue tear welled in her eye. "We talk on the phone, but it's not the same as being face-to-face. I don't doubt that he loves me. Or, at least I didn't until recently."

The tear escaped and Riggs thumbed it away.

"I can tell you that he's missing out on an amazing person," he said, his voice low and gravelly.

The air grew charged around them. Their chemistry had always been off the charts.

"He doesn't seem to be too bothered," she said. And that was the last time she was going to feel sorry for herself. "But it is what it is. I can't change other people no matter how much I wish I could." She paused and waited for Riggs to respond. Part of her expected him to judge her.

He didn't.

"I just miss having a family sometimes. You know?" she said.

"You have a family," he responded, sounding a little hurt. "Me. My brothers. My mother. We're your family now."

"Until—"

"There's no expiration date, Cheyenne. I'm not wired that way. The two of us had a child together. One I very much hope to bring home and raise together. I respect your wishes to do that from separate residences but that doesn't change the fact I'm your family now."

Those words spoken with such reverence literally raised goose bumps on her arms. She hadn't known that kind of unconditional love in far too long. Then again, it had been right under her nose with Riggs and she hadn't even realized the depths of it.

"I don't know what to say, Riggs. But I'll start with thank you." She could only pray their daughter was alive and well, and somewhere they could find her. "And I want very much to find her and bring her home. This child will be so loved between the two of us and your family."

"She will," he agreed. His belief was so strong that it gave Cheyenne hope. "Right now I need you to rest. This might be a long game, and you should know there is no length to which I won't go to find her and bring her home. At the very least, I will find out what happened to her if she didn't survive. Either way, we'll know. That much I promise you."

Cheyenne had no idea how she would sleep under the circumstances. He was right, though. They might be in this for the long haul. The first step of the journey was figuring out who killed Ally. That would lead them to the person who took their child. Was it Dr. Fortner? All signs pointed in his direction.

It felt almost too easy.

But then, sometimes solving a crime was as plain as the nose on a face. What had Colton said? *Follow the evidence.*

Would a wealthy traveling doctor drive a gray sedan? Surely he could afford a much more expensive vehicle? It was probably just her being naive, but she believed doctors made a whole lot more money than that. Of course, he could also use this cheaper car to mislead people.

Those thoughts needed to be tabled for now. Rest.

Riggs toed off his boots and she followed suit, kicking off her tennis shoes. He pulled back the covers and slipped out of his shirt and jeans. Ripples of muscles on his stomach provided plenty of eye candy. She'd mapped every line, every ridge. Fear she would lose him and everything good that had happened to her was a pit bull constantly nipping at her heels.

It was an exhausting way to live her life. Could she set it aside and just be in the moment? Not constantly figure out an exit plan or a way to deal with the disappointment when he realized his mistake and took off?

She made a promise to herself right then and there to get out of her head and into the present. More of the weight lifted and, for the first time, she didn't feel like the world would crumble at the snap of a finger.

Cheyenne decided to keep her clothes on but she curled her body around Riggs's the way she did when they used to sleep together. It was strange not having a huge belly in between them and also kind of nice for a change.

He wrapped his arm around her and closed his eyes.

The next thing she knew, there was movement beside her. She sat straight up, disoriented. A night-light emanated from the adjacent room.

"Hey, it's just me." Riggs's husky voice radiated calm in a storm.

"What time is it?" She rubbed blurry eyes.

"Noon," he said quietly.

"I slept five hours?" She shoved the covers off and hugged her knees into her chest. Tremors rocked her body as she slowed her breathing.

The mattress dipped underneath Riggs's weight. He moved beside her and brought her into an embrace.

"What's going on, Cheyenne? Tell me what to do to help," he said. His voice alone soothed more than he realized.

"It's okay. I'm fine." She could hear the shakiness in her own voice. "It'll pass."

He sat there holding her for more minutes than she cared to count before her body obeyed her request to calm down.

"It happens sometimes. Since…"

"Having the baby?" he finished for her.

"Yes. There are all kinds of fun things that come after…" She didn't feel the need to go into it all now. "It'll pass."

How many times had she heard the phrase? Dozens? More? *This too shall pass* were her least favorite words.

"Should we call your doctor?" he asked.

"No. It's nothing worth worrying over. My body has been through a lot of stress with the birth. That's all." She didn't want to go into the mental duress the whole ordeal had caused. And yet, part of her thought she would do it all again if things had turned out differently. "Anya."

Riggs shot her a worried look.

"We never say her name," she said.

"We need to change that," he agreed. Then came, "Anya."

Their daughter's name spoken out of his mouth was the sweetest thing Cheyenne had ever heard. He would be an amazing father whether the two of them lived under the same roof or not.

Speaking of fathers…

Hers was supposed to reach out to her. "What did I do with my phone?"

"I put it on the nightstand. Why?" he asked.

"My dad. I told him to call once he was settled," she said.

Riggs reached for the phone and she tried not to notice the flex and release of his muscles as he moved. His body was athletic grace in motion, and sinning-on-Sunday worthy.

She stopped herself from reaching out and seeking comfort. It would be temporary, at best. Damn good. But stoking the flames of the heat between them would only complicate matters even more. No need to tempt fate further. So why was it getting more and more difficult to fight what her body wanted and her mind knew better than to go for?

RIGGS HANDED OVER the cell, then sat by and watched the disappointment play out on Cheyenne's face.

"No messages and no attempts to call," she said, tossing the phone on top of the duvet.

There was nothing he could say to ease her pain. Rejection hurt like hell. He could only imagine how awful it would be coming from a parent.

"I'll never do that to my children," she said low and under her breath.

"Why don't you call him?" he asked, noting it was the first time he'd heard her mention the possibility there could be more kids since reuniting. Was she having a change of heart? Would she reconsider her position on the status of their relationship?

"You said the two of you were close once," he said.

"That's right," she confirmed.

"Have you tried to talk to him about how you're feeling?" he asked.

"Well…" She paused for a long moment. "No. Not really. I guess I figured that as the parent, he should know. I'll just text to make sure he's okay." She did. Confirmation came back a few seconds later with no additional explanation.

"I don't disagree with you, but if the relationship is important to you, I think you owe it to yourself to talk to him."

She lowered her eyes to the duvet and gave a slight nod.

"Any child would be lucky to have you as a mother, by the way," he said to her.

"Do you really think so?" She exhaled a shaky breath. "Because I'm not so sure that's true."

"Based on our talks during the pregnancy, you had a clear idea of the kind of mother you wanted to be," he said.

"You agree the most important thing for a child to receive is unconditional love. Your priorities have been clear."

"True." As confident as she was, everyone needed reassurance now and then.

"There's not a question in my mind," he said and meant it.

Cheyenne twisted the edge of the blanket in her fingers. "When I believed she was gone…it shredded me inside and out."

"Because you love her," he said. "Anya."

"Our Anya might be alive, Riggs." She brought her eyes up to meet his. Hers had an equal mix of heartbreak and hope.

"Yes," was all he could manage to say. As much as he didn't want to get either of their hopes up, after hearing Missy's statement, he had, for the first time, let himself go to the place where his daughter was really alive, and he might have the chance to hold her.

"We could get her back," she continued.

"That's the hope," he said.

"I know we can't exactly pick up where we left off and pretend the past couple of weeks didn't happen. I know that would be asking too much," she said.

"What if the news about Anya isn't what we're hoping, Cheyenne? What happens then? Do you move on with your life just like you'd planned, or do you try to come back home?" Those were fair questions that deserved answers.

She worked the hem of the duvet a little harder. "I guess I haven't thought that far ahead."

There'd been a determination in her eyes to keep him at arm's length from the get-go. Riggs couldn't stand to lose his child and Cheyenne twice. If he was going to seriously entertain the possibility of giving their relationship another shot, he needed reassurance that she wouldn't bolt if they got bad news.

"As much as I don't want to go down this road, there's a decent chance we won't get what we want, Cheyenne."

She put her hand in the air to stop him from going further, like she couldn't fathom it now that she'd dared to allow herself to believe their daughter might be alive.

"I think I know what you're going to say, and I completely understand where you're coming from." She dropped the material and clasped her hands. "My emotions get the best of me sometimes. You know?"

"It's understandable, after what we've been through."

"The truth is that I can't go through another birth if Anya's gone." Her admission caused more confusion.

"I understand not wanting to jump back on the horse in a manner of speaking, but why cut yourself off from the possibility of ever having a family because it didn't work out the first time?" He didn't even go into how hurt he was that she didn't view him as enough in a marriage.

"You want kids, right?" she asked.

"I haven't changed my plans to have a family when the time is right, if that's what you're asking." He saw the writing on the wall. Cheyenne refused to continue with plans to have a family if she lost Anya. Riggs might not like it, but at least he knew where he stood.

"I just don't see a middle ground here, Riggs."

Shame, he thought. Because he'd believed she was the one. And now? He couldn't fathom devoting his life to someone on condition.

Chapter Twenty

"We should think about something else."

Riggs wasn't wrong. And yet Cheyenne wanted to keep talking until they figured out a way to stay together. The disappointment in his tone told her just how badly she'd wounded him.

She hated it. But if she stayed married to him and refused to have children, he would resent her even more. Worse than that, he'd be denied having the family he was so ready for. The news of the pregnancy might have caught him off guard, as it had her, but he sure had risen to the occasion. Was he perfect? No. But then, neither was she.

They were both taking shots in the dark and coming up to the good more often than not. No matter what her heart wanted, she couldn't be selfish when it came to denying Riggs a child.

"I need a drink." She moved into the adjacent room and then splashed water on her face. When it came to her father, Riggs was right. She needed to have a conversation with him in private, just the two of them. She exited the bathroom after brushing her teeth. "Do you mind if I let a little sunlight in?"

"Not at all."

He grabbed a fresh outfit of jeans and a T-shirt from his dresser, and then threw them on.

Cheyenne stared outside, transfixed by the beauty of the land as he moved beside her.

"It's amazing you grew up here. Do you ever take it for granted?" she asked.

"Not me. I love this place. Of course, I'd prefer to sleep in my own bed but the view from the main house still takes my breath away." There was so much reverence in his tone.

"My mother would have loved waking up to this sky," she said, wishing her mother was alive to see it from this perspective.

"Texas is known for its incredible sunrises and sunsets." He put a hand on the small of her back and then seemed to catch himself when he pulled it back. He mumbled an apology and said something about muscle memory.

"I have decided to talk to my father." She wanted Riggs to know he was right about coming forward with her feelings. "In fact, I'm going to text him right now."

"For what it's worth, I'm proud of you." Riggs took a step back.

"What you said made a lot of sense. If he doesn't know how much I'm hurt by his actions he won't change them. If he does know and doesn't change them, I'll be able to move on," she said with conviction.

"If he's half the man I think he is, I have a feeling he'll do the right thing by you, Cheyenne."

"I hope you're right," she said on a sigh. Rejection was never fun but when it came from a parent it was devastating. She sent the text to her father asking for a meetup. The response came immediately.

When and where?

She blinked at her phone. "He wants me to pick a time and place."

"I'd feel better if he came on property for security reasons," Riggs said.

"That's probably a good idea. I'd hate for him to feel ambushed, though." She wanted her father to be as comfortable as possible during a conversation that might be anything but.

"How about if I drive you to him? That way, I can sit in the truck and keep watch. Make sure no one followed us or finds him," he said.

"When should I say? Half an hour? Forty-five minutes? I'd like to freshen up and grab coffee before we leave," she said.

"And a sandwich at the very least," he insisted.

"Deal. I'll just clean up." A shower sounded like heaven about now.

"Hand me your clothes and I'll run them through a quick wash-and-dry cycle. My mom has been bragging about her new machines that wash and dry a load in ten minutes each." His smile didn't reach his eyes.

"You have to find out if that's true. Hold on." She darted into the bathroom, undressed and then wrapped herself in a towel. Handing over her dirty clothes, including undergarments, should probably feel awkward. Except this was Riggs and he had a way of making her feel comfortable in any situation.

So she ignored the fact she had a towel wrapped around her when she cracked the door open and tossed her clothes toward him…clothes he caught on the first try.

"Thank you, Riggs." She realized she'd been saying those words often. Did he know how much she valued his help?

A quick shower revitalized her. Finding a new toothbrush and toothpaste in the top drawer made her want to pump her fists in the air from joy. She was learning to appreciate the little things—things she'd once taken for granted.

Realizing she'd taken the ladybug charm out of her handbag and tucked it inside the small key pocket in her jogging pants caused her heart to skip a few beats. It was small. Would it get lost?

Panic seized her as she searched for a robe in the attached closet. Most secondary bathrooms didn't have walk-in closets but then most homes didn't belong to an O'Connor. A hotel-sized white robe was folded up and tucked into a cubby. It was large enough to fit Riggs, so she wasn't worried about coverage. Running through the house with it on made her chest squeeze.

As she swung open the door to the bedroom, she nearly charged into Riggs's chest.

"Whoa there," he said. "Everything all right?"

"The ladybug charm…"

Before she could finish her sentence, he held his hand up, palm out. "I grew up with five brothers. My mother taught me to check pockets."

"Oh, thank heavens." She exhaled a shaky breath, trying to get her nerves under control. As it was, she seemed to go from normal to raging faster than a roller coaster could plummet down the first hill only to rise again a few seconds later. "I know I've said this a million times but I'm not sure what I would do without you, Riggs."

He stood there for a moment as the air around them grew charged. Then he turned and walked away without so much as a peep.

The move was probably for the best and yet it still stung. Besides, they needed to get on the road. As much as she dreaded having the conversation with her father, a growing piece of her wanted to get it over with.

Twenty minutes later, she'd washed and brushed everything that needed it, dressed, and then joined Riggs in the kitchen where a sandwich waited.

"My mom offered to take care of Ozzy today," he said.

"She's good with him." The little dog seemed to like Margaret O'Connor better than he liked Cheyenne. To be fair, she hadn't made much effort with him until losing Ally.

Cheyenne gobbled down the burrito and drained a cup of coffee in record time, eager to get out the door. She settled in the passenger seat as Riggs's cell buzzed.

"It's Colton," he said after checking the screen.

Riggs put the call on speaker as he navigated onto the road leading to the ranch's exit.

"Hey, Colton. What's going on?" Riggs explained that he was in his truck and that his brother was on speaker.

"Good. I want Cheyenne to hear this, too," Colton said. "I was able to track down Dr. Fortner and interview him."

"And?" Riggs and Cheyenne asked in unison.

"He started talking, expressing a suspicion he's had about one of the traveling ER docs he sometimes works alongside. Turns out they work for the same company and go wherever there's a shortage," Colton informed. "It wasn't uncommon for him."

"Ally worked in the ER," Cheyenne offered. "She would have worked with him at the very least. Did Dr. Fortner give a name?"

"Kyle Douglas," Colton supplied. "Sound familiar?"

Cheyenne smacked the armrest. "It sure does. He's the one who tried to hit on Ally a couple of times. I remember she thought he was cute, but something warned her against getting too close to him."

"Well, I learned another interesting fact about him. He drives a gray two-door sedan while traveling for work. He leaves his sports car at home in favor of something more practical, according to Dr. Fortner," Colton said. "I asked for a description and he matches both the one Missy provided and the one given by the clerk from the grocery store. He's our guy."

"What about the other nurses who came forward at other hospitals?" Riggs asked.

"Gert is on it but has confirmed the crossover in at least two instances," Colton said. "The hitch is that he wasn't working in the hospital the night Cheyenne gave birth."

"I'm betting Becca or Sherry was," Cheyenne said, remembering the two nurses she'd chatted with when she was trying to find Ally.

"That's right. I have a deputy on the way to pick Becca up for questioning at my office," Colton supplied. "I have no doubt in my mind about her involvement. In fact, I'm working the angle with the other hospitals, too. My best guess is that he has a network of nurses he cuts in on the deals."

"But Dr. Fortner was my attending," Cheyenne said. "How do you explain the amount of medication I was given? Or the fact I remember seeing him?"

"He was called away moments before the delivery and then told the baby didn't make it," Colton supplied.

"That's not how I remember it." Cheyenne blew out a frustrated breath.

"Given the amount of medication you were on, that isn't surprising. Dr. Fortner is calling for a review of the case. By the time he got back to your room the nurse said the baby had already been born. He said he had no reason to doubt her word," Colton added.

"Any idea where Douglas is now?" Riggs asked.

"None. The service he works for has been reaching out to him and he hasn't returned any calls yet." Colton white-knuckled the steering wheel as they thanked Colton before ending the call.

Disbelief and a sense of being violated caused anger to rip through Cheyenne. How could anyone do this to another human being?

RIGGS PULLED INTO the RV park, his mind spinning.

"We have a name," Cheyenne said. "And all the confirmation I need to know our daughter lived."

He didn't remind her of the fact one of the babies had died. The newborn very well could have been Anya. There was no way he could dash the hope and resolve in Cheyenne's voice.

"Which one belongs to your father?" There were half a dozen RVs sprinkled throughout the park.

She pointed to a white and orange number that looked straight out of the seventies. Riggs made a loop and pulled up alongside the vehicle. He could watch the entrance from this vantage point.

Cheyenne grabbed the door handle. "Are you coming with me?"

"I thought I'd stay out here to keep an eye out," he admitted.

She chewed on the inside of her cheek. "I'm not sure I can do this without you."

The RV door opened and a man who looked to be in his late fifties stepped out. He wasn't tall by Texas standards, coming in around five feet ten inches if Riggs had to guess. A tiny woman who, oddly, resembled Cheyenne's mother stepped out with him. She waved. Cheyenne's father had made an excuse about why he had to miss the wedding, so this was the first time Riggs was able to look his father-in-law in the eye.

Riggs thought about the irony of a man not wanting his

own daughter around because she looked too much like her mother but then marrying someone who did. Maybe Cheyenne's assessment was misguided.

"Hello, Dad." Cheyenne got out of the truck, but she didn't make a move to hug her father and vice versa. Instead, she leaned against the truck and folded her arms.

Riggs joined her so he could keep an eye on things.

"Cheyenne," was all her dad said in response.

Riggs walked up to his father-in-law and extended a hand. When her father took the offering, Riggs realized the man's palms were sweaty. He shot a look of fear and regret at Riggs.

"Good to meet you, sir," Riggs said.

"Same to you," her father said.

"Hi, Virginia." Cheyenne introduced Riggs to her stepmother.

"Ma'am," he said after a hearty handshake.

"I'll leave you alone. I just wanted to come out and say hello," Virginia said.

Riggs started toward the driver's side of the truck and was stopped by Cheyenne's hand. So he moved closer to her and noticed the tight grip she had on his fingers.

"Dad, I need to get something off my chest," Cheyenne started after sucking a breath.

"Oh," her father said.

"I still need you in my life and you're gone all the time. Most of the time, I can't reach you and when I do leave a message you don't get back to me for weeks. I've been married more than half a year, and this is the first time you're meeting my husband. I just have one question... why?" She'd clearly done her best to stay calm, but her words rushed out anyway.

"Because I can't stand seeing the disappointment in your eyes and not knowing what to say or do to make it better—just like when your mother died. I felt like I failed you by letting her die and I'm failing now." He threw his hands up in the air. "Renting the RV was supposed to help me heal from losing the love of my life, but I've learned one thing. I can't outrun the pain."

"Then, stick around and deal with it. Be here for me and I'll do the same for you." Her voice hitched on the last few words.

Her father stood there for a long moment before making eye contact with her.

"Is there any chance you can forgive a foolish old man?" he asked. "Because I feel like I lost the two great loves of my life when she died. Her and you."

Cheyenne released her grip on Riggs's hand before charging toward her father and wrapping him in a hug.

"It's never too late for forgiveness, Daddy."

Riggs wondered if the same could be true for their relationship.

Chapter Twenty-One

"Can you stick around?" Cheyenne's father asked when she finally released him. The torment in his eyes when she'd first seen him had softened. It was crazy how much they were able to clear up in one short conversation. Being face-to-face helped. It was so good to see her father's face again.

"We have to take care of something first. But I promise to spend as much time together as you can stand once we clear something up," she said. Her answer seemed to satisfy her father.

"I'd like to invite you and your wife to camp on the ranch. There's plenty of room and you'd be closer to your daughter," Riggs offered. It was a sly move because he would want her father in a secure location. She also believed Riggs was being honest about the two of them being closer. "I can call ahead and get you set up through security."

Her father's gaze bounced from Riggs to her and back.

"What do you think, honey?" he asked.

"I'd like it very much, Daddy."

Now it was her father's turn to beam. "Then, that's what we'll do."

Cheyenne sighed with relief.

"I'll get your father set up with directions if you'd like to say goodbye for now to Ms. Virginia," Riggs said.

Right again.

Cheyenne disappeared into the RV after first knocking. Riggs was a whole lot better at navigating family. Of course, with five siblings, he had more experience.

"I'm really happy to see you, Virginia," Cheyenne said.

"Well, it's good to be here." Virginia smiled through her surprise at the gesture.

Yeah, Cheyenne needed to get better about acknowledging her stepmother. Virginia made her father happy. Their relationship was different but that didn't mean it wasn't special. Cheyenne could see that now.

"I just wanted to let you know how happy you make my dad," Cheyenne said. She imagined her father would be so much worse off without his new wife.

"Do you think so?" Virginia asked and it was the first sign of insecurity Cheyenne had seen.

"Yes. I really do," she reassured her before adding, "My husband asked if you guys would like to camp at the ranch. The land is unbelievable, and I think you both would love it very much. I'd like it if you came."

Virginia smiled. "I'd like that, too."

Cheyenne said her goodbye as she exited the RV. Seeing her father and her husband standing there talking made her realize how much she wanted to be with Riggs. Could he accept her for who she was?

"We were just finishing up," Riggs said to her.

"Virginia and I will be on our way as soon as I run the idea past her," her father said.

"I just did. She was happy about it," Cheyenne assured him. "And so am I."

"We'll head out, then, since your husband has made all the arrangements," her father said.

"See you later." Cheyenne gave her father one last hug before claiming her seat on the passenger side.

Riggs got behind the wheel and put the gearshift into Drive.

"You didn't correct my father about being my husband," Cheyenne said to Riggs. "Was that on purpose or were you just being polite?"

"I am your husband, Cheyenne. You're the only one who can change that."

"And what if this doesn't turn out the way we'd hoped with Anya? Can you live with me not wanting to have children?" she asked.

"I married you and I meant it." He barely got the words out when he slammed on the brakes. "Hold on a second."

The entrance to the RV park was barricaded.

"Stay low," Riggs warned as he slid down in his seat.

She realized he was searching for a possible shooter as he grabbed his cell and slid it onto the bench seat toward her.

"I have a group text with my brothers. Send out an SOS and let them know where we are," he said.

"My dad," she said, firing off the text.

Riggs put the vehicle in reverse and flew backward, kicking up one serious dust storm. "Text your father and tell him to get inside the RV, lock the door and stay put until you call him."

Cheyenne did that next. Riggs's phone started dinging left and right with promises of help. Her father agreed to do as she asked. And yet her pulse still skyrocketed as panic squeezed her chest.

"Do you have anything we can use as a weapon in here?" she asked.

"Not sure," Riggs responded. "There has to be something around, though."

She unbuckled her seat belt and then hopped in back. Keeping low, she rummaged around. There were tools that might come in handy. Nothing like bringing a wrench into a gunfight. *Possible* gunfight, she reminded.

"I found these." She grabbed everything hard and metal that she could find, returning to the front with a fistful of options.

Riggs came to a roaring stop in front of her father's RV. The dust cloud made visibility next to impossible.

Cheyenne's cell rang, causing her heart to drop. She checked the screen. Her father.

"Hello, Dad. Is everything okay?"

"Someone's here. He wants to talk to you and said you should come inside." There was a mix of shock and fear in her father's voice that drilled a hole in her chest.

"I'm coming. Stay put and don't do anything to make him angry. Okay, Dad?"

Before her father could answer, there was a rustling noise on the line before it went dead.

As Cheyenne reached for the door handle, Riggs touched her shoulder. She brought her hand on top of his, needing the comfort of his touch.

"I'm not letting you waltz into a trap," he said quietly. "I can't lose you, too."

His phone was blowing up, but he didn't budge.

"I don't know what else to do, Riggs. It's my dad in there," she said before issuing a sharp breath.

He nodded. "Give me a few second to think up a plan. Okay?"

"I don't know how much time I have. If I don't head out of here in a second, he might get trigger-happy," she said.

"He was nervous before. His hand shook. He's not used to this. I think we have time," Riggs said.

"Yeah, but are you willing to bet my dad's life on it?"

A SHOT FIRED.

On instinct, Riggs ducked. And then he snapped into action. He jumped out of his truck as Cheyenne bolted out the passenger side. Sirens pierced the air; the cavalry was on its way.

Was it too late?

Without hesitation, Riggs opened the door to the RV. Inside, Virginia was on her knees with her hands clasped behind her head. Hoodie stood behind Cheyenne's father with the barrel of his gun pointed at his temple.

There was no sign of blood and that was the first bit of good news.

Cheyenne's father had his eyes closed and he looked to be whispering a prayer. There was a look of resolve on his face, like he was ready to join his first wife.

Not today, if Riggs had anything to say about it.

"Stop," Cheyenne said from behind him.

"You've gone too far. You keep poking around where you don't belong." Hoodie's voice had a hysterical note to it.

"You took an oath to save lives, Douglas," Riggs aid.

"How did…" The hood came off. The doctor would be considered attractive by most standards. He was a couple of inches taller than Cheyenne's father. He had sandy-blond hair and tanned skin, with a runner's build.

"Authorities know who you are, Kyle," Riggs continued. "Don't make this any worse than it already is."

The doctor's eyes were wild.

"Worse? It's a little late for that." He squeezed the trigger.

By some miracle, the bullet misfired. Riggs took advantage of the situation by diving headfirst toward Kyle. Riggs managed to shove Cheyenne's father out of the way a second before crashing into the doctor.

The gun went off in a wild shot again as Riggs struggled for control. He wrapped his arms around Kyle and body-slammed him onto the floor of the RV. The tile shook like there'd been an earthquake. Kyle tried to wiggle out of Riggs's grasp.

No dice.

Riggs clamped his arms around the guy like a vise. "You're not going anywhere but jail, where you belong."

"You'll never get her back," Kyle said through gritted teeth. He tried to point the barrel of his weapon at Riggs.

"The hell I won't," Riggs said. "My family won't rest until she's home where she belongs and you're rotting in a cell for kidnapping my daughter and killing Ally."

Cheyenne's father snatched the gun out of Kyle's hand unexpectedly. The older man took a couple of steps back before pointing the barrel at Kyle's head.

"Keep moving and I'll shoot," he warned and the tone in his voice said he meant every word.

In the next minute, the RV was flooded with O'Connors. Colton zip-cuffed Kyle and tossed him in the back seat of his service vehicle. Cash stood next to Cheyenne while she hugged her father and comforted Virginia. The afternoon had been traumatic for both of them.

Riggs walked over to his brother Colton, who stood next to Dawson.

"Why?" Riggs asked. "What would make a successful, well-paid doctor sell babies?"

"A gambling addiction for one," Colton said. "Once we got a name, we did some digging. He's in over his head in debt with men who don't take kindly to folks who can't clear their debt. And Becca was in on the take."

"Sonofabitch is willing to destroy people's lives to feed his own addiction." It had taken all of Riggs's restraint not to knock the guy out. He wanted him to be awake and aware of where he was going...jail.

"That's not all we found, Riggs. Caroline is alive and lives in Houston," Colton said.

"What? When? How?"

"Garrett hasn't stopped investigating and neither has Cash. I've been on it, too. We didn't want to say anything until we were one hundred percent certain. The trail came out of the alpaca farm. Turns out Dad was on the right trail," Colton said. "Arrests at the farm are being made as we speak."

"That's great news." Riggs was almost speechless. He thought about another mother and child who needed help. Loriann and her son would be well cared for. Riggs would put the wheels in motion with the family attorney when he headed back to the ranch.

A dirt cloud broke behind a vehicle that was moving toward them, catching their attention before Colton could answer.

Instead, he put a hand on Riggs's shoulder and said, "Go get your wife. We found something that belongs to you."

Riggs's pulse skyrocketed. He stared at his brother for a long moment before Colton urged him to get moving. He did, taking Cheyenne by the hand and bringing her to where Colton stood.

The vehicle Riggs recognized as Gert's came to a stop. His brother's assistant came out of the driver's seat. Instead of moving toward them, she went straight to the back and opened the door.

Riggs caught his brother's eye. Colton nodded. So Riggs turned to his wife.

"I love you, Cheyenne. I always will," he began, turning her away from the vehicle so she faced him.

Tears streamed down her cheeks as she looked at him

the same way she had on their wedding night...with love in her eyes.

"I wouldn't care if you couldn't have children. I married *you*. Plus, there are other ways to have a family," he said before locking gazes. "I want you to come home. I want to do better by you. I want to learn to talk to you when I think something's wrong. What do you think? Is that what you want?"

He didn't finish his sentence before she wrapped her arms around his neck and kissed him.

"Yes, Riggs. I love you more than I could express in a thousand lifetimes. But I'll take this one if you'll give it to me," she said. "I don't want to hang on to the rope any longer. I want to let go and fall into your arms."

"I love you with all that I am, Cheyenne," he said. "And there's one more thing you need to know."

Confusion knitted her eyebrows together.

"My brothers found *her*," was all he said. All he had to say before recognition dawned on her. "What do you say we go meet our daughter?"

More of those tears streamed now as Cheyenne nodded.

"Yes," she said, repeating the word a few more times as he turned her around.

There Gert stood, next to her car. A pink bundle in her arms. A smile plastered on her face.

Home. Their daughter was finally home. Cheyenne practically ran to Anya. Gert immediately handed over their child. Riggs followed and his heart swelled the minute Cheyenne turned around and beamed at him. He couldn't be happier to have Cheyenne and Anya together with him where they belonged.

"Meet our daughter," she said with the sweetest smile on her face.

The baby wasn't the only one who was finally home.

Chapter Twenty-Two

Margaret O'Connor sat in her library on the velvet couch. This was the place Riggs could normally find her—the place she loved most in the house. She'd said countless times how at home she felt among her books. Now that the house was filled with new life and new faces, she didn't spend as much time in the room as she used to. He saw that as progress, considering the innumerable hours she'd stayed here after her husband's murder.

He glanced at the long line of his brothers waiting behind him in the hallway, Cash, Colton, Dawson, Blake, and Garrett. They all seemed ready. He knocked lightly on the door, not wanting to surprise her or catch her off guard. Not in her sanctuary.

"Come in," her voice was less frail than it had been in the days after losing her husband. Finn O'Connor had left big shoes to fill on the ranch. Each of his sons, including Riggs, was now ready to take their rightful place on the ranch, working side by side as their father had intended when he'd built a successful cattle ranch all those years ago.

There was something very right about all of his brothers being home. Even Garrett was making the transition home with his new fiancée in a moment Riggs wasn't sure he'd ever see. His brother had always gone rogue. He'd always needed to buck convention and do his own thing. Of course, it didn't help matters that Garrett and Cash had been gas on fire for as long as Riggs could remember. Then there was Garrett's relationship with Colton, more fuel to the blaze.

"I have company." Riggs stepped inside the library, and then each of his brothers stepped inside the room. They made a half circle behind a very confused Margaret O'Connor.

No one wanted to miss this moment—a moment that had been thirty years in the making. Each of his brothers took a spot, hands folded in front of them like they were in church. This moment deserved that kind of reverence, Riggs thought, as emotion knotted in his throat. He figured his brothers were struggling just about as much as him, considering how many pairs of eyes were cast to the floor.

Finn O'Connor had died without ever knowing what happened to his daughter. Their mother would not suffer the same fate. In fact, she was about to see for herself.

"What's happening?" His very concerned mother looked around the room, a moment of panic darkening her eyes. "Is everyone okay?"

"We're fine. Never been better." Cash stepped forward. As the oldest son, he normally spoke on behalf of the family. He glanced at each of his brothers, waiting for the okay to continue. When he seemed satisfied that he got what he was looking for, he continued, "You already know Dad was trying to find Caroline when…" Cash's voice caught on the last word and he ducked his chin to his chest, no doubt to cover the emotion threatening to pull them all under. He cleared his throat and then continued, "I think we're all clear on what happened to Dad as a result of him renewing the search for our sister."

A moment of silence, of respect, passed before Cash

continued, "But his efforts to find Caroline weren't in vain and we understand why he chose to pick up the search when he did. The diagnosis meant he wouldn't be around forever. Granted, he should have had more time. We wanted more time with him. But we understand why he picked the timing he did to resume the search for her. And we've all learned more than a few important lessons because of his example. No one is guaranteed time on this earth. Every day is a gift that deserves to be embraced."

"Did you? Find out what happened to Caroline?" Mother asked, her back ramrod straight now.

Cash nodded.

"And?" their mother asked.

"We think you'll be pleased with what we learned." Cash moved to the doorway and waved in their guests as their mother sat perfectly still. A pin drop could be heard from miles around for how quiet everyone had become. "And we believe you should see it for yourself."

A very pregnant Caroline stepped into view. She stopped at the threshold and her mouth nearly dropped to the floor when her gaze locked onto their mother—the mother she never knew despite being a mirror image. It was one of the many things Riggs had first noticed when he'd met his sister for the first time. It was striking just how much she took after their mother.

Mother seemed to pick her jaw up off the floor. She blinked a couple of times like she couldn't trust her eyes. And then the tears slid down her cheeks as she pushed to standing, each of her sons at the ready in case she needed a hand up. She didn't.

"Caroline?" she asked but it was more statement than question.

Caroline nodded even though she didn't call herself by

that name anymore. She'd gone by the name Andrea for as long as she could remember. "I go by Andrea now."

Arms out, Mother practically bolted around the coffee table before bringing her only girl into a hug. There wasn't a dry eye in the room as their mother stroked her daughter's hair.

"It's been so long," Mother said quietly. "I was beginning to think I'd never see you again. That I'd never know what happened to my baby girl."

Andrea was crying now, too. Sniffles filled the air. No tears of sadness. Just sweet release and then joy.

Mother pulled back and then took Andrea by the hand. "Can you come sit?"

"I'd like that actually." Andrea wiped away her own tears with her free hand.

"Would one of you boys be kind enough to make us some tea?" Mother looked at Andrea before smiling at her pregnant belly. "Or whatever you and the baby would like to drink."

"Tea is good. Decaf if you have any." She practically beamed.

"I've got it," Cash said. He was standing closest to the door. Colton volunteered to help and the two disappeared a second later.

"What? How? I…" Mother covered her laugh. "I don't even know where to start."

Andrea held their mother's hand. "I can go back as far as I remember. But I'm afraid I don't remember this or anyone from here."

"Of course, you don't." If Mother was disappointed, she didn't show it. "You were a baby when you…" She seemed like she couldn't bear to say the words.

"I had a good childhood," Andrea said as though she realized that would be important to any mother. In fact, she rubbed her belly with her free hand and Riggs wondered if the move was subconscious on her part. "I'm sure it was nothing like this. I grew up in Santa Fe and we never moved. I had two parents who are still married. We grew apart when I went off to college in Houston. I'd always been drawn to Texas and now I know why they always looked at each other strangely when I brought it up. I always wanted to come here for vacation, but they refused." She shrugged. "I never understood why and, like all teenagers, became rebellious at a certain point."

Andrea paused for a minute and took in the room, the faces.

"I grew up an only child, but it never felt right to me. You know?" she asked with a hopeful look in her eyes.

No one in the room might understand, but every head nodded. Because being an O'Connor was in the blood. Ranching was in the blood. And each brother seemed to agree something would feel off if they'd been plucked out of this life.

"Going to Houston changed everything for me. It was a perfect fit, but it was the closest I'd ever been to feeling like I belonged somewhere," she continued.

Mother's smile was a mile wide as she hung on every word. She turned serious when she said, "A woman by the name of Ms. Hubert moved into the area about a year before you were taken from your crib."

Andrea sat there looking stunned. "It's going to take a minute for all this to set in. It must've been horrific for you."

Mother nodded as Andrea rubbed her belly again, and a look of horror overtook her face.

"How far along are you?" Mother asked, as though she realized Andrea needed a distraction from the gravity of the situation.

"Seven months." She sniffed away a few tears that seemed to be building. "Sorry. I'm just so emotional these days."

"It's understandable," Mother said without missing a beat. A kind of peace had come over her. She settled back into her seat, and her face glowed. "You don't ever have to apologize for feeling overwhelmed. This has to be a lot for you. I'm sorry we didn't find you sooner."

"Like I said, my childhood was good. I had a lot of friends. I did well enough in school to get a scholarship for college, which was good because my parents said that if I went to Texas, I'd have to figure out a way to pay for it myself." She exhaled and her shoulders slumped forward. "I think they were just scared I'd run into one of you guys and they'd be caught red-handed."

"It sounds like they loved you very much," Mother said.

Andrea nodded. "They weren't perfect by any means, but I never doubted they loved me. Not for one day. My mother became overprotective and it felt like I was being smothered. I think that's why I wouldn't consider any of the schools in New Mexico or Arizona. Too close to home."

"Do you still have communication with them?" Mother asked.

"Not really. Not since I refused to come home," she admitted.

Garrett stepped forward. "According to the investigation, her parents had no idea of the circumstances. They were high-risk for adoption because of their age and the fact Mr. Landis had a record. He spent time in a federal prison for a white-collar crime in the accounting firm where he worked. Apparently, he and one of his coworkers decided to skim money from the company accounts by padding expense reports that came in from the sales teams. The two of them got caught and he served five years."

"So they knew they were doing something illegal when they adopted me?" Andrea asked.

"They knew the adoption was shady but there's no evidence to suggest they knew you'd been kidnapped," Garrett said.

"Oh." Andrea sounded defeated. "You think you know people for your entire life and then, bam, you get hit with something like this out of the blue."

"The important thing is that they loved and cared for you, Ca—"

Mother caught herself. She couldn't finish and it seemed like she couldn't bring herself to call her daughter by another name.

"I guess," Andrea said before catching their mother's gaze. "But I can't imagine what you must have gone through as a mother. I mean, I haven't even met this little angel yet and I already wake up in a cold sweat at the thought anything could happen to her."

Mother sucked in a burst of air.

"A girl?" she asked.

"Yes." Andrea beamed.

Love was written all over Mother's features. "We have another little girl in the family now. Anya. She'll be a great older cousin. And now we have Missy." Mother's gaze shifted to Garrett. He smiled and nodded. He and his fiancée, Brianna, were a newly minted foster family. Missy had been separated from her parents at the age of four and brought into a kidnapping ring. She'd been returned when she couldn't "adjust" to the new family. When Missy was taken from her family, she'd been told her parents had gone to heaven. If that happened to be true, and no one believed it was, then she would live her life with Garrett and Brianna. But Garrett wouldn't rest until he had answers, because he knew firsthand how important it was for a child to be reunited with his or her parents if at all possible.

"But I'm getting ahead of myself, aren't I?" Mother asked. She straightened her back and continued, "You're a grown adult now. I have no idea if we fit into your life and I wouldn't judge you for a minute if you decided to go back to Houston and forget you ever knew us. You can't know what it means to me for you to be here, right now. And as much as I'd love for you to stay, you have a life that we're not part of in Houston."

Andrea waved her hand in the air like she was stopping traffic. "Right before I found out about the baby, that I was pregnant with her, my husband was killed in the line of duty. He'd been working deep nights and made what was supposed to be a routine traffic stop when it all went south. To make a long, sad story short, he was shot at point-blank range. I've honestly been wandering around ever since, not really certain what my next move was going to be. I used to work at the arboretum. I was always drawn to the outside, even when I was a kid." She smiled, but it didn't reach her eyes. "I guess now I know why."

"Why don't you move in here for the rest of your pregnancy?" Mother asked, her voice brimming with hope. "You'd have plenty of people to look after you until you gave birth and Houston isn't so far away."

"Are you sure about that?" Andrea studied their mother. "Because I'm tempted to take you up on the offer, but I really don't want to put you out or anything."

"I've never been more certain of anything in my life." Their mother was steadfast. Little did Andrea know their mother had been planning, hoping for this day since her daughter was taken from her crib where she peacefully slept. "In fact…"

Mother held her index finger in the air, indicating she'd

be right back. Her face lit up like Christmas morning and the skip in her step didn't go unnoticed.

Andrea looked up at each of Riggs's brothers as Cash and Colton entered the room.

"What did we miss?" Cash handed a steaming cup of tea to Andrea while Colton placed the other one on the coffee table for their mother.

"Mom took off to get a gift for Andrea." Riggs winked at his brothers as Andrea stared at them. The wrinkle in her forehead said she was clearly confused by what was going on.

"While your...*our*...mother is out of the room, I'd like to ask you six if you think it's a good idea for me...*us*...to stay here until she's born." She caressed the bump.

Cash made eye contact with each brother, including Riggs. Each gave a slight nod.

"I think I can speak for everyone when I say welcome to the family," Cash said. "You won't find a better bunch of people and we always have each other's back."

A tear slid down Andrea's face. She quickly wiped it away. Chin up, she smiled. "I'm looking forward to getting to know each and every one of you."

"We're a good bunch, but I wouldn't get too excited about getting to know each one of us personally. At least, not a few of us." Riggs elbowed Garrett.

"You definitely don't want to get to know this guy any better. Arm's length is good," Garrett shot back, jabbing Riggs in the side.

They both burst out laughing and the room followed suit, breaking some of the tension. Andrea laughed, too, and it was one of the best sounds. Their sister was home. Riggs let that thought sink in, which he couldn't do without thinking what a shame it was for their father to have missed this moment. If it wasn't for his investigative work, she might still be lost to them. The work had come at a heavy price and Riggs would miss his father for the rest of his days. Seeing the look on Mother's face...

It was exactly what his father would have wanted.

Mother bebopped into the room, her right hand fisted. She perched on the edge of the sofa next to Andrea. "I've been waiting a long time to give you this."

She opened her hand to reveal a key.

"You have your own house here on the property, Ca—" Mother's cheeks flamed. "Calling you Andrea is going to take some getting used to." She sat up a little taller. "But, you know, maybe it's time to move on and accept that Caroline is gone. Andrea is her own person and you're right here. And you're just as much part of this family as any one of us."

Andrea took the offering, the wrinkle on her forehead deepening. "I'm afraid I don't understand."

"Mother had a home built and decorated for each one of us. We get the key when we turn eighteen," Riggs explained.

"And do all of you live here on the property at your homes?" she asked.

"For the most part, yes," Garrett interjected. "Some of us are just now moving back home. A couple of us have always lived here. Point being, we've all made the decision to come home and take our rightful places running the family business. If you love the outdoors as much as you say, there's no better place to work and live than KBR and we'd love to have you here."

More of those tears streamed down their sister's face.

"I'd like that very much," she said.

"Welcome home, Andrea." Mother wrapped her daughter in an embrace. The brothers stood shoulder to shoulder, forming a circle around the pair of them. Each placed a hand on either their mother or Andrea's arms. There were wide smiles and overflowing hearts all around.

"It's good to finally be in a place where I feel like I belong," Andrea said.

And she did. KBR was home.

* * * * *

MOUNTAINSIDE MURDER

NICOLE HELM

To the kid who lives behind me who is always, always dribbling his basketball, for reminding me what it means to have dedication to something you love even if the thud, thud, thud while I'm trying to write drives me to distraction.

Keep thudding, buddy.

Chapter One

Sabrina Killian was *finally* free. The cast she'd been in for six weeks was off, and though she'd been ordered to take it easy, she had no plans to do so.

Not when there was *finally* an assignment to be accomplished.

Sabrina walked through the sprawling house that acted as North Star Group's headquarters. She knew Shay, the head of the group, and Elsie, lead on IT, had been working overtime to trace the dangerous weapons involved in their last successful mission. She expected this meeting to mean they'd made some progress.

She met Holden in the hallway to the conference room.

"You know it'll be me next. Shay's not sending you out on a mission when you're still banged up," Holden said, obnoxiously as always. It didn't matter that Holden was the reason she was here, and that she owed him...possibly her life, and surely her soul. She still liked to bicker with him.

After all, it was a bar fight that had led him to invite her to join North Star, instead of letting her wallow her failed life away on bar fights and bad elements. She'd helped bring down the gang she'd been considering joining up with. Because of Holden Parker.

She still gave him crap about his unwillingness to hit a girl, even when she could take it.

And boy, could Sabrina take it. She'd been *this* close to being one of the first female navy SEALs when a freak injury had ended her military career.

It might have ended her life if she hadn't happened to find fault with Holden Parker in a seedy bar in the middle of South Dakota. These days, she loved him like the big brother she'd never had, and she would never, ever admit that to him.

"We'll see," she muttered with a scowl.

"Hey, remember when I saved your butt a few weeks ago?" He slung his arm around her shoulder companionably.

She shrugged off the arm before giving him a fake saccharine sweet smile. "Hey, remember when I kicked your butt a few years ago? Besides, if you'd given me a little more time, I could have taken those guys on my own. Fractured arm and all." And she would have if Holden hadn't swept in trying to be a superhero.

She'd been ambushed by three brainless goons, and she'd been *this* close to taking all three of them when one had tripped her and she'd fallen wrong on her arm. It had incapacitated her, *briefly,* but she would have kicked their butts one-handed anyway. She knew it. Instead, Holden had taken care of it.

It still grated.

"Must be losing your touch. Want to try me now?" Holden offered, spreading his arms as if to offer her a free punch.

She tossed her long, dark ponytail over her shoulder. "When you've hung up your warped moral code about hitting women who were *this* close to being navy SEALs, I'll fight you."

Before he could respond to that, someone cleared their throat.

"Children," Shay said blandly, standing in the entrance

of the conference room, arms crossed. "If you'd enter so we could get this started?"

Sabrina sent Holden a haughty look, then sailed into the room in front of him. She took her usual chair and waited for Shay to come around to the front of the room. It was only her and Holden as field operatives in the meeting. Elsie sat at her computer in the corner tapping away.

It was weird without Reece. For two years now, it had been the three of them as the leads on all major missions. Shay always brought all three of them in to consult before she decided who to send.

Now, it was just Sabrina and Holden. Shay was going to have to promote one of the younger field operatives to take Reece's supervisory position so there was a trio again. But she hadn't yet.

Sabrina couldn't really blame her. There were some good options, but no one who'd been around nearly as long as Holden and her. Or Shay herself, who'd dedicated her life to North Star longer than any of them.

Sabrina *really* hoped she got this assignment. She was edgy and tired of being cooped up rehabilitating and thinking about all the changes North Star had been going through. She was a woman who needed to move, needed to act. Being injured and sitting around *thinking* suited her not at all.

"What we have in the wake of the whole situation from a few weeks ago is two highly dangerous weapons, in the hands of two highly dangerous individuals."

"So, let's go," Holden said.

"As if anything is that simple. From what our friends at the FBI can figure, we've just tangled with a highly specialized, complicated death machine."

"I thought it was a weapons dealer," Sabrina said with a frown. They'd taken down a group selling black mar-

ket weapons to the wrong kind of people six weeks ago.
She tested her arm. It felt weak, and she was still pissed a
group of muscle-bound thugs had gotten the better of her,
even if she would have been able to get herself out of that
mess eventually.

It wouldn't happen again.

"Turns out, the weapons being supplied were only a
small, tiny cog of a much bigger machine. Which means
they'll just replace their weapons dealer. The FBI is putting a team on finding out more about this machine, but
our job is much more urgent. While the FBI is trying to
smoke out the head of the big group, we've got to stop two
different hit men. Before we fully took down the weapons dealer group, they shipped off two untraceable, highly
powered guns—and distributed them to two ghosts. And
I do mean ghosts."

"Sounds like a challenge," Holden said, kicking back
in his chair and balancing it on two legs. Like Sabrina,
Holden was always ready for a challenge.

"Two hit men. Two guns that can make a joke out of
Kevlar. We don't know who the hit men are. We don't
know who the targets are. We don't even know how much
time we have before they act. We know nothing. Except
the guns themselves. The first lead we've gotten, thanks
to Elsie's tireless work, is the delivery of ammunition for
our weapon to two different PO boxes. Each equally untraceable as the owners don't exist and security footage
gives next to nothing away."

"So there's video of the ammunition being picked up?"
Sabrina asked.

"Elsie's hacked what she can, and I'll show you that in
a moment. Either way, you're going to split up and scout
each address out. Our first target is Wilson, Wyoming.
This is the only video we have of our suspect retrieving
the package from the PO box."

A grainy security feed showed up on the big screen in front of them. A man dressed head to toe for the winter weather walked over to one of the boxes. He kept his head completely turned away from the camera, and he was wearing too many clothes to make any sort of defining characteristic out.

"A bit overdressed, isn't he?" Holden murmured.

"It's still cold enough at the upper elevations, but you're right. Seems odd. Especially since we know what's in the package. And what makes it more shady…" Shay nodded to Elsie and another grainy video clicked on thanks to her manning the computers in the corner.

This video was similarly set up to the first, but definitely a different post office. "Evening, Nebraska."

Another person, dressed a bit heavy for May, came in in much the same way the man from the earlier video had.

"That gives us two targets. I want you both on it. You can take a team if you want, but the first stages might be best done alone until you actually find the target. Though I'd want a team close by for backup. And a full team completely in place before you take action."

"Define full team," Holden replied with a wide grin.

"We've got two people, at least, about to be killed, for reasons unknown to us. That might only be the tip of the iceberg based on what I'm getting from the Feds. Either way, we have very little to go on. It's important. But it's not more important than your own lives."

"Don't you think that depends?" Sabrina asked, without fully thinking the words through.

Shay fixed her with a hard look. "This is a dangerous mission. You're risking your life by taking it on, but that doesn't mean you have to play hero."

"How would we live with ourselves if we didn't?" Holden asked, with none of his usual humor or joking.

Shay blinked, and Sabrina knew that something about

Reece getting seriously shot last month, then leaving North Star to go live his happily-ever-after, had left Shay...altered. Sabrina would never call her boss *timid*, but there was something about her that seemed to think they were all more fragile.

Sabrina refused to be or feel fragile. She turned to Holden, bypassing Shay all together. "You take Nebraska," they told each other simultaneously.

"Not a snowball's chance in flat prairie hell," Holden replied.

She dug a penny out of her pocket. "Flip for it?"

"Who carries change around?"

"I found it yesterday." *Find a penny, pick it up, and all day long you'll have good luck.* Silly saying, but she hadn't been able to ignore the fact she needed some luck. "Thought it'd be good luck. Come on. Call it in the air. You win, you choose where you want to go."

Holden shrugged and grinned. "Sure. You should know luck always falls down on my side."

She flipped the coin, and Holden called heads. When it landed tails, she feigned humble surprise. "Oh, dear. It looks like I get to pick, doesn't it?"

"All right. Sabrina, you're headed to the Tetons," Shay said, clearly trying to head off any arguing. "Holden, that means Nebraska for you."

The look on Holden's face was darn near comical. Confusion dawning into horror and denial.

Sabrina reached over and slapped him on the back. "Don't worry. I'll send you pictures of the mountains."

SHE DID IN fact text Holden pictures. Repeatedly. It brought her great joy as she canvassed the area where the ammunition had been shipped. She posed as a police officer and questioned the post office employees. She got a few leads, and the current one had her taking a good ten-mile hike up the side of a mountain.

She didn't mind. Better here than sitting in a car at a dead end on Main Street, USA. She chuckled to herself, took a gorgeous picture of the sun rising over the mountains, purposefully cropping out the clouds that were quickly moving in. She sent it to Holden and added a *wish you were here. Oh, wait. No, I don't.*

She'd gone another mile or so when she got the text back.

I got a lead. $10 says I get my guy first.

We'll talk when you're confident enough to raise it to 50.

Which she wasn't. The plan had been to interview any hikers she found along the way to see if they'd seen the man she *thought* might be the suspect who'd gotten the ammunition from the PO box.

But the trail was mostly empty. Odd for spring, she thought. Then again she hadn't checked the weather forecast today as she had no plans of delaying following this guy. Maybe there was snow coming. She looked at the clouds quickly covering what little sunlight she had.

Maybe she'd get caught in a thunderstorm. She'd prefer the snow, but she'd deal with either. Weather wasn't going to stop her when she finally had a lead.

So, she hiked, and felt mildly comforted by the fact Holden hadn't texted back. Whatever his lead was, he was no more confident in it than she was in hers.

She was about halfway up the trail when she finally saw some people. A trio gathered around the edge of the cliff the trail currently skirted. Sabrina wondered if they saw wildlife or a pretty vista below.

They probably hadn't seen the man she was after if they were still on their way up, but on the off chance they were on their way down...

The faint sound of helicopter blades began to punctuate the air. Sabrina frowned up at the sky and then the people at the cliff. She moved toward them as the helicopter came into view, then was hidden behind trees and rock again.

Sabrina stood at the edge and looked down at where the people had their attention. A man was lying a good twenty feet below. He intermittently moaned and grabbed at his leg.

She couldn't decide if this was a boon or terrible timing that she was about ninety percent certain the man below was the man she was after. She'd have to wait for the SAR team to get him up here, then somehow convince the search and rescue guys she should get custody of the injured man. That was a challenge.

But she'd caught up to him.

"Everything all right?" Sabrina asked.

The woman next to her turned in surprise. She took her measure quickly. "We were hiking and heard someone moaning. We saw him down there and called the emergency number. Search and rescue is coming." She eyed Sabrina's pack. "Are you going up or coming down?"

"Up. You?"

"Same, or we were. Once the SAR team gets here, we're headed back. We just got word from our friends back at the resort that a nasty storm is coming through. Winds and snow. Avalanche warning, I guess. Isn't safe to hike here right now."

Sabrina didn't bother to hide her disappointment. Bad weather was going to cause her some problems.

She could tell the SAR helicopter had landed. There wasn't enough room on this part of the trail, but based on sheer noise, she'd say they had a spot not much farther up. She didn't know a thing about search and rescue, or how they'd get to the man below, but that wasn't her concern.

"Well, you and your friends should head back," Sabrina said, adopting a tone of authority.

The woman glanced worriedly at the two people she was with, older and not in as good shape. "We should, but I thought maybe the search and rescue team might need to talk to us."

"Did you see it? The fall, I mean."

"No, but—"

"Then you're good. But if you're worried you can leave your contact information with me." Sabrina flashed her fake badge. "I'm with the local PD. Off duty," she said pretending to be disappointed her time off was interrupted. "But I can handle it from here on your behalf. Wouldn't do having tourists stuck up here." Sabrina offered a friendly smile.

The woman's face lit up. "Oh, isn't that handy? Well, here." She showed Sabrina her phone and Sabrina took a picture of the number on it. "We're staying together in Jackson Hole. We'll be there through the week. Longer if the weather is as bad as they're predicting."

"We'll be in touch if we need to ask you any questions. Otherwise, you hurry back and enjoy the rest of your vacation."

"Oh, that's so great. Thank you."

The trio discussed then tramped off, disappearing around the curve of the trail just as a man and a woman with search and rescue gear appeared on the opposite side of the trail. Sabrina waved them over, and pointed to the man below.

"You made the call?" said the man, a tall, broad-shoul-dered...*god* was the word that came to Sabrina's mind, but no matter how good anyone looked, no man was a god. Most were barely human.

He had thick, light brown hair slightly poking out of a bright orange ski cap. He wore layers, but she could tell he was in just *fine* shape underneath. His eyes were the color of the sky, and his mouth...well, it was hard not to get a little fluttery over a soft mouth pressed into a grim line when a guy had a jaw like that.

"Uh, yeah, I made the call," Sabrina offered, looking away from the mouth and the jaw back to the man moaning below them. "I didn't see him fall. Don't know the guy. Just heard him moaning and saw he'd fallen. So I called the emergency number." Sabrina figured using the other woman's story as her own was good enough.

He got to work with his female partner. Ropes and pulleys and all sorts of things Sabrina didn't have much experience with. It was interesting though how it could all work together so that the man could rappel down the sheer face of a mountain certain all would hold his weight.

And the injured man below.

The partner and the man on the ropes spoke into little comm units much like the ones Sabrina might use with her team if they were moving in together on a target.

Sabrina watched from the edge of the mountain as the rescue guy strapped the injured man to a board. Sabrina still wasn't sure that was the man *she* was after, but it was the only lead she had.

She couldn't let this SAR team whisk the injured guy off to a helicopter and then to a hospital. Especially with a storm coming in. She had to stop this somehow.

By the time the SAR partners had pulled the man up to the trail, Sabrina had her plan.

"Not as injured as he seems to think," the SAR man

was muttering to his partner as he started to unstrap the injured man.

But Sabrina watched the victim. He kept his gaze on the bonds on his legs and arms. There was calculation in his expression as one leg was freed. Like he had some kind of plan.

This was her guy. She didn't *know* it, but she *felt* it, and that was good enough for Sabrina. She marched forward, pulling out the fake badge again. "Excuse me." Sabrina stopped the SAR guy from unstrapping another restraint. "Police." She flashed the badge quickly in his face, hastily returning it to her pocket so he couldn't examine it. "I'm going to have to take it from—"

"Well, that's fake," the rescuer said, gesturing at her pocket.

Even though it *was*, Sabrina couldn't ignore the spurt of outrage that he'd seen through her quick flash of the badge. "Excuse me, I think—"

"Out of the way, miss."

But she would not *get out of the way*. She stood firm. "I'm afraid I can't let you transport him anywhere, *mister*. This man is a danger to society, and I'm in charge of—"

He stood, and though she was a tall woman, this SAR guy had a good few inches on her. And was all well-packed, *excellently* honed muscle. "You can take that up with him once we've transported him to the hospital."

"Can I see your badge?" the rescue woman asked, politely.

Sabrina glared at the dark-haired woman, noticed her partner was doing the same.

"It's fake," the guy said between clenched teeth. "I don't know why, and I don't care. You take whatever up with him once we've done our job and dropped him at the hospital."

"How do you know the badge is fake?" the woman whispered to the man.

SAR god held Sabrina's gaze, eyes cold and assessing. He crossed his *very* impressive arms across his chest. Seriously, Sabrina was going to have to get herself in need of being searched and rescued once this was all over.

But for now, she had a job to do. Whether he believed her fake badge or not. "The guy's mine. Thanks for rescuing him and all, but your job is done." Sabrina moved forward, sure the man wouldn't put up a fight.

But he stopped her. Bodily.

Sabrina's jaw dropped. "Did you just *touch* me?" She'd been spending too much time with Holden if that surprised her.

"I rescued him, as I was called to do. I'll continue to rescue him until I've finished the job. Again, I'll invite you to visit him at the hospital if you have some sort of actual official business. But as of now? I'd recommend getting the hell off this mountain before the storm blows in and I have to come and search and rescue *you*."

She had a half thought to grin at him and offer a far more enjoyable suggestion, but again, the assignment came first. If she got to the potential hit man now, she'd bet Holden that $50 for sure.

So, she'd just have to take the rescue dude out. Judging by the nervous woman next to him, she wasn't going to fight back. And they didn't have weapons, so Sabrina gave no warning, she struck out.

The man dodged her punch, immediately followed up with a grab that Sabrina ducked. They grappled like that, neither landing blows, and predicting the other's move right before the other did it.

They had the same moves. The same style.

Sabrina blew out an irritated breath and dropped her hands. "Oh, God, you're *military,* aren't you?"

He didn't relax or drop out of the fighting stance. "Same goes, huh?"

"You guys?" the woman said, her voice a little timid. "The fighting is a real meet cute and all, but our guy is gone."

Sabrina whirled at the same time the man did. The board was empty.

The SAR guy swore, furious blue eyes meeting her own furious ones. "You let him get away!" they shouted at each other.

"Iona," he barked to the woman he worked with. "Get in the helicopter and search. I'm taking it by foot." The woman immediately jogged away, but Sabrina wasn't done with this guy.

"I'm a police officer, and I—"

"And I'm Bigfoot, lady. I'm SAR, so I'll search and rescue and you can go off and lie to someone else."

He strode off, a big, broad-shouldered man with a foul temper. Yeah, he was *hot.*

But there was no way he was going to find her quarry first.

Chapter Two

Connor Lindstrom knew he hadn't gotten rid of the woman pretending to be a police officer. She was following the same tracks as he was. She held back so he couldn't see her, but he knew she was there all the same.

There and probably planning how she could get around him. Considering it was clear she had a military background, and likely a mind under all those lies, he figured she'd probably manage it.

But *his* job was to search, and to rescue. So, regardless of what was up with her, and what she wanted from their escapee—*his* job was rescue. Plain and simple. With the weather ready to turn, Connor had to work fast. Before this turned into a more complicated rescue than it already was.

The man he'd brought up from the cliff face had essentially escaped a rescue. It didn't sit right with Connor, but it wasn't his job figure out why. Search. Rescue. The end.

He wished he had Froggy with him. She could run ahead and cut the guy off at the pass, but as it was, she was back at his cabin. Connor eyed the sky. Luckily he had a dog door in the back, because Froggy would need some cover before Connor managed to return.

"Are you sure about tracking him on foot?" Iona's voice crackled through his comm unit.

"Yup."

"The storm is going to be bad. If we get up—"

"Get the helicopter back to base. The guy wasn't hurt as bad as he was acting, so he could get a bit of a lead on us. I'll keep searching."

"Storm is coming, Con. You can't outrun it."

"Yeah, well, I know how to weather a storm. You drop the heli. If I need backup, I'll radio."

"I don't like this."

Connor eyed the sky again. No, he didn't like it either, but she didn't have time to argue with him about it. "Tough. Get in the air." Iona was a fine pilot and she'd get the helicopter back to base in one piece as long as she got off soon. For him, he'd survive whatever spring storm the Tetons threw at him and get to the man who'd...

Well, he hadn't been that injured. Connor had also noticed a few ropes on the cliff below the one he'd rapelled onto. Had the man been doing some rappelling of his own? And this woman after him. Military? Former military?

It made his back itch, between his shoulder blades, where no good feelings ever settled. Mostly, he'd like to pretend to ignore the woman's existence. Do his job and disappear, never to have those sharp brown eyes vaguely mocking him again.

He grunted irritably. There was no use pretending she wasn't there. Somewhere. "Are you really going to follow me the whole time?" he called out.

She appeared, off to his right. She was closer than he'd thought she'd be, he'd give her that. Tall, slim, but the way she walked, moved and tried to fight him—it all spoke to a muscular body underneath the warm hiking layers.

Probably shouldn't be thinking about that.

"I know your job is rescue," she said, flicking a thick black braid over her shoulder. She should be wearing a hat and gloves, but wasn't and didn't seem worse for the wear over it.

She would. Once the storm hit.

"But my job is stopping this guy. So, you could just leave off. Jump in the helicopter. Let me…"

She trailed off as the sounds of the helicopter pulsed through the air, then its body became visible. Iona taking it back to base. *Thank God.*

"No such luck, lady."

The woman scowled and shoved her hands into the pockets of her coat. She wore dark, drab colors but there was something about her that was a bit like a beacon. Maybe it was because of the snow around them, the brightness still holding on against the incoming clouds. She was the opposite of all that. Dark. Quiet. Sharp like a blade.

Except there was an *energy* about her, pumping off of her. Much like the impending storm, she looked determined to cause some damage. She hiked right next to him, matching him stride for stride. Her profile was strong, her eyes stubborn. There'd be no getting rid of her.

But there'd be no getting rid of him either. He saw the job through. Always.

As if she sensed that, she blew out a breath. "So, how about this? He's a hit man. A highly trained hit man, equipped with some nasty gun and ammo that can rip up Kevlar. Still want to rescue him?"

Connor didn't even pause to think it over. "It's my job. You know what's *not* my job? Believing anything you say." Though he wondered if she might at least be telling part of the truth. *She* didn't need to know he thought that though.

"But you know as well as I do that he wasn't as hurt as he was pretending. There were ropes he'd dropped and tried to hide. The dude was faking it."

So she'd noticed those details too. "If he's so bad, and so dangerous, why are you following him? Alone?"

"Because I'm so bad and so dangerous too, baby." She flashed a grin at him.

He almost believed her, and that was…uncomfortable. "You're not armed."

She raised an eyebrow, following him up the side of the rock—clearly not worried about going off trail. "Think again."

Connor would have, but he realized the direction the man's tracks were taking them. The moron had gone in about the worst direction possible. He pulled up off the rock and onto a long sheet of snow and ice. The tracks continued up.

"He's heading for high ground," the woman said. "To get a shot off," she murmured, coming to stand next to him again. "Hit man, remember?"

Connor'd give her credit, that was the only reason he could think of someone would head this way, alone, and in this weather. Unless someone was completely lost. But… "He didn't have anything on him. I would have seen it. Felt it when strapping him to the board."

"Doesn't mean a weapon, specifically his gun, isn't hiding somewhere. Cave? Buried? I sure wouldn't climb up that unless I had a really, *really* good reason."

"Who's he going to shoot out here?"

"I wouldn't know. But I know I'm going to stop him."

Connor would have questioned her, but the shift in the wind had his internal senses going off. He stopped abruptly. When she made another step and he *heard* the hollow echo of it, he began to see the cracks. The danger.

"Stop," he ordered, quietly but with enough gravity to have her doing just that.

"What is it?" she demanded.

"We have to get out of here. And not the way you came."

"Why?"

He sized her up, how far they had to the beginning of the trail. Nope, he'd have to take her with him. And fast. "I don't particularly want to be buried alive in an avalanche, that's why."

SABRINA WOULDN'T SAY she was *scared* exactly. She was tough. She could survive.

She just didn't think surviving an avalanche sounded like a lot of fun. It was a step above being taken out by a sniper though.

So, when the man moved quickly, she followed. He scooted down the mountain, and then she began to hear what she thought maybe he'd heard back there that had made him stop. An odd, hollow echoing every time their footsteps landed on the snow.

"Pick up the pace, or you're going to be buried."

"I'm *right* behind you."

He all but leaped from one rocky surface to another and Sabrina paused for half a second, maybe. With the cold and the jump, she was in danger of re-injuring her hip— the whole reason she was here rather than on some military mission as a SEAL.

Here was better. At first, she'd only told herself that, only *tried* to make herself believe that because the one thing she'd wanted in the world had been taken away from her in a freak accident that had shattered her hip six years ago.

She took the jump, and though she felt the twinge, nothing broke, nothing shattered. No time to be grateful for it. She broke into a jog to keep up with mister SAR.

Here was better. She repeated it to herself as everything about the man in front of her *screamed* military, and she felt a bit like she was back in BUDs training, desperately trying to prove herself.

Here was better. She believed it now. Most days. There was a freedom to being part of North Star. She got to have her own life, make friends and not constantly have to prove herself as the only woman in the field—considering her current boss was a woman. She loved what she did, loved what she'd done.

She'd had a part in taking down a huge and dangerous biker gang. Now, she was going to get that hit man.

Once she survived what she could only assume was the beginning of an avalanche. She glanced behind them briefly and found it freezing her in place.

She saw the snow simply *move*, a huge big sheet of it.

The man she'd been running with grabbed her arm and jerked her through the haze of unadulterated fear to look away from the huge piles of snow getting ready to unload on them. He pointed to a little dot a ways away. "That's our target. Just run. Do *not* look back."

He moved, so she followed doing what he said. Just ran. Didn't look back. Of course, she desperately wanted to, but she could hear the crackling of nothing good. The wind howled. A freezing rain started to fall, pelting her face with stinging cold.

Still, she ran, until the dot became clearer and clearer as a small cabin. Wouldn't that cabin just be swallowed up by the snow too?

But, much as she didn't trust anyone, she trusted a SAR guy to know where to go to not get buried alive by an avalanche.

Her breath puffed painfully in and out of her lungs, the air so cold it felt like knives everywhere it touched.

They were almost to the cabin and Sabrina couldn't help it. She looked behind her and the big wall of snow…

"Do you have a death wish?" the guy yelled above the din of storm and avalanche.

She hadn't stopped running, so she didn't think the look behind was *that* bad. Except for the terror that had invaded her at the sight of what was bearing down on them. Still she kept up with him and noticed there was an odd triangular stone structure behind the cabin. Would that keep them from being buried alive in the cabin?

She didn't have the breath to ask, so she simply ran with him all the way into the tiny cabin.

It was warmer inside, though not expressly *warm*. They both stood inside, breathing raggedly. Sabrina couldn't get a sense of her surroundings at first. She was too busy trying to catch her breath, trying to weather the weakness that had flooded her after she had been an idiot and looked back despite his warnings.

She heard the roar, the *thumps*. But the cabin didn't shudder or shake or come apart around them like she half expected.

She wasn't sure how long they stood there, panting and not saying anything. It gave her some gratification that it was taking him as long as her to be able to breathe normally again.

When she had some wits about her, she looked around the room. It was spartan. A stone fireplace, a couch and a rug. No artwork on the walls. A few books piled up on the floor in the corner.

A big dog, a silky golden retriever, padded into the room from somewhere deeper in the cabin. It gave Sabrina one look then let out a low *woof*.

"Froggy. Sit," the man ordered through deep breaths.

Froggy. Everything inside of Sabrina recoiled as she eyed the man with disgust. "Oh. God. You *were* a navy SEAL," she muttered. Figured of all the dang people to get stuck in an avalanche with, she'd be trapped with a damn *SEAL*.

Connor raised an eyebrow. "Something against SEALs specifically?"

"Yeah. Specifically." She gestured to the outside, wanting to change the subject. "We going to be buried alive in here or what?"

"Or what. Deflection wedge should keep us safe."

"Should?"

He shrugged, and walked over to the fireplace. He began to build a fire as his dog walked over to where he crouched and curled up on the rug.

"What now?" Sabrina demanded.

"We wait until it's safe. Then you go back to whatever hellhole you crawled out of, and Froggy and me here go save your friend."

"He's a dangerous assassin."

"Yeah, well, for all I know, he's dead as a doornail. But we'll find him, one way or another." He stood, the fire crackling away. He shrugged out of his coat and *yowza*.

Underneath he wore a heavy sweatshirt, likely over another layer. Thermal probably. But *dang* the guy had a set of shoulders on him.

Navy SEAL, remember? You hate those.

She did. A lot. Didn't mean she couldn't enjoy appreciating the hardware, did it?

He strode out of the room, so Sabrina followed. She was trailing wet tracks through his house, but then again, so was he, so she didn't feel too bad.

He walked into another room, a small, cozy kitchen. Off the kitchen was another tinier room where he hung his coat. He pulled off the comm unit he'd had attached to it, then spoke into it, still saying nothing to her.

"Iona. Copy?"

"You okay? That came out of nowhere, huh?" the woman—the pilot—said in return over the unit. She seemed very...casual about an avalanche and a guy being caught out in it.

Sabrina supposed that was their job. To be calm and casual about what they did. She understood that, certainly.

"I'm good. At my cabin. We'll give it time to settle, then Froggy and I will head out and try to find our target."

"What about the woman?"

The man looked back at her, scowling. "She's with me. I plan on getting her out of my hair ASAP."

Sabrina smiled sweetly at him. "Good luck with that, sailor."

Chapter Three

Connor was hardly surprised this woman was going to be difficult. She practically had *pain in the butt* stamped across her forehead.

"I'll let you know when I head out again," Connor said into the unit, then turned to face the woman currently screwing with all his plans. This tall, mouthy stranger dripping in his kitchen.

"You're going to want to take all that off."

She fluttered her eyelashes on him. "Don't you think you should at least give me your name first?"

A nameless hookup wasn't his style. It didn't appeal. Or at least, it usually didn't. Still, he didn't mind using her own tactics on her. He smiled. "Some of us have work to do, *baby*."

She didn't scowl exactly, but her fake flirtatious expression got harder. "You can search and rescue all you want, but that guy is mine. I don't rest, or leave you be, until I've got him."

"You're not going to leave me be? Well, that *is* a threat." He moved past her and down the short hall to his bedroom. She followed, because of course she followed. He pulled the sweatshirt off. The freezing rain hadn't penetrated his waterproof coat, but the run and all the layers had caused him to work up a sweat. He needed warm, dry clothes fit for an avalanche rescue as that would be next on the agenda. Once the most dangerous part of the snow pile-up had settled.

She hadn't entered his room, but she leaned in his doorway, arms folded over her chest, one ankle crossed over the other. *Dripping* on his hardwood floor.

He sighed. "Do you mind?"

She raised her eyebrows all faux innocence. "I don't mind at *all*. Might be quite a nice show. I enjoy a good show."

He shook his head, appalled he wanted to laugh at her brazenness. "You've got to be freezing," he muttered.

"I've survived worse."

"Haven't we all." He jerked a drawer open, found a dry Henley and tossed it at her. Then went pawing through the next drawer for a pair of sweats and threw those in her direction too. "Bathroom is at the end of the hall. Change. We'll throw your gear into the dryer, then decide what's next."

"I know what's next. I—"

He simply walked over to her leaning in his doorway, gave her a gentle thrust backward, then closed the door in her face. Locked it for good measure.

He was half convinced she'd knock it down, except there was nothing but silence on the other side of the door, then the sound of footsteps retreating.

It gave him the chance to change completely, and put on a fresh pair of boots. It gave him a chance to *breathe*.

He didn't know what she was. Not a cop. Maybe some kind of mercenary. Not unheard-of for someone to leave the military and use their skills to go that route. But her excuse was that she was looking for a hit man. Though he supposed mercenaries didn't have to always be looking to do harm. Maybe she was the kind that hunted down the bad.

If he believed her story. Unfortunately, what she'd told him matched with the way his rescue escapee behaved. Except why here? The Tetons might be well visited, but he hadn't picked a busy trail or the part of the park closer to Jackson Hole and its never-ending spate of tourists.

Didn't add up, and Connor really hated when things didn't add up.

But that had to come secondary to the task at hand, which was a post-avalanche rescue. *If* there was a guy to save after the avalanche.

Fully dressed, Connor moved back into the kitchen. He tried to forget about the woman in his cabin as he made coffee, got out one of his print maps and turned the emergency radio on. Froggy curled up under the table he worked at while Connor made notes, got himself some coffee and formulated a plan. He glanced at the time and knew loss of daylight would be the biggest challenge.

He looked up as she entered his kitchen. This strange woman in his clothes, holding a dripping mass of her own. Something he refused to identify tightened in his gut.

"Dryer's back through there," he said, nodding his head toward the utility room off the kitchen.

She nodded and disappeared. When she returned, he tried to pretend she wasn't there, but he just couldn't manage it with all that *energy* pumping off her. She'd unbraided her hair, and it was still damp, but she must have run a towel through it because she wasn't dripping anymore.

"You got any extra mugs, or do I have to drink that right out of the pot?" she asked with a nod toward the coffeemaker.

"Please, make yourself at home. You're a guest after all," he said, sarcasm dripping from every word.

She laughed, low and smoky. "In that case," she said, opening the wrong cupboard, "I'll just poke around until I find what I want."

"Fantastic," Connor muttered. He didn't bother telling her what cabinet the mugs were in. She'd probably just open them all even if she knew.

So, he focused on his map and left her to it. When she slid into the other chair at his kitchen table, he had to fight back a grimace.

He really preferred to be alone.

"Sabrina," she said, out of nowhere.

He blinked and looked up at her. "Huh?"

"My name is Sabrina. So while you're inwardly cursing me, you've at least got a name to go along with it. Now yours? I want to inwardly curse you, too."

Again, he wanted to laugh. But there was no way he was going to let himself. "Connor."

"Connor the navy SEAL."

"Former navy SEAL," he amended, going ahead and flipping off the radio since she was apparently going to *chat* now. Iona or someone at base would notify him when it was safe to go out.

"Little young to be former, aren't you?"

He lifted his gaze to hers. "I assume you're former *some* kind of military. Aren't you calling the kettle black?"

She kicked back in her chair. "So, injury then?"

Didn't he wish. But that was the cover. "Yeah, injury. You too?"

She nodded.

"Yet here you are outrunning avalanches and allegedly chasing down the bad guys, without so much as a limp."

She raised both hands. "You can take the gal out of the military…"

There was more to her story. He could tell by the steely

glint in her eye, the way her entire posture had gone a little rigid, like she was ready to fight something off.

But it was none of his business, and he didn't want it to be.

"Look, lady. Avalanche rescue is serious work. You—"

"Sabrina. Not to be a cliche, but I ain't no lady."

Connor rolled his eyes. "Look—"

"Gotta make a call." She pushed away from the table and walked out of the room.

Connor allowed himself the full-on scowl. How he'd gotten saddled with her was beyond him. He could lose her. Here, or on the trail. He knew how to disappear. A man like him had to know how to disappear.

It was what he *should* do. But he had the sinking suspicion it wasn't what he'd end up doing.

Sabrina stepped out of Connor's cabin and onto a small porch covered in snow. The whole *world* was covered in snow. The white was nearly *blinding*, but the little stone triangle thing had kept Connor's cabin from being buried. They were surrounded on all sides by walls of snow, except this little front area. It was like being in an igloo.

Interesting. Except Sabrina had no clue how they were going to get out of here, surrounded by walls of snow and mountain debris, but she figured she'd trust Connor to figure that out. She didn't trust *people* as a rule, but she knew when to trust someone's skills.

Sabrina pulled out her phone and dialed Shay.

"Shay—" Shay answered the phone in something of an irritable bark.

"Well, things got interesting on my end. You sound annoyed."

"Yeah, that's a word for it. Holden got a lead, now he's MIA and I might hunt him down and take him out myself."

Sabrina's chest clutched in alarm, but she kept her voice steady. "How MIA?"

"It hasn't been long enough to worry," Shay said, calmer now.

But you're worried, Sabrina wanted to say. She held her tongue though. Shay was one of the few people in this world she'd do it for.

"I'm just irritated because if I know that brainiac he's done something stupid like turn off his phone. He'll pop up before the allotted time, probably with some new, good lead, and I won't be able to curse at him."

"You'll let me know when it is long enough to worry?"

Shay sighed. "You've got your own mission. Let's focus on that. Fill me in."

Sabrina had to stop herself from asking more questions about Holden's lead. About what trouble he might have gotten himself into. Shay was right. She had her own mission.

That you'd leave in a heartbeat to save Holden, given the chance.

True enough. Holden had given her a life by bringing her into the fold of North Star. She thought he might be the only man who'd cared about her without wanting to get in her pants, and that was…sacred.

But she had a mission in the here and now, and there was no way a woman survived being a North Star agent by being distracted. She filled Shay in on her day, where she was now, what the plan was.

"Former navy SEAL and current SAR," Shay said, her tone considering. "Well, not a bad partner to have, all things considered."

"I haven't told him anything. He didn't buy the cop story, but I can probably make something up about being a bounty hunter or whatever."

"Good."

"He's *hot*."

Shay snorted out a laugh, as had been Sabrina's hope. Levity had its place, and ever since Shay had become leader of North Star, she'd lost that. Sabrina knew Holden thought it was the pressure of the job, but Sabrina had always figured it laid on Shay more like guilt.

What she was guilty over, Sabrina didn't know.

"I'd worry about that," Shay said blandly, "but I know how you feel about military guys."

"Regardless, I won't quit until the job is done. He's in there poring over maps and whatnot, so I imagine we'll head out soon. Might not get back on messages right away while we're hiking. So, don't worry about me if I go radio silent."

"All right. Be careful. Don't fall for any hot military guys. Losing Reece was bad enough."

"You're stuck with me for the long haul." Sabrina hesitated before ending the call. "Even if I don't answer, give me a heads-up when Holden's accounted for."

"Will do. Take care of yourself. Check in when you can."

"Roger." Sabrina ended the call. She squinted out at all that blinding white. She couldn't worry about Holden when she had her own mission to attend to, but she gave herself a minute to worry, to think of him, and to hope he was okay.

Then she turned back into the cabin and left it behind. Right now, the only thing she could think about was hunting down her quarry before he killed whoever his target was.

Maybe he was buried under a pile of snow and rock, but Sabrina didn't think there was any way she was going to be that lucky.

When she entered the kitchen, Connor had cleaned up everything. He had two packs on the kitchen table—one of them was the one she'd been wearing earlier. There were some new supplies stacked up next to it.

The man in question was crouched eye-to-eye with the dog, murmuring sweet nothings.

Something in her stomach did a strange roll. It wasn't the lust thing. It was something softer, wistful almost. Which meant she was going to ignore it. Hardcore.

He stood slowly, staring at her, a mix of disgust and glare in his expression. "All right," he said on a sigh she might have told him was a bit dramatic if he didn't keep speaking. "I'd tell you that you can't come with me, but I'm not stupid enough to think you'd be smart enough to listen. Then I'd likely have to save your butt and I'm not in the mood to dig two people out of an avalanche. So, you'll follow along and do as I say. And before you argue, understand that if you get in my way, I can have you arrested."

"I do really bad with threats, hotshot. Really bad."

"And I do really bad with mouthy pains in the butt. I didn't ask for you to join me on a mission, but here we are."

She laughed, couldn't help it. There was something about his dry give-and-take that amused her. "All right, Con. Here's the deal. I'll follow the rules and instructions the entire time we're out there, up until we get the guy. Once he's free and good, I'll fight you for him." She held out a hand. "Deal?"

Connor heaved out a sigh. "Fine," he muttered, and shook her hand.

When she tried to pull her hand away, his grip tightened. "But if you break that deal, I'm having you arrested."

She thought about lifting up on her toes and pressing her mouth to his, just to see what he'd do. But if she was honest with herself, she was a little afraid of what *she* might do.

"One thing you're going to learn about me, Mr. navy

SEAL, I keep my word." And she would. But that didn't mean she couldn't continue to be a pain in the butt *while* keeping her word.

Chapter Four

Connor double-checked his pack, ordered Sabrina to add the supplies he'd set out to hers. He checked in with Iona, then attached Froggy's special harness for avalanche rescue onto the dog. The bright orange-and-black harness allowed for leash attachments, including a load-bearing harness in case they should need to do another high line rescue.

Connor didn't like the fact that his job involved people being in danger, but he did love the act of his job. Even more than he'd enjoyed being a navy SEAL. While he'd joined the military to serve his country, to put his strength and discipline to the test, much of the actual real-life stuff he'd encountered hadn't been so cleanly about *helping* people.

War and conflict were gray areas and death and bureaucratic red tape and unfairness complicated all of that. Search and rescue were simple. You did the job. Sometimes you saved the day. Sometimes you didn't. But he didn't have to suffer a lot of deep personal moral dilemmas. Things were success or failure. He liked the black and white of it.

"Doesn't the dog get cold?" the woman—Sabrina— asked.

He was having a hard time thinking of her as *Sabrina*. She was all sharp edges and brash grins with the occasional innuendo tossed in for good measure. Sabrina seemed like a name better suited to someone…proper. Feminine. This woman looked like a slim, honed weapon in his Henley and the sweatpants that bagged on her. She was pure energy.

It was a shame he liked that in a woman.

"Froggy's fur keeps her warm," he said, running a hand over the dog's back. "The gear helps. She's trained for this, and as her handler and partner I pay attention to how she's faring. If the search goes on too long, we'll call for backup—both in terms of handlers *and* dogs."

"I'd like to avoid that."

So would he, but he wasn't going to let her know that. He shrugged negligently. "Search and rescue is rooted in *safety* for all involved. Searchers, dogs, victims. Everyone's well-being is taken into account. Because the whole principle behind it is *rescue*. Not creating bigger problems."

Sabrina pretended to yawn. It should offend him. Instead he had to stifle a grin.

He needed to get this guy saved and fast so this strange woman would be out of his hair. For good.

"You'll need to put your clothes back on now that they're dry. I dumped them in the bathroom with some other stuff you'll want to wear. I've got your boots in the dryer. So, they'll be last."

"Awfully bossy."

"Yeah, well, I'm the boss. If this is going to go smoothly you might as well get used to it."

"If you're expecting a 'yes, sir' you read the room way wrong, babe."

"And if you think I'm going to get all flustered every time you *babe* me, you read the room wrong, sweetheart."

"Oh, come on, you can't honestly call me sweetheart with a straight face." She flashed him a grin and sauntered down the hallway with one last simmering look over her shoulder before she disappeared into his bathroom.

He really didn't want to like her. She was in his way, after all, but it was hard not to admire a woman with that much…*personality.*

When she finally came out, she'd put her own clothes back on, plus a few of the layers he'd thrown in there.

"You'll have to wear one of my coats. And a hat. And gloves. Who goes hiking in the cold without a hat and gloves?" He moved into the mudroom to gather the rest of the supplies he'd collected for her.

"My mistake, not planning for an avalanche."

"It was, yes," he agreed, handing her the coat, hat, gloves. She shrugged into the gear without complaint. They were a little big on her, but she was tall enough that the apparel wasn't swimming on her body. "A smart hiker checks the weather forecast, the potential for danger."

"I ain't no hiker. I'm—" She stopped herself, the first flicker of annoyance aimed at herself rather than him.

It was a kind of triumph, to Connor's way of thinking. Any time he could make this woman off balance enough to almost reveal some information, maybe he could understand what she was getting him roped into.

Connor opened the dryer and tested out her boots. "They'll do." He tossed them at her.

She shoved her feet into them, and he waited impatiently for her to lace them up. When she stood there after she was finished, he rolled his eyes. "The gloves. Unless you like frostbite."

"Okay, dad." She pulled the gloves on. "We ready yet? Or is it policy to let the guy suffocate?"

"Safety is the policy. The end."

"Damn, that's *so* hot."

"I don't have to take you along with me. You realize that, right?"

"But I'd go anyway. As you said yourself, that would only lead to you having to rescue me too. So, really, I'm doing you a favor."

Connor could not fully believe she was somehow spinning it that way, but she looked so pleased with herself, clearly she believed it. "God help me," he muttered, heading for the front door.

She trailed along much like Froggy did. Outside everything was the blinding white he'd expected. It was going to be a hell of a hike back to where they'd left any signs of their guy.

"You going to spill the reason you're after this dude?" he asked, marching through the snow as he eyed the sun through his sunglasses. They only had a few hours to get this accomplished before dark hindered their efforts. Iona would be putting together a night team, but Connor wanted this done, and Sabrina out of everyone's hair.

"I already did," Sabrina replied, squinting against the sun. "Bad guy with a bad gun, recall?"

He grumbled irritably to himself then dug a pair of sunglasses out of his pack and handed them to her. "You told me maybe half of why someone's after him, but you didn't tell me why you, specifically, are ineffectually tramping around mountains trying to…what, kill him?"

"I'm going to ignore the fact you said 'ineffectually tramping' because you're a guy and so obviously operating on half a brain. But for your information he's the hit man. Not me."

"That doesn't answer my question."

"I wasn't planning on answering your question."

"You know, I could hike you around, ditch you and leave you to the elements if I really wanted to. It wouldn't be hard." It was a threat he'd never act on, but maybe she wouldn't know that.

She snorted, clearly not taking him seriously. "You aren't the only one who went through navy SEAL training. I know how to survive."

SABRINA *REALLY* WISHED she hadn't said that. She had a mouth on her, so she was used to things flying out of it that she hadn't planned on, but she tried to keep personal stuff on the down low.

The way he stopped, turned and stared at her with his eyes wide, mouth open, she wanted to hunch away from his reaction. Instead, she lifted her chin at him. "What?" she demanded.

"You're Brina Killian."

She paled. No one had called her Brina in years. She'd left her nickname behind when she'd had to give up her SEAL dreams. She tried to fight off the cold slither of dread that worked its way up her spine. Tried to be smart in the face of swamping emotion.

There were a couple ways she could play it. Deny it. Admit it, flippantly. But the fact he knew her, or knew *of* her, was something she had to get to the bottom of. "How do you know that?"

"You shattered your hip." He eyed her suspiciously. "Healed up okay."

"Eventually. And I'll repeat myself. How do you know that?"

"Nathan Averly ring any bells?"

This time Sabrina didn't just blink in shock, she was pretty sure she blushed. "What about him?" Sabrina knew how small the military world could be, but the fact that this guy knew the ex-boyfriend that she hadn't treated all that well in the aftermath of her injury was…well, quite the twist of fate.

Shouldn't you be used to the cruel whims of chance by now?

"We were in a unit together. Came out the same time. He mentioned you."

"Super."

Connor went back to hiking, thank God. She could focus on moving her way through the high, hard-packed snow. Not on anything to do with an old life she hadn't just left behind, she'd forgotten all about. Purposefully.

She shook her head at herself. Sometimes a woman could lie to herself, but sometimes it didn't actually do any good. "Where is old Nate if not navy SEALing his way through life?"

Connor shrugged. "Not sure. Lost touch."

Sabrina opened her mouth to tell him he was lying, and that he was bad at it. But she thought better of it. Maybe she didn't want to know what had happened to Nate. Ignorance could absolutely be bliss. Especially when it came to old flames she'd done wrong.

They trekked in silence. Sabrina paid more attention to the dog than the man in front of her. Both because she was fascinated that a dog could have such an important job, and because she knew staring at Connor's backside was not good for her decision-making.

She wasn't sure how long they walked before Connor stopped and crouched next to the dog. He murmured something to the retriever. The demeanor in the dog changed, sharpened. Like she'd just gotten orders.

Sabrina looked around. Everything was still white. She got the sense they'd gone up in elevation, but mostly everything looked the same here as it had back at Connor's cabin.

The dog took the lead now, Connor following her, Sabrina behind him. Connor didn't look back to see if she was following him. Maybe he knew instinctually that she was. That she would.

"Wish I'd gotten Nebraska after all," she muttered to herself.

"What about Nebraska?" Connor asked, clearly more to annoy her than because he cared.

"Don't worry about it."

"The only thing I'm worried about is if you can really hack this."

She tried to keep the snap out of her voice since she knew he was purposefully needling her. "Do I sound winded?"

"Nate made that injury sound pretty major."

Go figure Nate would be haunting her still. "It was. It was also years ago. Injuries heal."

"Most major ones leave scars."

He had *no* idea. She also got an idea of what he was trying to do now. Irritate her with other topics so she'd answer his questions. But North Star was not public knowledge. Her personal involvement with the group even less so.

Back when Granger MacMillan had run the group, you got four years tops, then were a goner. If anyone ever made you, or you told someone about your job, you were out. The only one who'd ever gotten around that edict had been Shay herself.

Sabrina had respected Granger, but Shay loosening the stringent requirements of involvement in North Star, *and* how long a person could stay active in North Star, certainly made her future a lot more secure.

No one could get her kicked out of North Star except herself. Even with an injury she could transfer to some kind of intel job. She liked having that kind of control.

She thought about Shay's call earlier, and Holden, and pulled her phone out of her pocket.

"You won't get reception out here," Connor informed her.

She smirked at his back. Showed what he knew. Still, there were no messages. So Holden was still MIA. She slid her phone back into her pocket and pictured herself shoving her worry about Holden into its own compartment.

She had to focus on the task at hand. If she got this guy today, before the sun went down, she could be in Nebraska helping Holden by tomorrow.

She used that as fuel. It kept her hiking despite the way the cold bit into her. It kept her from snarking at Connor just for the sake of it. Focused. Determined. She'd get the job done.

She was starting to *feel* the elevation change, the way the air got thinner. "Are we higher than we were to start?"

"Yeah, but he was going up when the avalanche started. So, makes sense."

She wasn't convinced. Something about the tone in his voice had her wondering if he was lying to her. Whether for the sake of it or for some other reason, she didn't know.

It was when Connor paused to take a swig of his water bottle that Sabrina started to feel…exposed. She couldn't have said why. Just a tingling at the base of her neck, a heavy, throbbing *wrongness* to the still, the quiet and how completely open they were. An easy, easy target. "We need to get out of this open space. Now."

Connor scoffed. *Scoffed.* "There's no way someone somehow survived that avalanche *and* got a gun *and*—"

Sabrina could have let him go on with his *and*s, with his reasonable responses, but she had her gut feeling, and she went with it. She gave him a shove, and stuck her foot in just the right place to trip him in the force of her shove. Then launched her body so she'd land on top of him.

The gunshot ringing through the eerie silence before they'd fully hit the hard-packed snow beneath them was a relief. Her instincts were still always right on target.

"Told you," she muttered into the snow around them.

Chapter Five

It took Connor a few seconds to fully grasp what had just happened.

She'd been right. She may have even saved his life, pushing him out of the way, though he wasn't sure where the bullet landed and therefore what or who the presumed target was.

She'd been *right* either way. Connor had to sit with the fact that he'd...lost his touch. There'd been a time he could have sniffed something like that out. He would have felt it. Predicted it.

Maybe instead of being horrified he should be relieved. He'd left the navy SEALs feeling like a hunted dog. In the few years he'd been here he'd let that feeling go. Convinced himself his mountain was safe.

Now, it wasn't.

He thought of Nate, who'd never found that safe feeling. Who'd let that hunted feeling rule his life. Strange, the zigs and zags of this. His connection to Nate. Her.

No more shots rang out, though Sabrina stayed awkwardly splayed over the top of him. Like *she* was protecting *him*. He nudged her off of him, though made sure he kept her in the small hole they'd made in the snow—the force of their bodies making enough of an indentation in the hard pack.

Froggy sat, waiting for orders, as he and Sabrina thought about what the next move was.

The snow wouldn't protect them from gunfire, but if they stayed low enough, it might prevent the gunman from a good angle—depending on where the person was.

"If you wanted me underneath you, you could have asked," he said, because otherwise he was afraid he might thank her. He wasn't sure his pride could take the beating this woman would dole out if he *thanked* her.

"Ha. Ha. Maybe next time you'll listen to me. Or thank me for saving your life."

"How do you know he was shooting at me? Maybe he's shooting at the woman after him."

"Maybe," she muttered somewhat distractedly. "You got any binoculars in these packs?"

He rummaged around for them then handed them to her. She poked her head slightly above the edge of snowpack hiding them. Connor scanned the world around them. Wide open space here, with a big sheet of snow-covered rock to the west. That's where the shot had to have come from.

It was where Sabrina trained the binoculars. She looked out of them for what felt like several minutes, but he didn't rush her.

It had been a long time since he'd been on a military mission, but that's exactly what this felt like. Sniper. Interminable waiting in uncomfortable conditions. Teamwork that meant a little bit more because both of your lives were at stake.

Even if he hadn't predicted it. Even if his instincts had failed him. *This* felt right. It fit like an old glove. No matter how long it had been, he knew how to be the hunted. He knew how to fight it.

"Gone. Running or hiding." Sabrina made a considering sound before handing the binoculars back to him. "I think he'd have taken us both out if he'd hit one of us."

Connor noted she wasn't calling him the specific target, so she'd taken his point to heart. Surprising.

"But since he missed, thanks to me, he didn't want to stick around and risk getting caught?" She shook her head. "Not sure that makes sense, but not sure it doesn't."

"I'm not going to thank you."

"Then don't." She shrugged, surprisingly casual about the whole thing. "Just admit that my superior intelligence saved your very nice butt."

He snorted. "Did you just call my ass *nice* after getting shot at?"

She shrugged, humor lifting some of the gravity in her expression. "You could probably make a case for spectacular, but hard to tell with all those layers."

"You are something else," he muttered, irritated with her for being…something else, and irritated with himself for feeling a bit flustered. This was not a time to short-circuit.

"Look, I know what you're going to say to this and all, but I've got to give it my best shot. This guy is dangerous. Doesn't need rescuing. Go back to your cabin. Give this one up. I'll handle it, because he's my job. You don't need to make him yours."

She was serious. Not trying to poke at him. Not flashing her humor or sexual innuendo as some kind of weapon. No, this was a soldier. Through and through.

Harder to pretend or argue with a straight-forward woman just trying to get the job done—whatever her job happened to be.

Connor looked up at the rock face in front of them. He knew it would bother her, but he took his own time searching the place the gunman would have been with the binoculars.

No, there was no one visibly up there right now, but that didn't mean someone wasn't hiding. Hiding or running, either way, he and Sabrina wouldn't be able to pinpoint where he'd gotten the shot off. No matter what her skills were, she needed more than just her sharp brain and determination.

Froggy might be able to help with a search, but there were a few other options to exhaust before he went that route. "It might not be the same guy."

Sabrina gave him a doleful look, and he could hardly blame her. Of course it was the same guy. No one else would have been up on that mountain. Still, he'd had to offer the slim chance the two events of today were unrelated.

Less than unlikely. More and more, her dangerous hit man story held water. Didn't mean Sabrina herself was on the up-and-up, but he doubted someone who *was* on the side of right would be out there shooting at him and her, no matter how bad *she* might be.

She'd trusted her instincts to push him down and avoid the gunshot. Well, he had his own instincts, even if they'd apparently dulled a bit when it came to finding himself the potential target of a gunman.

"I can't let you—I couldn't let anyone—go out in this alone. It isn't smart, feasible, and like I said before, would probably end up in me being called to rescue you anyway. I'll stick it out. Froggy will help track the guy down."

"It's dangerous. Life and death of the shooting kind, not the buried alive kind."

"I got that."

She nodded, serious and focused. "If your SAR friends send reinforcements, it puts them in harm's way."

Connor cataloged all the people he worked with. He wasn't the only one with military experience, but he definitely had the most recent experience. His team was tough, focused and dedicated.

But there wasn't even one of them he'd want to risk. Too many had families, responsibilities, lives outside this little mountain range that had become Connor's entire world.

"I'll call them off," he said gruffly. Her raised eyebrows were the only sign she was surprised by his assessment. "But I don't think we should go into this unarmed."

"I'm not."

"You keep saying that—"

She patted her coat at her chest. "One holstered here." Then she pointed to her pack. "An arsenal in there."

"A bit heavy."

"I do just fine." She paused to consider something, then shrugged her pack off. She rifled around, then pulled out a secured Glock. "You know how to use one of these?"

"Yeah."

"This ain't a navy rifle."

He tried not to let her purposeful barbs land, but she sure knew how to aim them. "I can shoot a Glock. Want a demonstration?"

"Maybe later when I've got time to get all hot and bothered. Got anything to carry it with?"

"No," he muttered irritably.

"I think I've got a back holster in here." She dug some more in her pack.

"You can't really think you're going to hike around a mountain with all that weight on your back."

"Why not?" She pulled out a holster that would indeed fit onto the back of his pants. Not really where he wanted a gun, but it'd have to do.

"In this weather, in the distance we might need to go, you want the lightest pack possible."

"Sure, but I'm not hiking for fun. I'm hiking to take down a guy before he kills anyone. I'll have my arsenal with me, thanks."

"Speed should be a consideration."

"It will be. But the weight of the pack's not holding me back yet. Want to bet how long it will take me before it does?"

He looked her up and down, and realized before he'd finished the sweep this woman would always be too contrary to admit she was wrong if there was a bet. "No."

She grinned. "Good. Now, you got any safe ways we can follow him without walking through this big open get-yourself-shot-in-the-head clearing here?"

Since he could see that eventuality just a little too clearly in his head, Connor sighed. "You have such a way with words."

SABRINA CHUCKLED. SHE wasn't sure about the guy's skills, but at least he wasn't too much of a bore to be around.

"It'll take longer to take the safe route. You have enough prepared in that backpack of horrors if we have to be out here through the night?" he asked.

She had no doubt the Boy Scout here was. Beyond that, she'd prepared for everything she could. Anything to bring this guy in. "Yup."

"All right. If we move east here, we can wrap around the mountain with some decent cover." He pointed at the direction he wanted to go, looking big and authoritative in black and orange in the midst of all this white. "They'll be some clearings to cross, but unless he follows our path, we should be okay."

Sabrina nodded. She maneuvered from lying on her

stomach into a low crouch. The top of her head would likely be visible from wherever the hit man had been, but as no shots rang out, she had to believe he'd run off.

She wasn't the target after all, and there'd be no reason for Connor to be one. Oh, a hit man hired by this kind of shady black market group would no doubt kill them both if they were in the way, but she and Connor weren't the *target*.

She'd hold onto that. It was a shame she didn't have *snow* camo to see her through this part. "I'll get up first. If there's no shooting, you come up behind."

"You may have been right about the whole someone's about to shoot us thing, but hiking this mountain is *my* expertise. You're going to let me lead."

Sabrina had to bite back her initial, knee-jerk response to that. The fact she *could* meant her tactical training had finally taken over. Instead of sniping with him, she considered. And realized he was right, no matter how irritated she was by it. Or the heavy-handed way he was trying to *order* her. It had been a long time since Sabrina had taken orders from someone she didn't fully trust and respect.

But desperate times called for desperate, self-controlling measures. "All right. You lead us to the rock face over there. Then what?"

"We'll use Froggy to track. Probably going to be edging toward nightfall anyway, so even if there were *actual* tracks, we won't be able to see them."

"You need to call off your team."

He'd agreed to do it, but there was a hesitation in him now. She had the sense he was doing the same thing she'd just done—fighting off knee-jerk arguments in favor of considering what was best for their situation.

He lifted the comm unit attached to his coat to his mouth. "Iona. Copy?"

"Copy."

"I'm calling off the search. All signs point to this guy getting off the mountain on his own. But you saw him, right? You could describe him?"

"Well, sure."

"Give a description to the local police, and let them know he escaped rescue, and therefore might be dangerous."

There was a long pause of static as Sabrina had to fight with the rising need to rip the comm unit out of his hand and demand to know what the hell he thought he was doing. Getting cops involved was a terrible idea.

"Dangerous?" the woman's voice said carefully.

"It's possible. And they should know," Connor said, but as he spoke the words he maintained eye contact with Sabrina.

She wanted to punch him.

"Are you sure about this, Connor. What about the wom—"

"I'm sure. I'm headed back to the cabin. Do not send out another team. Understood?"

"Connor—"

"Understood?" Connor repeated, and Sabrina could all but see him in tactical gear barking orders at a navy SEAL team. She hadn't been needling him when she'd said he looked too young to be a retired SEAL and she had to wonder what kind of injury could have taken him out of commission. Much like her, he'd clearly recovered from it.

"All right. If you're sure."

"Get the description to the police, then forget about it. Over and out." He didn't reattach the unit to his coat. He took the whole thing off, and turned a switch Sabrina had to assume shut the unit off completely.

He shoved it into his pack. Cutting ties. That was good

for what she was trying to do, but she had to wonder. "You sure she'll listen?"

"Mostly. This lasts too long she's going to send a group after me, but I imagine she'll wait a few days."

"Why'd you involve the cops?" Sabrina tried to keep the scathing note out of her tone. She could be equitable for the sake of teamwork. "Basically signing them a death warrant," she added. Okay, maybe not *equitable*.

"No, I'm covering my bases," Connor replied. "If he gets off the mountain without us knowing about it, they'll have a heads-up. And so will we."

Sabrina shook her head. For a former SEAL this guy really seemed to underestimate how dangerous the bad guy could be.

"You ready?" he demanded.

"Ready."

Even though he was leading them, she still stood first, gun cocked and ready.

He stared at the gun. "Where'd you... How'd you get that out without me seeing?" he asked, eyebrows drawn together.

It lifted her spirits some. She smirked. "Magic, baby."

Chapter Six

No shots rang out when Connor stood up alongside Sabrina. So, he led her and Froggy on the path that would give them the most cover. They walked in silence except for the crunching of their feet on the snow. Even that was muted.

They both knew how to move through a landscape with stealth and care. To be aware of their surroundings. But the gunman seemed to have run or hunkered down, because there were no more sightings, and no more gut feelings from Sabrina having them hit the deck before shots rang out.

The quiet and the hike gave Connor time to think. Really think. In a way he hadn't been able to since he'd gotten the rescue call this morning. The way he preferred to. A lining up of facts and thoughts that would clarify some things for him. Because even though he'd agreed to help Sabrina, there was this nagging feeling he needed to know *what* she was, not just who.

The fake cop thing she had pulled at the rescue site wouldn't be out of character for some kind of bounty hunter, and a military background would be beneficial in that kind of work. Though bounty hunters could skirt the law a little bit, they were usually bringing in someone who should be brought in. It fit.

But it didn't.

What he knew about Brina Killian from Nate, was that she was—or had been—a woman with superior drive who'd blow up her life after her SEAL goals had been ended by a freak injury. In Nate's estimation, Sabrina was an all-or-nothing type. Bounty hunters lived in a gray area that didn't quite work with that personality.

Granted, Nate could have been wrong about Sabrina. He'd been wrong about other things, which was half of why Connor was here and not a SEAL. Still, while Nate blamed himself for everything that had gone wrong, Connor didn't. He'd had free will. He'd trusted Nate's assessment of a dangerous situation.

They'd both been wrong. They'd both paid the price.

That was way beside the point of what he was trying to figure out now. Sabrina Killian was his focus, and he didn't think she was a bounty hunter.

The situation itself screamed mercenary to him. And yet, that didn't ring true. There was something about her— no matter how brash, no matter how happy to lie about the cop thing or irritate him on purpose—that he couldn't equate with mercenary. She had a sense of fairness about her. An ease at working with him, even when she didn't fully want to be.

Maybe the facts added up, but his instincts told him *false*.

In search and rescue, fact was more important than instinct. And yet, instinct always played a role in decision-making. When it came to people, Connor had always found it imperative.

But when instinct warred with fact, especially when he had time to think, a lot of past failures undercut the clear truth, or the right way forward.

Did it matter what she was? When they'd been shot at?

So clearly whoever she was hunting was equally as bad as whatever she was up to. When every time he had the chance to decide to let her go off alone, to let this be out of his hands, he refused?

"Tell me why I should think you're anything but a mercenary," he said as they weaved through a thicket of whitebark pine.

"I never said I wasn't."

Which clarified the argument he'd been having with himself. "But you're not." He might not know this woman, but based on the way she'd acted, what he could glean from having been friends with her ex-boyfriend once upon a time, that wasn't the way she operated.

Mostly because if she *was* a mercenary, she wouldn't let him think she was.

She didn't say anything else. Didn't argue with him or explain. She just kept hiking. He snuck a look over his shoulder at her, wondering if the weight of her pack was getting to her. But she followed him with easy strides, not breathing too heavily even as they went up in elevation. She looked calm and collected and at ease. The only sign this wasn't a leisurely walk on a nice day was the fact the very tip of her nose was red.

They came to a series of boulders. Connor eyed them, thought about the terrain he knew like the back of his hand. He brought up a mental map of the area in his mind. They'd have to climb this series of rocks to give them cover to get to the main cliff face they were headed for.

He started to climb, thinking about what might get through to her. No matter what he'd told her, or anyone else, he didn't know what it was like for an injury to ruin his military career. Still, his had ended abruptly and because of a mistake, so he knew what happened in the aftermath of sudden loss. Whatever she was doing here, whoever had sent her, this *had* to connect to the end of her military career.

"Leaving the military is rough," he said, trying to strike a conversational tone. "Finding something to do with those skills is a really lucky thing." He climbed over the next rock easily enough, holding Froggy's leash and watching her with an eagle eye to make sure the dog wasn't over-taxing herself.

Sabrina snorted behind him. She eyed the rock between them. "Luck doesn't have a thing to do with where I am."

"Then what do you call it?" He considered her standing below him. "Sheer force of will to build your life into something different than you planned, but equally fulfilling?" Because the way this job meant so much to her that she wouldn't give up spoke to it being some kind of satisfaction for her.

She frowned up at him for a moment. He couldn't possibly read what was going on in that brain of hers. "Some of it's will, sure," she said, climbing up the first rock between them. She shrugged as if will was nothing.

Definitely not what he would have expected.

She scrabbled up a rock taller than her. When she got the top, she looked down at him from her crouched position. "Don't you believe in destiny?"

She went from crouching to standing at her full height at the top of a rock, the sun haloing her body in gold. Loose tendrils of dark hair danced around her face and her expression was fierce and goddess-like.

Something heavy and irrevocable seemed to flip over in his chest. "Hell no," he said, but his voice came out rusty.

She hopped down so they were on the even ground again. That odd moment gone, thank *God.* Though he wouldn't mind her not being so close.

"I do. Sheer force of will. Luck." She waved them both

off. "If I believed in those I'd have given up on life the minute my hip shattered. And I tried. Boy did I. But some things are *meant*, Connor. Destiny is where you're meant to be, knowing who you're meant to know, doing what you're supposed to do."

"With no choice?" he asked blandly. She was trying to pull one over on him, surely.

"There's always a choice. It's all we've got on this crazy ride around the sun. But destiny is where you end up when you make all the right choices." She tilted her head, studied him from below and managed to make it seem like she was a queen inspecting a commoner. "Do you really think you survived the military, got into SAR, because of *luck*?"

She sounded so dismissive he had to fight the need to bristle. The need to argue with her. What did her opinion matter? He hadn't meant everything was about luck anyway. And what was the difference between luck and "destiny" anyway?

"Well?" she asked, pointing to the route ahead. "What's the holdup?"

She wanted him to keep walking, keep leading her to the hit man. And he should. That's absolutely what he should do. But he found himself studying her, trying to puzzle her out first.

"I'm not going to tell you what I am, Connor. Why I am. And if that bothers you, you're free to vamoose."

Vamoose.

"I'm not going anywhere, *Brina*."

She had a knife in her hand, pointed at him, and he had *no* idea where it had come from or how she'd gotten it there. She could move, that was for sure. He supposed he should feel more fear than admiration but he couldn't quite work past awe.

"I want to make something very clear," she said, her

voice as sharp as the blade she held. "You don't call me that. It's not my name. That's a past I left behind and nobody, and I mean *nobody*, gets to remind me of it. We clear?"

HE DIDN'T APPEAR to be worried, threatened or even scared at the fact she'd only need one good jab to take a piece out of him. Which poked at Sabrina's temper even more.

"Clear," he eventually said.

She should have been gratified he'd stand down. Happy he understood she was *dangerous* if she wanted to be.

But she felt small and foolish and *pissed*. Because she'd given too much of herself away. He'd pushed a button and she'd allowed herself to explode, rather than play it cool and win the game in the end.

Exhaustion tried to sneak over her. She'd been working hard following this guy and she finally had this lead, but in the midst of all this cold, and the heavy weight of her pack, she wanted to curl up and sleep.

Which wasn't an option. Nor was getting all worked up that he'd used her old nickname. She'd give herself a break at the overreaction. What did it matter in the short run? They were working together. Better he know her sore spots and avoid them.

If he tried to poke at them, she'd just leave him in the dust. She eyed the dog. Maybe even take Froggy with her. The dog was on a leash, and Sabrina knew a few dog commands. All she'd have to do was snatch it and run. Oh, the guy would fight for his dog, but Sabrina might be able to win the fight.

She shook her head. Bad habit, always trying to find ways to escape the situation she was in. Ditch the partners she was supposed to be working with. If there was anything North Star had taught her, it was that teamwork could be invaluable. She couldn't dismiss it out of hand just because the other person was a jerk. Especially if they were a skilled, knowledgeable jerk.

Unfortunately, Connor fit the bill.

"What's your last name?" she demanded, searching for equilibrium and a place her past wouldn't haunt her. All these years at North Star she'd been able to leave Brina behind. Why was that iteration of herself back to haunt her now? Why did she *care*?

"Why do you want to know my last name?" Connor asked, easily climbing another boulder and jumping to the next.

"You know mine. Why shouldn't I know yours?" She followed him, knowing her leaps weren't as graceful, but they got the job done. *Story of your life, Sabrina.*

"Because I don't know what your business is or who you'll pass my last name along to."

"It'd be easy enough to find out your name whether you tell me or not."

"Probably."

"So why don't you just tell me?"

"I'd rather you have to do the work. Which you won't be able to do while we're out here."

"That's what you think," she muttered. Thanks to Elsie's IT expertise, Sabrina's North Star phone could do a whole heck of a lot.

But she didn't tell him that. She followed him. Through the cold and the white. It would have been pretty and exhilarating if they weren't following and on the lookout for an assassin. She'd always loved the mountains. A sharp contrast to the Kansas flat she'd grown up in.

She'd always thought she could have enjoyed that flat, felt at home there. But her father's strict rules and expectations had made her feel as beat down as that hardscrabble patch of land he'd tried to use her as a tool to farm.

The navy had been her escape. She'd run away, joined up and found a purpose that had finally, *finally* felt like freedom. The rigidness, the orders, she'd understood all that thanks to dear old Dad. But getting to go places, set her own goals and strive toward them had been all the freedom she'd ever wanted.

Her throat felt tight and her eyes burned. The altitude getting to her, surely. Either way, if she wasn't going to think about her life as Brina, she really wasn't going to think about her father.

She felt her phone vibrate in her pocket. She considered Connor's easy gait. She'd struggle to keep up with him if she surreptitiously stopped. She'd likely fall and break her neck if she tried to jump boulders and talk on her phone.

"Hold up, Connor," she said, imbuing the casual statement with enough bite to sound like an order. Just the way she hoped would irritate him. She brought the phone to her ear.

"You're not going to have serv—"

"Shay? What's up?"

Connor's voice was obnoxiously loud next to her so that Sabrina didn't quite pick up on Shay's words.

"I don't believe you've actually got anyone on the line," he said irritably. "You're just trying to—"

"Do you *mind*?" she retorted. She hit speaker, and Shay's voice echoed in the space between them. She smirked, clicked speaker off, then turned away from Connor. "Must have lost you for a second, can you repeat that?"

"I just needed to give you an update on some things. First, we've got Holden. He's got a lead, and it's taking a team of us to work through it. I've had to pull some of the team I had closer to you as backup. I'm going to have to call in some outside help to send your way if—"

"I don't need any backup. I got this."

"Sabrina." There was censure in Shay's tone, but Sabrina didn't need it.

"Seriously. I've got this SAR guy working with me. Former navy SEAL. He wants to track down the guy as much as I do. But until we do, and even once we do, it's two against one. Holden may need a team. I don't."

"It's not a competition."

No, it wasn't. It was Holden's life. "I'm good, Shay. I promise."

There was a pause. A sigh. "I'm glad you've got someone with skills helping you, but we're talking about a hit man."

"We're talking about me," Sabrina replied, trying to sound her brash and cocky self even as relief Holden was okay made her feel a bit too soft. "Look, you want to pull some outside help and station them close as an emergency to make yourself feel better, that's fine. But you know I'm not going to call on strangers. Take care of Holden's lead first. Mine's pretty straightforward."

"Do you remember that I'm in charge here?"

Sabrina laughed. "Yeah, I also remember some things you did when Granger was in charge that weren't exactly 'sir, yes, sir.'"

It was Shay's turn to chuckle. "Yeah, that feels like a lifetime ago. Listen. I'm putting some people on standby. When I think I can spare Gabe or Mallory, I'm sending them your way. If you need help, it'll be close. I know you'll avoid it at all costs, but I also know you're smart enough, and care about getting this guy enough, that you'll call in backup if you need it."

"Low blow," Sabrina muttered.

"That's why I'm the boss. Watch your back, Sab. This might be a little bit more complicated than we were planning on it being."

Sabrina eyed the angry mountain man former SEAL staring at her with blue eyes the color of spring skies. Yeah, *complicated* was no joke.

Chapter Seven

She ended the call. He'd gleaned she was talking to her boss or some kind of leader. Though clearly Sabrina could make a lot of her own choices when it came to how to proceed.

He was slightly surprised that Sabrina had told the person she'd talked to about him. That she hadn't tried to pretend she was handling this alone, or that her boss hadn't demanded more information about who he was.

Mercenary seemed less and less possible.

"How do you get service up here?" he asked. That was another odd piece to the puzzle.

She fluttered her lashes. "Magic."

He'd figured she wouldn't tell him, but it had been worth a shot. "Yeah, you keep saying that. So strange how I don't buy it. You're not some secret government group, are you?"

"Why, Con, you got something against Uncle Sam?"

Boy, did he. But he wasn't about to air that here, or with her. Still, if she had moved into some government group... Distaste moved through him. He would have preferred working with a mercenary.

"You *do* have something against Uncle Sam," Sabrina said, seeming delighted with the idea.

"Didn't say that."

"Didn't have to. Your sneer says it all."

"I am *not* sneering. Even if I was, you're walking behind me and can't see my face."

"But I can see your posture. That's a sneering posture."

"You're one strange lady, you know that?"

"Been told that a time or two. Doesn't bother me much. Usually all strange means is different than so-and-so, and who wants to be so-and-so?"

"We're going to have to find a place to camp soon."

"Don't you think we should hike through the night?"

"Not unless you want to break a leg. Either in the dark or tomorrow when you're dizzy from lack of sleep."

"For a former SEAL, you're kind of a baby."

Connor did not huff out an irritated breath though he wanted to. He wasn't going to be needled into forgoing safety precautions. "We break for dark. Non-negotiable."

"You don't seem to understand this guy is a hit man. Meaning he has a target he's trying to kill. It's life or death we stop him before he does kill."

"Who exactly is this man after in the middle of the Tetons? What innocent bystander is going to get offed in the middle of the night with a storm threatening?" Connor spread his arms out. "No one is out here but the three of us. On a good day—" This time he pointed at the sky. "If you haven't noticed, it's not a good day. So who would he be after?"

"I don't..." She bit off the remainder of the sentence, but he could tell by her frustration exactly what she'd been about to say.

"You don't know. You don't know who his target is." Great. Just *great*. She probably *was* with the government with this level of ineptitude.

"Not exactly. And it isn't my job to know. It's just my job to stop him. We spend the night, he puts more miles between us. He reaches that target, kills him and disappears. You don't know how hard it was to track him down in the first place."

He turned to face her, to stop their forward progress. "What do you know about this guy?"

"What I need to," she retorted.

But he didn't think so. "You don't know *anything* about this guy." Not a question. Clearly, she was acting in the dark.

"I know he's the guy I'm after. That's all I need to know."

"CIA? Some stupid offshoot where the minute you screw up you're out on your butt? I'd say FBI, but that mouth of yours wouldn't last a day."

She raised her eyebrows, let out a low whistle. "Man, what exactly happened when you left the SEALs? They mess you up? Didn't give you the sendoff you'd come to think you deserved?"

"Keep trying." She'd never guess, and he had to be careful to guard his temper so it didn't come spilling out, all pointless vitriol that didn't change a damn thing.

Nothing she was involved in changed what had happened, and it certainly didn't help that she was connected, no matter how much ancient history, to Nate Averly.

Which was all over and done and not what mattered in the here and now. He jabbed a finger in her direction. "You need me. You can't track him out here on your own. Not when a storm's about to unleash. So, pretend like you're going to run off. Two things will happen—you either come crawling back, or you freeze to death."

"Actually, there's a third option." She nodded meaningfully at Froggy.

Connor's hands tightened on the leash and he couldn't

old back a sneer. "You try to touch my dog, I won't be responsible for what I do in return."

She rolled her eyes. "Take it easy, hotshot. You got responsible etched into the fiber of your being."

He wanted to shout. To fight. He *wanted* to turn back the clock and make a whole bunch of different decisions. Ones that kept this woman far, *far* away from him.

But he couldn't do that, and shouting and fighting was a waste of energy when they were facing tough roads ahead.

Someone had to be even-tempered. *Someone* had to do the right thing. And that someone was him. Beginning and end of story. *Always.*

"He's either going to have to find shelter himself, or he's going to die of the elements. I know this mountain. I know those clouds. Unless his target is within a five-mile radius of him, he can't get to anyone before this storm hits. That I can guarantee you."

For the first time Sabrina didn't retort right away. She looked up at the sky, kept quiet and seemed to really *consider*.

"Guarantee, huh?" She studied him skeptically.

He nodded. "If he knows what he's doing, and based on what we've seen, I think he does. He knew how to fake an injury by rappelling down a cliff. He knew how to take off and disappear when you were about to get to him. He's not out here by accident. He's out here by design. So, let's take the leap he knows what he's doing. He's going to camp. It's what I'd do. Even if my target was close. Because no matter how close the target, if you can't finish them off, there's no point risking giving yourself away."

"He gave himself away when he shot at us."

"Only because we were already after him. What if the target doesn't know he's a target?"

"I don't think they do."

Connor nodded. "Then he's got time. Or thinks he does
We're a wrinkle, but again, storm's coming. Maybe he'll
assume we're not as smart as him. Maybe he won't. But
you don't survive, you can't kill the people and get the
payoff. Right?"

She scowled, not answering the question, which he
knew meant he'd scored a point.

"And if *you* don't survive, you can't stop the guy." He
tapped his temple. "So, use your head."

"I'd like to use your head as a battering ram," she muttered, clearly because she couldn't out-reason him. Not
when he was right.

But all that scowling and irritation melted off her face
and she smiled brightly up at him. "You got a tent built
for two in that big pack of yours?"

Hell.

SABRINA KNEW SHE'D scored a point when Connor's superior
expression went a little lax. Because naturally he'd have
a tent, but one of those flimsy backpacking deals meant
to be light and certainly not built to shelter two people.

Especially when one of the people was as tall and broad
as he was.

But he recovered, quickly enough. "We'll need a lookout anyway, just in case your friend decides to take some
interest in us. We'll take turns. Froggy will rest when I do."

"Don't trust me with your dog?"

"Lady, I don't trust you with my *hat*."

She smirked, because it wasn't precisely true. He was
trusting her with some things or he wouldn't be here. Still,
the wind was screaming and her pack was damn heavy.
There hadn't been any snow or other precipitation yet, but
Sabrina figured it was a matter of time.

She'd survived just as bad, if not worse, and sometimes

alone. Bad weather, cold weather didn't scare her. Didn't mean she was going to enjoy herself overnight.

"We need to find a good place to camp. Some shelter from the wind. Some cover from the hit man wandering about."

"Not wandering. Whatever he's doing. He's got a plan." That she was sure of now. "Unless he had a gun on him when you lifted him up?"

"He didn't," Connor said gravely, ducking his head against the wind as he headed forward toward another cluster of boulders. "Could have had a knife or something on him, but no gun. I would have felt it when I boarded him."

Sabrina nodded though she knew he couldn't see her. Still, it proved her point. "He had a gun hidden up here. Did he have something on him that could have been ammo?"

Connor's stride didn't hitch, but she sensed him go back over the course of events. "He had stuff in his pockets. I didn't pat him down."

"So, he could have had the ammo he picked up—which is how I tracked him. Gun hidden somewhere up here on the mountain."

Connor stopped and turned to look at her. He had to raise his voice against the howling wind. "Why the fake rescue then?"

That was the question.

He shook his head and went back to hiking. "You don't know either."

"No. I don't. But it's something we should think about. He didn't have a gun. Then he had one."

"I still maintain it could be two different guys."

"But you know it's not."

When he didn't respond to that, she figured it was as good as assent. But *why the fake rescue* was something she hadn't had time to fully turn over in her mind yet. "What if the target is someone in SAR?"

This time Connor came to an abrupt halt. Then he shook his head. "Why the hell would you say that?"

"Because the only way the fake rescue makes sense—having that kind of contact with people in an uncontrolled situation without a gun—is to see how someone would be rescued or who would be doing the rescuing. Don't know why a hit man would care about the first. We both know why a hit man would care about the second."

Connor started walking again. He said nothing, didn't even grunt. Sabrina had to assume that meant he was thinking about it. So, Sabrina continued to roll it over in her mind.

"You got any cops or the like in your group? That seems the most obvious option. Someone in law enforcement. Someone who could have ticked off some criminals."

"No one who's in current law enforcement. Possibly someone has it in their history. I'm not in charge of hiring, so unless someone mentioned it, I wouldn't know."

"Could you find out?"

"I'd have to use that fancy phone of yours."

Sabrina considered it. "No, we don't want to raise any red flags." Elsie might be able to look into it, if she wasn't caught up in Holden's mission. Sabrina would send her a text later.

"Here," Connor said. "We'll camp here."

She didn't care for the *order*, like he was in charge of her or something. She surveyed the area. Flat. Sort of. Surrounded on most sides by boulders. It would certainly protect them from the wind. She turned in a slow circle looking at higher ground. She didn't see any good places that someone would be able to get a shot off from. Granted, those peaks and cliffs could be concealing places to hide or shoot from, but she didn't think they were going to get a better spot.

"You really think stopping is our best course of action?" Normally she would have flat-out argued with him about it, but he was the expert when it came to this stuff, and he'd brought up some good points earlier. She was torn. Not certain.

Something she really hated.

"It's the *only* course of action."

Sabrina rolled her eyes, but she didn't argue with him. Dark was encroaching. God, she was cold. And tired. And *hungry*. Taking care of her basic needs would allow her to complete her mission without making a critical mistake.

Didn't mean stopping and waiting suited her any.

Before Connor did anything he pulled some contraption out of his pack, which turned out to be a foldable water and food bowl for the dog. He filled both, and Froggy eagerly ate and drank to her heart's content.

Only then did Connor set about securing them some shelter. He set a little tarp down then put his backpack on it and began to spread out supplies.

"What can I do?"

He looked up at her as if surprised she could be helpful. Cooperative. And, okay, his surprise was probably warranted. Working with a partner didn't come naturally to her, especially one whose skills outmatched hers in this one small particular area.

Still. She could do what she had to do to survive. Even be helpful and ask questions.

"I'll get the tent set up. You can handle food. I've got an MRE in each of our packs. Probably be good for us both to do the heating up rather than eat them cold."

"An MRE. I haven't had one of those in eons. I didn't miss them." The ready-to-eat meals that had been part of her military career did not inspire excitement for the meal ahead.

"They'll keep you full."

"I know what they'll do," Sabrina muttered. She pulled out the tarp Connor had made her pack back at his cabin. She spread it out to keep herself from having to kneel or sit in the snow.

She got out the MRE pouches from her pack and then Connor's and followed the instructions to utilize the flameless heater to warm the food while Connor built up the flimsy-looking tent.

"That thing going to hold in all this wind?"

He stepped back and studied his work. "That's why we camped here. Won't keep us out of the wind completely, but the boulders should block the worst of it. Sleeping in shifts won't just be to keep a watch for our hit man, it'll be imperative to make sure the winds don't damage the tent."

She handed him the warm part of his MRE and he took a seat next to her on the spread-out tarp, though kept enough space between them to almost be laughable. Sabrina was about to make a joke about sharing body heat, but Froggy curled up in between them, which turned out to be a nice warmth.

Darkness was encroaching, spreading across the world around them. The stars winked to life, bright beacons of peace. Sabrina didn't care much for peace or stillness. Much as she'd love to appreciate the beauty of a night sky spread out before her without being dimmed by city lights or human interference, the quiet and the stillness required often led to reflection.

Sabrina tried to avoid reflection at all costs. It made her think about her father, and how even though she'd cut off all ties, even though he'd been a terrible dad, she'd mourned when she'd heard he'd died.

It made her think about how she'd put everything she was into becoming a navy SEAL. So sure it would be the thing that magically made her feel *right* in her own skin. In this world.

It made her think about the pain of her injury. Which made her think about Nate. And how the man next to her knew and had been a SEAL side by side with Nate. What were the chances?

The world was small because whatever higher power was up there sure liked messing with people.

"Does search and rescue make up for it?" she found herself asking, when she knew she shouldn't. But star shine was as good as a couple whiskey shooters in her world. Loosened her tongue and her inhibitions. Made her feel big and bright and too aware of the loneliness inside of her she'd been burying since her mother had died when she'd been five.

"Make up for what?" Connor asked roughly.

"You know what."

He heaved out a sigh. She couldn't see him in the dark. He was just a faint shadow in the silvery light of stars and moon. But she sensed…a similar restlessness inside of him.

Or you're cold and tired enough to be delirious.

"Doing SAR… At first, it helped. Suddenly not being able to *do* anything was hard, so search and rescue felt like doing. Now, I think it's better than anything I could have done as a SEAL."

"You're saving dummies who didn't follow directions."

Connor snorted out a laugh. "Sometimes, sure, but those dummies are just people who overestimated their own abilities. Haven't we all been there?"

"You're nicer than I am, Con."

"No doubt."

And she'd blame it on the stars that it made her feel a

little mushy toward him. Though he took care of that pretty quick as the stars shone and the wind howled and the first flakes of snow began to fall.

"I think I know who the target could be," Connor said quietly. So quietly she almost convinced herself he hadn't spoken at all.

"Oh yeah? Someone on SAR, yeah? You should probably contact them. Forewarned and all that."

"Right."

Sabrina dug her phone out of her pocket. "Here."

He shook his head. "Don't need it."

When she only stared at him in confusion, he huffed out a breath.

"Buy a clue, Sabrina."

Chapter Eight

"You?" Sabrina demanded. "Why you?"

Connor rubbed a gloved hand over his face. Both were cold. Because of the weather. Because ever since she'd said the target could be someone on his team he'd known...

"Law enforcement aren't the only people who make enemies." Not that he'd understood he *had* enemies, but it made sense. More sense than Iona being some kind of target.

"Explain."

It was an order, and he didn't have to obey any orders from this woman, but it seemed they both had information the other needed. She knew something more about this hit man than she'd let on, and he knew...

Nate had warned him, hadn't he? That they were in danger. That getting rid of them hadn't been enough for whoever was pulling the strings.

Connor had listened to his friend and convinced himself Nate had paranoia born of PTSD. But this fit every single thing Nate had said that Connor had brushed off as the ravings of someone who needed professional help.

It made his stomach twist and turn, but he'd been warned that he could be a target. He just hadn't listened. "And if it's connected to me, it's connected to Nate. He'd be a target too."

"What?" Sabrina demanded. She got to her feet and began to pace. "Explain this."

"I'm not sure I know how." His own mind reeled with possibilities, and had since he'd begun to work through the options. It didn't *quite* make sense, but it made more sense than anything else.

"Try," she gritted out through clenched teeth.

He noted she was *working* to keep a lid on her temper, which he knew meant this was important. But the truth was words escaped him. There was only feeling and instinct.

He could be wrong. God, he hoped he was wrong, but this was the kind of thing he'd always been waiting for. Not a hit man. Not the *danger* Nate had always been going on and on about, so much Connor had pulled away, called him less and less, answered his calls less and less. Until they were barely friends.

But he'd always been subconsciously waiting for something from that confusing time to pop up and finally make sense.

"I'm not sure I can work out exactly *why* I'd be a target, but if I line up all the evidence, I'm the only one who fits. The truth is, I've always wondered, waited for…something. Not a hit out on me, but *something*. Because the way Nate and I were not so honorably discharged has never set quite right with me."

She stopped pacing and just stared at him, even though she couldn't have seen the expression on his face in the dark any more than he could see hers. "You said you were injured. That's why—"

"I lied," Connor sad flatly. "I've had to lie. I was *told* to lie." Which was why he hadn't gone home like Nate had. Lies didn't come easily to Connor, so he'd had to carve out a new, isolated life away from his family and the people he'd want to tell the truth to.

"That doesn't make any sense."

"No, it didn't. It doesn't," Connor agreed. He was ↓oing his level best to remain calm, to reason this out, ↓nd weirdly Sabrina...helped. She was all edges and angles ↓nd he felt the need to be calm and smooth in response.

"Start at the beginning. If you weren't injured, why ↓ere you discharged?"

"Nate and I were part of an operation. A lot of ground-↓ork in this village. Nate thought he had an in with a ci-↓ilian. He—*we*—trusted the wrong guy. We learned this ↓esulted in a major intel breach. We were blamed, ousted, ↓hen told to pretend it was an injury that ended our SEAL ↓areers."

"That doesn't make any sense. Doesn't the military love ↓scapegoat?"

"Yeah, they do. That's why it never set right. Why not ↓ust...blame us and be done with it? Sure, you'd have to do ↓he trial thing, but if it was true—wouldn't they win the ↓rial? Why did we have to pretend? It always felt...wrong. ↓ike we'd stumbled into something bigger than what we ↓ere doing. Or knew we were doing."

Sabrina was quiet for a while, and Connor felt the need ↓o...fill in the silence. He didn't want to tell her about Nate, ↓bout how little he'd believed him. Not so much because ↓t hurt his pride to be wrong, but because she could very ↓ell have the same opinion he'd held for so long.

"Nate's always said there was more to it, and to watch ↓ny back. The more I settled into my life here, the less I ↓elieved him. But the guy coming when *I'd* rescue him? ↓When no one else was out that far on the trail? It adds up." *Hell*. It added up. Nate had been right. Not paranoid. *Right.*

"Couldn't someone else in your SAR group have some ↓secret they're hiding? I'm not discounting your story, I

just don't understand... What I know doesn't make sens
with the military."

Connor let himself consider, beyond his own persona
feelings and instincts. "Possible, but not probable. If thi
hit man or whoever did their homework enough to know
who they'd have rescue them, the group is small. Ion
is our only helicopter pilot—and the location was prett
much only reachable quickly by helicopter. She doesn'
have anything in her background. I'd know."

There was a slight, tense pause. "Would you?"

"Yeah, I would." Uncomfortable with her implication
God knew why, Connor rubbed a gloved hand over Frog
gy's head. "We've been working together since I started
She's got a husband and three kids. We spend a lot of tim
together." Frustrated he felt the need to defend himsel
he grumbled the rest. "I'm her youngest kid's godfathe
for Pete's sake. I'd know if she had something going on."

"Would she know the same about you?"

Connor considered. "She wouldn't know what, but I'
bet a lot of money if someone asked her if I had somethin
lurking in my past, she'd say yes."

"There's no one else who would have been called ou
to rescue?"

"Today? No. I was on call for this precise sort of thing
through the end of the week. We don't exactly publiciz
our schedule, but it wouldn't be hard to find out either. I'n
the only full-time guy on our crew."

"So you really make the most sense, even aside from
your macho pride."

She said it so glibly, it poked at his temper. "My..
You're a real piece of work, Sabrina."

"Yeah, don't forget it. So, you get blamed for an inte
breach. You and Nate. No one else in your team?"

"No. We were the only ones involved in communicating with this civilian."

"You know anything about the civilian?"

"Aside from the fact he's likely a terrorist, and the name he gave us was fake, no."

"You're blamed for this breach. Dishonorable discharge, but they tell you to fake an injury."

Connor debated the rest of it. He wasn't sure she needed the truth about Nate when this was about him. Except if it *was* about him, it'd be about Nate too. Nate might be a target too. He might not know who Sabrina worked for, but stopping this hit man was more important than pretty much anything at this point.

"I was told to fake an injury. Nate didn't have to."

"What?" Sabrina said, a breathlessness like she'd been delivered a blow. Maybe she still had feelings for Nate. That certainly shouldn't *bother* Connor. And didn't. At all.

"The informant, or supposed informant, had shot him. I was discharged and sent back to the States before Nate was. He had to recover. They told me not to contact him, so I assume they told him the same."

"But you did."

"Of course I did. He went home to Montana and…" Connor wasn't comfortable with the level of subterfuge he'd used to contact Nate. It had been for the sake of Nate's paranoia, but Connor had done it. Now, it seemed he'd actually made the right choice. "I made sure no one would be able to find out I did, but we got in touch. We both knew it was fishy, but neither of us knew what to do about it." Nate had wanted to press. To investigate secretly. To wage their own war. Connor had suggested gently he see the therapist at the rehabilitation facility he was at.

He couldn't feel guilty about that now. There was no

time for it. But he also didn't need to let Sabrina in on the specifics. "We agreed to let it go. Get on with our lives."

Sabrina laughed. Which was so incongruous to the situation, Nate could only stare at her shadow in the dark. "Why are you *laughing*?"

"I mean, maybe Nate had a personality transplant, but if he didn't, there's no way that stubborn mule let *anything* go."

Connor sighed. Then just rested his head in his hands. "No, he didn't let it go. I just didn't believe him."

SABRINA FELT SOME sympathy for Connor. The resignation in his voice was guilt and blame, heaped only on himself. But she didn't have time to try and deal with the feeling. "So, Nate keeps digging. Whatever and whoever was hiding something, well, they'd have a reason to silence you two, wouldn't they?"

"I... I guess. I don't know. Silence us? We don't know anything."

"They sure think you do." Whoever *they* were. And how did it connect to the military? "Jeez, this is a cluster. But I need to share it with my group."

"You're with the government."

He said it so flatly, so devoid of any and all emotion it was almost comical. Especially since he was wrong. She could have let him think it. Part of her thought she should, just to prove she didn't have a soft spot. But she *did* have one. Sadly for her, an epically big one for do-gooders. "No, you're safe there."

"So, what then?" he asked suspiciously. "Not a cop. Not the government."

"I work for a private group. With private interests— ones that work for the good guys. Only and always."

"Like the bad guy is ever that clear-cut."

"Maybe not, but it can be." She'd never doubted North Star. The work they'd done to take down the Sons of the Badlands hadn't always been clear-cut, but taking down a vicious, powerful group had been. And they'd done it.

Then they'd gotten involved in whatever this was. They'd stopped a weapons dealer, and now they had to stop some hit men. *Men.*

"Nate would be the other target." She frowned. Connor had said Nate had headed back home to Montana. But Holden had been dispatched to Nebraska. She might have thought that was a false alarm, or a distraction, but Shay had the whole team with Holden. He'd found something too.

"You don't think there's another hit man out there after Nate?"

"There could be. Or our guy could be offing you first, then Nate." But that didn't fully make sense. Connor hadn't been digging. Had he? "You're not lying to me? About keeping your nose clean since you've been out."

"I never saw the point. Thought it was better to move on, but…"

"But what?"

"All they'd need to know was I kept in touch. With Nate. I kept tabs. On the team. On the brass. If anyone left the military, I'd get in contact and figure out what happened just in case it matched. It never has, but I haven't fully kept my nose out of it." Connor reached out and grabbed her arm. "You've got to use that magic phone of yours and get a message to Nate."

Sabrina shook her head, then realized he wouldn't be able to see it in the dark. "No, we have to be more careful than you've been about this."

He pulled his hand away. "Than *I've*—"

"I'm not blaming you." She cut him off quickly. "God

knows I would have blown it all up, not kept my wits about me. I'm just saying, now that we know there's a real threat, we have to be more careful than a phone call. It can't be traced on my end, but I don't know about Nate's. The message we get to him has to be done as carefully and untraceably as possible."

"And if there's someone out there right now five seconds away from pulling the trigger?"

Sabrina felt a pang—fear, concern and, worst of all, some sort of empathy for Connor worried about his friend. "We have to trust Nate's abilities. Once a SEAL, always a SEAL, right? Besides, if he's been poking into this, he has to know he's in some kind of danger."

"Maybe he thinks he's been careful."

"He knows better." God, Sabrina had to hope. "Look, the one thing we know is this isn't about…speed. They've taken their time. This hit man we're after has had his ammo for days. They're setting it up so it's airtight. Luckily for you, I saved your butt by coming along when I did."

"I think an avalanche saved my butt, thanks."

She appreciated the dig. It kept them on even ground. Kept her from feeling like she needed to reassure him. "I know it isn't easy to sit back. But we have to play this carefully. It's an operation with one goal. Keep everyone safe. Which we can't do if we panic. Here's where we rely on what we were and what we learned, and Nate's going to do the same. Nate *is* doing the same. I'm sure of it. Unless you have some reason to believe he wouldn't be?"

"No, I don't."

"Good." *Thank God.* Bad enough to have innocent blood on her hands, she'd rather not be responsible for collateral damage.

"I take it you're not still hung up on him or you'd have *some* kind of emotional response here."

The *no* was on the tip of her tongue. Even though she'd felt some guilt over the way she'd treated him, she'd accepted long ago that whatever she'd felt for Nate had been…immature. It never would have lasted even if she'd handled her injury well. But why did *Connor* need to know that? "What's it to you?"

"Nothing. Just commenting."

"Well, comment on this. I have a mission, and my personal feelings on *anything* don't matter. All that matters is we stop the hit man before he takes you or Nate out. Now, if you'll excuse me, I have a call to make."

Not that she had anywhere to go, but she walked as far away from him as she could in their little camp space, and got out her phone to call Shay.

When she got Betty, North Star's doctor, and a bunch of vague, try-again-tomorrow answers, she didn't swear or stomp or let on that she was dissatisfied.

She just went back to camp, and focused on what had to be done.

Chapter Nine

Chapter Nine

They took turns sleeping and watching out, even as the storm dumped inches of snow and icy winds on them. There was no other choice when it came to the weather, and Connor supposed there was no other choice when it came to what he now knew.

Connor figured all the revelations of the evening gave him an element of trust in Sabrina he might not have had otherwise. He knew too much. She knew too much. There was no separating now. Especially with the storm raging around them.

As for letting go of his stress and worry enough to sleep for a few hours, well, he was well versed in that. They both were well versed in that and having a few hours of rest prepared them for another long day of hiking.

They didn't talk. Not when they cleaned up the campsite or started out again. Connor quietly gave Froggy the order to track. She was trained to find bodies—live and otherwise—buried in the snow, but that didn't mean she wouldn't be able to suss out a man on a mountain when there was only the three of them.

And if the hit man *was* after him, Connor doubted he'd gone far.

So, they hiked. Through as much cover as they could find. The only difference between today and yesterday was the sky was a clear blue. The sun shone and the air was frigid since they kept climbing in elevation.

It was an absolutely breathtaking untouched world.

He wished he could enjoy it.

Instead, his mind twisted itself in circles trying to work out what he knew—or what some random hit man might *think* he knew—that could get him killed. Which led him to uncomfortable potentials Connor really didn't want to consider.

But didn't he need to? This wasn't civilian life anymore. He was being thrust back into his military one. Which meant turning off his emotions. Turning back into a soldier.

There was a time being a soldier had been natural. A time when he'd even enjoyed it. He found it no longer fit comfortably and he didn't know what to do about it except suck it up.

Which meant not being afraid of worst-case scenarios. "Nate could already be dead. And they could think he told me something."

He said it without working up to it, because he didn't know how to soften the blow of that possibility for himself. She'd been unaffected by Nate's involvement yesterday, so she either truly didn't care about her ex, or she was an excellent actress.

He didn't care either way.

But she stopped dead in her tracks as the words seemed to sink in. "That's worst-case scenario," she said carefully. Like she was weighing every word before she said it.

"Yeah, it is. But it makes more sense to me than anything." Connor shut off the part of himself that wanted to pre-grieve. No use before he knew anything. "Why come after me first?"

"Because you're the easier target? As a warning? Especially if you don't actually know anything. You don't know how deep Nate is into this."

"It'd help if we did. If we got in contact with him."

She was walking again, trudging through the snow with that overly heavy pack. But they were past the casual bickering and sniping they'd started off with. This was serious now.

"I'm working on it," Sabrina said. She didn't sound so much defensive as...irritated.

"You need to work faster."

"Look, if he's already dead, too late. If he's not, we have to be careful we don't lead the hit man to him. Are you sure they'd be able to find him?"

"They found me."

"You work in the public, Connor. I bet your pretty face is splashed all over your SAR group's website. What does Nate do?"

Connor hesitated to answer, because it was irritating she had a point. "He's at a ranch in his hometown," he grumbled.

"A ranch? I mean obviously I knew Nate before you, but back in the day his plans were definitely not go home to the family ranch in nowhere Montana."

"It's not his family's. It's...a ranch for injured military guys. A rehab type facility."

"Oh, so you're telling me he's *surrounded* by other military guys and you're all alone? Gee, I wonder which one I'd off first."

"Because you can predict how a hit man, potentially working for the US military to off its former soldiers, would think, act and plan?"

"First, it's not the military. Not saying the guys involved might not be *in* the military, but there's no way the brass sent a hit man after you when you don't even know anything. Unless they themselves were involved in something shady."

"You so sure about that?"

"Based on what I know? Yeah. I am. Just like I know my next suggestion is going to sound crazy, but I think we should—"

But her words were cut off by a sharp, decisive bark from Froggy. Connor grabbed Sabrina's shoulder and pushed her down into a crouch. They both had their guns ready, eyes scanning the blinding white around them.

"I don't see anything."

"She might just smell a track, a campsite or something like that. But we'll want to proceed with caution."

Sabrina sent Froggy a sidelong glance. "You don't want to send her forward first."

"Worried about my dog, Sabrina?"

She scowled. "Just saying. If she can give you some idea of direction, I'll go first. Maybe I can pick up some tracks."

"Just a big old softie, aren't you?"

"Trying to protect your dog here. You really want to make fun of me over it?"

"Kind of." And only because the fact she'd care about Froggy's well-being made him feel a little too soft toward this woman currently upending his life.

Or saving it.

Yeah, he wasn't going to think like that. He crouched next to Froggy, stroked her head, and murmured a few commands to her. The dog sniffed the ground, began to catch a scent. Connor held her back. "This way."

Sabrina went ahead, searching the ground with an interminable attention to every detail. He'd never seen her so careful or still. Each move was measured. Controlled. All that energy usually pumping off of her contained.

It was fascinating. Way too appealing. Especially when

despite the layers and packs, it was no challenge to imagine the lithe, athletic body beneath.

"Kind of a dead end here. But look." She pointed ahead of them a few yards. There was a small cave mouth at the base of two boulders.

"That'd be a good place to camp. Especially last night."

"It'd also be a good place to hide right now," Sabrina replied. "You got a light handy?"

Connor nodded and pulled the flashlight from its loop on his backpack. She held out a hand for it, but he ignored her and turned the light on himself, inching toward the cave mouth. He stayed on one side of the opening, and Sabrina stayed on the other, weapon at the ready.

She kept Froggy behind her, and again Connor had to pretend that sort of thing didn't matter to him. He crouched, inched into the cave as soundlessly as possible.

The air was colder in here, but there was no wind, so it was definitely protected. Damp, but if you had the right gear that'd be okay. His light swept carefully over the dark space.

"Clear," Connor said. The opening was small enough he didn't see anywhere someone could hide. And the remains of a campfire were in the middle, long since put out. Connor crouched next to it as Sabrina and Froggy entered the cave too.

He touched the fire remnants. "Cold."

"Must have been up earlier than us."

"It's cold enough in here it wouldn't take long to cool the embers off. Or he could have had a fire last night and not this morning. A lot of options." Connor sat back on his haunches and considered. He didn't really know where to go from here. They could keep following the guy, but it seemed like they'd continue to be just out of reach.

Until the hit man decided to make the hit, he supposed. "What was your crazy plan?"

"I'm not sure he knows that the people he shot at are me and you. Me, maybe. You? Why would he?"

"He knew I wanted to rescue him."

"Sure, but would he assume you'd keep searching for him? When it was obvious he'd run away on his own two feet?"

"Then where's he going? Higher and higher. That's not the way to me."

"No, it's not. Not to you *here*." Sabrina agreed. Too easily. "But wouldn't this, in a roundabout way, lead back to your cabin?"

Connor tried not to jerk at how right on she was. Because if he thought about the mountain terrain, the direction they were going, the easy thing would have been to get to his cabin the way they'd *left* his cabin. But going this way would also lead to the same general area, but with a lot of tree cover.

"So, what are you suggesting we do?" Connor asked, still staring at the blackened remains of a fire.

"Stop chasing him higher. Stop exhausting ourselves. I say we go back to your cabin and wait for him to come for us."

"Stop chasing. Wait for him to come for us."

"Yes, those are the words I just said." The way Connor repeated them, like they were so foreign he didn't even know what they meant, almost made her laugh.

"You're the one who—"

"The original plan was to follow him, stop him, yeah. Then I figured out *you* were the target. Things have changed. What do we get out of chasing him?"

"Knowing where he is."

"We know he's after you. Isn't that enough? We go back to your cabin. Hunker down for the duration. Set up some traps of our own. Maybe even convince him we *don't* know he's after you. That you were never out here chasing him." She'd have a chance to get a real hold of Shay or *someone* at North Star who could send her some backup.

"He saw us. He has to know—"

"At best, he saw two figures. If he'd had any kind of scope or binoculars, one of us would be dead."

Connor shook his head. "You know that isn't true. *You* knew something was about to happen. That's why I'm not dead. You knew something was wrong and pushed me down."

An odd satisfaction swept over her. She didn't need external praise. Didn't need anyone else to see she'd done her job and tell her, but it was weirdly…nice that he understood she had been the one to save his life. "Maybe."

"Maybe," he snorted irritably. "Yes, that is what happened." He stood up from the crouch, though he had to tilt his head to one side not to hit it on the cave ceiling.

"Okay, that's what happened. Still, that doesn't mean he knows that you were his original target. If he knows who I am, he might have thought you were someone working with me. There's a lot of what-ifs. But if he is after *you*, and I don't think that's one of our ifs, following him doesn't do much for us. He'll always have higher ground, a head start, and the upper hand. Why not make him come to us?"

"So, you want to go back to my cabin and hide?"

"I want to go back to your cabin and lay a trap, Connor. It's tactical. I wouldn't mind being tactical *and* warm, would you?" She looked at the dog. She could probably handle it, what with the fur and training and all, but Sabrina couldn't help but feel sorry for the animal. "I think Froggy and I are in the same boat."

He huffed out a breath. "And what if we go back to my cabin. Fortify, lay a trap, whatever. What prevents him from going off to take out Nate?"

"Time? Distance? At some point, he's going to figure out we've figured him out, which means he'll realize he's got to get rid of us before we can tell Nate he's a target too."

"Which you refuse to do."

"I don't refuse to do it. I just know we have to do it carefully, and you know, I can be a lot more careful getting messages if I'm in a house with electricity."

"That's *if* all our guessing is right."

She wanted to pummel him, but she took a deep breath and slowly let it out. She'd keep her calm. She had to. "Yeah. Sometimes you've got to take decisive action on what information you've got. Maybe it's wrong. But what's the other option?"

He was quiet for a long while, his gaze on the dog standing between them. Sabrina didn't know if he was thinking about her, or just thinking in general, but she waited. Pestering him into agreeing with her wasn't going to work. So, she bit her tongue and waited.

She really tried to wait.

"Look. If we go back to your cabin, I can probably get some backup. Not right away or anything, but maybe a team. We could surround the place, and—"

"A *team*?"

Sabrina tried not to wince. "Yeah, a team."

"Why don't you have a team right now?" he demanded angrily. Though it was undercut by the way he had to keep his head to the side to stand in this cave.

Sabrina thought about Holden. She didn't know anything about the lead he'd found. She'd think it had something to do with Nate, but why Nebraska? "Was there anyone else in on this thing with you and Nate? Anyone else who would be a target?"

"Yeah, change the subject," he muttered irritably, but he eventually answered her question. "We had a team of sixteen, but we worked in partners. Nate was mine. No one else was discharged when we were. It seems unlikely they've got a hit man out there trying to take out an entire navy SEAL team. Especially when a good half of us are still SEALs."

"And you know that because…?"

"Because I keep track."

"Uh-huh."

"It's not the same as digging into what happened."

"Isn't it?"

"What about this *team*, Sabrina?"

"They're currently occupied. But by the time we get back to your cabin, who knows?"

"Who knows. Shouldn't you know?"

"Look, I'm not going to stand here watching you get a crick in your neck while we argue about this. My plan is to go back to your cabin and make our guy come to us. You got a better one?"

He stood there glowering, there was no other word for it, and even with his head cocked at an awkward angle that glower had some *effect*. Too bad it was all south of the border effects.

"Come on, Connor. Let's go set a trap."

Chapter Ten

Connor hated feeling out of his element. Like he was walking through some maze he didn't know all the parts to. But Sabrina had a point with one thing—he didn't have a better plan.

Besides, if they got back to his cabin, *he* could get his own message to Nate. Regardless of all her concern. Back home, he'd have access to communications and making some of his own decisions, with or without Sabrina's agreement.

So, it made sense to leave the cave and hike back to his cabin. Or if not *sense*, it was the only option. They could keep hiking after the hit man, but to what end? A standoff they couldn't control? A trap of the hit man's own?

"He won't expect this, you know," Sabrina pointed out as they hiked through the quietly sunny day. The wind was still bitterly cold, but only blew occasionally. It might have been an enjoyable walk.

If not for all the impending death hanging around them.

But she was right. This was not the expected response. The guy had to know he was being tracked. A sudden about-face would leave him confused.

But Connor wasn't fully convinced that would work in their favor even as he led Sabrina back to his cabin. "Won't he know we're trying to trap *him*?"

"Maybe." Sabrina shrugged next to him as if she didn't have a care in the world. "But as long as he's here, playing our game, that means he's nowhere near Nate. Doesn't it?"

"There could be two."

"There could be." Sabrina took a deep breath, squinted at the world around him. "Look. I work for this private group, right? I was sent here looking for this hit man. It's a long, complicated story, but basically I was tracking the ammo for this gun, and very little information from another group. But it wasn't just me or this guy. Another one of my teammates was sent to Nebraska to track another shipment of ammo. Another hit man."

"Nebraska? But—"

"There *are* two hit men. The other one is in Nebraska. So, he's either after someone else, or Nate isn't in danger yet."

"That doesn't make sense. Nate wouldn't be hard to track." He'd gone to his hometown. Surely that would make him even easier pickings than Connor himself. "Maybe there's a third."

"Maybe there is, but he'd be using different ammo and a different MO? Doesn't add up. Maybe this doesn't all make sense big picture, but small picture? That's what we've got to work with."

She spoke and moved with a confidence Connor couldn't find within himself. Had he gone soft? Was that the price of civilian life?

"How'd you get involved in this group?" Maybe if he understood her, her group, this whole *operation*, he might find that confidence again. That sure footing. Because it wasn't about trust. He had to search and rescue with people he didn't necessarily *trust*, but he understood what both parties were after. He knew all about their training.

Sabrina was a big question mark. And she'd probably stay that way.

"You don't have to worry about my group. We're on the up-and-up. I promise you that."

"My life and my friend's life are on the line here. Why should I just trust some stranger's promise? Would you?"

She seemed to ponder that. "No, I wouldn't. It'd take a lot for me to trust anything. I get it. And this goes better if we trust each other." She blew out a breath. "Getting involved with my group goes back to when I got hurt. The recovery would take too long to keep my place in my SEAL class. I could have stuck it out, worked hard and maybe stayed in the navy, but… I'd wanted to be a SEAL. There was no runner-up that would have satisfied me at the time. I was young. I was angry. And I'd lost the one goal I'd ever set myself, aside from get the hell off my dad's farm."

He listened, tucking away the details he didn't know if she was purposefully giving him to build that layer of trust, or if she was just letting things slip. But she wasn't the kind of person who let things slip, so he had to believe the first.

She mentioned her father's farm, she mentioned how much the SEALs meant, because she was allowing him to understand this enough to believe her. To trust her.

Sneaky, because if they really trusted each other, going their own way without the other knowing about it would come with guilt.

"Your dad's farm. Not your family farm?"

She laughed. Bitterly. "It was never mine. Some people have families, I suppose. The real kind. Some people are just separate entities sharing the same space until one can escape."

Connor couldn't say he knew what that was like, so he kept his mouth shut.

"My crappy childhood isn't the point. Except that it's

why the SEALs was so important to me. I didn't just want to escape and the military was there. I wanted to do something big. I wanted to be *elite*. A middle finger to the old man. So, losing that, it was a failure on a lot of levels, and this may come as a surprise to you as I'm such a retiring, rule-following paragon of womanhood now."

Connor snorted.

"But I blew up my entire life. Top to bottom. Nate tried to be sweet about it. Which was the worst thing to do, for me, in that situation. So, I kicked him to the curb, and I just…took off. Didn't realize I was headed back to that godforsaken farm until I was crossing the Kansas border. Since I wasn't that much of a masochist, I took a sharp left north instead and ended up in South Dakota. Got a job at a gas station. Got in fights at bars at night to work out all that anger. Picked a fight with the wrong guy."

"Surprised to hear you admit you could come up against the wrong guy."

"Oh, I kicked his butt, more or less, don't get me wrong. Just turned out this guy, who I'd just sliced with a broken bottle, had sort of been there done that in terms of being the young moron on the wrong path. He offered me a job."

She laughed, and it wasn't bitter. It was like she was recounting a fond memory. Of slicing a man with a broken bottle. Yeah, that seemed about right with this woman.

"Didn't believe him at first. Obviously. But he kept pestering me, got his boss to come meet me." She adjusted her pack a little as they walked. "He was… Older. Not old enough to be my dad, but had that…vibe, you know? Like when you have a horrible dad, you always have a vision of what a good one looks like, and he just…fit. Not paternal. He was straightforward and gruff, but said he'd done his research and thought I'd be a good fit. Believed in my skills. They both did. They had all this faith in what I could give to their group."

Connor could tell, even as she hurried to keep talking, that had been one of the most meaningful parts of her life. Not anything warm or fuzzy, but someone believing in her skills.

"Still didn't believe them, but I figured I could give it a shot and keep one foot out the door. Maybe even fight some people without getting myself thrown in jail. So, I did the first mission, then the second. Eventually, we did some real good in the world and I realized I believed them. And I belonged. And I knew, fully down-in-the-gut knew we were doing the right thing. And helping people."

She cleared her throat, sliding him a look. It wasn't calculating or anything. It was almost…embarrassed. It was that more than anything that made him believe she was giving him the full, unvarnished truth.

"There. Now you have my story. Sabrina Killian in a nutshell. Your turn."

He didn't have to tell her. That much Connor knew. And if he kept himself somewhat separate, or if he even made some stuff up to lie to her with, he'd have an easier time doing what he wanted to do.

But it felt wrong.

Connor didn't do a good job of hiding his thoughts. It was all over his face. She could practically *hear* him thinking, wondering if he should lie to her.

He could. Sabrina had faith that she'd know if he did. She also had a pretty good dose of faith that he'd tell her the truth. Guy was that true-blue Captain America type.

"My parents are pretty decent. Had too many kids for what they could afford, but they loved us. I didn't leave to escape, but I did leave to make something of myself. I get that. I wanted to make them proud."

It gave her a pang. Something like longing. Silly, to still wish she'd had what she never would.

"And you did," she supplied for him.

"I did. In fairness, I could have done just about anything and made them proud. Still, being something they could brag about felt good. And I got to be away from that crowded house, send some money home and see the world. Navy life and then SEAL life wasn't a joy or a picnic, but I felt like I was doing something…good. At first."

The *at first* surprised her when she didn't think he would. When she thought she had him pegged. "You're not saying you got disillusioned?"

"The missions I went on didn't leave room for much else. It's not like what you said about your…group. I didn't know I was fighting for the right side. It's too muddied. Too complicated. So, yeah, I was feeling a little disillusioned there. But I had a mission, and I was going to complete it. Do my time. Do the right thing."

Yeah, he was a man who would—always—do the right thing. She was a little surprised he'd been good friends with Nate. Nate was a good guy and all, but he'd had an edge to him. Like her, he'd had some…willingness to bend the rules. To follow their own drummer beats.

"I've told you the story. Nate finds this civilian he thinks is going to help, but instead the guy takes everything Nate tells him and gives it to his insurgent group." Connor's eyebrows drew together, even as he kept marching along. "It wouldn't have been enough for a serious intel breach. It just…wouldn't have. I was there. I would know."

Sabrina thought about it, like she'd been turning it over in her mind all night. "I have a theory. And that supports it. Maybe there was nothing you and Nate did wrong. Maybe someone else, higher up, was doing something wrong. And they framed you two."

"To what end?"

"To make it look like they'd found the bad guy. To get you out of the way. So, they could keep doing the bad thing. Your discharges didn't make sense. Nate's not the kind of guy who just accepts that—especially since he was the one trusting this civilian, and you got caught up in it. Nate's warped sense of responsibility wouldn't let that rest."

"Warped?"

She shook her head. She wouldn't argue semantics when her theory made *sense*. "Nate gets close to the truth, and he has to be taken out. Or threatened, depending on who the bad guy is and what they want. Silence. Cooperation."

"I don't know why they'd go after me first."

"No, I don't either."

"We have to get in touch with Nate. We *have* to."

"I agree." She still wanted to do it carefully, but the truth she believed at this point was that Connor was some kind of target because of Nate. Which meant getting an understanding of what Nate knew. What he'd done.

"You agree? No buts?"

"I still want to work out the best way to do it. The most careful way. If I'm right, Connor, Nate knows. He knows exactly the kind of danger he's in. What he might not know is that you're in danger too."

Connor glanced at her, a considering and not completely kind perusal. "You don't want to split his focus," he said flatly.

She didn't understand the tone of voice. Or the way her chest pinched. "It's not that simple."

"None of this is simple," Connor muttered.

"Exactly." She blew out a breath. "We have to—"

But Connor's arm shot out, stopping her progress. He

lifted his nose to the air, sniffed. Sabrina watched him in confusion, but took a deep sniff of mountain air too... except it wasn't just the smell of snow and pine needles.

"Smoke," Sabrina said, a shiver of fear working its way through her. "He's close?"

"That isn't campfire smoke." Connor jogged forward and climbed up onto a large boulder. She tried to follow, but she didn't have the same kind of climbing skill, and he'd left Froggy down here with her.

"What is it?" she demanded, rather than try to scramble up after him and leave the dog on her own.

He didn't answer her right away. He climbed down from the rock first. When he stood face-to-face with her, she saw a bleakness and a fury that had that shiver of fear working through her again.

"It's my cabin," he said, his voice gruff.

"What?"

"I can't see it from here, but I can see where the smoke is coming from. I'm willing to bet it's my damn cabin that's on fire." He started marching forward, long strides she had to scurry to keep up with.

"Connor."

"He set fire to my damn cabin," Connor said, shaking off her hand when she tried to grab him and stop his quickening pace.

"Connor, we can't go there."

He whirled on her. But all that fury and rage on his face disappeared after a few seconds. Like he'd carefully locked it all away. When he spoke, it was with a carefulness that made her...cold. "All my stuff. Froggy's food. I need—"

"We can't go back," Sabrina said, not sure why her voice was so *gentle*. "It's either a trap or a warning. Either way... Our hit man didn't get back to your cabin *that* fast. Did he?"

Connor seemed to consider. "We're still miles off. He'd had to have… No, he couldn't have gotten there *and* set a fire." He closed his eyes as if that could block out the bad news.

"There's more than one," Sabrina said out loud, even though she knew he'd figured it out himself. "Our hit man has backup. We can't go back. We have to…"

"Run away? Hide?" Connor demanded angrily.

She felt for him, she really did. Which wasn't comfortable…all this *empathy*. "We have to be smart. We have to be careful. For ourselves. For Nate." And she had to get rid of all these soft feelings careening around in her chest. "There's got to be somewhere we can go and…recalculate."

But he wasn't listening. She could tell he was somewhere else. Somewhere she understood. An impotent rage at things that were already done. He stood there, looking like fury personified, and her heart softened.

Very much against her will.

Chapter Eleven

Connor couldn't remember the last time he'd had to fight so hard against the rising tide of fury. Some nameless, faceless nobodies had set fire to his cabin. Though he couldn't actually see his cabin due to the rises and falls of the earth and how far away they were, he knew that rising smoke could only be that one thing.

He knew.

There was nothing else to set fire to around there, and setting a fire in the snow-covered woods would require so much work it wouldn't be worth it. But a house fire could be set from the inside out.

It was as senseless and frustrating as his sudden and confusing discharge had been, but not having to serve his final enlistment year had been something of a relief too. He'd been done with the SEALs, with the military, but was going to gut it out. Do his duty. Because it was the right thing to do. Nevertheless, there'd been no grief at it being ended early. Only confusion.

He wasn't done with his cabin. With his things. This was personal, beyond any of the offensive things that had happened to him in his discharge from the navy. This was personal, and there would be grief.

Sabrina touched his arm. Gently. Her expression was… sympathetic. It was the antithesis of everything she'd been up to this point and that... It wasn't good. It loosened things in his chest he couldn't afford to loosen.

"I'm sorry," she said, and her voice sounded like it belonged to someone else. Someone soft and kind. "Losing your cabin is..."

He stepped away from her hand. He looked down at Froggy to keep his focus where it needed to be. "My cabin isn't accessible by car or truck," he said, ignoring Sabrina's apologies. "They would have had to have something all-terrain. And since they're at my cabin, they've likely either destroyed my ATV or used it for themselves. I keep a Jeep at SAR headquarters in Wilson. Hiking there would take...days. At best."

She nodded, as if she understood both what he was saying, and what he was doing by putting some distance between them. "I'd say we could radio your SAR buddies, but—"

"No, they stay away. No one's getting shot at over me." Though he had some concerns that if news of his cabin burning down got out, they'd start looking for him. Iona definitely would. He needed to get a message to her to hold her off, but first they needed a plan.

"Any other cabins around here?" Sabrina asked.

"Here and there, but they've got people. They're too far and... Wait." Connor cut himself off as he remembered one place that might work. "There's a ranger cabin. Not close, but walkable." He eyed the sky, the area they were in. "We can probably get there before afternoon. The park rangers use it for summer interns so it should still be empty for a few more weeks. Not sure what kind of provisions it'll have, but we can set up there and figure things out."

"Lead the way."

He did. At a pace just shy of reckless. But the sooner

they got there, the sooner they could really sort this mess out. Contact Nate. Tell Iona to stay the hell away.

Would she? Connor had his doubts. So, he had to find a way to convince her he didn't need her help.

"What about the fire?" Sabrina asked while they hiked. When they were higher up, the smoke was visible, even though they were going in the opposite direction now. "Do you think emergency services will be called? Or that your friends might come looking for you?"

"News of the fire should take some time to spread. I'm pretty isolated. So, unless these guys set the fire and called the fire department, it's likely going to go out on its own before anyone notices. Especially with all this new snow and the avalanche. Hikers won't be out to see and call."

"You're *that* isolated?"

"Yeah."

"Interesting choice for a guy who says he's got a nice family."

It was none of her business, but it seemed they'd reached this place where they weren't strangers anymore. They knew each other's backgrounds. Motivations, to an extent. Hopefully it would help them work together, trust each other, because this was getting messier and more complicated by the minute.

"I didn't want to lie when I got home. Not to anyone's face. I'm not that great at it when it comes to people I care about. So, I found this place. I found SAR training. By the time my fake injuries would have healed, and I could have gone home without too many lies, I found I liked my solitude. I loved what I was doing. I visit my family when I want. They come to Jackson Hole in the summer. It works." It did, and because it did, a heavy weight of worry settled itself on his chest. Connor sucked in a breath, tried to think rationally. "You don't think they'd get roped into this, do you?"

"Obviously I can't promise you that, but if you've kept your distance? I don't see any reason to kill a bunch of innocent civilians. They wanted to scare you, they'd have done it already. You're a target, the kind they want to kill, not scare, because they must think you know something. They have to think you know something."

"We have to get in touch with Nate," Connor muttered. Knowing what she would say. "We have to know what he has. What he knows. What these people might think *I* know. Because if he doesn't know anything…"

"I think I've got an idea on that score. But I need to use my computer. How long do you think it'll take us to get to this cabin?"

"Good Lord, you're carrying a computer in there?"

"Small one. For emergencies. This counts."

He was going to question her about wifi, then thought better of it. If she got cell service out here, chances were her group had some sort of futuristic way to connect to the internet. "A good three hours. But even if we slow down, not more than four."

"Okay. And you really don't think anyone's going to know about the fire for that long?"

"It's unlikely. Highly unlikely."

Sabrina nodded. "Then let's book it."

Connor agreed, but that didn't mean he was going to wait for the cabin to hear how a computer was going to put them in touch with Nate any more untraceably than a phone call.

"So, what's the idea?"

"I've got a program on my computer that can send untraceable emails. If I can figure out a way to get Nate's email address, one he'll actually check, and use some kind of coded language to let him know what's going on, it's possible we can get a message to him—even one that's intercepted—that no one will think twice about. Something like that. But I've got to fiddle with my program."

"Nate's not big on email."

"Yeah, that's part of the problem. But maybe…someone he's living with is? I just need to sit down and do like thirty minutes of research and maybe we can get a lead on how to tug that line without putting him in danger's way. Or you."

"I'm already in danger's way apparently. You aren't worried about you? Or your group?"

"I'm a ghost, Con. Even if they find my name, they won't know who I work for or where I came from. But like you said, you have family. You have connections. So, we don't want them looking any harder at you than a double tap, you're dead."

He laughed. Couldn't help it. All the sympathy and kindness was gone and *thank God*. Her irreverence made him feel far more sturdy than her *emotion*. "You're a constant comfort, Sabrina."

She sent him that quicksilver grin. "I try."

SABRINA DIDN'T BOTHER wishing her pack was twenty pounds lighter. She didn't curse at the ache in her back. She didn't even grumble at Connor for this never-ending hike to some *supposedly* abandoned cabin.

It damn well better be after all this.

But she swallowed it all down, kept her complaints to herself, because she'd made her heavy pack bed, and now it was time to lie in it.

"Let's trade packs for an hour," Connor said. Casually. Deceptively casual.

"Not on your life," she returned, focusing on her breathing so it didn't sound all huffy and puffy like it actually was.

"You're slowing down," he said, and this time his voice was not casual. It was pointed.

And right on target, which stung her pride. She'd once carried heavier rucksacks across much more difficult terrain, but it wasn't something she had to do often with North Star. "I carry my weight."

"Stubbornly. With no regard as to if it's the smart thing to do."

"Pretty much."

He grumbled something under his breath, but he let it go. Sabrina wasn't letting herself check the time. It would just depress her how few hours they'd been at it, but she followed the path of the sun in the sky. It was past noon. They had to be getting close.

She still hadn't heard from anyone at North Star, and that made her edgier than she'd like. What she really wanted to do was get in contact with Elsie and get her advice on how to email safely, or even have Elsie do it. But if she was working on Holden's side of things, Sabrina was just going to have to trust her own instincts there.

Which made her nervous. Which made her irritable. She wanted to snap at Connor, but he looked a bit like he was about to snap himself. Too many unanswered questions.

They needed to talk to Nate. She should be thinking about that and only that. Though, she had to admit, watching Connor's butt was a nice distraction from the way her pack dug into her shoulders.

"There," Connor said, looking like some sort of god standing on a rock, pointing off into the distance. "See it?"

She climbed up on top of the rock with him and Froggy. She could make out a small, brown structure if she squinted. "How far you think that is?"

He eyed her. "Far enough."

Sabrina huffed out an irritated breath. "*Fine*. You win." She unsnapped her pack, shrugged it off and handed it to him. He handed her his, and they worked to adjust the straps on both their new packs.

Once it was on her back she scowled. "This isn't that much lighter."

"But lighter," he said. "Come on now, let's make good progress this last mile."

"*Mile*." Sabrina allowed herself one childish moan, but kept up with him and the dog as they hiked the remaining distance. The building they reached was small and clearly old. The yard around it was overgrown with grasses and summer wildflowers. There was a towering pine tree to the side that gave off considerable shade.

The porch creaked precariously as Connor walked up the stairs. He opened the storm door, then looked back at her. "I could break it down, but I'm going to go out on a limb and guess you probably know how to pick a lock."

She smiled at him and batted her eyelashes. "Your faith in me is *so* sweet." She dug the Swiss Army knife out of her pocket and then crouched next to the door and got to work.

When she swung the door open without any damage to the knob, she gestured Connor inside dramatically. "Entre."

"My hero," he said, deadpan. Which made her laugh. He stepped inside first, and she followed, eagerly dropping the pack off of her sore shoulders.

Connor did the same, then bent down to unclip Froggy's leash. Inside the house was dark, and a flip of the light switch did not do anything to alleviate dark or cold.

"Electricity must be shut off," Connor said. "I'll see if I can do anything about that, but for now figure out your computer stuff. I'm going to water and feed Froggy, then put together something for us to eat."

"Back to giving orders?" she asked, but it was a good-natured dig, because she was already pulling her computer out of her pack. Finding a way to carefully contact Nate was now her number one goal. "You said he's at a ranch? Or a rehab facility or something."

"Yeah. Both. In Blue Valley, Montana."

"I'll see what I can do." She tuned everything else out. Connor talking to Froggy. The lights suddenly coming on. She focused only on finding this rehab center—easy enough—and then a way to get a message that would be delivered to a man at such a place.

Once she thought she had a reasonable target to get a message to Nate, she opened the program Elsie had installed onto her computer a while ago. Sabrina hadn't fully listened to what the program did, but she knew whatever email she sent—usually to North Star staff—couldn't be hacked or traced.

Now, when she sent something to North Star, she knew it was going to a similarly safe program. Sending this email to Revival Ranch's contact email meant that someone could and would read it. But as long as they didn't track it back to North Star, or Sabrina's current location, it should be fine.

So, why did she feel so nervous?

Big stakes. Nerves were par for the course.

Before she figured out how to code a message to Nate, she wrote an email to Elsie about what she was doing with the hopes Elsie would be able to hack in and fix any mistakes Sabrina might make.

She thought about emailing Shay, or sending her yet another text, but she mentally talked herself out of it. She'd called. She'd left messages. Betty knew she was trying to get in contact with everyone. If no one had gotten back to her, they were busy.

She refused to think about that meaning Holden was in significant trouble.

She leaned back and rolled her shoulders. A bowl appeared next to her, steaming and full of a hearty-looking stew.

Sabrina glanced up at Connor. "Got a beer to go with it, sweetie?"

"Cute," he said, rolling his eyes. He went back to the kitchenette and brought another bowl of stew to the table. He sat next to her and gestured at the computer. "So, what have you come up with?"

"We're going to have it be from me." She took a spoonful of stew. Clearly some canned concoction, but good enough. "That way he might be curious to read it. And it makes sure nothing connects to you that someone might trace."

"Okay. So start off with something super personal. Any cute nicknames from your relationship?"

Sabrina pulled a face. "Don't be a weirdo."

"Apparently your pet name for me is sweetie. Surely you had one for Nate."

She laughed, and knew that's what he'd wanted. To loosen her up some. She appreciated it, not that she'd tell him that. "No nicknames. I used to call him Nathan to tick him off."

"There you go. Be yourself and start with that."

"I don't *always* try to tick people off."

"Don't you?"

She looked over at him and couldn't stop herself from grinning. "Only the special ones."

He shook his head, but his mouth curved. She could tell he was trying to fight the grin, the amusement, but it didn't work. He took a bite of stew, and she was still staring for some unknown reason. Maybe it was because his eyes had a measure of warmth in them, and that was a first. One that had things fluttering around in her chest and pulsing dangerously lower.

She looked back down at the email, focus shattered. But she started typing, anything that came into her head. *Press on*, she told herself.

Definitely don't dwell on any heart racing or *sudden shivers*.

Chapter Twelve

Connor shouldn't be fascinated at the slight rise of color in Sabrina's cheeks as she looked back at the computer. Kind of abruptly. Like sharing a smile might have affected her in some way.

Which was not something he could even remotely consider right now. He was in mortal danger. His friend was too. And by luck of the draw, so was Sabrina. "We can't use military code," Connor said, working very hard to keep the tension out of his voice.

"You're right," she said after a pause. "This all connects too much to the military. We have to assume whoever is after you two is well versed. But, at least on my end, the relationship I had with Nate was very much centered in the fact we both were in the military."

"What about people you both knew? Since the mission I had with Nate is presumably the crux of this, anyone he and I knew could be figured out. But if you guys knew some people during your time in the military, presumably whoever is potentially reading this aside from Nate might not be able to put the clues together."

Sabrina took a few more spoonfuls of stew. Her braid had come out of its tight coil, wisps of black hair falling forward. There were rays of sun falling over the table from the window where he'd pulled back the curtains earlier.

When the weak sunlight caught those strands of her hair, they shimmered into a shade that edged toward purple.

Why was he noticing the color of her *hair*? The slight warmth to her cheeks which could just be due to the cold.

"We need to get across the fact that he is in danger in a way only he would understand." She frowned at the laptop screen, her fingers tapping idly against the table before she took another spoonful of stew. "Real danger. Ideally he has a clue what's going on, so he'll read into a weird email from me, but I don't want to take the chance he just sweeps it away."

Connor ate his stew without tasting it. He didn't feel hungry, but knew he needed the fuel. "So, it's got to sound serious enough, without being too...possible I guess. What about a mutual friend being sick? A funeral he should attend that doesn't make any sense?"

"Yeah. Yeah, I like that. A funeral of someone he wouldn't actually want to go to. That way he's confused. Confusion will get him to dig into it. It's why we're in this mess, right?" She rolled her shoulders. "Now I just have to pick the right target."

"We don't want to accidentally drag an innocent bystander into this though. The name you choose has to be someone who—"

She waved him off. "I know who." She started to type. The expression on her face went from intense and energetic to blank. Contained. Like that glimpse of her up on the mountain.

Connor set aside his now empty bowl and got out of his chair so he could read over her shoulder. At first, she didn't stop, but eventually she sighed and gestured at the screen.

"He knows how I felt about my dad. I don't know if he knows he's dead. Of course, someone could look into it. Find out he died about five years ago. That's a red flag, but I have to wonder if anyone would dig that deeply." She chewed on her bottom lip as she considered. "So, I tell Nate—*Nathan*—I could use the moral support at my dad's memorial service or whatever. First of all, Nate will know it's me. Second of all, he'll wonder what the hell I'm smoking. So, he'll dig."

Connor knew he should focus on if it was a good plan or not, if her email made sense or not, but he couldn't help but add that to everything he knew about her. What she'd told him about her dad. "Your dad died five years ago. Isn't that about when you had your injury?"

"Yeah, little after."

"So, you lost the SEALs and your dad in one fell swoop?"

She shrugged. "My dad was already dead to me anyway. More or less."

He found he didn't believe her, but dwelling on it wasn't going to do either of them any good. "Maybe use that. A change of heart these years later. You're going to give him the funeral he never had and need some attendees. Did he ever meet your dad?"

"No, but that's good. I could pretend like he did. No one would be able to verify one way or another. Except Nate, who's going to wonder what I hit my hard head on." She started typing again. Deleting some things, adding some. They spent a good hour on it, occasionally taking breaks to eat or clean up after themselves. Connor let Froggy out at one point, and watched her lope off into the dark to do her business.

She returned after a while, and Connor let her back in and closed and locked the door behind them. Likely they wouldn't be heading anywhere tonight. They were fed, then they would rest once Sabrina was satisfied with the email.

She sat back as Connor tossed Froggy a treat.

"All right. Read it one more time and if you give it the thumbs-up, we're done."

Connor came to stand behind her, leaned close and read over her shoulder.

"Good?" she asked.

He didn't know what else to add. Couldn't discern anything that might tip the wrong people off. It wouldn't make sense to Nate as far as Connor could see, but she was right that Nate was the kind of person who wouldn't let that go. He'd get to the bottom of it. One way or another.

If he knew he was in danger, hopefully he'd make *some* kind of connection to that. Either way, he'd be trying to get in touch with Sabrina now. It put her in the spotlight.

Connor found he really didn't like that, even knowing she and her bag of tricks could take care of herself.

"If it looks good to you, looks good to me."

She hit Send with a flourish then scraped back from the table, practically knocking into him in the process. But she just got to her feet and moved away, though there weren't too many places to go in the tiny kitchen area.

"There. Dad finally came in handy for something." She said it with a flippancy he wanted to believe, but her dark eyes were too…soft to really get there.

He thought about the way she'd touched his arm and offered a simple apology and found himself wanting to offer her the same kind of sympathy, even though he'd balked at her gesture. God knew she'd balk at his.

Didn't stop the need. "Guess your mom's not in the picture?"

"Died when I was five." This time when she shrugged, she crossed her arms, holding her elbows tight at her sides.

"Haven't caught too many breaks, have you?"

Her gaze met his for the briefest of seconds, all that

grief bright and alive before she turned and squinted out the window into the dark night. "I'm here. So, I figure I've caught my fair share." She held herself so tense, so rigid, but he knew she wasn't lying. She truly felt like she hadn't gotten such a bad hand, even though she had.

Sure, there were worse. There always were. But someone who'd had the bad from the beginning who came through it believing they'd done okay…

Something tumbled in his chest, felt a bit like falling. Falling where, he didn't know—didn't want to know. Knew that the best thing he could do for himself right here, right now, was create distance. "We should rest, while we wait."

"I'm really bad at waiting." She dropped her arms, shook them out a bit like a fighter might before taking some test punches. Her face changed, from that blank control to something sly, something…hot.

Connor had to fight the urge to curl his own fists in defense. As if they were going to square off. But they weren't. They were on the same team.

She sauntered toward him, her brown gaze direct on his. She hadn't fully shed the sadness. It lurked there behind this…act.

Didn't diminish the potency of the act when she kept walking, practically right into him. Pressing her body to his.

He didn't swallow at his suddenly dry throat. Wouldn't give her the satisfaction. Whatever this game was, he was more than capable of playing.

Maybe.

She trailed a finger up the center of his chest, looked up at him through her lashes. "So you're going to have to distract me."

He held himself still. Not tense. Just still. And he waited

until he knew he could speak without his voice cracking. "How would I do that?"

"Oh, Connor, don't disappoint me by playing coy." She curled her arm around his neck, fully molding herself to him. She was lithe and lean and yet soft and warm against him.

Okay, *now* he was tense. It wasn't that his brain was a little scrambled, between the feel of her and the warmth of her surrounding him, that kept him from kissing her. Though he was very definitely scrambled. It was that sadness she'd shed—not shed so much as buried. Concealed.

He opened his mouth to tell her this wasn't the way to deal with any of what was going on, but before he could say anything she lifted onto her toes and pressed her mouth to his.

And he forgot all his protests.

SABRINA HALF THOUGHT he'd jump back. Pull away. *Run* away. Likely followed by a lecture about burying her feelings in distraction.

Maybe she'd kind of hoped for that, because it would make her feel powerful. In control. Maybe even a little superior. And that was what she was after.

She needed to find equilibrium, and the only place she'd been any good at finding that was in the middle of a fight. Win or lose, the physical release of fighting did the trick. It released the tension. Left her loose and ready for the next.

Since she couldn't physically fight with Connor, there was one other physical interaction they could have that might offer the same results.

But she hadn't counted on the *punch* of it. Of him. The way his arms wrapped around her, and to feel the strength there. She hadn't counted on the rasp of his stubble or the smooth, slick slide of his tongue in her mouth.

Something deep inside of her trembled as heat swamped any thoughts of power and equilibrium. His hands slid up her back, big, powerful, and she found herself simply clinging to him, arms around his neck, like he was some kind of anchor.

His hands tangled in her hair, angled her head to take the kiss deeper. Wild.

It exploded into something bigger than she'd expected. Way bigger than she'd meant. She didn't feel equilibrium. She didn't feel power.

She felt *lost*. Which was what had a tiny trickle of icy fear piercing the fear of warmth. *Too much. Way, way, way too much,* her brain seemed to scream at her. She wrenched her mouth away from his and fought off the panic when she pushed at him and he didn't let her go.

But it only lasted a second. Then he was unwinding his fingers from her hair and she was stumbling back.

Get it together.

She was breathing too heavily to hear the sound at first. But Connor seemed fine. Oh, he was clearly *affected*, but not like he'd been bashed over the head with something he didn't understand.

He reached over and picked her phone up off the table where she'd laid it next to her computer. He handed it to her.

Her hands were shaking. She knew they would shake even harder if she reached out and took it, but what choice did she have? The phone had stopped ringing, but she took it anyway, fighting with everything she was to keep the tremor out of her hands.

God, what had that *been*? No one had ever kissed her with all that… What? She didn't even have a word for it.

Her phone began ringing again. She cleared her throat. "Killian," she answered, irritated her voice was still rough.

"Sabrina. Thank God."

"Shay?" Relief would have flooded her, but her boss's voice didn't sound all that steady.

"Listen. I don't know what you've found, but Holden's mission led him to one of the names of the hit man's target. Unfortunately, we know there's another hit man and another name out there. We only got intermediaries. I don't know when we'll get the second name, but your assignment is the first one. Listen carefully, the first target's name is Connor Lindstrom. I haven't had time to—"

"Shay."

"Sabrina. Don't interrupt. Time—"

"Shay. I'm *with* Connor Lindstrom. He's the SAR guy. The one I told you about."

"Oh. Oh... I... Well."

Sabrina wished she could be amused she'd surprised Shay of all people, but there were too many things jangling around inside of her to find any humor. "We figured out he was the target just last night, and we're pretty sure we know the second target. His name's Nathan Averly. He's in Blue Valley, Montana. I need Elsie to—"

"Els was hurt, Sabrina."

"Elsie?" Sabrina's heart clutched painfully at how grave Shay sounded. "Hurt? But how? Why?"

"We had her doing some computer work on-site. Unfortunately she got caught in the middle a little bit. She's going to be fine, but for right now she's in the hospital."

Sabrina closed her eyes. It was both relief and pain. Elsie would be fine. That was great. But she was no agent. She was IT. She should be safe, not in the hospital. "Did anyone else get hurt?"

"We're all okay, more or less. We'll give you more details soon, but there are more strings to tie up here. I needed to get you that name. And you're… You're with him. Geez. That's a stroke of luck."

Sabrina wished she felt lucky. "His cabin got burned down. We're laying low. I've made careful contact with the second target. We need more information from him to understand who's after them."

"We'll get you more information on that angle as soon as we can. Are you safe? Can you sit tight for a few?"

"We're good for tonight. But I need someone to dig on Nate without anyone knowing they're digging. I need…" She needed Elsie, damn it. "I don't want us digging to come back on anybody. Or let them know we're after them and have whoever is doing this escalate. I might have names, but I don't feel close to figuring this out. Do you know where the second hit man is?"

"No. We know there was an ammo tradeoff a day ago. So the person who picked it up here in Nebraska isn't the shooter. But that does mean they've had a day to get to this Blue Valley, Montana."

Sabrina wouldn't allow herself to panic. It was better than a hit man already being there, but not by much. "Someone could have gotten to Montana by now."

"Yes. You've warned the second target?"

"I've sent a message. I don't know that he's gotten it." Maybe she shouldn't have been so careful. Maybe warning Nate ASAP would have been the better course of action.

"We'll clean things up here. I'll get a team to Blue Valley. You focus on the hit man after Connor Lindstrom."

"We need to know why, Shay. We need to figure this out. It's got something to do with their time together in the navy SEALs. The way they were discharged wasn't on the up-and-up."

"Got it. Look, I know Elsie's the best, but one of her IT team can handle this. I'm sure they can. So, we'll get one of them on it. We'll get a team to Montana ASAP, and I'll get you some backup."

Sabrina eyed Connor. He hadn't moved. Perhaps not a muscle. He stood there like some mountain of immovable stone. "I'm not saying no to backup, but we're good here. So, we're the last priority. As long as we're here, and they're burning down his cabin, they're going to stay put and look for us." Whoever they were. How many and what skills and weapons was a mystery, but Sabrina had to believe she and Connor could handle it. For now.

"All right. I've got to take care of things here. I'll be in touch. Stay safe."

"You too." The line went dead. Sabrina found herself delaying pulling the phone away from her ear. Found herself…not quite ready to face Connor and what had transpired before that phone call.

But she was not a coward. She wasn't going to be nervous over a kiss that hadn't gone the way she'd planned. "Don't know how much you heard, but we got some information. Mostly intermediary stuff or confirming what we already know. I think the best course of action is to sit tight here tonight and then hope we've got some more to go on in the morning. My group will be sending a team to Nate, so we don't have to worry too much about him. A warning and backup. It's the best we can do."

He didn't say anything to that, and she found no matter how she told herself not to be a coward, she couldn't quite force herself to look at him. "So, we've eaten. Now we should rest." She started walking past him to find if there was a bedroom or, please God, two separate rooms to sleep in.

But as she tried to brush past him, his hand shot out and grabbed her arm. Hard.

"What was it you said to me? Don't disappoint me by playing coy?"

Both his grasp and words irritated her enough to snap her gaze to meet his. She had a million brilliant, cutting rejoinders on the tip of her tongue. She did, she *really* did.

But he used all that strength to jerk her against him, haul her up and crush his mouth to hers, and the words just melted away.

Everything did.

Chapter Thirteen

Connor hadn't meant to find himself back here. He'd meant to prove something. That he could be as aggressive and flippant as she. That he wasn't a coward who was just going to pretend the first kiss hadn't happened. No, things weren't going to go down that way.

But he hadn't meant to kiss her again. It was too dangerous. Just a little touch, and a verbal jab that would leave her off kilter. That had been the plan. He'd been certain it would work.

But she'd looked at him with all that fire, and she hadn't fought him off like he knew she could have. And he just…

Went with it.

Whatever she'd been thinking when she'd originally kissed him, he didn't know, but it had unlocked something inside of him. Because here, with her mouth meeting his kiss for kiss, nip for nip, he didn't think. *Couldn't* think.

It was just her and lust and greed and absolutely no thought to anything beyond having his hands on her. His mouth on her. *Having* her.

"I want you," he found himself saying against her mouth, hands tangled in her hair as she wound herself around him—arms banded around his neck, legs vised around his waist.

"So have me."

She was wrapped around him so he only had to shift his grip on her to lift her up, walk her deeper into the cabin.

"Bedroom somewhere," he muttered, his brain feeling a bit like it had been fried. He was okay with that as long as her body kept pressed against him, all that heat, all that strength.

He stumbled into a dark room, and only bothered to find a light switch because if he was going to be this stupid, he was damn well going to enjoy it. He flipped the switch and headed straight for the bed, never quite taking his mouth from hers.

How could he? Here was power and he wanted all he could drink of it. He dropped her to the bed, and before he could follow her hands were busy pulling his shirt over his head. He accommodated her, then pulled her shirt off. They stripped each other, touching every inch of skin exposed like two people lost in the desert finding water after days.

She was perfect. Lean and toned. Soft, with all that hair. He couldn't keep his hands out of it. Couldn't seem to take his mouth off her. Dimly he was aware this was a *terrible* idea, and they had far more important things to busy themselves with.

But her hands closed over him and there went any thoughts—dim or otherwise.

Then there was nothing but a wild need neither one of them seemed to know how to satisfy. It was all tangled limbs and rolling bodies and muttered curses that didn't quite make sense. They joined together in a storm that overwhelmed him completely, when he'd always had his two feet under him—good weather or bad.

But she was something wholly unique. He wasn't sure he'd survive it—or that he wanted to. Pleasure was an avalanche he wanted to be buried in. She rolled with him,

oming apart in his arms, and he could only think to find
way to drive her higher, and higher, until something big-
er cracked. Exposed them both.

She panted his name, but it wasn't enough. She set her
eeth to his shoulder, shuddering and moving against him.
ut that wasn't what he was after either, even as she cried
ut. Over and over again.

"Connor. *Please.*"

Apparently that was what he'd been waiting for. Some-
hing exploded. Maybe his entire being. He was wholly
nd completely overtaken by light and sensation and some-
hing that felt oddly comparable to joy.

They lay sprawled out on the bed, breathing heavily.
Connor stared up at the ceiling and could only assume she
vas doing the same.

"Don't get a big head, but I think I see stars."

He huffed out a laugh. He doubted Sabrina would ever
et anyone have a big head, but he didn't mind the compli-
nent. "I'll let you know what I see when I'm not dead."

She laughed in turn and rolled onto her side to look
t him. He eyed her, not moving since he wasn't sure he
ould quite yet.

"That was fun. I figure it could keep being fun when
ve're given the chance. That being said, I want to make it
lear that fun is all I'm after."

He couldn't quite *laugh*, though the statement was in-
leed laughable. There was an odd pressure in his chest,
ut he ignored it and worked to sound as dry as possible.
And here I thought you were going to propose."

Her eyes narrowed a little at that. "Just trying to be
lear."

"Well, you're crystal." And he was glad he was ut-
erly relaxed enough not to delve into the odd pressure
nd be annoyed. No, he'd hold on to satisfied and loose.

He nudged her onto her back, her dark hair spilling ou
over the pillow.

"I've got to let Froggy out." He looked down at her
balanced on his elbow. He couldn't read that expression
what odd mix of emotions swam in her eyes, and she didn'
say a word.

She was strength and a brash confidence. She *was* th
storm, and she wasn't going to let anyone forget it. Bu
there was a beating heart at the center of all that. One with
a big old melting pot of hurts and issues even he could tel
she hadn't worked through. Why that should appeal to him
on any level was beyond him. But it did.

She stared up at him—no snippy rejoinders or snark
smirks. Just…looking. She probably saw too much, but h
figured he saw too much in her too. There was *somethin,*
here, between them, and neither of them probably wante
it or were comfortable with it.

But neither looked away. He kissed her before he full
thought it through, and didn't rush through it. He lingered
and something in his chest flipped, filled up, much like i
had when she'd stood on that rock talking about destin
of all things.

He did not, would not, believe in destiny. And that in
cluded whatever this was. He ended the kiss and got of
the bed.

"Get some sleep, Sabrina." He pulled on his pants and
stalked out of the room to let his dog out. And hopefull
get his head on straight. But he was a little afraid bein,
with Sabrina had irreparably changed him, and he'd neve
be on even ground again.

SABRINA WOKE UP SLOWLY, burrowing into the pillow that…
didn't feel or smell familiar. She yawned, not quite read

o open her eyes. She always woke up knowing where she was, but she found today her head was a bit scrambled.

Oh, right. She allowed herself ten seconds of pure satisfied smile. The guy had *moves*, and he used them *effectively*. She sighed because there was no time for a repeat performance.

Then she pushed out of bed because the sense of loss she felt over that was a little too close to her heart for comfort.

It was utterly dark, and the bed was now empty. Likely he'd stayed up to keep watch. Which meant it was his turn to sleep and hers to watch. And check her email.

If Nathan had responded maybe she could figure out a good next step. They had to move forward. They had to...not dwell here. In what had happened between them.

Inexplicably she thought more of that gentle kiss before he'd left her than the actual sex. Sex had been reaction. Great. A revelation, if she was being honest in the inside of her own thoughts. But that kiss...

It had been...

Nope. She wasn't going to think about that. She was going to think about her mission. Chalk up last night to a good time, *fun* just like she'd told him, and forget everything else.

She pulled on her clothes, ran her fingers through her hair. She didn't know where her hair tie had gone and her bag was still out in the kitchen. So, she'd just go get one. Go check her email.

Easy. Casual. No big deal. So, they'd had sex? Two unencumbered people who were attracted to each other could do that sort of thing and not have it *mean* something. Just because she'd never actually been able to go through with any one-night-stand type things even though she routinely pretended she did didn't *mean* anything.

Connor didn't *mean* anything besides a hot guy at the

right place in the right time. She rolled her eyes at her self. She doubted that many people would consider *thi* the right time.

She stepped into the kitchen area certain she was i charge of what she felt. He stood at the front door. It wa open, though the screen door was closed. He was look ing out into the night. The faintest hint of dawn was o the horizon. She could tell by his relaxed demeanor h was watching or waiting on Froggy rather than prime for a threat.

His hair was mussed. His feet were in thick hiking socks. She could smell coffee. It was like...living wit someone. She didn't know why it was different than th other times in her life she'd shared quarters with a guy, bu it was somehow more domestic. Cozier. Homier.

Or maybe it just felt different. What would it be like t just...watch the sunrise? With someone?

She shook her head, a little violently, hoping weir thoughts like that might just fall right out. She'd neve had a thought like that in her life. And certainly didn' *want* to. There was no way she was pulling a Reece Mont gomery and giving up her life at North Star for some sor of domestic bliss.

She'd be bored within an *hour*. North Star was her ev erything. The kind of risks she took were *necessary*. T her very soul. She barely knew Connor. She only knew his last name because *Shay* had mentioned it.

Take it down a few notches, Sabrina.

"Coffee's on," Connor said, rough and rumbly enough to have a flash of what it had felt like to have him inside her. "I figure you'll see if Nate emailed you back. If he did we'll hopefully have a next step to move forward with. I not, I'll grab a few hours' sleep."

He opened the screen door and whistled. Froggy came pounding in, tongue lolling out to the side.

It looked like… It felt like… Like home. Not one she'd ever had, but the kind people with real families talked about.

She was really, really losing it. Coffee. She needed coffee. Maybe a lobotomy while she was at it.

"You okay?" he asked, and she realized belatedly he was looking at her. *Studying* her as she stood here and had some sort of break with reality.

She forced one of her snarky grins, though she wasn't sure it landed. "Peachy."

He quirked a smile. "I'll pour. You check."

She nodded and headed for her computer sitting there on the table. She ignored the irregular beat of her heart. How her hands were unsteady enough to type her password in wrong at first. She ignored everything except getting to her email.

Once she had coffee, everything would be fine. He put a mug at her elbow. She didn't look at him, though she grumbled a thanks. The email program booted up and Sabrina took a sip of the coffee as she waited for it to load.

Caffeine would fix the jangling feeling inside her chest. It would balance her right out. So she took a deeper sip, scalding her tongue in the process.

She put the mug down and swore quietly. "Nothing. Guess you can grab that sleep."

He didn't say anything, but after a moment or two his hand passed over her hair. Gently, not like the lusty tangle of last night. Her heart pinched dangerously.

"You better put this into one of those braids or it's going to be a problem."

She shook back her hair, eyed him. "Well, you know that makes me want to *never* put it up, right?"

"Because you like the problem, or because you jus couldn't ever do anything someone else suggested?"

She didn't like how easily he saw through her, big sur prise. The thing that was a surprise was that no matter how she told herself she didn't like it, she felt a bit like leaning into it. All of it. "I guess it's both."

"I don't mind both."

She had to say something mean. Something distancing Something… Anything to stop this horrible feeling inside of her. Foreign. Weird. *Scary.*

Because it felt like hope.

But Froggy began to growl, low in her throat. All feel ing had to be forgotten. The dog clearly sensed someone or something outside.

Connor muttered something to the dog and got the gun Sabrina had given him back when they'd been hiking She already had hers in her hand. He signaled that he wa going to check the back of the cabin and she should stay here in the front.

She nodded, surprised when the dog sat where she wa and didn't growl anymore. Could have been an animal out there she was growling at, Sabrina supposed, but then again better safe than sorry.

She watched Connor melt into the shadows of the back of the cabin. Turned out, big, hot guy prowling with a gun was very much a turn-on. But she didn't have time to in dulge it. Her phone was buzzing.

She looked at the screen. A text from Holden.

Don't shoot. Let me in.

Sabrina closed her eyes for one second. Just one, to try and find her equilibrium. What the hell was *Holden* doing here? "At ease, sailor," she called to Connor. "I know who's out there."

She was already jumbled up, thanks to Connor. But Holden showing up here... She had to get her head on straight somehow. She went to the front door as Connor reappeared. She opened it and Holden appeared out of the shadows like an apparition.

He stepped into the cabin as Sabrina held the door open for him. "What are you doing here?" she demanded.

"Had to save your ass, Killian." He grinned. "So you can come to my wedding." His eyes tracked over to Connor while Sabrina tried to make sense of *that*. "This our target?"

Sabrina looked back at Connor. The gun he'd been holding wasn't in his hand any longer. He had his arms crossed over his chest, Froggy standing next to him as if ready to attack. He looked nothing like a target and everything like the kind of guy who took targets out.

He said absolutely nothing, and Sabrina didn't know why she had to fight off the wave of a *blush*.

"Connor, this is Holden Parker. We work for the same group. Holden, this is Connor." She was about to say he was a former navy SEAL and could take care of himself. Like she wanted to defend him somehow. But that was stupid. *Everything* jangling around inside of her right now was extraordinarily stupid.

So, it was probably best just to keep her mouth shut.

Chapter Fourteen

Connor didn't like Holden Parker on sight. He knew it wasn't fair, and he found he didn't care. He watched Sabrina fetch the guy some coffee and a snack. They joked, took potshots at each other, and *clearly* enjoyed each other.

Connor found he kind of wanted to punch the guy.

He didn't, of course. He maintained his utter silence, no matter how many questioning glances Sabrina threw his way while she explained to Holden what they were doing.

This was their deal. Connor wasn't going to insert himself. He wasn't part of their group. He wasn't going to be *the target* either, but he'd handle that on his own. Their group could do whatever.

Connor was going to take care of himself. And Nate if it came to it. So, he stood in the kitchen, Froggy at his feet, listening to them and saying nothing.

Sabrina and Holden worked together like a well-oiled machine. Finished each other's thoughts, moving like partners in some kind of dance they'd been practicing for years.

No, Connor didn't like Holden. In fact, he wasn't ashamed to admit in the privacy of his own head that he downright hated the guy.

"I can't believe you're not asking about my wedding," Holden said after Sabrina had caught him up completely, down to the fact they were waiting on Nate's response.

Sabrina frowned at Holden. "I thought that was some kind of weird joke."

"Nope."

"You're...pulling a Reece?"

Connor didn't know who Reece was, but Sabrina was clearly shaken by the news of her coworker getting married.

"Not exactly," Holden said, the first sign of discomfort in a slight adjustment of how he sat. "Not exactly *not*. But regardless, we're finishing this first. I need to finish it for her as much as me and you. Her parents are spies."

"Her. This her got a name?"

"Willa. Willa Parker soon enough. Her parents are spies and they're the reason we got a name."

"I already had the name."

"Okay, sure." Connor didn't miss Holden's considering glance at him before it returned to Sabrina. "And you figured out the second target. But the mission I completed connects to this one. It's all part of a bigger picture. I want to finish it. For her."

"The bigger picture isn't my job." Sabrina stood abruptly, clearly irritated about something.

Connor could only assume it was the *her*, the wedding. That shouldn't matter to him. It *didn't* matter to him. He wasn't going to let it.

She paced, but then stopped herself and jabbed a finger over her shoulder to point at Connor. "My job is to save this guy's butt. And Nate's."

"I think we could save our own," Connor said, being careful to keep the acid out of his tone.

She whirled on him. "No, you couldn't. Because if I hadn't come along, you'd be deader than a doornail."

He hated that she was right. Maybe he would have sensed something was wrong in the moment. But her crashing his rescue had been the real thing that had saved his butt, and he couldn't be petty enough to argue with her about that.

"Gonna take Froggy out."

Sabrina looked at him like he'd grown a second head. "Aren't you going to add your two cents?"

"You two are doing just fine." He whistled for the dog and walked straight out the front door, Froggy at his heels.

He found a stick Froggy would get a kick out of chasing as the sun rose in the sky. It was going to be warmer than the past few days. Which of course put them at risk for another avalanche. Among other things.

He had to get rid of this edgy mood. He heaved the stick a few times, really putting some strength behind it. Froggy yipped and raced through the snow in perfect dog heaven, and it helped Connor even out.

At least until the door squeaked open and he looked back to see Holden there, studying him and his dog.

"She's in there taking a shower," he offered, coming up to stand next to Connor.

"Okay." Connor slid his hands into his pockets. He didn't know what to say to the guy. Didn't really feel like figuring it out.

"Just to be clear, it was never like that between me and Sabrina. Can't explain why exactly. It just wasn't. Isn't. So no need to be jealous."

"I'm not jealous." He wasn't so basic as all that. He just didn't like Holden. He had his reasons. He'd think of them. Eventually.

Holden slapped him on the back. A little too hard to be considered friendly. "Well, you're giving an *excellent* impression then." He sauntered back inside, and Connor felt no less like punching the guy in the nose.

Even if the fact Holden and Sabrina had *never* been

something more than coworkers and friends to each other *did* ease something inside of him.

Last night had been a one-off. *Fun,* as she'd put it. That suited him fine. *Just* fine. What the hell other options were there? Zip, zero, zilch.

He turned to go back inside, beyond irritated with himself more than anything, but he heard the faint sound of…a helicopter.

He frowned and searched the sky. Surely he was hearing things. Or it wasn't really a helicopter. He'd sent Iona a text to stay far away. She wouldn't be so crazy as to…

Of *course* she would. She was a dog with a bone. Why was he surrounded by frustrating, irritating, *stubborn* women?

He swore. And stormed back inside to grab his radio and Froggy. Holden and Sabrina had their heads bowed over the computer. Sabrina's hair was wet and pulled back into a braid.

No matter what Holden had said, Connor didn't like it. Just plain old didn't like it. Because maybe Holden hadn't been interested in Sabrina, but that didn't mean the opposite wasn't true.

And it was absolutely neither here nor there, he reminded himself as he dug his radio out of his pack. "I hear a helicopter. I think it's Iona."

Sabrina swore herself and immediately hopped out of her chair. "You've got to get her out of here."

"I know it." He flipped his radio on. "I'm going to try to get her through this, but I've got to follow the helicopter."

"Con—"

He shook his head. "If she doesn't answer the radio, I've got to show her I'm okay and she's got to get out of here. She won't look at her phone up in the air. She's going to head for my cabin. See the fire remnants. If she doesn't hear me, she's going to have to see me, or this could get bad. Fast."

Sabrina was on his heels, but it wasn't necessary. "Stay here," he said, jerking his chin toward the table. "Keep working on this angle."

"Like hell I will."

He wanted to argue with her, but there was no time. He didn't need help trying to get over to Iona with the radio. He jogged north. It'd be a harder hike, but the straightest shot to his cabin was this way.

"You don't know what's out there," Sabrina said, hurrying to keep up with him. "They burned down your cabin. They could be lying in wait and you're going off half-cocked."

He glanced back at her. "I thought half-cocked was the name of the game."

She huffed out an irritated breath. "I don't know what bug crawled up your butt."

"That's funny because I know exactly what bug crawled up yours."

She stopped, but he didn't. "What's that supposed to mean?" she called after him.

The sounds of the helicopter were getting closer. He looked up, not bothering to answer her. It didn't matter. Him being an absolute *idiot* about her did not matter. Iona mattered. He pointed at the sky. "There," he said, calculating how far away from the cabin she was. How far away from him right now. "That's too damn close to my cabin." He got on the radio again. Tried to reach her. But there was no response. Connor swore.

A gunshot rang out and the helicopter jerked, the engine making a terrible sound as it hovered there, but only for a few moments before it began speeding to the ground.

SABRINA DIDN'T THINK Connor realized he was yelling as he ran. Making himself a bigger target than they already were.

Still, she couldn't blame him. His friend was going down and if the situation was reversed, she'd be doing the same thing.

Holden caught up with her. She'd asked him to pack everything up, hide her computer, and get all the weapons he could while she went after Connor. It hadn't taken him long to accomplish it.

"What's going on?" he demanded.

"Helicopter pilot is a friend he works with on Search and Rescue. She's not military. Shouldn't be mixed up in this. But the bad guys can't be too far off, Holden. And if she crashes that tin can..." Sabrina thought of the calm woman with the dark hair, that Connor was her kid's *godfather*.

It was all wrong.

"If she's a good pilot, she'll make a decent enough landing," Holden said, running right next to her. Her pack on his back, no doubt loaded with most of her weapons. He had his own gun in his hand as they ran after Connor.

What neither of them said was the possibility that the gunshot hadn't just hit the helicopter, but had hit the pilot. That the helicopter could very well explode before landing.

There were a lot of bad scenarios that could happen regardless of how good a pilot Iona was.

Still, they ran after Connor. Sabrina had to force herself not to think about him or the mom of three. She focused on their surroundings. On places a sniper might be situated. Connor would focus on helping his friend. *She* would focus on making sure they didn't get killed in the process.

They heard the crash, a loud, echoing thud, the sound of metal crunching in on itself. All three of them seemed to find an extra gear inside of themselves to run just a little bit faster than they'd been running, but the dog still made it there first—just out of view—and let out a bark of alarm.

She could see the smoke, smell the acrid burn of it all. But when the wreckage came into view, it didn't appear to be on fire. Yet. And it wasn't completely crushed. There was a chance, if Iona hadn't been shot, that she could be pulled from the wreckage and be okay.

Please, God.

Still a good few yards ahead of them, Connor threw himself onto the helicopter and wrenched open the door not skidded into the ground.

Before they could reach him, he'd dragged Iona out. Her eyes were open and she seemed to be moving some of her own accord as Connor began to stride back the way they'd come, Iona in his arms.

"Chance it'll blow," he said through gritted teeth. "Get as far back to the cabin as we can."

"I'm okay," Iona said, though she sounded thready. Definitely in shock.

She was bleeding profusely from her head. But she was talking. White as death but alive. It was *some* relief. But until they really examined her, it was hard to feel relieved fully.

"She needs a doctor," Sabrina said, following behind Connor.

"I'll call Betty," Holden said simultaneously, his phone already out and at his ear.

They walked quickly, though not at the same clip. Connor was clearly doing everything he could not to jostle Iona as Froggy stayed at his heels, with an unerring and surprising ability to keep out of the way of quickly moving feet.

"I'm really okay, you know, considering."

"Considering I pulled you out of—"

The explosion echoed through the white world around

them. Bits of debris scattered about them, but nothing sizable as they were far enough away. Still, an echoing rumble came from farther off and Sabrina eyed the mountains warily.

"Great, another damn avalanche and our best pilot needs a hospital," Connor said through gritted teeth, clearly struggling to carry Iona without further injuring her. "Do you ever think?"

"Your concern is touching," Iona said dryly. But her eyes were drooping.

"She's losing it."

"I'm fine," Iona said. But she clearly, *clearly* wasn't.

Holden was talking to Betty on the phone in low tones as they reached the cabin. Sabrina rushed forward to open the door. Connor took her straight into the bedroom and Sabrina worked very hard not to think about what had occurred in said bedroom last night.

"I'm putting Betty on video." Holden held out the phone so Betty could have a decent view. Sabrina opened all the curtains she could, trying to suffuse the room with more light.

"Someone pull her hair away from the worst of the wound. Carefully," Betty instructed through the phone.

Sabrina watched as Iona tried to do it herself, but her hands fell limply at her sides after a moment. Connor obliged, carefully rearranging Iona's hair.

"I didn't lose consciousness," Iona said, but even Sabrina could tell her coloring was getting worse.

"Consciousness is good, but it could be fleeting." Betty instructed Holden where to hold the phone, Connor what to do. After a few moments of considering silence, Betty sighed.

"That head wound is nasty, and you're losing a lot of blood. You've got to get her to a hospital. They'll be able to see if there's a skull fracture. Dangerous swelling. All that. She needs tests I can't do remotely, and she might need a transfusion. You've got to get her to a hospital. How far's the nearest one?"

"A lot closer if I had a helicopter," Connor muttered.

"You'd need someone to pilot it," Iona pointed out.

Her eyes were drooping again, and Sabrina noticed Connor was holding her upright more than he had been. But she was still talking. Cognizant of her surroundings. It had to be a good sign. It had to mean she'd be all right.

"Closest hospital would be a good thirty-minute drive. But we don't have a vehicle," Connor said. His icy sheen of control was beginning to crack, but Sabrina watched him work hard to keep it in place.

"I do," Holden said. "Hid it a ways down the road."

"You'll want to drive her as quickly as possible. Keep her awake if possible, but if she loses consciousness it's not the end of the world. The most important thing would be getting her to a hospital that has available blood in less than an hour."

"I'll take it and get her to the hosp—"

"No, Connor, you're the target," Sabrina interrupted as Holden ended the call with Betty. "You can't take her. They could follow you. Connect you to Iona, and then what? She's a target, that's what. Holden will do it."

Holden frowned. "I came here to help you on this mission."

"This helps me on this mission. Betty said it herself. She needs a hospital. You know Connor and I can't take her. We're already too mixed up in this. But if you take her, they can't connect it."

"They can when I come back."

"Don't come back. Go to this future wife of yours. Go get married and live your life, Holden." And she found…

Even as weird as it was, as reticent as she was for change, she meant it. The way he'd talked about Willa... Holden should have that.

"Do I have a say in it?" Iona asked.

"No," the three of them snapped at her.

Sabrina put her hand on Holden's arm. This was imperative. To everything. "Holden. Please."

He inhaled and didn't look pleased about it, but he eventually nodded. "All right. What's the name of the hospital?"

"Wilson West," Connor said, clearly not liking the direction this was going. "I don't think—"

"I'll put it in my GPS and get her there. You contact her family. Once they arrive, I'll take off. I'll..." He shook his head as if he couldn't believe he was going to say it. "I won't come back. But you're using the backup crew. Gabe and Mallory especially. They were on my mission. They understand some of it, and they're good. You use them, Sabrina. Give me your word."

It was Sabrina's turn to suck a breath in and agree to something even though she didn't want to. "All right."

"Don't do anything crazy." He grabbed her shoulder and gave it a squeeze. "Promise me, Sabrina."

"I promise." Which wasn't hard. Taking a chance wasn't always reckless.

Holden nodded. "I'll bring the car up. You know they're going to be looking for that chopper they shot down."

"And hopefully the wreckage and the avalanche will keep them busy enough to get you out of here with Iona. We'll handle whoever follows us here," Connor said. He was all military stoicism, but Sabrina knew. Whether she saw something in his expression or she just...*felt* it, she knew he was holding on by a thread.

Holden eyed Connor, and then Sabrina. "Good luck," he muttered, then disappeared.

There was a tense silence Sabrina didn't know how to fill. Even Froggy seemed torn with indecision, standing between them uneasily. When Holden returned with the car, they got Iona loaded up as best they could. She was in and out of consciousness and Sabrina found herself saying a little prayer as they drove away—something she hadn't done much of since her mother had been alive.

"If anything happens to her I'm holding you and your boyfriend personally responsible," Connor finally snapped out.

Sabrina didn't know what she was feeling. She should be mad. Snap back at him. Or even keep her head and coolly dismiss him. But her heart just *ached* and when he tried to storm past her, she simply couldn't... She couldn't let it go.

She wrapped her arms around him. "I know you're afraid, but he's going to get her to the hospital and she's going to be okay. I'm sure of it." She wasn't sure she'd ever tried to comfort anyone in her entire life. It was more uncomfortable than healing from a career-ending injury.

She nearly let him go, nearly bolted, but that rigid hold he had on himself loosened, slowly, glacially. He rested his cheek on the top of her head, his arms coming around her. His breath came out in a tortured sigh.

"Hell, Sabrina, Iona shouldn't be part of this."

"I know."

"Why are they shooting at random helicopters?"

"That I don't know." Which was hard to admit. A little less hard when he was leaning on her.

"They'll be coming for us now. They'll want a body. They'll see our foot trail and blood. They'll know."

Sabrina pulled back, though she kept her arms around him. She looked up at his handsome, stoic face. Only something in the blue of his eyes seemed to give away that he was torn up over this. Worried about his friend. Stuck in something that had never had anything to do with him or what he'd done. Because he was just…a good, decent guy. Who wasn't afraid to fight for the right thing. To protect because it was *right*.

She moved onto her toes, pressed a light reassuring kiss she'd have to find some regret over later. "Then let's be ready for them."

Chapter Fifteen

Luckily his time in the military had taught Connor how to compartmentalize. Because he had been away from it, though, and because Iona had become as close as family, it was harder to simply set his feelings of guilt, anger, blame and worry aside. And he knew her husband and kids would be worried sick.

Sabrina helped. He wasn't sure how exactly. A hug shouldn't have helped. He couldn't remember a time he'd needed soft comfort to get through something difficult.

But it helped.

It also helped when she stepped back, seemed to physically shake all the hard stuff away, and sharpened. Like the weapon she was.

"All right. Here's what we know. We've got one hit man who shot at us. What we don't know for sure, especially now that we know they're shooting at *anyone*, is if he knew it was *you*—his target, or just knew he was being followed."

"I'm not sure it matters *why* he shot at us."

"No, I'm not sure either. But it might. The more information we have, the more we don't just stop them from killing you, the more we get to the bottom of it. Because you're not safe until we get to the bottom."

"Cheering."

She smiled. Not that flashing grin. It was softer that had the tiniest dimple winking to life on her cheek. Something in his chest turned over with a flop. He really wished that annoying feeling would stop happening.

"Why did they shoot the helicopter? They didn't know Iona was looking for me, and even if they did somehow figure that out, wouldn't it make more sense to follow the helicopter? Think she knew where I was and follow it?"

"They're here, on your turf, I think, because it's isolated. They could burn down your cabin and like you said, no one might know for days. But if someone sees it, they have to leave. Without you."

Connor shook his head. Something felt off about that. "If they wanted to burn down my cabin, and knew where it was, they would have come to it right away. Not tried to get me on a search and rescue ploy. Easier to off me when I'm sleeping in my bed, wouldn't it be?"

"Yeah, easier. Maybe they had to double-check identity first. Maybe they couldn't find your cabin."

"I'd be easy enough to find and verify."

"Okay. So, it seems like the hit man was supposed to kill you. But they burn down your cabin without you in it. Do they think you have something? Something they need to destroy?"

"If they think that, they're wrong."

"This all connects to Nate. And they're after you. Burn down your cabin…keep people away at all costs." Sabrina paced, and it clearly helped her think, process, but it made the headache at his temple pound with a vicious throb.

He rubbed his head, trying to work his way through everything that had happened in a short period of time. The hit man had missed. Then there'd been a team to burn down his cabin. Or had it been more simultaneous than that. Not totally, because of the avalanche, but by the time they'd seen the fire, it had been mostly finished. His cabin had been toast. They'd been there at least by the evening he and Sabrina had camped out.

"What if—"

But Connor knew where her brain had gone. His had gone to the same place. "Nate sent me something. Or they think he did. The hit man's on me, but you made things trickier. They still need that evidence destroyed, if it's evidence, even if I'm still alive and kicking."

"You don't get mail delivered to the cabin this isolated. So, what? A PO box?"

Connor shook his head. "I use the SAR office as my address. If it was important enough to burn something down over, would Nate really send it through the mail?"

"Who knows? It'd certainly make it *look* unimportant. So, I'd say we've got to get to the SAR office. Without the bad guys knowing that's where we're headed, and without anyone connecting anything."

"But I didn't have anything in that cabin. They torched the place and I didn't have anything."

"Maybe they assumed you did. Maybe Nate made them think you did? There's a lot of maybes."

Maybes. It wasn't all that different than his search and rescue job. A lot of factors, a lot of possibilities. Instead of one target though, he didn't know *what* his target was. And that was just like the military.

"We've got to get it. Whatever it is. *If* it is." Sabrina raked a hand through her hair. "First step, use my phone to call headquarters and see if they have anything."

"*And* to warn them."

"Yeah, okay. But be careful and vague about it. My number is untraceable, but we don't know what kind of surveillance these guys might be doing at your SAR place. We don't know how long they've been tracking you."

"Not long enough, or I'd be dead. Or so you keep reminding me."

She smiled again, sharper this time, but it didn't last when she handed him her phone. "Really careful, Connor. Not a whiff that anything is wrong."

He tried to take the phone, but she held strong as she looked at him like a scolding teacher.

Why he *felt* admonished was beyond him. "They probably already know. Iona would have radioed when she was going down."

"You act like you don't know. You act as dumb as possible. You hear me?"

"Yeah, I got it." He yanked the phone and she finally let it go.

He dialed the number to headquarters, thought about who would be there this time of day. Probably Gene Branch. Older guy, retired firefighter, who did more coordinating than anything else. He'd know if Iona radioed. He'd know if Connor had a package. And he'd be easy enough to talk around.

"Hey, Gene. How's it going?" Connor asked casually when Gene answered.

"Con. Good. Good. Quiet, which is good with you out of commission. Iona said you were taking a few days off. Kinda sudden."

"Yeah, sorry about that." Since he didn't mention Iona's crash, Connor had to assume he didn't know yet. *That* didn't add up, but he didn't know how to bring it up without tipping him off. "Had some family stuff come up. Just wanted to call and check to make sure I don't have a bunch of mail piling up there?"

"Matter of fact, a package came yesterday. Iona thought it might be important so she took the heli out to drop it off your way. Figured you were stuck in because of the avalanche. She hasn't gotten to you yet? Should have."

Connor knew he had to lie, but his mind remained stubbornly blank. Iona had the package. Iona had...

"Con?"

"Gene? Gene? You there? I'm getting nothing but static." It was a crappy lie, but at least it was *something*. Connor hung up and handed Sabrina her phone.

"What is it? What's wrong? You went pale there."

"Iona had the package. In the helicopter. You know, the one that *exploded*."

SABRINA SWORE. NOT only was the package no longer hypothetical, but it was...gone. Real but useless to them. "We have got to get a hold of Nate. He's got to email us back."

"We don't have time for that, Sabrina. You know it as well as I do. We're going to have to call him and screw the consequences."

She was leaning toward agreeing. "Let me check the email one more time. Talk to..." God, she wanted to talk to Elsie about what they could do to protect themselves. Protect Nate. But this kept spiraling to some new place she couldn't quite get a handle on.

He was right. No time. "Okay, we'll call. But we play it my way." She had *no* idea how she was going to play it, but they didn't have time to plan it out. Connor had been right about those guys coming after the helicopter wreckage and then them. They needed some kind of direction and then they needed to get the hell out of here before the bad guys caught up.

She'd already put the number to the ranch Nate was supposed to be at in her phone. Just in case. Just as a precaution. And here they were, needing it.

She felt nervous. Not about calling or even speaking

to Nate. But that she was making things worse. Making the wrong choice.

But she was officially out of choices. She hit Call and listened to the ring with her stomach pitching restlessly.

"Revival Ranch. Becca speaking," a perky voice answered.

"Hi. I'm trying to get a hold of an old friend of mine. I don't have his cell phone, but I know he's staying at your ranch."

"Well, I'll see if I can help you out there. Who are you looking for?"

"Nathan Averly."

"Oh, sure. I think Nate's around." There was the shuffle of papers, then the plaintive wail of a child somewhere. "*Mooooom.*"

"Shh, you're fine, Dane," the woman hissed in a whisper. Then immediately used that pleasant voice again. "Just, hold on one second. Who should I say is calling?"

"Brina. He'll know who I am."

Another muffled whine from a child and the sharp whisper of a mother scolding her kid. Sabrina muttered a curse under her breath, then covered the receiver. "Let's pack up. Be ready to hit the road when this is over."

Connor nodded and Sabrina put the phone on speaker and on the table. They began to work as silently as possible to get all their gear together and back in the packs as they waited for the woman on the other end. There were muffled words, children shrieking, a few barks.

"Sorry about that," the woman said. "You still there?"

"Yeah, I'm—"

"Here you go then. Nate. Phone for you."

There was the sound of rustling and Sabrina and Connor moved for the table, both positioning themselves over the phone, staring at it as if Nate himself might actually appear before them.

"Hello?" The voice was low, raspy and suspicious. And so very much Nate Averly that Sabrina almost felt like her knees gave out. They were getting somewhere.

"Heya, Nathan. Your old pal Brina here." She wasn't sure the flippant tone she was going for really landed, but hey, she gave it a shot. "You didn't answer my email."

There was a long, fraught silence before he spoke again. "The office manager here showed it to me just a few hours ago. I hadn't quite figured out what to make of it."

"Yeah, well, when I didn't hear back figured I'd give you a call. Catch up, you know? Funny thing. I got an old friend of yours with me."

At Connor's horrified look, she waved him off. "From the navy. Said you called him Skidmark back in boot camp."

Connor glared at her, but clearly got the message. "Hey, Nate. Bob...here."

God he was bad at making up names. And lying, apparently, based on the name Bob No Last Name and the way he'd hurried off the phone with the SAR headquarters. Why was that adorable?

"Ah, Bob. Good old Skidmark," Nate said, sounding half amused, half baffled. But he played along. "Haven't seen you since boot camp. And you're there with Brina. That's some...coincidence."

"Oh, yeah. Small world and all that," Sabrina said. "Bob's in trucking, just like I am these days."

"Trucking," Nate echoed. "That's...interesting."

"Uh-huh." *Think, Sabrina, think.* "Listen, I figure you can't come to the thing and all. That's fine. But Dad left me something he wanted me to send you. I was getting all ready to mail it out and there was a bit of a mix-up."

"A package."

"Yeah, my fault," Connor inserted himself. "I meant to deliver it, but there was a bit of a problem and the package got destroyed. Sucks to have a package destroyed like that when you can't retrieve the contents."

Sabrina nodded at him. Maybe he *could* lie.

"Destroyed. Well, Skidmark, that sounds about like your luck."

"Or yours," Connor returned.

"Listen, I've got to go."

Sabrina couldn't let him get off this call until she really knew that he understood what she was trying to relay. Until she knew he'd try to get them the information they needed. "Nate—"

"No, I get it, Brina. Sorry about the destroyed package. Good to hear from you. Take…care of yourself. Both of you."

"If I needed to get in touch with you again—"

"I'll get in touch with you when I need to. Got chores." He ended the call before she could protest any more. She swore.

"Look, it's frustrating, but I don't think we have time for this," Connor said.

"Right." She rubbed at her chest. "Damn, I hate an unfinished puzzle."

"I think I'd hate having my head blown off more."

She rolled her eyes at him. "Well, I'm not going to let that happen to you, hotshot."

He huffed out a breath, not quite a laugh but close. "We got in contact. I think… I think he recognized my voice. I think he got the package hint. Or at least he'll place it in this whole thing. I can hope. We can hope. But we've got bigger fish on our tail for the moment. Let's go."

"We can't just run."

"I wasn't planning on running. At least not away."

Sabrina eyed him. "You want to go to your cabin?"

"I want to see what we're dealing with."

"I've got a team coming. They'll canvas—"

"Until that team is *here*, Sabrina, let's do what needs to be done."

She rubbed at her chest again. Everything was all off. But he was right. They had to move. She'd prefer to lead him away, just because… Just because. But it would be pointless. He needed answers as much as she did.

She shouldered her pack and Connor attached Froggy's special vest leash thing. Sabrina moved for the door and looked back when he didn't follow. He stood there, looking right at her. Then he said the most…confusing thing he could have said.

"Thanks."

"For what?"

"Hell if I know, but I feel a little less like tearing after Iona and punching your guy's face in."

"He's not *my* guy. He's my friend. Like a brother."

"You sure about that?"

"Yeah, I'm pretty sure how I feel, jerkweed."

"Jerkweed. That's a new one." He stepped forward, but only to hover there in front of her like some kind of hulking mountain. "You seemed worked up about him getting married."

"Because I literally saw him a week ago and he had no plans to *ever* get married. What happens in a week to change a guy's mind? With some woman he's never met. It's weird."

Connor shrugged.

"If Iona had waltzed in here, with no warning, tells you she's divorcing her husband and leaving her family to join the circus, you'd wonder what the hell was wrong with her, right?"

"Yeah. Point taken."

She smirked at him. "Jealousy looks good on you, though."

"Not jealous."

"Then what would you call it?"

He only grunted, which made her laugh. Lightened her spirits some, but she turned to open the door. He stopped her by cupping her face, that big hand curling under her chin and holding her in place. She could have smacked it away. Could have done any number of things to get his hands off her.

She never seemed able to though. He touched her, looked at her, and she felt pinned in place.

"I don't want you taking any unnecessary chances on my account," he said, blue eyes blazing. "I need you to understand that. You're not my savior. I don't need one of those. We work together."

"You're the target."

"I was a navy SEAL, Sabrina. I can take care of myself. I don't need you to do it for me. I don't *want* you to do it for me. Any more than you'd want me to do it for you."

She didn't want to be hurt by that. A silly thing to be hurt by. Luckily, when she tried to turn her face away he held tight, which let anger fill in all those hurt spaces. But before she could unleash it, he kept talking.

"I couldn't *live* with it, if you took some chance *for* me. You get that?"

And *that* was different than not wanting her help, or thinking he didn't *need* her help. That was...

Well, things she supposed she didn't have the right or time to think about.

"We have to go, Connor," she said, her voice tight.

"Yeah, we do."

But he pressed his mouth to hers, for far longer than they had. When he released her, he brushed past her and out the door. "So, let's go."

Chapter Sixteen

They hiked. Again. It was a nicer day, the cold was just cold instead of bitter. But the melting snow made for harder hiking. Things were slick, muddy and amidst all that reminded Connor of what he'd found here. A peace in nature and the comforting cycles of it. Cold followed by warmth followed by cold. The simple struggle of man against nature. And the wide expanse of all that sky, framed by those craggy mountains that reached for it.

Now, all that peace was ripped up because some guy had taken a shot at him and blown up his cabin over some military thing he'd thought he'd left behind. And Nate had given him no answers, no clues, nothing. Connor couldn't even take confirmation away from it. He *thought* he'd heard understanding in Nate's voice, but maybe all he'd heard was someone trying to get off the phone with his ex.

A woman Connor had now slept with as well. Not exactly a comforting thought. But he found he couldn't care the way he thought he should. You didn't go after your friend's ex, but the thing with Sabrina was... Well, out of his hands.

He wouldn't go so far as to call it destiny. She'd have to be alone in that belief. But it was something bigger than thinking she was good-looking. Something deeper.

He could smell the acrid smoke from the helicopter

crash even as they hiked away from it. Distance was key until they had an idea how many men they were up against.

Men. Burned-down cabins. Assassins. What *had* Nate gotten him into?

Sabrina hiked behind him, talking to her boss on the phone, coordinating this team of hers. Connor knew he should be grateful for the numbers, but he didn't know Sabrina's team. Couldn't trust random, faceless members of some *group*.

He was wound too tight. He knew it. The conversation with Nate hadn't helped, because all it had really done was make it seem like maybe Nate knew what was going on but couldn't tell them.

The conversation with Sabrina hadn't helped because when he said things like that to her that gave some hint to what insanity was going on inside of him, when he kissed her, he had to start analyzing *why*.

And there was no good answer. Not one that made any damn sense when it came to a woman he'd known for less time than the average shelf life of a banana.

"My boss is sending a team to Montana to help Nate," she announced when she hung up her phone. "My team is already here. But they're on the other side." Sabrina cracked a small tree branch off a tree and used the snow as a canvas. "This is your cabin," she said making a big X in the snow. "Where would you say we are in relation?"

He took the stick she handed him and made his best estimate.

"Okay, so I've got four on the ground here-ish." She made four Xs. "They're going to have to hike around. They should be able to get a read on how many men are guarding your cabin and what they're doing. Watching? Waiting? Tracking? We should sit tight, let my team meet us here."

He eyed her in surprise. "When have you ever sat tight?"

She grimaced. "Not often. Definitely not my strong suit. But it's the smartest course of action. And before you get all snarky about me following the smartest course of action, remember I'm holding a gun."

"This isn't how you'd normally handle a situation like this. You're handling it on the safe side because of me." He wasn't sure if it was his pride that poked at, or something else he couldn't identify. But he didn't like it.

She raised her dark eyes to his. "And if I am?"

"Don't," he bit out, doing everything to keep the rising tide of anger banked down. He didn't even understand why he was angry. She was making a smart, safe decision. They should both be smart and safe.

But his cabin was gone and someone had upended his life. Not just these "bad" guys. Not just the military, but at this point, his own damn friends.

"So, I should go risk both our necks, instead of just my own?" Sabrina demanded.

"Yeah, if that's what you'd do anyway."

"Did it occur to you that *I* might not be able to live with it if my disregard for my own life hurt yours in some way?"

That surprised him enough to sidestep the anger for a minute. "What do you mean disregard for your own life?"

She shrugged restlessly, pacing again. Always with the pacing. A ball of energy. All those sharp turns of her mind. A recklessness, and yet a core of determination to get the thing—whatever the thing was—done. And under all those rough edges a vulnerability, not just in what had happened to her, but in her need to give comfort. Even if she didn't want to admit that's what drove her, there *was* a need. Or she would have stamped out any softness toward anybody by now.

He understood it, even though they were so different, he seemed to understand her. Even when she baffled him, she made sense. She felt right. Like some missing puzzle piece. Too bad the past few days had torn the puzzle apart.

"I didn't really think my life mattered all that much for a while there," Sabrina grumbled, then whirled and pointed a finger at him. "And you know what? That wasn't so bad. Because I turned myself into a badass because of it. But I also built myself a family because of it, and I can't say I'm at all comfortable with that realization, but there it is. So, we'll wait, Con. We'll wait."

He didn't have the first clue as to what to say to that. Mostly because he understood. Deep in his bones. He'd been there. Maybe in a different way. He had to assume her disregard came from her rough upbringing, when his had come from an immature cockiness that time and maturity had cured.

Then he'd come here and, because he hadn't been able to lie to his own family, had built something of his own.

"Two peas in a pod, aren't we?" she said with a smirk.

Because it felt a little too much exactly like that, he scowled. "Something like that." He stood in the trail they'd forged, and looked around. Trees and rock, sky and cloud. And he was waiting for strangers to help him stop this threat against him.

There were questions he hadn't asked, because they'd been moving too much. Because he'd been too worried about Nate or Iona. Because he'd fallen into bed with this woman and inexplicably wanted to keep her around.

"Your group is sending some people to help Nate. Sending some people to help us. What's the endgame?" he asked, unclipping Froggy's leash so the dog could sniff around for a bit.

"Stop them. Figure out who they are and who they work for so that whatever this is, is over."

"Why?"

She wrinkled her nose. "What do you mean why?"

"What does it matter to your group? Why did they send you here? How do you all connect?"

"I was supposed to stop the hit man."

"But *why*, Sabrina?"

She heaved out a sigh. "I'm not in charge."

"Don't pretend like you don't know. Or like it might not matter. We've been focused on what Nate can tell us. What about what *you* can tell us?"

She pressed her lips together. "It's not going to give you anything, but a couple months back, we—my group—was contacted to figure out a mystery for this small…government agency."

"Government. Mother of God, Sabrina—"

"Let me finish. I wasn't point on that mission, just backup." She looked down at her arm then shook her head. "But what we discovered was a black-market arms dealer supplying a bigger bad guy organization."

"Are you sure it wasn't the government?"

She rolled her eyes at him. "Which led Holden and I to *our* assignments. Before we stopped the arms dealer, they shipped off some high-powered weapons. We followed the weapons with the assignment to stop the hits. From what Shay told me, Holden's assignment didn't stop a hit, but found an intermediary. The intermediary has been able to give my group some information, but we're still mostly working in the dark."

"For a government agency."

"Yeah, one that didn't want you offed, Connor."

"I left that life for a reason, you know. Not just because they kicked me out for no good reason, but because the red tape, bureaucracy BS doesn't help *anyone*."

"You're alive, aren't you?"

He didn't know what to say to that, or what to do with

the direct, *sympathetic* way she looked at him. So, he said nothing. Did nothing.

"What's interesting, to me, is that they sent a hit man for you before they sent one to Nate," Sabrina continued. "That we know of. I'm thinking whatever blew up in that helicopter was pretty darn important. It's why you became the target above Nate."

"Great."

"It means we have to make it look like we have whatever it was. We have to pretend like we know more than we do until we can get more information safely from Nate."

"Fantastic."

"Aw, don't be grumpy." She reached up and ran her fingers over his cheek, mischievousness lighting up her dark eyes.

She was trying to poke him out of his dour mood, but he didn't want to be poked out of it. He wanted to *brood*.

Hard to hold onto when she was this close, when she was grinning up at him.

"I don't need your protection." Maybe that was the crux of it, much as he hated to admit it even to himself. He didn't like being at the mercy of other people. Didn't like feeling like the helpless victim. Maybe it wasn't even a *like* thing. He'd never been in this position before. He didn't know what to do with it.

Sabrina's mouth touching his jaw eased some of those uneven edges though. Even as she said obnoxious things. "But I *am* your protector, Con. Need one or not."

It was hard to argue with her when she'd wound her arms around him and was pressing her distracting mouth to his neck. But there was something important at stake here.

"I'll take a partner, Sabrina. How about that?"

Her eyes flickered, all that smooth confidence scattered for just a moment. "I can be a partner, but I'm warning

ou I've never been a good one. Too cocky, too nasty and
vay too intent on doing things my own way."

"Yeah, like I haven't figured *that* out." He shrugged,
ot quite able to stop himself from tucking a stray strand
f hair behind her ear. A gentle move when this was re-
lly not the time or place for gentle. "Something I seem
o like about that."

She rose to her toes to kiss him, but a man appeared
ut of the trees and Connor gripped her by the shoulders,
bout ready to toss her behind him like he was some kind
f human shield.

But the guy didn't shoot and even as Sabrina made eye
ontact with the man, she didn't bother to unwind herself
rom Connor.

"God, not you too," the man said, sounding disgusted.

But Sabrina only grinned. "Hey there, Saunders."

T WAS A good team. Gabriel Saunders was former military
imself, but a marine. Holden had handled a lot of Ga-
riel's training, so Sabrina trusted Gabriel to know what
vas what. The other three were more part-time North Star,
ke a reserves situation, they came to help when there
vas a need.

But they hadn't dedicated their entire beings to North
tar like Gabriel and she had. She trusted them to follow
rders, but it was Gabriel whose mind she'd use.

She'd prefer to plan with Connor, and that was a sur-
rising development. She was supposed to trust North Star
bove all else, and she *did*. She just also trusted Connor
s much.

God, she wanted way too much when it came to him.
he didn't know what to do with it. It reminded her of the
avy SEALs. She'd wanted that with her whole being and

look where that'd gotten her. And *that* was just a thing
People were even less controllable than freak injuries.

And boy, did she not have time to deal with any of *that*

After Gabe gave a general update to her and Conno
and the team now that they'd met here, Sabrina pulle
him aside. She wanted his input without the input of th
reserves or, if she was honest with herself, Connor. Jus
to make sure she wasn't letting her feelings interfere wit
her decision-making skills.

"We're evenly matched," Gabriel said in a low voice
"I think we could easily take them out, but if we still nee
answers, we need more than to just take them out."

"You said they have four men," Sabrina replied. "We'v
got six."

"No, we have four."

She glared at him.

"Sorry, you're the handler here. Your job is that guy
not taking down the men."

"Does that guy look like he needs handling?"

Connor watched them with an expression she couldn'
read. It certainly wasn't a happy or hopeful expression
Resentment almost? But that would be dumb. He wasn'
dumb.

"Look—"

"No, Saunders, you look. He's the target, sure, which
means we keep an eye on him. But let's not pretend th
former navy SEAL over there is some run-of-the-mill ci
vilian who can't protect himself. He can act like part o
the team as easily as these reserves you've brought along.'

She'd thought she wanted Gabe's opinion, thought she'
doubted her own impartiality, but it turned out, when pus
came to shove, trust was the only thing that mattered to
her. And she trusted Connor. She might prefer to keep hin

t of harm's way, but she knew he wouldn't stay there. st as if she was in his position, she wouldn't.

Better to use him. Use them both. "Six against four. We an that way." When he looked like he was about to argue, e flashed a grin at him. "I'm the boss, Gabe."

He gave her a doleful look, both at her shortening his me and at using her position against him. "Six against ur is still tough odds if we're not taking them out. hey're standing around that cabin waiting for *something*."

For Connor. And maybe her if they'd rendezvoused with e hit man and had figured out Connor was with her. 'as the hit man one of the four men? Or was there a fifth an in hiding? There was no way to be sure. She didn't ive a picture or enough of a description to give Gabriel his team.

"We need more intel." That was all there was to it. Irtating and obnoxious to have to wait. But there were no her options. "We stand down until we get word from the ontana team."

Gabriel raised his eyebrows. "You, Sabrina Killian, are ggesting we *wait* until we have more information, rather an wade into the fray and knock some heads together?"

The disbelief poked at her confidence, because she ew she was far too wrapped up in Connor for anyone's od. But even as she tried to sort out feeling from fact, e only knew how to listen to her gut.

She glanced at Connor. Froggy stood next to him. He d his arms crossed and that disapproving look on his ce. She wanted to be somewhere else. Where she could ritate that brood off him. Where it could just be them.

Never in her life had she wished to be somewhere else a job. Never. She should let Gabriel take over. Trust 's instincts over her addled ones. She even opened her outh to do just that.

But she couldn't. She looked at Gabriel and she *couldn*
Addled by feelings or not, her gut was her gut. She'd a
ways trusted it. She couldn't stop now. "This is the rig
thing to do. I know it."

Chapter Seventeen

onnor knew Sabrina trusted her team, but he'd taken
ome time to observe each of them. To decide if he was
oing to trust them too.

It was the way they deferred to Sabrina that did it. She
ld them to wait, they waited. Even the head guy. Con-
or knew he didn't agree with Sabrina's plan, but he didn't
rgue. He didn't huff off and do his own thing.

He listened. He followed. Connor had to believe if they
usted and followed Sabrina, he should trust and follow
em too.

When Sabrina took a phone call, walking a ways away
om the group, Connor watched her. She paced. Then,
ill talking, she looked up at him and her eyes unerringly
et his. She kept talking in low tones as she walked to-
ard him.

And even knowing whatever she was going to tell him
as bad news, even knowing they were surrounded by her
am watching them very carefully, he *wanted* her. With
visceral pull he simply couldn't—or wouldn't—fight.

She stopped in front of him, and he didn't touch her. He
idn't say any of the things he wanted to say to her. But
e way she looked at him, it was almost like she *felt* it.

And boy, he was losing it.

"Yeah," she said into her phone. "Got it. Here he is." She

handed him her phone. "Your old pal Nate. Secure lin␣
Feel free to tell him whatever you need to. Make sure ␣
tells you what we need to know too."

He looked at her, a few beats too long. She didn't mov␣
Didn't look away. When he finally took the phone, he he␣
her gaze. "Hello."

"Care to explain how you got mixed up with my ex?␣

Oh, you don't know the half of it. But the question, ar␣
the edgy drawl of it almost felt normal. Almost. "Care ␣
explain why my friend's in the hospital and my cabin␣
obliterated? Oh, and why I got shot at?"

There was a pause. "I know you told me to let it go..␣

"I told you to build your life. That's different. Sort o␣
He couldn't keep looking at Sabrina and have this conve␣
sation. And still he couldn't break the connection witho␣
some kind of acknowledgement. He hoped it didn't co␣
her any kind of tough points in front of her team, but ␣
took her hand and squeezed it before turning away.

"Yeah, well..." Nate's voice went muffled. "You su␣
this is secure?" Then he sighed. "Okay, Brina's friend he␣
says I can be assured I can tell you anything without an␣
one being able to trace, hear or whatever. I guess I ha␣
to trust her. I wanted to keep you as out of it as possibl␣
Con. I tried. But this is bigger than me. Bigger than u␣
It's huge. We're talking military corruption on a scale..␣

Connor winced. It sounded a little too much like wh␣
he'd been worried about. Nate being a little too...conspi␣
acy theory. A little too obsessed. Paranoia. PTSD. The␣
was a guilt that wound through Connor that he'd nev␣
fully been able to work through. He hadn't believed h␣
friend.

Nate wasn't his responsibility. Nate had gone hom␣
healed and worked on this ranch. He had family an␣
friends there. Connor had trusted them to help him.

And all this time, Nate had just been right.

"I know I sound crazy," Nate said, frustration edging his tone. "I know it. It's why I can't go to anyone. But I also know what I've found. What I sent you was evidence Rear Admiral Daria was selling off weapons to the highest bidder. It's what my informant back in the Middle East was *this* close to telling me, or if not telling me, getting me to the place I'd see it myself. It explains everything."

Connor could only blink. Rear Admiral Daria. The guy had been no different than any other officer Connor had come into contact with. Serious. Hard. Maybe a little vindictive at times, but what officer wasn't? It wasn't a job for the fair or faint of heart, that Connor had learned. Weapons. Military weapons to…anyone.

"I know it sounds like I'm making it up, but I'm not. After they kicked me out, all trails led to him. So, I dug. And dug. I finally got what I needed to prove it. I sent it to you because I wanted to have it in a secure place before I went after them. I didn't want to involve you, but you were there. You were discharged. You were already involved. So, I sent you the evidence I had—"

"It's destroyed."

"Yeah, Brina told me." There was another pause, as if Nate was deciding what to tell him. "I might have some backup of most of what I sent you."

"Nate…"

"You don't believe me."

"I've been shot at and my cabin is blown up. I believe you." He just didn't *want* to believe Nate. Still, wanting to bury his head in the sand didn't mean he would. "I just don't know what the hell we're going to do about it. They want me dead. They're really going to want you dead."

"It's not the first time people have wanted us dead."

But it was the first time they were specific targets, not just a uniform.

"I'm sorry you got dragged into this."

Connor looked at the Tetons towering around him. Then he looked at Sabrina, clearly needling that Gabriel guy over something and enjoying the hell out of herself. Sorry? "I'm not." Even frustrated, tired and lost... Connor couldn't be sorry. "Have you seen any sign of people after you?"

"No. I think they want that evidence taken care of first. Before I sent it off to you I'd think...maybe. It felt like paranoia more than actual threat, though."

But if he took Nate's paranoia at face value, that meant *all* roads led to him because they thought he could prove Daria was the bad guy here. "You'd think they'd have a bigger..."

It hit him then. They had a bigger presence. Somewhere close, but not close enough for Sabrina's team to notice. Suddenly Connor knew that had to be true. These men didn't know the evidence had been damaged, and that meant they thought he had it. If they thought it was in the cabin and they'd destroyed it, they wouldn't still be here.

He was their biggest target. He was what they were after. What they were willing to kill for. Which meant Connor knew what had to be done.

"I know what I have to do. You sit tight. Watch your back. And let this...team of Sabrina's help you. They want to help."

"They sent me their computer geek."

"The person who could get us a secure line so I actually knew what was going on? How dare they," Connor said dryly.

"All I'm saying is you got the baddest badass, almost navy SEAL."

"Yeah, it's a real shame your ex-girlfriend couldn't

come save your butt. Would have been a real nice reconciliation story." It was bitterness that coated his voice, and self-loathing that had him stalking away from the woman in question.

Nate let out a short bark of a laugh. "Brina and I would *never* reconcile. Whatever we had was all…kid stuff. Doesn't matter now."

But it did. Somehow, it had to. "Yeah, well, I slept with her."

"I… I do not know what to say to that."

Nor did Connor himself. Just that it had to be on the table. Just that… Everything had to be on the table. "Just felt like clearing the air."

"Oh, no. No. *No.* Don't you go play hero, Con. No need to clear the air. No getting crap off your chest. Because you're going to come out of this in one piece and tell me to my face you fell for my ex."

"I plan to." He did. But there were risks, and since he planned on Sabrina's safety falling just a hair ahead of his own, the clearing the air had been necessary. "Listen to the computer geek. I don't understand this group at all, but I know they're doing the right thing."

"You sure about that?"

Connor looked at Sabrina, talking to her team. He didn't know why or how, but… "Yeah, yeah I am."

SABRINA WATCHED CONNOR talk to Nate with an intensity that she figured the situation warranted. Probably.

When he ended the call, he walked back to her slowly. He said nothing as he handed her the phone.

"Well?"

"I know what Nate's trying to prove that could get us both killed. But more important, I know that the four guys you saw are just the tip of the iceberg," he said to Gabriel.

Gabriel stood, and Sabrina knew he was about to bluster about how his team hadn't missed anything. Because in his position she'd do the same. Still, she slapped a hand to his chest. "Wait," she said to Gabriel. "Explain," she ordered Connor.

His mouth thinned. Guy did not like an order. He'd have to suck it up for today.

And he did. Connor explained his phone call with Nate, what they were dealing with, and the fact that he was the main and perhaps only target for as long as they thought *he* had the evidence.

Sabrina absorbed the information. She appreciated Connor's delivery. It was straightforward and devoid of any emotion or…interpretation. He laid out the facts so they could all form their own opinions.

She knew he had his own, but for the time being he kept them to himself.

There was a few moments of silence as everyone took on Connor's information. Sabrina didn't get the sense he was leaving anything out, per se, but he was holding something back

"Maybe we're dealing with a small group. And *that's* why no one's after the other guy yet," Gabriel pointed out echoing Sabrina's own feelings on the matter.

"Maybe. We've got a hired hit man, that we know for sure. Some kind of explosives expert, because that cabin was blown to *hell*. We've got a navy SEAL rear admiral implicated." Connor held up three fingers. "Maybe I'm wrong, but if I'm a dirty military higher-up, I'm not fooling around with a couple random guys. I'm sending out everyone I can to end the threat to my position, my reputation, hell, my life. Because you're not just looking at getting kicked out of the military, you're looking at getting tried for treason."

"You'd want your group small though. Too many people know, too many possible slipups," Gabriel said. Which he would have told anyone was Gabe's biggest weakness. Once he had a theory, he didn't want to deviate from it.

Sabrina had the uncomfortable worry lodged in her gut though that if Holden left North Star as Reece had, she wouldn't have much of a say in who became the other field team lead. A worry for another time.

"You're selling military grade weapons to the highest bidder, you've got a direct pipeline to some of the worst humanity has to offer," Connor said. He was calm. Not rattled or frustrated he was arguing his point with someone. Just setting out the information. Weighing it.

"He's got a point," Sabrina said, trying to match Connor's calm so she and Gabriel didn't start a pissing match. "People who'd do anything for a price, and won't talk, because they've got their own skeletons. You wouldn't only take four of those to save your butt. You'd take as many as you could get."

"We only saw four," Gabriel insisted.

"Here," Connor returned, as bland as ever. "Watching my cabin. There's probably some watching SAR. There might even be some tracking our hike through the mountains. We've got four *here* to deal with, but that doesn't mean that's all we'll have to deal with. And this guy, this military guy, he's somewhere too."

"You don't think he's doing his own dirty work," Sabrina said.

"No, but if there was evidence you wanted to have your hands on, wouldn't you want to be close?"

She hated that he was right. The kind of guy who risked everything for some extra money, who used the military and his position in it to pad his pockets... Then was willing to kill over it?

He probably wasn't doing the dirty work, but he wasn[t]
hiding either. Not when he knew everything was at stake[.]

"Which is why we need to set a little bit of a trap," Con[-]
nor said, bright blue eyes straight on hers. Only on her.

She knew what it meant, and she had to fight, real[ly]
fight, to keep her tone and gaze calm in return. "Let m[e]
guess. You're offering yourself up as bait."

"Let me guess," he said, matching her attempt at a bore[d]
tone. "You're going to argue with me about it."

She wanted to. Desperately. But that was knee-jerk[,]
and she had to think it through. "The problem with tha[t]
is they're just going to kill you. It's hard to be bait whe[n]
they just want you dead."

"Not if they think I have the evidence stored some[-]
where."

"Risky, because they could take a gamble that Nat[e]
knows where it is."

"They could, but if it's important enough to kill ove[r]
would they?"

"They'd have to believe you," Gabe said, piping up fo[r]
the first time in a while. "They'd have to believe it wasn[']t
a trap. That you're actually scared or desperate or *some*
thing enough to give yourself up."

"I'm not talking about giving myself up. I'm talkin[g]
about getting myself caught."

Chapter Eighteen

Sabrina whirled away from him. It was her only outward sign of distress. She kept the rest locked down, and Connor could sense how hard that was for her.

He probably shouldn't have been soothed by that reaction.

When she turned back around, it was with clear, fierce eyes and a determination he knew he'd struggle to fight his way through.

"They know I'm with you," she said, as if she'd won a point.

"Sabrina, we don't know that for sure."

"We know there's a pretty high probability they know you're with a woman. That hit man shot at *us*. We can't risk that they know about me just for the sake of your ego."

He scowled at her. "It's not my ego. This is *my* problem."

"The way I see it? It's Nate's problem. He made it North Star's problem, and that made *you* my problem. So buckle up."

"Your group is called North Star?"

She blinked. Paled. "I…" No other words came out of her mouth. Just a kind of strangled noise before she grabbed him by the arm. Roughly.

"Stay here," she ordered her team as she dragged Connor away from them. Froggy whined and Sabrina rolled her eyes. "You can come, too," she muttered.

So, Froggy trotted after them as she pulled him away from her wide-eyed team and into a small grove of trees.

"As much as I'm keen, this probably isn't the time to have your way with me."

"Don't be cute now." She slapped his chest in one final shove. Froggy whined between them.

"He deserved it," Sabrina told the dog, immediately starting to pace as he stood there watching her work through...whatever was going on in that hard head of hers.

And maybe it was inexplicable but all this frustration, worry and anger calmed his own.

"Do you ever get tired of pacing?" he asked casually.

"I pace so I don't punch you in the face," she muttered, and then if possible, paced *harder*.

"You slipped up and told me your secret group's name."

She stopped pacing, looked at him with nothing but fury and maybe some self-loathing on that beautiful face of hers. "Yeah, well, I trust you. So, bite me."

Maybe she hadn't said it softly, or with any *positive* emotion, but he understood enough to know what her trust meant. Or at least what it meant to him.

"Sabrina—" He reached out for her, but she sidestepped him.

"I can't..." She scrubbed her hands over her face. "Look. I need you to listen to me. Seriously listen. Put aside the ego and the macho nonsense and—"

"I would, but since I wasn't relying on any of those things..."

She scowled at him. "Okay. Whatever. Just... I can't let you be the bait in a trap when the chance of survival is something like fifty percent at best. We don't know enough, except how dangerous they are. I cannot let you waltz in there knowing they could know more about us than we know about them—which definitely leads to your death, by the way."

"Would you let yourself waltz into the middle of it? Alone?"

"I would have. Once." She looked at him and that fury melted into something…softer. He couldn't say he understood it, only that it made his chest ache. "It took me a long time to figure out…" She sucked in a breath and let it out. "The thing is you spend your childhood getting kicked around, you figure that's the way of the world. That kind of behavior is what you expect from people and it's what you give people. It took me a long time, a really, *really* long time to believe there could be another way. So, I won't lie to you and say I would never do such a thing, but in the here and now, Con, we need to depend on each other. We can't do this alone. It's a death wish."

"It's not a death wish. I get killed in this, Nate blames himself to the end of his days. I don't want that for my friend. I also have a feeling you'd blame yourself, and I don't want that for you either. This isn't a disregard for my own life. It's the only way we figure out what we're dealing with."

"Then you have to let me go with you," she said stubbornly enough he wished he could beat his head against the nearest tree.

Instead, he dug in. "If we're worried about each other, we're not focused."

"Is that what they taught you in the SEALs? Not to depend on anyone? I've been there, Connor. It doesn't work. I… It's taken me years to fully get that through my head. Hell, a few months ago I managed to break my arm because

I wanted to handle things on my own, and I was ticked off at Holden for a few good more weeks after that for stepping in and stopping the situation from getting worse."

He shoved his hands in his pockets. "I'm not jealous or anything, but I sure am tired of hearing about how great Holden is."

Some of that heartbreaking *earnestness* lightened on her face, and he supposed his, yes, stupid jealousy was worth it if it made her smile.

She stepped forward, curling her hands around his arms as if she was going to shake him. But she only held on. "If you've got a team at your back, you've got to use it."

He jerked his chin toward the people they'd left behind. "They're your team."

"And I'm yours." She tightened her grip, looked right at him. "I don't know what the hell I'm going to do about it. But I am your team and I am sticking. You hear me?"

"Yeah, I hear you. Hard not to when you're yelling in my ear." And he heard something in her words that she wasn't saying. So, he figured he'd be the bigger person and say them first.

He cupped her face with his hands. "I care about you, Sabrina."

She jerked a little in his grasp, like he'd punched her rather than said something nice and meaningful.

"I guess I care about you too," she muttered. Then she pulled herself away, shoving at his arms. "So, we go together. Stop arguing and let's get this over with."

"Then what?"

She stopped and though he couldn't see her face he figured there was a little bit of fear sneaking over her features. He had to believe it.

"Let's live through this first."

Connor planned on it.

ABRINA HATED THAT she felt jittery as she outlined her plan
vith her team. They would each try to take down one of
ne lookouts. She and Connor would move in toward the
abin. The assumption being that as long as the North Star
eam could get the four lookouts around the cabin taken
ut, the other teams would be called in.

Maybe even the head honcho. They'd rearranged Con-
or's pack so he had some smaller bags inside he could
retend housed the evidence they were looking for.

The vests Gabe doled out made Sabrina feel marginally
etter about walking into an open field. Of course a good
it man would just take the headshot, but…

God, she couldn't think about that. She had to tuck it
ll away. Focus on the mission, just like she always did.
s the North Star team had come to mean more and more
o her, she'd had to fight side by side with what had be-
ome her family and worry about them. She was used to
nis clawing feeling of panic and setting it aside to do what
ad to be done.

She didn't know why being used to it meant she couldn't
radicate it completely.

Her phone buzzed and she pulled it out, read the text
nessage from Holden, then showed the screen to Connor.

las to be hospitalized a few days, but prognosis good.
he husband here now. I'll stick around make sure no one
onnects her. Take care of yourself.

Connor's expression betrayed nothing, but because
he'd been staring at the guy for a few days now she saw
ne slight relaxation in his shoulders. He was letting one
vorry go.

"Guess I'll have to thank the guy," Connor grumbled
s Sabrina put her phone back in her pocket.

"Guess you will."

He grunted irritably, making her smile.

They situated the comm units in their ears. Anothe connection. Another safety. Every piece of North Sta armor helped her set aside her worries and nerves an focus on what she had to do.

She stood in front of her team and Connor once the were all packed up and ready to head out.

"All right, team, no one takes any chances. You tak down who you can take down. You stay with your partne You get anyone to talk? Dandy. They're tight-lipped, we' figure it out. Our end goal is to get as many of this grou here in this area with us, then capture as many of them a we can until we have someone who can get us the mai guy. We want to avoid casualties if we can, but remembe *your* life and the team's life is most important."

She looked at her team, all grim-faced and determine She trusted them to follow orders. To make the best choice for the team. She wasn't sure she trusted her partner to d the same, but she cared about him and would do what ha to be done to protect him.

Whether he liked it or not.

"Connor and I will move into the clearing by the cabi remnants. A lot depends on who comes after us, so yo keep those comm units in. You update all changes in po sition and all men you take down. We have to be flexibl and ready to change gears at any moment. If we lose ou communications, it's your job to keep tabs on us. Stay wit your partners. Rely on each other. Let's go."

There was a murmur of assent, then everyone paired of and moved in different directions. *Here we go.*

"Nice speech," Connor said as they headed straight fo the heart of things.

"I do what I can."

"You would have been a hell of a SEAL, Sabrina."

The remark didn't hurt as much as she'd thought it might. Because didn't she know? She *would* have been. But it hadn't worked out. Still it was some kind of comfort or healing or *something* to hear someone who'd been there say it.

"I'm sure as hell glad you're here to fight by my side instead."

She'd known for the past few years that things had probably turned out better this way than if she'd been a SEAL. North Star suited her better, and she had the feeling she'd done more specific good as a field operative than a SEAL.

And *still* some little piece of bitterness she'd held onto, deep inside, finally smoothed out into acceptance.

Destiny. Here it was. She looked at Connor out of her peripheral vision. He didn't have Froggy leashed, but the dog moved by his side as if they were one.

She listened to her comm unit with half an ear. Teams saying they had targets within sight. Still, she and Connor moved forward stealthily until the cabin ruins came into view.

She looked at Connor. His expression was grim, but he kept moving forward.

"Target one taken out. No shots fired."

"Good," Sabrina murmured into her mic. "Move onto the next."

The next three went down in quick succession, and a cold ball of dread settled in Sabrina's stomach. "Well, that was easy."

"Too easy," Connor said.

"Way, *way*, too easy."

"Do any of the men match the hit man's description?" Sabrina asked uneasily as she and Connor began to slowly, calmly move for cover.

She felt as though they were being watched, but that was the whole point. Someone finding them. Someone they could use to get to the head guy. Someone they could use to take the whole thing down.

Surely they wouldn't just be picked off. Not without the evidence. Of course if the people watching them assumed they had the evidence, they could just kill them and take it. But that was quite the risk.

At least...to kill Connor over.

Sabrina's heart stuttered uneasily in her chest. *She* was the expendable one. Had they been shooting at her in the beginning too?

"I've got one that matches your description," one of the part-timers said into the comm unit. "The gun and ammo we've been looking for. Should be our hit man."

It was a relief, and yet Sabrina didn't *feel* relief.

"I don't like being out in the open like this," Connor said into the horribly stifling silence around them. "They're going to take us out, not take us in."

"Yeah." Not *us*, so much as *her*, but if he didn't see that, she wasn't going to point it out to him. Especially when she could *feel* something really bad was about to happen. Sabrina spoke quietly into her mic. "We're going to pull back. Something is off. We'll rendezvous in that wooded area on the east side. Pick one guy to bring and we'll try to get some information out of—"

Something exploded into her. A searing bright pain she couldn't make sense of. She stumbled back, fell, her legs unable to keep her upright.

The snow was cold. So cold. God, she was cold. She writhed in pain, trying to escape the burning, tearing inside of her.

There was a high bark, a harsh curse. Then Connor's face wavered in her vision.

"What the hell happened?" he demanded.

She didn't know. She hadn't heard anything. But she looked down at the same time Connor did. Blood. So much blood.

Silencer.

"Sabrina. Sweetheart."

"Oh, God, don't call me that. I'm not that." She tried to look away from the unbearable pain. The hot spill of her own blood. But all she saw was a gaping hole in the vest that was supposed to protect her and the seeping wetness of her own life slipping away.

Connor was ripping the vest off of her, dragging her out of the open area. They wouldn't know if they were still being shot at until the bullets landed. "Silencer," she rasped.

"I know it." He swore some more. Just a constant stream as he pushed some wadded-up fabric to her wound. She didn't know how he was doing it, then realized somehow he'd gotten the dog to help drag her by the shirt.

Connor pushed one hand to the lump of fabric on her wound. She cursed a blue streak to match his own as he used his other hand to fire back.

Sabrina wanted to tell him to run. She wanted to tell him it was no use. She wanted a million things, but she felt her vision going gray. Everything just dissolving in front of her.

"Told you," she said, trying to fight the gathering darkness, the fade even as her teeth began to chatter. "It makes a joke out of… Kevlar," she managed to finish. But the pain was buzzing in her head and she couldn't see anymore. Everything was black. Everything was gone.

And then so was she.

Chapter Nineteen

Connor had never known such terror. But he bore down on it. There was no place for it here. Not when Sabrina's life was spilling out of her in front of his very eyes.

He concentrated more on putting pressure on the horrible bullet wound in Sabrina's side than the direction he was shooting at. He didn't have time to worry about the hit man. He just had to get Sabrina to safety as quickly as possible.

Good Lord. The bullet had torn through her vest. Just tore the protective gear to pieces. Like she'd said.

He babbled things into his comm unit. Who knew what. The rat bastard had used some kind of silencer. They'd made a grave, grave mistake thinking the hit man was one of the four men the North Star team had taken out. Made a grave mistake thinking Sabrina was invincible.

Blame wanted to bubble up, but how could he focus on blame when she was torn apart like this?

It took too long. Too damn long for the North Star team to appear as Connor, with Froggy's help, had pulled her behind a boulder.

"Good God." Gabriel started shouting into his comm unit. "We need immediate medical attention. Immediate. Sabrina's been shot. It's bad."

Bad didn't begin to cover it.

"There is a hit man out there with a gun and ammo that can shoot through Kevlar. She got a gut shot. You have to get her to medical attention. Now. There's no time to find these guys. Just get her some help."

One of the women in the team pushed forward. "Let me field dress it. Then we'll carry her out to somewhere we can get transportation. Helicopter?"

"They'll shoot it down," Connor said, wanting nothing more than to lie down next to her. Than to carry her out of here himself.

He saw the flash of something out of the corner of his eye, far off, and knew exactly what and who it was. "Hide. He's got a silencer. And that ammo cuts through anything. So you get somewhere you can hide. Get her somewhere. Get the hell out of the way." Connor grabbed Froggy's face, looked into the dog's dark eyes. "Stay with her."

Connor got to his feet, but Gabriel grabbed him by the arm before he could take off. "Where the hell do you think you're going?"

Connor jerked his arm away, and narrowly held back from decking Gabriel. "To kill the son of a bitch." Nothing and no one would stop him now. "Watch after my dog."

"You'll get killed yourself," Gabriel said after him.

"I wouldn't bet on it," Connor muttered, though he'd broken into a run so doubted Gabe had heard him.

There'd have to be a team of hit men with that ammo out there. Maybe there was. So bright and bold was his anger, his fear, Connor was sure he could take them all down. Piece by piece with his bare hands.

He shut off everything going on with North Star. Shoved away the feel of the woman he loved's blood on his hands. Loved. He'd used that stupid word *care* because he'd been a coward. He'd been too overwhelmed by something as stupid as a *feeling*.

And now he was going to pay the price. But if he had to pay, so would the man who had shot her.

Everything faded until there was only the cold grip of righteous anger.

The hit man wouldn't get away with shedding one drop of Sabrina's blood.

So Connor moved through the trees, around boulders, with only one goal in mind. Get to the hit man before he got another shot off. What he'd do once he incapacitated the man? Well…

It wasn't like being back in the military. This was no team mission. It wasn't the partnership Connor had agreed to back before Sabrina had been shot.

This was him. And vengeance.

He had the place where the hit man had been in his mind, and he worked toward it with a single-minded ferocity that left room for nothing else. Not worry. Not grief. Not pain. Not even the sound of his own footsteps.

He moved with a stealth he hadn't had since his days as a SEAL, but it all came back to him. Because he needed it.

As he closed in on the area he knew the hit man had to be in, or had to have run from, Connor made careful circles. He had a gun in his hand. He'd lost his pack somewhere along the way. If he'd had time, he would have lost the vest too.

It didn't matter except that he simply didn't have the time to shrug it off. Connor heard a sound. The faintest scrape of boot against rock. He stilled, listened, then crept forward with all the silence of a shadow.

When he skirted around another boulder, there was the man he'd rescued just a few days ago. He was laid out flat on a rock. Even if they'd had a sniper of their own, they wouldn't have been able to shoot him from anywhere except exactly where Connor was.

The man either didn't know Connor had left the group, or didn't think he'd come after him. He didn't look concerned at all. He had the rifle positioned to shoot, and he patiently watched through the sight.

Connor didn't know if he saw anyone. It didn't matter. He was a dead man.

Bigger fish to fry.

Alarming that his inner voice now sounded like Sabrina. Snarky and sharp and fully capable of sending this guy to hell, but choosing not to because there were bigger fish to fry.

Connor breathed through that rational thought. A deep, dark, desperately afraid part of him wanted to forget rational thoughts. Wanted to act only in violence. As long as he wasn't sure Sabrina would live, what did getting the bigger fish matter?

But it mattered. To Nate. To the people he didn't know who had been hurt or killed or left behind because of what Rear Admiral Daria had done just because he *could*. Just for some extra money.

It took time to wrangle those messy emotions. To separate them. To focus. He moved the aim of his gun from the man's head to the hand that was wrapped around the high-powered rifle.

Then for his own satisfaction, he whistled. And shot only when the hit man's eyes met his.

THERE WERE VOICES. Jostles. The pain made her want to fade back into that black world where nothing hurt. Where there was nothing.

But there was something she needed to do. She had to figure out what it was. Where was Connor? Where was Froggy?

Where was *she*?

She blinked, trying to make her vision work. People were carrying her, but she couldn't quite feel all the parts of her body. And everything was swirly with gray around the edges. Unfocused and dull. "What's happening? Where's Connor?"

"Don't move, okay?" It was Gabriel's voice. Strained. Because he was carrying her over his shoulder while someone pressed something to where the pain in her centered. "Almost there."

"Almost where?" She didn't know if no one answered her because they couldn't or because they didn't hear her. She wasn't even certain she had managed to get sound to come out of her mouth.

But she was alive. The pain. The jostling. Trying to make sense of anything meant she was alive.

"Connor?"

But he didn't come into her vision. She didn't hear his voice. She saw Froggy's paws, trotting alongside Gabriel's long strides. Surely Connor was here if Froggy was.

"Close your eyes," a calm, female voice said.

"Betty?" How had North Star's doctor gotten here?

Betty didn't answer. She was busy shouting instructions as she did things to Sabrina's body that she couldn't feel.

"Come on, close your eyes. Do it for me, Sabrina. Now."

Sabrina was a little afraid she was going to never open them again if she closed them, but she always trusted Betty to patch her up.

God, she needed some patching up. She couldn't even move her arms. Couldn't get her brain to do more than circle. So, she closed her eyes, and fought not to give in to the dark.

"There's a girl." Betty's voice. "Gabriel, gently as you can, she goes on the stretcher. Keep those eyes closed, Sabrina."

Sabrina did as she was told and the world around her

seemed to move. Her stomach pitched. Pain stretched out from so deep inside of her she almost thought of reaching for the black instead of fighting it away.

But she was alive. Alive. She kept her eyes closed and tried to focus on the voices. Betty's especially. Though it was just coming to her in snatches. The word *hospital. Too late. So much blood.*

Too late.

Too late.

It seemed like everyone around her was chanting it. Only when the stretcher seemed to jerk then settle, and Betty shouted, "drive," did Sabrina realize the "too late" chants were her own.

"I'm going to die," Sabrina said flatly. *That* was her destiny. Finally got her head on straight, found a decent guy where she didn't screw everything up by kicking him to the curb, and she was doing to die.

"You're going to let this puny bullet wound take you out? That's not the Sabrina Killian I know," Betty said, but Sabrina knew that tone.

It was the tone she used when she was lying to someone about how big the needle was going to be.

"Gabe. Hold her still. I'm going to sedate her."

"No. No, you can't—wait. Gabe? Where is Connor?"

She tried to focus on him, but he said nothing and his face was just a blur.

Which meant Connor wasn't here. Oh, God. He'd gone off to… No. No, it couldn't be happening.

"Damn it, someone has to get to Connor. Someone has to—"

"We're taking care of it," Gabriel said.

"You're here. You're *here*. You're not taking care of…" The pain was so all-encompassing it was like a blinding bright white light and she couldn't get the rest of the words out.

"Hold her down," Betty ordered.

But Sabrina didn't feel it. Something fluid and warm moved through her, and she lost what little grasp she had on the here and now.

Chapter Twenty

The hit man did not take getting shot in the hand very well. Not only did he howl and thrash, but also the guy wasn't even smart enough to grab his rifle before it went flying off the cliff he'd spread himself out on.

Worked for Connor.

He stood over the man, who was holding his hand and keening in high-pitched waves as he held the bleeding, mangled hand. Connor didn't want to touch him, so he didn't. He pressed his boot to the man's neck.

The man shrieked, wiggled and tried to roll away, but since his hand had been shot and he was using the other one to hold it, he didn't use his hands or arms to push Connor's leg away.

"What? You never been shot before?"

That seemed to get through to the guy. Some of the thrashing stopped. Some calculation began to filter into his expression amidst the pain. Cold eyes looked up at him.

Connor pressed harder. Revenge kept working its way through him, making him forget the promises to himself. "Tell me where your boss is."

"You'll kill me whether I tell you or not. So go to hell," the man rasped. He started using his good hand to try and push Connor's leg away, but it was no use.

God, Connor wanted to kill him. He had to believe Sabrina's team had saved her, would save her, but she could be dead.

Dead.

He pressed harder against the hit man's windpipe as the man choked and gasped for air. Pulling at Connor's leg with his good arm, but ineffectually.

If Sabrina was dead, this man should suffer the same fate.

But this wasn't who Connor was. A life for a life wasn't his decision to make. No matter what happened, he wouldn't let that be the man he was. It would make him no better than this subhuman life form. "Actually, no matter what you tell me, you're going to rot in jail. One route is just going to be more painful than the other. You tell me, I tie you up and leave you here to be picked up by the authorities. You don't tell me, I keep pressing. Maybe I should press somewhere else."

Connor repositioned himself meaningfully, giving him the right angle to crush his boot in between the man's legs if he let go some of the pressure on his neck.

The man shrieked and bucked under the boot at his neck. "Don't. Jeez. You want to go one on one with the boss? Fine. You want to send me to jail? Fine. Daria's in an off-grid cabin on Albert's Peak. Good luck, you dumb SOB."

Connor knew the spot, thought he had a good idea where the cabin was. Miles away. It was a disappointment, but he could cover miles. He could cover the whole damn earth if he had to. He would end this. No matter what it took.

Connor kicked the guy onto his stomach, ready to tie him up, but the guy *had* to just keep yammering on.

"They'll get me out, you pissant nobody. This is futile.

You're *nobody.* High and mighty nobody. I'll be out of jail in seconds. Then I'll come for you and—"

Connor laughed darkly. "You keep dreaming. You're a murderer. No one's getting you out of that."

"Murderer." He scoffed as much as a man being held down in the snow could scoff. "So are you. Military, right? You kill, but I do it for profit and I'm the bad guy? I don't think—"

Connor timed and executed the hit perfectly so that the guy lost consciousness from one nasty blow. Then he didn't have to hear the rest of his crap or tie him up. He searched the guy for weapons or ID or anything. Found a wallet with nothing but cash in it, and some ammo. Connor shoved both into his own pocket then shimmied down the cliff face and picked up the gun the hit man had lost. Wouldn't be easy to maneuver with, but he wasn't about to let it stay here for when the moron woke up.

Connor looked around, oriented himself to the area, then set out. The biggest problem wasn't terrain—he'd climb, ford, plow through anything in his way. The biggest problem wasn't miles, he'd cover every last inch without a break. Maybe he hadn't been a SEAL for a while, but he'd been trained for precisely this. He could, and would, hack it through sheer force of will.

The problem was he was one man, with two guns, an out-of-range comm unit, and absolutely no idea what awaited him at this off-grid cabin. Daria wouldn't be alone. He might even know Connor was coming if the hit man had some way of communication.

But there hadn't been any communication device on the hit man that Connor had found. Not even a cell. How were they communicating?

Connor hoped to God there was *no* communication. It could give him the element of surprise.

He would use whatever came his way. Face whatever came his way. No matter what.

But he had to focus on the facts. The cool, grounding weight of them. What had happened? *Sabrina* had been shot. A trained hit man with a major weapon had shot *Sabrina* while they'd been out in an open area, moving slowly. Easy pickings, if he'd wanted them both. If he'd wanted Connor.

The hit man had hit her, because they *wanted* him and didn't think she was worthwhile to them. But they needed him. Alive and ready to take in.

Connor could use that. He had to use that.

He wasn't sure how long he'd walked before he heard something, or maybe even felt something. Just suddenly he knew he was not moving through the mountains alone. He curled his finger around the trigger of his gun, the bigger one loose in his other hand. He kept moving. Ready. Waiting.

A footstep. Connor didn't whirl at the sound, he carefully turned his body, aiming the gun toward the sound, scanning the area and—

"Hey, wait up."

Connor spun at the voice, ready to shoot. But the voice hadn't come from the same place the footsteps had come from. But he thought he…recognized it. And when the figure appeared, Connor felt some mixture of irritation and relief.

Holden. "What are you—"

From the side he'd heard the footstep someone else moved into vision. Connor whirled on the unknown quantity.

The guy held up his hands as Holden spoke.

"Connor, this is Granger McMillan," Holden said. "He's

with me. Well, us now. Granger, this is Connor. Former SEAL. Desperately in love with Sabrina."

"What are you doing here?" Connor growled, scowling back at Holden.

He bit his tongue to keep from demanding how Sabrina was. He didn't want to know if she was dead. Better to keep moving forward with the belief she was alive, and he was fighting for something. If she was dead…

"She's in surgery," Holden said, far too gently to have Connor snapping at him for ruining his delusions.

Connor swallowed. "Will she…" God, how was he supposed to ask? How was he supposed to deal with this weight? He wasn't. They should move. They had to…

"We don't know. But she made it to the hospital and she's in surgery." Holden nodded toward the way Connor had been going. "So, let's end this for her. God, she's going to *hate* that. She'll live just to be mad about it for the next century. The big strong men saving the day."

Connor knew this guy who'd been friends with Sabrina for far longer than Connor had known her was trying to bolster him. It might have shamed him if he had any emotions left.

"Don't get too cocky just yet." It was a woman's voice this time, as a built blonde stepped out of the trees.

The two men who'd joined Connor frowned at her, but they didn't point their weapons at her so Connor supposed it was another one of these North Star people. Not the ones he and Sabrina had worked with either. New ones. They were slightly older-looking with more aura of…authority, he supposed.

She smiled coolly at Holden and then Granger. "Can't let you boys have all the fun, can I? As you said, Sabrina would really hate that."

"Who's manning the group while you're here?" Granger demanded.

The woman narrowed her eyes at Granger. "Not your group. Not your problem. Now, what's the plan?"

Connor could question it, or he could take the help. There was only one choice that brought Daria down faster, and him back to Sabrina faster. "If I believe the hit man, the head guy—the rear admiral who started all this—is in a cabin over here."

"Do you believe the hit man?" Granger asked.

"I don't know, but if he's not here, something or someone is."

"Then let's go," the woman said.

SABRINA FELT LIKE she was swimming through gray mists. Sometimes they'd part and she'd see lights. Hear an incessant beep. Someone's voice. But it was hard to stay in those moments because the gray crept back in.

When she finally managed to open her eyes and keep them open, it was Betty's face swimming in her vision.

"Guess you saved the day," Sabrina said, but the sounds that actually came out of her mouth didn't sound anything like the words she was trying to articulate. She frowned, tried to shift in the bed, but Betty's hand softly yet firmly touched her shoulder.

"There you are," Betty said, smiling kindly. "Stay still now."

Sabrina liked Betty. Much as she didn't like being hurt or sick, Betty had always been a soothing, calming presence. Holden always got bent out of shape about having to sit for the good doctor, but Sabrina didn't mind.

She stilled under Betty's hand, tried to hold on to the fact she had her eyes open, understood who she was with and what was happening, even if she was struggling to speak.

"I had to sedate you in the field so they could operate right away once we got to the hospital. Bullet went straight through, but it nicked some organs on the way, which isn't the best. They stitched you up. You're pumped full of drugs so you might feel woozy, sick, confused. You won't be able to move quite the way you're used to, but that's all right. It'll all wear off."

"I'm going to be okay?" This time her mouth seemed to work, though her voice was weak and scratchy. Slow and slurred to her own ears.

"You're not quite out of the woods. Infection is always a concern, among other things. But you're strong and a fighter, so my money's on you."

"What happened? I mean, got shot, I know. But after? Where's Connor? Did we get the guys?"

Betty's smile stayed in place, but something flickered in her eyes that had Sabrina's blood running cold. "No need for you to worry about that. Your focus is healing and—"

"Betty, you have to tell me what's going on."

Betty sighed. "Well, it was worth a try. They're still out in the field. Shay sent Connor some backup."

"Who? Gabriel? The part-timers are fine enough, but—"

"Not the part-timers. Not Gabriel. Sabrina, you have to stay calm. Really, really calm. Okay? If you can't, I'll have to get the nurse to sedate you."

"Tell me what backup she sent," Sabrina said through gritted teeth, happy her voice was coming out stronger. She wanted to grab Betty's hand. Demand and squeeze and rage, but she couldn't get her body to work in quite that way yet.

"Holden went," Betty said, eyeing the machines hooked up to Sabrina.

"I told him not to get involved! I thought he was quitting! Shay sent him alone?" Everything hurt. Her brain was fuzzy. But Sabrina knew this was all wrong. And felt twin pangs of relief that two of the best men she knew were working together, and horror that two of the people she cared about most in the world were out in harm's way.

"You can't get worked up, Sabrina. You just had major surgery. And Holden's not alone in helping Connor."

"*Who?*"

"Well... Shay called Granger in for a favor on Holden's case. Then she figured you almost dying was reason enough to call him in again."

"Granger? But he quit. He refused to come back. He..." Exhaustion washed over her, but there was relief in it. "Holden *and* Granger?" She felt like crying. Everything hurt. She wanted that oblivion again, but tears filled her eyes. Holden and Granger had put themselves in danger to help Connor. To help *her*.

Three men she would have trusted with her own life. Quite the feat for someone who never thought she'd trust anyone just a few years ago.

"And Shay," Betty added.

That did it. That really did it. A tear leaked over her cheek, but just one. She fought the rest back. "Who's running the group then? Didn't anyone tell her when you're the boss you're not supposed to go back to field operative?"

"Sabrina, honey? Right now, we're a family, not a group. And the people who love you and are in a position to are out there making sure the guy who hurt you doesn't hurt anyone else. Also, Holden said you were in love with this Connor guy."

"Love?" Sabrina made a scoffing noise that made her

body hurt, and her eyes sting even more. But one tear was all they got. Just the one. "Who falls in love in a few days?"

"Apparently, you. And Holden. I can't wait until you meet this woman he's going to marry. She's… You're just going to have to meet her. And visit her farm."

"Farm?"

"Yeah. A farm."

That didn't make any sense, but that somehow made it better. That it was nonsensical. Love sure felt nonsensical, and not just because she'd been shot.

But none of this was okay until they were all back. "When will I know they're okay?" Not if. Never if. Only when.

Betty took her hand. "You worry about resting up. You're not out of the woods yet. Sewing up organs is not easy on a body."

"Betty…"

"It'll take time, honey. You just rest up so when they get back, you can kick their asses for taking care of this without you."

Sabrina sighed. She couldn't relax, but she let herself stop trying to *will* her way into the situation she couldn't be part of. "You always know the right things to say." She thought about everything that had happened. "What about the dog?"

"We've got her. She's being taken care of."

Okay. Okay, she could deal with this. She could figure this out. Holden, Granger and Shay were out there helping Connor. Froggy was taken care of.

Now she had to figure out what she could do. "I need to talk to Elsie."

"You need to rest."

"Bet, I can't rest until they're okay. So, I'm going to need you to get me Elsie on the phone. And everything

North Star has on this Daria guy. And… Look, if I can't be in the field, you've got to give me this."

Betty's lips were pursed. "Fine, but I'm warning you, you won't have the energy for it."

They'd see about that.

Chapter Twenty-One

About a mile away from where Connor thought the cabin was, they met their first guard, dispatched easily enough. And, even better, a comm unit stolen to give them an idea of what the enemy was doing.

They stayed together in teams of two. Holden with him, Shay and Granger together. Though he hadn't seen them interact with Shay, except for Holden, Connor found trusting them was easy. They were part of Sabrina's team. Her family.

They were all here for her.

Dark was beginning to descend, but they were getting close. Connor could hear the guards occasionally talk to each other. It didn't give a clear picture of where they were all stationed, but evidently it was serious business.

The guards didn't seem to have a sense of what they were guarding. Only that they were waiting for something, and Daria was holding all the strings.

"They don't know anything," Holden said after they listened to two guards have a conversation about wondering how long this would last. He scanned the area, nodded toward a tiny pinprick of light. "You think that's it?"

Connor looked around. At the moon. At the mountains. "Should be." There was only darkness and moonlight and that tiny orange glow. There weren't any lights on the guards, which would make it difficult.

"Something is lit up in your pocket," Holden whispered to him. "Might want to take care of that before we get any closer."

Connor looked down at his leg where the cargo pocket held his phone. The display shone through the fabric. Connor scowled and jerked it out, ready to turn it off completely.

But he stopped at the unknown number on the screen. Could be some spam call, but with everything so...turned upside down, he wasn't sure he could just ignore... "Hello."

He heard Holden curse bitterly next to him, but that was immediately forgotten at the voice in his ear. "Connor..."

He thought his legs might give out, but they didn't. Words piled up, but none of the important ones would squeeze out of his throat. "How do you even have my number?"

"Magic."

He nearly crumbled right there. She sounded tired. Raspy and drained, but she still infused that sassy, irritable note to her voice and God, she was okay. Going to be okay.

"Now, you have to listen to me. He's got explosives."

Connor's mind was reeling. He couldn't quite follow. She was...alive. In his ear. Warning him about... "Who's got explosives?" Connor held the phone out between him and Holden so they could both hear what she had to say.

"Daria. He's been stockpiling them. I think they're in that cabin. The guys we caught on our initial move didn't know anything about it, but Elsie's been unearthing evidence on Daria and the explosives can't be ignored. I think he's going to blow the whole thing up. He's going to end the whole thing, destroy all the evidence, including the witnesses. But he's waiting for you, because he thinks

ou've got the evidence on you, and maybe even thinks
ou know everything."

"What about Nate?" Connor demanded, even as Holden
yped something into his phone.

"Elsie's working on that angle. You need to worry about
ou. Connor, you go anywhere near that cabin, he blows
t up. I'm sure of it."

"I'm not backing off of this, if that's what you're get-
ing at."

"Why not? I had to."

"Yeah, because you almost *died*."

"I'm still here, aren't I?"

"Thank God."

There was a slight pause. "You have three of North
Star's best field operatives with you. Work with them.
Please."

Please. He'd only heard her say that once before. A
memory he couldn't afford right now.

"They're your family," he murmured, understanding
what she was asking. Not just to work together, but to keep
them safe. To not risk them because he wanted to end this.

"Yeah, they are," she said, but surprised the hell out of
him by taking it farther. "I love them, but I love you too.
So don't get exploded, hotshot."

Love. "Did you just say—"

"Gotta go. End it. Safely. Bye."

Connor had mostly forgotten Holden was next to him,
listening in. He might have felt discomfort over the love
thing. Holden hearing it. Sabrina saying it. Love in general.

But there was no time for that. There was only ending this.

"Texted Granger and Shay to come back. If we're talking explosives, we need a new plan."

"You know anything about explosives?"

Holden grinned in the shining moonlight. "You happen to be looking at an expert."

"Okay, so, we'll put you on finding them. Disarming them. What about the other two?"

"The other two," Shay began mildly, coming into view on a quick run that was almost utterly silent, Granger behind her, "and you, will take out the guards. Daria probably has a gun or something, but there's no way he's some kind of fighter hiding in a cabin like this. He's the weak link. Once we get to him."

"Except the part where he can probably detonate whatever explosives Sabrina was telling me about."

"Holden and I move to the cabin. Holden searches for the explosives and I take out any guards who try to stop him," Granger said, clearly used to being in charge. "Connor and Shay take out the guards around the perimeter. Once it's clear, I will enter the cabin—"

"Daria wants *me*. I'll be entering the cabin," Connor interrupted.

"Daria wants you so it's a risk to give him you," Holden argued. "Granger and I go. My bet is the explosives are inside. You let *me* go into the cabin and—"

"You're not immune to explosives any more than Sabrina was immune to that special ammo ripping a hole in her Kevlar and her *body*," Shay said, barely restrained fury in her tone. "Any of us die, she's going to feel that on her head. We're not letting that happen. Plus, we need Daria alive. He's supplying these stolen weapons to *somebody*, and we need to figure out who."

"I don't care who. I care about ending the man who wants to end me."

"Fair enough, Connor, but our missions overlap. Take out Daria, without loss of life." She gave Connor a meaningful look. "And then build on what we learn from here to move up the chain."

"I can stop the explosives. I should—"

"We don't know the explosives are in there. We don't know what Daria does if somebody he's not counting on bursts in there." She took a deep breath. "Connor is right. It should be him."

Holden and Granger both mounted arguments, but they stopped whispering them harshly into the quiet night when Shay held up a hand.

Connor took the pause as an opportunity to plead his case. Not because he needed permission, but because if they were all on the same page... Well, that's what Sabrina would want. "He wants me, yeah, but he also wants the evidence he thinks I have. I go in there, and tell him I have the evidence hidden, maybe we can draw him out. I have what amounts to a bulletproof vest. He needs me, or thinks he does."

"You took the chance at laying bait when you and Sabrina walked into that open field. Didn't work so well, did it?" Granger said gruffly.

Shay eyed Granger, an exchange Connor couldn't begin to understand. But it wasn't the point.

"No, it didn't. But it proves my point. The hit man shot her, not me. Here I am, totally unscathed, and he had ample time and opportunity. They don't want me dead. Not yet."

"That's the plan then. Granger, Holden and I fan out and take out all the guards we can. Connor, you head for the cabin. You walk in, try to draw him out. Ideally by that time Holden's got a handle on the explosives and can work on defusing."

Shay pointed to the light. "Granger, east, Holden, west. I'll head forward then circle around the back. Got it?"

Everyone agreed, so she sent them on their way. Holden

and Granger first. Before Connor could run forward, she stopped him. "You die, Sabrina is going to kill me. So keep your head about you."

Connor thought of Sabrina saying she *loved* him. Then hanging up. "She's not rid of me that easily."

Shay's mouth curved. "All right, let's go."

She disappeared into the night, and Connor followed at his own pace. He had two guns and his head about him, as Shay had said.

He didn't come into contact with any guards, which he figured meant North Star had taken care of them all. A good sign. Connor made it to the cabin. He took a second, only one, to take a deep breath and focus.

This was about apprehending Daria without getting everyone blown up. Without getting himself killed. With the guards taken out, carrying two weapons of his own, Connor figured he had a good shot to come out on top.

He crept up to the cabin. He gave a brief thought to trying to rendezvous with the other North Star operatives just to make sure, but taking out guards might call attention to people coming. Connor had to use surprise to his advantage, and not let Daria get off any explosives before he and North Star were out of here.

Though the windows glowed, it was around pulled curtains. So, Connor couldn't get a look inside. He would have to break in, guns at the ready. No other option.

He really hoped Daria didn't have one of these Kevlar piercing guns. But, no other options. This had to end. He didn't want to die and let that be on Sabrina's conscience, but he couldn't live with this falling through his fingers.

He took one breath, then kicked down the door in one quick slam. He ducked back out of the doorway, ignoring the flashback to the Middle East and missions there.

He was in Wyoming. Cold to the bone, and about to take down his former superior.

No gunshots exploded. No guards came running. Connor led with the gun. He didn't have the tactical gear he would have had a SEAL, but he still had the moves, the knowledge, the understanding.

Rear Admiral Daria stood in the middle of a rough cabin. There was no furniture, no explosives, no debris. There was only a man Connor had once saluted.

"Rear Admiral. I'd salute, but my hands are full."

The man who'd once calmly told him he was being dishonorably discharged and had to lie about an injury merely sneered. He held no weapons. Wore no vest. He had what appeared to be a phone in his hand, that was it.

But he didn't seem scared.

"I would have preferred my guards to bring you here in chains, but I suppose the ends negates the means," Daria said, all cool, practiced authority. "I want that evidence Nathan Averly sent you. Or you're dead."

"Seems like to blow me up, you'd have to blow yourself up too."

Daria shrugged. Calmly. So calmly Connor's gut turned to ice.

He held up the phone, and that was when Connor understood that would set off the explosives. Daria might not look armed, but oh... He was armed. Where were the explosives? There didn't appear to be any doors to other rooms, and mountain cabins—especially off-the-grid ones—didn't tend to have basements.

Still, Connor knew they were somewhere. Had to be. "Put it down, Daria."

Maybe the explosives weren't here. Maybe Daria was holding someone else's lives in his hands.

But there was such a...resigned set to his shoulders.

To his mouth. He might be calm, he might be authoritative but…

"I don't care if I have to blow myself up in the process."

There was a deadness in Daria's eyes. A lack of hope. A lack of will. This was a man at the end of his rope. A man willing to die rather than face the consequences of his actions.

And that was the most dangerous thing Connor could have come face-to-face with. Because he wasn't going to win the bluff, which meant he had to hope to God Holden had figured out the explosives. Where they were. How to defuse them.

Connor swallowed. Sweat dripped down his back even though it was cold. "All right. You got me. I've got the evidence right here. Put down the detonator and I'll hand them over to you. You can take them. Escape. Kill me. You can do all that. We don't both have to die."

The man's smile told Connor everything he needed to know.

They were dead already if Holden hadn't been fast enough.

"See you in hell, Lindstrom." And Daria pressed the button.

Chapter Twenty-Two

Nothing happened.

Connor nearly sagged in relief. Even as Daria began to press the button harder and harder, just plain old relief swamped Connor.

"It can't be. It can't be. I'm not going in. I'm not…" He trailed off, looked up at Connor and the guns.

The calm, resigned man was gone. His eyes went wild and then he flew at Connor.

Connor didn't shoot him. He thought about it, but that was what Daria wanted. To be dead. To have nothing touch him. Connor simply moved out of the way, but Daria only pivoted, reaching for the guns.

"It doesn't matter now, Daria," Connor said, fighting the man back. He was surprisingly agile, though he couldn't beat Connor for strength. "The evidence we have on you isn't even here."

Daria tried to wrestle the smaller gun out of Connor's hand. Connor tossed the bigger one toward the door. He couldn't fight with no hands, so he needed one free. Daria lunged for it, but Connor tackled him to the ground before he could get it. Then he went ahead and tossed the other gun too.

Threatening to kill the guy wasn't going to end anything. He wasn't afraid of dying, and that made for a very dangerous man indeed. Connor didn't need guns. He only needed his strength.

A figure appeared in the door. Connor couldn't look more than peripherally as he wrestled with Daria to keep him away from the guns.

"Don't kill him. It's what he wants," Connor ground out.

"No problem," Shay's voice replied. She stepped in, unerringly reached down and grabbed Daria by the arm—Granger doing the same to the other arm—in an easily choreographed move. Connor panted and watched as they tied him up.

"You two are quite the team."

They looked at each other, another one of those charged exchanges Connor didn't understand.

"FBI should finally be getting up here in the next thirty," Shay said, once Daria was effectively bound and gagged. "They'll take him."

Connor got to his feet. Looked at Daria. His eyes were wild and he still fought his bonds, but it was no use. It felt anticlimactic almost. They'd found him. Stopped him. No explosions.

Now what?

Shay and Granger stepped out of the cabin to meet with Holden. They spoke in low tones, but as Connor stepped outside, he didn't listen. He looked up at the sky.

Now what? It was over, but it didn't feel over. Because he was stuck here, while Sabrina was…

Alive. She'd not just spoken to him, she'd warned him about the explosives. Somehow, even bedridden with a bullet hole in her, she'd saved the day.

Shay approached him as they heard the sound of an incoming helicopter. FBI coming to clean up the mess.

"We did our part." Shay clapped Connor on the shoulder. "Now they'll do theirs."

Connor let out a long breath. Stars winked. The night air was cold. And this was over.

Or almost over. He still had one loose thread to tie up. He looked at Shay. "You got some time to talk about something unrelated to this mission?"

"I'll drive you to the hospital. That should give us some time."

THE SOUND OF the door opening made Sabrina want to scream. She was so tired of being poked and prodded every five seconds. The beeps. The machines. She just wanted out.

She wanted to be in the field with everyone. She wanted to be side by side with Connor ending it. God, he had to end it. Not *die* in the process.

And she couldn't deal with any well-meaning nurses when she was this churned up. When she didn't have any answers to what was going on up on that mountain and probably wouldn't until morning.

"My blood pressure is fine and I don't want any drugs. Could you please leave me the hell alone and let me get some sleep?"

"Well, that's some way to greet the guy you dropped the L-word on in the middle of a deadly mission. I guess I could let you get some sleep, but—"

She whirled, nearly ripping out her IV and causing a lot of pain in the process. She moaned in agony and closed her eyes against the burning ache of it.

"Sorry, shouldn't have surprised the gunshot wound victim. Shh. Shh. Lie still." She felt the bed move as he came to sit next to her. His hand touched her face. "Sorry, sorry."

"You're here," she said, keeping her eyes squeezed shut. "You're okay. Gabriel said it would take hours. It would… You're alive. Everyone?" *Please God, don't let me be hallucinating.*

"Everyone's okay."

Then she just started *sobbing.* It was possibly the most embarrassing experience of her life, but she couldn't stop. The tears poured out, even as Connor carefully, so carefully, gathered her in his arms. She covered her face with her hands, but the sounds coming out of her didn't stop.

It was *humiliating.* But he held her. Tight. He was okay. Everyone was okay. It was going to be *okay.*

"Geez, Sabrina. You gotta stop that. You're going to kill me."

She sniffled, miserably embarrassed and yet so damn relieved she couldn't do anything but cling to him. "I mean, I almost died, feel like it's only fair."

He chuckled into her hair. And just sat there and let her hang all over him like a dope. "I don't want to hurt you."

"Just tell me what happened."

"Well, you know, Holden and I saved the day."

She pulled back enough to look up at him. So broad and sturdy and here. Blue eyes calm and *here.*

She wouldn't cry again, couldn't survive the embarrassment. But it was a hard-won fight to find her normal self in the midst of all this relief. "Except for the part where I warned you about the explosives and Shay made the three of you hardheaded men actually work together rather than race in as the sole savior."

He frowned. "How did you know that?"

"Woman's intuition. Now, tell me the rest."

Connor blew out a breath. He studied her face, as if looking for some sign she was really half a step away from death. But he spoke as he studied her. Held her carefully. "He would have blown us up, that's for sure. So, credit where credit is due. Shay had the best plan, Holden deused the explosives, the three of them took out all the guards and I…"

"Brought the bad guy in," she finished for him.

"He's not going to talk. They'll have to put him on some kind of suicide watch. He was ready to kill anyone in his path, including himself, to make this not stick to him. Don't know what it'd matter if you're dead, but I guess some people care more about their legacy than others. Nate's got the evidence to make sure it sticks, though. Daria bought and sold weapons on the side. There's more to it beyond him, and I don't think Nate's going to give up on this until he goes all the way up the chain, but the threat to the both of us, the specific threat of Daria, is over."

"Over," Sabrina repeated.

Connor swallowed. Hard. He leaned forward and pressed his forehead to hers. "I love you, Sabrina."

She blinked. She refused to cry any more tears, but that didn't mean they weren't there. She'd said it to him. Over the phone. But he'd had to know and now he…

She didn't know what the hell they were going to do about it, and she was too tired to figure it out, but it was enough now. She loved him. He loved her.

"Say it again," she murmured.

He chuckled, humored her and even kissed her gently. Too gently for her tastes, but as long as she was hooked up to half a dozen machines, she'd give him a pass.

"I'm in the hospital for a few more days. Out of North Star commission for a lot longer than that, so I guess we've got time to figure out how this love thing works."

He got an odd expression on his face, but he smiled. "Yeah, we've got time."

Epilogue

Sabrina was a little irritated Betty was the one driving her from the hospital in Wilson to North Star base farther northeast.

Surely, Connor could have made the trip. He visited her every other day, but only in the mornings. Like he had things to do.

Probably back SAR-ing. Living his life. *Not* worried about her at all. And good for him. What did *love* matter? They had two separate lives and that was that.

She wanted to pound something to dust, and worst of all, didn't have the strength for it. Betty even had to help her out of the car. She had to *lean* on someone to walk.

"You want to go say hi to everyone, or you want to rest first?" Betty asked as she unlocked all the security features and ushered Sabrina into North Star headquarters.

"I want to burn everything to the ground," Sabrina muttered.

"Aw, just like old times," Betty said, her eyes dancing with laughter. "But maybe a rest would do you some good."

Sabrina grumbled something. She was home and Connor was *somewhere*. Holden was *somewhere*. And no one apparently gave two flying pigs that she had been released from the hospital.

Or they're avoiding because they know you'll be in

foul mood. She scowled at her inner voice, knowing it was right.

Sabrina leaned on Betty as they walked deeper into the house, but frowned when she heard the low sounds of a female voice she didn't recognize, followed by Holden's voice shouting out orders.

Sabrina scowled. "What's he doing here?"

"Guess you'll have to go find out."

Sabrina scowled deeper, but pulled away from Betty. She took ginger steps toward the big room they did training exercises in when the weather was bad.

"Stop," Holden was yelling at two fighting figures. "You gotta let the military stuff go. Stop fighting fair."

A red-haired woman sat next to Holden, and glanced up when Sabrina walked in. She poked Holden's shoulder and he turned around to look.

He crossed his arms over his chest, looked Sabrina up and down. "Look who's decided to finally join us."

Sabrina couldn't look at who Holden had been instructing because she could only stare at the woman next to him. She was willowy with green eyes and freckles.

Holden pointed at her.

"This is my wife. Willa. You missed the impromptu wedding, by the way."

Willa smiled, beaming with a sweetness Sabrina normally wouldn't trust. "I've heard a lot about you."

"I wish I could say the same." She blinked. "Betty told me you have a farm."

"I do. And we'll be having a more traditional wedding for you to come to eventually." Willa and Holden had their arms around each other's waists. Casually. Like they fit, and Sabrina found she understood that. The way someone could just click into your life.

She wasn't sure she'd understand how to give up North

Star and live on a farm or whatever. How to give up who she was but...

Then she had to pay attention to who had been fighting, because they walked around Holden and Willa, sweaty and panting and...

Connor.

He said nothing. He didn't smile. He just took the bag of medicine Betty had been carrying for her and slid his arm around Sabrina's shoulders. "I can handle it from here," he said cheerfully.

Cheerfully.

Then he was leading her out of the room, into the hallway. She hadn't said a word. Couldn't. Didn't know what on earth she could say.

She was dreaming. Hallucinating. Or he was. She looked up at him. "Are you drunk or something?"

But he simply maneuvered her through the house. The house he shouldn't have known how to maneuver her through. Certainly not to her room.

Which, she realized as he gently nudged her inside, was hardly *her* room anymore. Her twin bed had been replaced by something much bigger. The bedding was hideous. But there was a dog curled up at the end of it.

Froggy.

Her throat clogged, but no. No, she'd already cried all over him. That was a once-in-a-lifetime thing.

She turned—couldn't quite work up a whirl—and pointed her finger at him.

"Tell me what's—"

"Shay didn't think anyone else was ready to step in to take your spot while you're rehabilitating. So she offered me the job."

Sabrina found her knees couldn't hold her and she simply sank down. Luckily the bed was right there to catch her. "But..."

"Obviously with years' seniority, you get the lead position back when you're back to a hundred percent," Connor continued casually, even as Froggy wiggled her way to her side, laying her head on Sabrina's lap as if she'd gotten the message she couldn't be jostled just yet.

"Seniority. Job. I don't…" She pressed a hand to her temples. "Are you telling me *you're* part of North Star now?"

"Of course. Rumor is you guys used to have three leads anyway, so I figure as long as I earn my keep while you're hurt, I can just keep being a lead too when you're back."

She blinked. None of it made sense. Or if it did she didn't know how she felt about it making sense. She didn't know…anything. Except he was standing there, his dog in her lap, and he was *smiling.*

"Why are you grinning at me?" she demanded, stroking Froggy's ears.

"Because I know you well enough to understand that despite the look of horror on your face and your demands for information, you're actually going to be happy about this."

"Oh, am I? And why would that be?"

"Because you love me. And you love North Star. And this way, you get both."

She swallowed. "What do you get?" she asked, her voice a squeak, if that. No tears. *No* tears, but she couldn't control the way they fused in her throat like a lump. Still, better there than on her face.

"The opportunity to do good. Not just save people who made a mistake, but innocent people." He crouched in front of her, meeting her eye to eye. "But most of all, I get you. I'd do a hell of a lot to have you, Sabrina."

She sniffed. Shaky and tired and…soft. So damn soft. "Don't know why I'd ever fall in love with a cocky, grumpy, former navy SEAL."

"Yeah, I couldn't say. But here you are."

"Here we are." She leaned forward, wrapping her arms around his neck, pressing her forehead to his just like he'd done to her in the hospital. "Just so you know, I'm never crying like that ever again," she said, even as one more tear escaped. It'd be the last one.

He wiped it away. "Good, I'd rather have a gun to my head than watch you cry again."

"You're North Star now. That just might happen."

"We'll deal."

"Yeah, we will." Side by side. Doing what she loved, with the man she loved.

It was better than all the dreams she'd lost, all the dreams she'd barely let herself have before him. "You believe in destiny yet? Because if the coin flip had gone the other way, I'd have been in Nebraska with the farm girl and Holden would have been saving your butt."

He made a noncommittal sound, nudging her back so she could lie down on the bed. *Their* bed. She looked up at him, eyes already drooping. "Admit it. Destiny."

He dropped a kiss on her mouth then stood up, patting his leg so Froggy jumped off the bed.

"Maybe just this once, destiny had something to do with it."

She smiled, but she couldn't keep her eyes open. Too much for one day, and her bed was so much more comfortable than the hospital bed. A bed she'd share with him. She reached out and he gave her hand a squeeze.

"I love you, Sabrina."

But she'd already fallen asleep, dreaming about a future of love and kicking butt. Side by side.

* * * * *

COMING SOON!

MILLS & BOON

THE HEART OF ROMANCE

A ROMANCE FOR EVERY READER

MODERN

Prepare to be swept off your feet by sophisticated, sexy and seductive heroes, in some of the world's most glamourous and roman locations, where power and passion collide.

HISTORICAL

Escape with historical heroes from time gone by. Whether your passio for wicked Regency Rakes, muscled Vikings or rugged Highlanders, a the romance of the past.

MEDICAL

Set your pulse racing with dedicated, delectable doctors in the high-p sure world of medicine, where emotions run high and passion, comfo love are the best medicine.

True Love

Celebrate true love with tender stories of heartfelt romance, from the rush of falling in love to the joy a new baby can bring, and a focus o emotional heart of a relationship.

Desire

Indulge in secrets and scandal, intense drama and plenty of sizzling action with powerful and passionate heroes who have it all: wealth, s good looks…everything but the right woman.

HEROES

Experience all the excitement of a gripping thriller, with an intense mance at its heart. Resourceful, true-to-life women and strong, fearl face danger and desire - a killer combination!

To see which titles are coming soon, please visit

millsandboon.co.uk/nextmonth

LET'S TALK
Romance

For exclusive extracts, competitions
and special offers, find us online:

f facebook.com/millsandboon

🐦 @MillsandBoon

📷 @MillsandBoonUK

Get in touch on 01413 063232

For all the latest titles coming soon, visit
millsandboon.co.uk/nextmonth

MILLS & BOON

MODERN

Power and Passion

Prepare to be swept off your feet by sophisticated, sexy and seductive heroes, in some of the world's most glamourous and romantic locations, where power and passion collide.

Modern stories published every month, find them all at:

millsandboon.co.uk/Modern

MILLS & BOON
MEDICAL
Pulse-Racing Passion

Set your pulse racing with dedicated, delectable doctors in the high-pressure world of medicine, where emotions run high and passion, comfort and love are the best medicine.

MILLS & BOON
True Love
Romance from the Heart

Celebrate true love with tender stories of heartfelt romance, from the rush of falling in love to the joy a new baby can bring, and a focus on the emotional heart of a relationship.

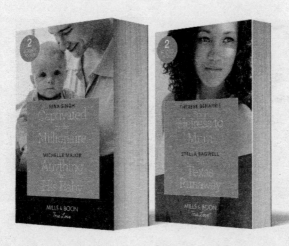